Praise for Jeffrey Archer

'The ability to tell a story is a great – and unusual – gift
. . . Jeffrey Archer is a storyteller'   *The Times*

'If there were a Nobel Prize for storytelling, Archer
would win'   *The Daily Telegraph*

'An unputdownable story'   *The Cairns Post*

'The man's a genius . . . The strength and excitement of
the idea carries all before it'   *Evening Standard*

'Stylish, witty and constantly entertaining'
     The Times

'Jeffrey Archer has the strange gift denied to many
who think themselves more serious novelists. He can tell a
story'   *Scotsman*

'A storyteller in the class of Alexandre Dumas'
     The Washington Post

'Probably the greatest storyteller of our age'
     The Mail on Sunday

'Arch   without
distra

    f Books

PATHS OF GLORY

JEFFREY ARCHER, whose novels and short stories include the Clifton Chronicles, *Kane and Abel* and *Cat O' Nine Tales*, is one of the world's favourite storytellers and has topped the bestseller lists around the world in a career spanning four decades. His work has been sold in ninety-seven countries and in more than thirty-seven languages. He is the only author ever to have been a number one bestseller in fiction, short stories and non-fiction (*The Prison Diaries*).

Jeffrey is also an art collector and amateur auctioneer, who has raised more than £50 million for different charities over the years. A member of the House of Lords for over a quarter of a century, the author is married to Dame Mary Archer, and they have two sons, two granddaughters and two grandsons.

ALSO BY JEFFREY ARCHER

THE WILLIAM WARWICK NOVELS
Nothing Ventured   Hidden in Plain Sight
Turn a Blind Eye

THE CLIFTON CHRONICLES
Only Time Will Tell   The Sins of the Father
Best Kept Secret   Be Careful What You Wish For
Mightier than the Sword   Cometh the Hour   This Was a Man

NOVELS
Not a Penny More, Not a Penny Less
Shall We Tell the President?   Kane and Abel
The Prodigal Daughter   First Among Equals
A Matter of Honour   As the Crow Flies
Honour Among Thieves
The Fourth Estate   The Eleventh Commandment
Sons of Fortune   False Impression
The Gospel According to Judas
(*with the assistance of Professor Francis J. Moloney*)
A Prisoner of Birth   Paths of Glory   Heads You Win

SHORT STORIES
A Quiver Full of Arrows   A Twist in the Tale
Twelve Red Herrings   The Collected Short Stories
To Cut a Long Story Short   Cat O' Nine Tales
And Thereby Hangs a Tale   Tell Tale
The Short, the Long and the Tall

PLAYS
Beyond Reasonable Doubt   Exclusive   The Accused
Confession   Who Killed the Mayor?

PRISON DIARIES
Volume One – Belmarsh: Hell
Volume Two – Wayland: Purgatory
Volume Three – North Sea Camp: Heaven

SCREENPLAYS
Mallory: Walking Off the Map   False Impression

JEFFREY ARCHER

PATHS OF GLORY

PAN BOOKS

First published 2009 by Macmillan

This paperback edition first published 2023 by Pan Books
an imprint of Pan Macmillan
The Smithson, 6 Briset Street, London EC1M 5NR
EU representative: Macmillan Publishers Ireland Ltd, 1st Floor,
The Liffey Trust Centre, 117–126 Sheriff Street Upper,
Dublin 1, D01 YC43
Associated companies throughout the world
www.panmacmillan.com

ISBN 978-1-5290-5998-4

1 3 5 7 9 8 6 4 2

A CIP catalogue record for this book is available from the British Library.

Printed and bound by CPI Group (UK) Ltd, Croydon, CR0 4YY

Visit **www.panmacmillan.com** to read more about all our books
and to buy them. You will also find features, author interviews and
news of any author events, and you can sign up for e-newsletters
so that you're always first to hear about our new releases.

In memory of

CHRIS BRASHER

who encouraged me to write this book

My special thanks go to the mountaineer and historian

Audrey Salkeld

for her invaluable help, advice and expertise.

My thanks also go to

Simon Bainbridge, John Bryant, Rosie de Courcy,

Anthony Geffen, Bear Grylls, George Mallory II,

Alison Prince and Mari Roberts.

Inspired by a true story

Elegy Written in a Country Churchyard

The boast of heraldry, the pomp of pow'r,
And all that beauty, all that wealth e'er gave,
Awaits alike th' inevitable hour:
The paths of glory lead but to the grave.

THOMAS GRAY (1716–1771)

PROLOGUE

1999

Saturday, May 1st, 1999

'Last time I went *bouldering* in my hobnails, I fell off,' said Conrad.

Jochen wanted to cheer, but knew that if he responded to the coded message it might alert a rival group tuned in to their frequency – or even worse, allow an eavesdropping journalist to realize that they'd discovered a body. He left the radio on, hoping for a clue that would reveal which of the two victims the search party had come across, but not another word was spoken. Only a crackling sound confirmed that someone was out there, but unwilling to speak.

Jochen followed his instructions to the letter, and after sixty seconds of silence he switched off the radio. He only wished he'd been selected as a member of the original climbing party, who were out there searching for the two bodies, but he'd drawn the short straw. Someone had to remain at base camp and man the radio. He stared out of the tent at the falling snow, and tried to imagine what was going on higher up the mountain.

–◦–

Conrad Anker stared down at the frozen body, the bleached skin as white as marble. The clothes, or what was left of them, looked as if they had once belonged to a tramp, not a man who had been educated at either Oxford or Cambridge. A thick hemp rope was tied round the dead man's waist, the frayed ends showing where it must have broken during the fall. The arms were extended over the head, the left leg crossed above the right. The tibia and fibula of the right leg were both broken, so that the foot looked as if it was detached from the rest of the body.

None of the team spoke as they struggled to fill their lungs with the thin air; words are rationed at 27,000 feet. Anker finally fell to his knees in the snow and offered up a prayer to Chomolungma, Goddess Mother of the Earth. He took his time; after all, historians, alpinists, journalists and the simply curious had waited over seventy-five years for this moment. He removed one of his thick fleece-lined gloves and placed it on the snow beside him, then leant forward, each movement slow and exaggerated, and with the index finger of his right hand gently pushed back the stiff collar of the dead man's jacket. Anker could hear his heart pounding as he read the neat red letters displayed on a Cash's name tape that had been sewn on the inside of the shirt collar.

'Oh my God,' said a voice from behind him. 'It's not Irvine. It's Mallory.'

Anker didn't comment. He still needed to confirm the one piece of information they had travelled over five thousand miles to discover.

He slipped his gloveless hand into the inside pocket of the dead man's jacket, and deftly removed the hand-stitched pouch that Mallory's wife had so painstakingly made for him. He gently unfolded the cotton, fearing that it might fall apart in his hands. If he found what he was looking for, the mystery would finally be solved.

A box of matches, a pair of nail scissors, a blunt pencil, a note written on an envelope showing how many oxygen cylinders were still in working order before they attempted the final climb, a bill (unpaid) from Gamages for a pair of goggles, a Rolex wristwatch minus its hands, and a letter from Mallory's wife dated April 14th, 1924. But the one thing Anker had expected to find wasn't there.

He looked up at the rest of the team, who were waiting impatiently. He drew a deep breath, and delivered his words slowly. 'There's no photograph of Ruth.'

One of them cheered.

BOOK ONE

NO ORDINARY CHILD

1892

1

St Bees, Cumberland, Tuesday, July 19th, 1892

If you had asked George why he'd begun walking towards the rock, he wouldn't have been able to tell you. The fact that he had to wade into the sea to reach his goal didn't appear to concern him, even though he couldn't swim.

Only one person on the beach that morning showed the slightest interest in the six-year-old boy's progress. The Reverend Leigh Mallory folded his copy of *The Times* and placed it on the sand at his feet. He didn't alert his wife, who was lying on the deckchair beside him, eyes closed, enjoying the occasional rays of sunshine, oblivious to any danger their eldest son might be facing. He knew that Annie would only panic, the way she had when the boy had climbed onto the roof of the village hall during a meeting of the Mothers' Union.

The Reverend Mallory quickly checked on his other three children, who were playing contentedly by the water's edge, unconcerned with their brother's fate. Avie and Mary were happily collecting seashells that had been swept in on the morning tide, while their younger brother Trafford was concentrating on filling a small tin bucket with sand. Mallory's attention returned to his son and heir, who was still heading resolutely towards the rock. He was not yet worried, surely the boy would eventually realize he had to turn back. But he rose from his deckchair once the waves began to cover the boy's knee breeches.

Although George was now almost out of his depth, the moment he reached the jagged outcrop he deftly pulled himself out of the sea and leapt from rock to rock, quickly reaching the top. There he settled himself, and stared out towards the horizon. Although his favourite subject at school was history, clearly no one had told him about King Canute.

His father was now watching with some trepidation as the waves surged carelessly around the rocks. He waited patiently for the boy to become aware of the danger he was in, when he would surely turn and ask for help. He didn't. When the first spray of foam touched the boy's toes, the Reverend Mallory walked slowly down to the water's edge. 'Very good, my boy,' he murmured as he passed his youngest, who was now intently building a sandcastle. But his eyes never left his eldest son, who still hadn't looked back, even though the waves were now lapping around his ankles. The Reverend Mallory plunged into the sea and started to swim towards the rock, but with each slow lunge of his military breaststroke he became more aware that it was much further away than he had realized.

He finally reached his goal, and pulled himself on to the rock. As he clambered awkwardly to the top he cut his legs in several places, showing none of the sure-footedness his son had earlier displayed. Once he'd joined the boy, he tried not to reveal that he was out of breath and in some considerable discomfort.

That's when he heard her scream. He turned to observe his wife, standing at the water's edge, shouting desperately, 'George! George!'

'Perhaps we should be making our way back, my boy,' suggested the Reverend Mallory, trying not to sound at all concerned. 'We don't want to worry your mother, do we?'

'Just a few more moments, Papa,' begged George, who continued to stare resolutely out to sea. But his father decided they couldn't wait any longer, and pulled his son gently off the rock.

It took the two of them considerably longer to reach the safety of the beach, as the Reverend Mallory, cradling his son in his arms, had to swim on his back, only able to use his legs to assist him. It was the first time George became aware that return journeys can take far longer.

When George's father finally collapsed on the beach, George's mother rushed across to join them. She fell on her knees and smothered the child in her bosom, crying, 'Thank God, thank God,' while showing scant interest in her exhausted husband. George's two sisters stood several paces back from the advancing tide, quietly sobbing, while his younger brother continued to build his fortress, far too young for any thoughts of death to have crossed his mind.

The Reverend Mallory eventually sat up and stared at his eldest son, who was once again looking out to sea although the rock was no longer in sight. He accepted for the first time that the boy appeared to have no concept of fear, no sense of risk.

1896

2

Doctors, philosophers and even historians have debated the significance of heredity when trying to understand the success or failure of succeeding generations. Had a historian studied George Mallory's parents, he would have been hard pressed to explain their son's rare gift, not to mention his natural good looks and presence.

George's father and mother considered themselves to be upper middle class, even if they lacked the resources to maintain such pretensions. The Reverend Mallory's parishioners at Mobberley in Cheshire considered him to be High Church, hide-bound and narrow-minded, and were unanimously of the opinion that his wife was a snob. George, they concluded, must have inherited his gifts from some distant relative. His father was well aware that his elder son was no ordinary child, and was quite willing to make the necessary sacrifices to ensure that George could begin his education at Glengorse, a fashionable prep school in the south of England.

George often heard his father say, 'We'll just have to tighten our belts, especially if Trafford is to follow in your footsteps.' After considering these words for some time, he enquired of his mother if there were any prep schools in England that his sisters might attend.

'Good heavens no,' she replied disdainfully. 'That would simply be a waste of money. In any case, what would be the point?'

'For a start, it would mean Avie and Mary had the same opportunities as Trafford and me,' suggested George.

His mother scoffed. 'Why put the girls through such an ordeal, when it would not advance their chances of securing a suitable husband by one jot?'

'Isn't it possible,' suggested George, 'that a husband might benefit from being married to a well-educated woman?'

'That's the last thing a man wants,' his mother responded. 'You'll find out soon enough that most husbands simply require their wife to provide them with an heir and a spare, and to organize the servants.'

George was unconvinced, and decided he would wait for an appropriate opportunity to raise the subject with his father.

--<o>--

The Mallorys' summer holiday of 1896 was not spent at St Bees, bathing, but in the Malvern Hills, hiking. While the rest of the family quickly discovered that none of them could keep up with George, his father at least made a valiant attempt to accompany him to the higher slopes, while the other Mallorys were happy to wander in the valleys below.

With his father puffing away several yards behind, George re-opened the vexed question of his sisters' education. 'Why aren't girls given the same opportunities as boys?'

'It's not the natural order of things, my boy,' panted his father.

'And who decides the natural order of things?'

'God,' responded the Reverend Mallory, feeling he was on safer ground. 'It was He who decreed that man should labour to gain sustenance and shelter for his family, while his spouse remained at home and tended to their offspring.'

'But He must have noticed that women are often blessed with more common sense than men. I'm sure He's aware that Avie is far brighter than either Trafford or me.'

The Reverend Mallory fell back, as he required a little time to consider his son's argument, and even longer to decide how he should answer it. 'Men are naturally superior to women,' he eventually suggested, not sounding altogether convinced, before lamely adding, 'and we should not attempt to meddle with nature.'

'If that is true, Papa, how has Queen Victoria managed to reign so successfully for more than sixty years?'

'Simply because there wasn't a male heir to inherit the throne,' replied his father, feeling he was entering uncharted waters.

'How lucky for England that no man was available when Queen Elizabeth ascended the throne either,' suggested George. 'Perhaps the time has come to allow girls the same opportunity as boys to make their way in the world.'

'That would never do,' spluttered his father. 'Such a course of action would overturn the natural order of society. If you had your way, George, how would your mother ever be able to find a cook or a scullery maid?'

'By getting a man to do the job,' George suggested guilelessly.

'Good heavens, George, I do believe you're turning into a free-thinker. Have you been listening to the rantings of that Bernard Shaw fellow?'

'No, Papa, but I have been reading his pamphlets.'

It is not unusual for parents to suspect that their progeny just might be brighter than they are, but the Reverend Mallory was not willing to admit as much when George had only recently celebrated his tenth birthday. George was ready to fire his next question, only to find that his father was falling further and further behind. But then, when it came to climbing, even the Reverend Mallory had long ago accepted that his son was in a different class.

3

George didn't cry when his parents sent him away to prep school. Not because he didn't want to, but because another boy, dressed in the same red blazer and short grey trousers, was bawling his head off on the other side of the carriage.

Guy Bullock came from a different world. He wasn't able to tell George exactly what his father did for a living, but whatever it was, the word *industry* kept cropping up – something George felt confident his mother wouldn't approve of. Another thing also became abundantly clear after Guy had told him about his family holiday in the Pyrenees. This was a child who had never come across the expression *We'll have to tighten our belts*. Still, by the time they arrived at Eastbourne station later that afternoon they were best friends.

The two boys slept in adjoining beds while in junior dormitory, sat next to each other in the classroom and, when they entered their final year at Glengorse, no one was surprised that they ended up sharing the same study. Although George was better than him at almost everything they tackled, Guy never seemed to resent it. In fact, he appeared to revel in his friend's success, even when George was appointed captain of football and went on to win a scholarship to Winchester. Guy told his father that he wouldn't have been offered a place at Winchester if he hadn't shared a study with George, who never stopped pushing him to try harder.

While Guy was checking the results of the entrance exam posted on the school notice board, George appeared more interested in an announcement that had been pinned below. Mr Deacon, the chemistry beak, was inviting leavers to join him on a climbing holiday in Scotland. Guy had little interest in climbing, but once George had added his name to the list, he scribbled his below it.

George had never been one of Mr Deacon's favourite pupils, possibly because chemistry was not a subject he excelled in, but as his passion for climbing far outweighed his indifference towards the Bunsen burner or litmus paper, George decided that he would just have to rub along with Mr Deacon. After all, George confided to Guy, if the damn man went to the trouble of organizing an annual climbing holiday, he couldn't be all bad.

-◄O►-

From the moment they set foot in the barren highlands of Scotland, George was transported into a different world. By day he would stroll through the bracken and heather-covered hills, while at night, with the aid of a candle, he would sit in his tent reading *The Strange Case of Dr Jekyll and Mr Hyde* before reluctantly falling asleep.

Whenever Mr Deacon approached a new hill, George would loiter at the back of the group and think about the route he had selected. On one or two occasions he went as far as to suggest that they might perhaps consider an alternative route, but Mr Deacon ignored his proposals, pointing out that he had been taking climbing parties to Scotland for the past eighteen years, and perhaps Mallory might ponder on the value of experience. George fell back in line, and continued to follow his master up the well-trodden paths.

Over supper each evening, when George sampled ginger beer and salmon for the first time, Mr Deacon would spend some considerable time outlining his plans for the following day.

'Tomorrow,' he declared, 'we face our most demanding test, but after ten days of climbing in the Highlands I'm confident that you're more than ready for the challenge.' A dozen expectant young faces stared up at Mr Deacon before he continued, 'We will attempt to climb the highest mountain in Scotland.'

'Ben Nevis,' said George. 'Four thousand four hundred and nine feet,' he added, although he had never seen the mountain.

'Mallory is correct,' said Mr Deacon, clearly irritated by the interruption. 'Once we reach the top – what we climbers call the summit, or peak – we will have lunch while you enjoy one of the finest vistas in the British Isles. As we have to be back at camp before the sun sets, and as the descent is always the most difficult part of any climb, everyone will report for breakfast by seven o'clock, so that we can set out at eight on the dot.'

Guy promised to wake George at six the following morning, as his friend often overslept and then missed breakfast, which didn't deter Mr Deacon from keeping to a timetable that resembled a military operation. However, George was so excited by the thought of climbing the highest mountain in Scotland that it was he who woke Guy the next morning. He was among the first to join Mr Deacon for breakfast, and was waiting impatiently outside his tent long before the party was due to set off.

Mr Deacon checked his watch. At one minute to eight he set off at a brisk pace down the path that would take them to the base of the mountain.

'Whistle drill!' he shouted after they had covered about a mile. All the boys, except one, took out their whistles and heartily blew the signal that would indicate they were in danger and required assistance. Mr Deacon was unable to hide a thin-lipped smile when he observed which of his charges had failed to carry out his order. 'Am I to presume, Mallory, that you have left your whistle behind?'

'Yes, sir,' George replied, annoyed that Mr Deacon had got the better of him.

'Then you will have to return to camp immediately, retrieve it, and try to catch us up before we begin the ascent.'

George wasted no time protesting. He took off in the opposite direction, and once he was back at camp, fell on his hands and knees and crawled into his tent, where he spotted the whistle on top of his sleeping bag. He cursed, grabbed it and began running back, hoping to catch up with his chums before they started the climb. But by the time he'd reached the foot of the mountain the little crocodile of climbers had already begun their ascent. Guy Bullock, who was acting as 'tail-end Charlie', continually looked back, hoping to see his friend. He was relieved when he spotted George running towards them, and waved frantically. George waved back as the group continued their slow progress up the mountain.

'Keep to the path,' were the last words he heard Mr Deacon say as they disappeared around the first bend.

Once they were out of sight, George came to a halt. He stared up at the mountain, which was bathed in a warm haze of misty sunshine. The brightly lit rocks and shaded gullies suggested a hundred different ways to approach the summit, all but one of which were ignored by Mr Deacon and his faithful troop as they resolutely kept to the guidebook's recommended path.

George's eyes settled on a thin zigzag stretching up the mountain, the dried-up bed of a stream that must have flowed lazily down the mountain for nine months of the year – but not today. He stepped off the path, ignoring the arrows and signposts, and headed towards the base of the mountain. Without a second thought, he leapt up onto the first ridge like a gymnast mounting a high bar and agilely began making his way from foothold to ledge to jutting outcrop, never once hesitating, never once looking down. He only paused for a moment when he came to a large, jagged rock a thousand feet above the base of the mountain. He studied the terrain for a few moments before he identified a fresh route and set off once again, his foot sometimes settling in a well-trodden hollow, while at other times he pursued a virgin path. He didn't stop again until he was almost halfway up the mountain. He looked at his watch – 9.07. He wondered which signpost Mr Deacon and the rest of the group had reached.

Ahead of him, George could make out a faint path that looked as if it had only ever been climbed by seasoned mountaineers or animals. He followed it until he came to a halt at a large granite slab, a closed door that would prevent anyone without a key from reaching the summit. He spent a few moments considering his options: he could retrace his steps, or take the long route around the slab, which would no doubt lead him back to the safety of the public footpath – both of which would add a considerable amount of time to the climb. But then he smiled when a sheep perched on a ledge above him let out a plaintive bleat, clearly not used to being disturbed by humans, before bounding away and unwittingly revealing the route the intruder should take.

George looked for the slightest indentation in which he could place a hand, followed by a foot, and begin his ascent. He didn't look down as he progressed slowly up the vertical rock face, searching for a finger-hold or a hint of a ledge to grip on to. Once he'd found one and pushed himself up, he would use it as his next foothold. Although the rock couldn't have been more than fifty feet high, it was twenty minutes before George was able to yank himself onto the top and gaze at the peak of Ben Nevis for the first time. His reward for taking the more demanding route was immediate, because he now faced only a gentle slope all the way to the summit.

He began to jog up the rarely trodden path, and by the time he'd reached the summit it felt as if he was standing on top of the world. He wasn't surprised to find that Mr Deacon and the rest of the party hadn't got to the peak yet. He sat alone on top of the mountain, surveying the countryside that stretched for miles below him. It was another hour before Mr Deacon appeared leading his trusty band. The schoolmaster could not hide his annoyance when the other boys began cheering and clapping the lone figure sitting on the peak.

Mr Deacon marched up to him and demanded, 'How did you manage to overtake us, Mallory?'

'I didn't overtake you, sir,' George replied. 'I simply found an alternative route.'

Mr Deacon's expression left the rest of the class in no doubt that he didn't want to believe the boy. 'As I've told you many times, Mallory, the descent is always more difficult than the climb, not least because of the amount of energy you will have expended to reach the top. That is something novices fail to appreciate,' said Mr Deacon. After a dramatic pause he added, 'Often to their cost.' George didn't comment. 'So be sure to stay with the group on the way down.'

Once the boys had devoured their packed lunches, Mr Deacon lined them up before taking his place at the front. However, he didn't set off until he'd seen George standing among the group chatting to his friend Bullock. He would have ordered him to join him at the front if he'd overheard his words, 'See you back at camp, Guy.'

On one matter Mr Deacon proved correct: the journey down the mountain was not only more demanding than the ascent, but more dangerous, and, as he had predicted, it took far longer.

Dusk was already setting in by the time Mr Deacon tramped into camp, followed by his bedraggled and exhausted troop. They couldn't believe what they saw: George Mallory was seated cross-legged on the ground, drinking ginger beer and reading a book.

Guy Bullock burst out laughing, but Mr Deacon was not amused. He made George stand to attention while he delivered a stern lecture on the importance of mountain safety. Once he had finished his diatribe, he ordered George to pull his trousers down and bend over. Mr Deacon did not have a cane to hand, so he pulled off the leather belt that held up his khaki shorts and administered six strokes to the boy's bare flesh, but unlike the sheep, George didn't bleat.

At first light the following morning, Mr Deacon accompanied George to the nearest railway station. He bought him a ticket and handed him a letter which he instructed the boy to hand to his father the moment he arrived at Mobberley.

—◇—

'Why are you back so early?' George's father enquired.

George handed over the letter, and remained silent while the Reverend Mallory tore open the envelope and read Mr Deacon's words. He pursed his lips, attempting to hide a smile, then looked down at his son and wagged a finger. 'Do remember, my boy, to be more tactful in future, and try not to embarrass your elders and betters.'

1905

4

The family were seated around the breakfast table when the maid entered the room with the morning post. She placed the letters in a small pile by the Reverend Mallory's side, along with a silver letter opener – a ritual she carried out every morning.

George's father studiously ignored the little ceremony while he buttered himself another piece of toast. He was well aware that his son had been waiting for his end-of-term report for some days. George pretended to be equally nonchalant as he chatted to his brother about the latest exploits of the Wright brothers in America.

'If you ask me,' interjected their mother, 'it's not natural. God made birds to fly, not humans. And take your elbows off the table, George.'

The girls did not offer an opinion, aware that whenever they disagreed with their mother she simply pronounced that children should be seen and not heard. This rule didn't seem to apply to the boys.

George's father did not join in the conversation as he sifted through the envelopes, trying to determine which were important and which could be placed to one side. Only one thing was certain, any envelopes that looked as if they contained requests for payment from local tradesmen would remain at the bottom of the pile, unopened for several days.

The Reverend Mallory concluded that two of the envelopes deserved his immediate attention: one postmarked Winchester, and a second with a coat of arms embossed on the back. He sipped his tea and smiled across at his eldest son, who was still pretending to take no interest in the charade taking place at the other end of the table.

Eventually he picked up the letter opener and slit open the thinner of the two envelopes, before unfolding a letter from the Bishop of Chester. His Grace confirmed that he would be delighted to preach at Mobberley Parish Church, assuming a suitable date could be arranged. George's father passed the letter across to his wife. A smile flickered across her lips when she saw the Palace crest.

The Reverend Mallory took his time opening the other, thicker envelope, pretending not to notice that all conversation around the table had suddenly ceased. Once he had extracted a little booklet, he slowly began to turn its pages while he considered the contents. He gave the occasional smile, the odd frown, but despite a prolonged silence, he still didn't offer any opinion. This state of affairs was far too rare for him not to enjoy the experience for a few more moments.

Finally he looked up at George and said, 'Proxime accessit in history, with 86 per cent.' He glanced down at the booklet, 'Has worked well this half, good exam results and a commendable essay on Gibbon. I hope that he will consider reading this subject when he goes up to university.' His father smiled before turning the next page. 'Fifth place in English, 74 per cent. A very promising essay on Boswell, but he needs to spend a little more time on Milton and Shakespeare and rather less on RL Stevenson.' This time it was George's turn to smile. 'Seventh in Latin, 69 per cent. Excellent translation of Ovid, safely above the mark Oxford and Cambridge demand from all applicants. Fourteenth in mathematics, 56 per cent, just one per cent above the pass mark.' His father paused, frowned and continued reading. 'Twenty-ninth in chemistry.' The Reverend Mallory looked up. 'How many pupils are there in the class?' he enquired.

'Thirty,' George replied, well aware that his father already knew the answer.

'Your friend Guy Bullock, no doubt, kept you off the bottom.'

He returned to the report. '26 per cent. Shows little interest in carrying out any experiments, would advise him to drop the subject if he is thinking of going to university.'

George didn't comment as his father unfolded a letter that had been attached to the report. This time he did not keep everyone in suspense. 'Your housemaster, Mr Irving,' he announced, 'is of the opinion that you should be offered a place at Cambridge this Michaelmas.' He paused. 'Cambridge seems to me a surprising choice,' added his father, 'remembering that it's among the flattest pieces of land in the country.'

'Which is why I was rather hoping, Papa, that you'll allow me to visit France this summer, so that I might further my education.'

'Paris?' said the Reverend Mallory, raising an eyebrow. 'What do you have in mind, dear boy? The Moulin Rouge?'

Mrs Mallory glared at her husband, leaving him in no doubt that she disapproved of such a risqué remark in front of the girls.

'No, Papa, not rouge,' replied George. 'Blanc. Mont Blanc, to be precise.'

'But wouldn't that be extremely dangerous?' said his mother anxiously.

'Not half as dangerous as the Moulin Rouge,' suggested his father.

'Don't worry yourself, Mother, on either count,' said George, laughing. 'My housemaster, Mr Irving, will be accompanying me at all times, and not only is he a member of the Alpine Club, but he would also act as a chaperon were I fortunate enough to be introduced to the lady in question.'

George's father remained silent for some time. He never discussed the cost of anything in front of the children, although he'd been relieved when George won a scholarship to Winchester, saving him £170 of the £200 annual fee. Money was not a subject to be raised at the breakfast table, though in truth it was rarely far from his mind.

'When is your interview for Cambridge?' he eventually asked.

'A week on Thursday, Father.'

'Then I'll let you know my decision a week on Friday.'

5

Although Guy woke his friend on time, George still managed to be late for breakfast. He blamed having to shave, a skill he hadn't yet mastered.

'Aren't you meant to be attending an interview at Cambridge today?' enquired his housemaster after George had helped himself to a second portion of porridge.

'Yes, sir,' said George.

'And if I recall correctly,' added Mr Irving, glancing at his watch, 'your train for London is due to leave in less than half an hour. I wouldn't be at all surprised if the other candidates were already waiting on the platform.'

'Undernourished and having missed your words of wisdom,' said George with a grin.

'I don't think so,' said Mr Irving. 'I addressed them during early breakfast, as I felt it was essential they weren't late for their interviews. If you think I'm a stickler for punctuality, Mallory, just wait until you meet Mr Benson.'

George pushed his bowl of porridge across to Guy, stood slowly and ambled out of the dining room as if he didn't have a care in the world, then bolted across the quad and into college house as if he were trying to win an Olympic dash. He took the stairs three at a time to the top floor. That's when he remembered he hadn't packed an overnight case. But when he burst into his study he was delighted to find his little leather suitcase already strapped up and placed by the door. Guy must have anticipated that he would once again leave everything to the last minute.

'Thank you, Guy,' said George out loud, hoping that his friend was enjoying a well-earned second bowl of porridge. He grabbed the suitcase, bounded down the steps two at a time and ran back across the quad, only stopping when he reached the porter's lodge. 'Where's the college hansom, Simkins?' he asked desperately.

'Left about fifteen minutes ago, sir.'

'Damn,' muttered George, before dashing out into the street and heading in the direction of the station, confident he could still make his train.

He raced down the street with an uneasy feeling he'd left something behind, but whatever it was, he certainly didn't have time to go back and retrieve it. As he rounded the corner onto Station Hill, he saw a thick line of grey smoke belching into the air. Was the train coming in, or pulling out? He picked up the pace, charging past a startled ticket collector and onto the platform, only to see the guard waving his green flag, climbing the steps into the rear carriage and slamming the door behind him.

George sprinted after the train as it began to move off, and they both reached the end of the platform at the same time. The guard gave him a sympathetic smile as the train gathered speed before disappearing in a cloud of smoke.

'Damn,' George repeated as he turned to find the ticket collector bearing down on him. Once the man had caught his breath, he demanded, 'May I see your ticket, sir?'

That was when George remembered what he'd forgotten.

He dumped his suitcase on the platform, opened it and made a show of rummaging among his clothes as if he was looking for his ticket, which he knew was on the table by the side of his bed.

'What time's the next train to London?' he asked casually.

'On the hour, every hour,' came back the immediate reply. 'But you'll still need a ticket.'

'Damn,' said George for a third time, aware that he couldn't afford to miss the next train. 'I must have left my ticket back at college,' he added helplessly.

'Then you'll have to purchase another one,' said the ticket collector.

George felt desperation setting in. Did he have any money with him? He began searching the pockets of his suit, and was relieved to find the half crown his mother had given him at Christmas. He'd wondered where it had got to. He followed the ticket collector meekly back to the booking office, where he purchased a third-class return ticket from Winchester to Cambridge, at a cost of one shilling and sixpence. He had often wondered why trains didn't have a second class, but felt this was not the time to ask. Once the collector had punched his ticket, George returned to the platform and bought a copy of *The Times* from the newspaper seller, parting with another penny. He settled down on an uncomfortable slatted wooden bench and opened it to find out what was happening in the world.

The Prime Minister, Arthur Balfour, was hailing the new *entente cordiale* recently signed by Britain and France. In the future, relations with France could only improve, he promised the British people. George turned the page and began to read an article about Theodore Roosevelt, recently inaugurated for a second term as President of the United States. By the time the nine o'clock train for London came steaming in, George was studying the classified advertisements on the front page, which offered everything from hair lotion to top hats.

He was relieved the train was on time, and even more so when it pulled into Waterloo a few minutes early. He jumped out of his carriage, ran down the platform and onto the road. For the first time in his life he hailed a hansom cab, rather than wait around for the next tram to King's Cross – an extravagance his father would have disapproved of, but Papa's anger would have been far more acute had George missed his interview with Mr Benson and therefore failed to be offered a place at Cambridge.

'King's Cross,' said George as he climbed into the hansom. The driver flicked his whip and the tired old grey began a slow plod across London. George checked his watch every few minutes, but still felt confident that he would be on time for his three o'clock appointment with the senior tutor of Magdalene College.

After he was dropped off at King's Cross, George discovered that the next train to Cambridge was due to leave in fifteen minutes. He relaxed for the first time that day. However, what he hadn't anticipated was that it would stop at every station from Finsbury Park to Stevenage, so by the time the train finally puffed into Cambridge, the station clock showed 2.37pm.

George was first off the train, and once his ticket had been punched he went off in search of another hansom cab, but there was none to be found. He began to run up the road, following the signs to the city centre, but without the slightest idea in which direction he should be going. He stopped to ask several passers-by if they could direct him to Magdalene College, with no success until he came across a young man wearing a short black gown and a mortar board, who was able to give him clear directions. After thanking him, George set off again, now searching for a bridge over the river Cam. He was running flat out across the bridge as a clock in the distance chimed three times. He smiled with relief. He wasn't going to be more than a couple of minutes late.

At the far side of the bridge he came to a halt outside a massive black oak double door. He turned the handle and pushed, but it didn't budge. He rapped the knocker twice, and waited for some time, but no one answered his call. He checked his watch: 3.04pm. He banged on the door again, but still no one responded. Surely they would not deny him entry when he was only a couple of minutes late?

He hammered on the door a third time, and didn't stop until he heard a key turning in the lock. The door creaked open to reveal a short, stooping man in a long black coat, wearing a bowler hat. 'The college is closed, sir,' was all he said.

'But I have an interview with Mr AC Benson at three o'clock,' pleaded George.

'The senior tutor gave me clear instructions that I was to lock the gate at three o'clock, and that after that no one was to be allowed to enter the college.'

'But I—' began George, but his words fell on deaf ears as the door was slammed in his face and once again he heard the key turning in the lock.

He began thumping on the door with his bare fist, although he knew no one would come to his rescue. He cursed his stupidity. What would he say when people asked him how the interview had gone? What would he tell Mr Irving when he arrived back at college later that night? How could he face Guy, who was certain to be on time for his interview next week? He knew what his father's reaction would be: the first Mallory for four generations not to be educated at Cambridge. And as for his mother, would he ever be able to go home again?

He frowned at the heavy oak door that forbade him entry and thought about one last knock, but knew it would be pointless. He began to wonder if there might be some other way of entering the college, but as the Cam ran along its north side, acting as a moat, there was no other entrance to consider. Unless . . . George stared up at the high brick wall that surrounded the college, and began to walk up and down the pavement as if he was studying a rock face. He spotted several nooks and crannies that had been created by 450 years of ice, snow, wind, rain and a thawing sun, before he identified a possible route.

There was a heavy stone archway above the door, the rim of which was only an arm's length away from a windowsill that would make a perfect foothold. Above that was another smaller window and another sill, from which he would be within touching distance of the sloping tiled roof, which he suspected was duplicated on the other side of the building.

He dumped his case on the pavement – never carry any unnecessary weight when attempting a climb – placed his right foot in a small hole some eight inches above the pavement, and propelled himself off the ground with his left foot, grabbing at a jutting ledge which allowed him to pull himself further up towards the stone archway. Several passers-by stopped to watch his progress, and when he finally pulled himself up onto the roof, they rewarded him with a muted round of applause.

George spent a few moments studying the other side of the

wall. As always, the descent was going to be more difficult than the ascent. He swung his left leg over and lowered himself slowly down, clinging onto the gutter with both hands while he searched for a foothold. Once he felt the windowsill with a toe, he removed one hand. That was when his shoe came off, and the grip of the one hand that had been clinging to the guttering slipped. He'd broken the golden rule of maintaining three points of contact. George knew he was going to fall, something he regularly practised when dismounting the high bar in the college gym, but the bar had never been this high. He let go, and had his first piece of luck that day when he landed in a damp flower bed and rolled over.

He stood up to find an elderly gentleman staring at him. Did the poor fellow imagine he was confronting a shoeless burglar, George wondered.

'Can I help you, young man?' he asked.

'Thank you, sir,' said George. 'I have an appointment with Mr Benson.'

'You should find Mr Benson in his study at this time of day.'

'I'm sorry, sir, but I don't know where that is,' said George.

'Through the Fellows' archway,' he said, pointing across the lawn. 'Second corridor on the left. You'll see his name printed on the door.'

'Thank you, sir,' said George, bending down to tie up his shoe lace.

'Not at all,' said the elderly gentleman as he headed off down the path towards the masters lodgings.

George ran across the Fellows' lawn and through the archway into a magnificent Elizabethan courtyard. When he reached the second corridor he stopped to check the names on the board: AC Benson, Senior Tutor, third floor. He bolted up the steps, and when he reached the third floor he stopped outside Mr Benson's room to catch his breath. He knocked gently on the door.

'Come,' responded a voice. George opened the door and entered the senior tutor's domain. A rotund, ruddy-faced man with a bushy moustache looked up at him. He was wearing a light checked suit and a yellow-spotted bow tie under his gown, and seated behind a large desk covered in leather-bound books and students' essays. 'And how may I help you?' he enquired, tugging at the lapels of his gown.

'My name is George Mallory, sir. I have an appointment to see you.'

'*Had* an appointment would be more accurate, Mallory. You were expected at three o'clock, and as I gave express orders that no candidate should be allowed to enter the college after that hour, I am bound to enquire how you managed to get in.'

'I climbed over the wall, sir.'

'You did *what*?' asked Mr Benson rising slowly from behind his desk, a look of incredulity on his face. 'Follow me, Mallory.'

George didn't speak as Mr Benson led him back down the steps, across the courtyard and into the lodge. The porter leapt up the moment he saw the senior tutor.

'Harry,' said Mr Benson, 'did you allow this candidate to enter the college after three o'clock?'

'No, sir, I most certainly did not,' said the porter, staring at George in disbelief.

Mr Benson turned to face George. 'Show me exactly how you got into the college, Mallory,' he demanded.

George led the two men back to the Fellows' garden, and pointed to his footprints in the flower bed. The senior tutor still didn't look convinced. The porter offered no opinion.

'If, as you claim, Mallory, you climbed in, then you can surely climb back out.' Mr Benson took a pace back, and folded his arms.

George walked slowly up and down the path, studying the wall carefully before he settled on the route he would take. The senior tutor and the college porter watched in astonishment as the young man climbed deftly back up the wall, not pausing until he had placed one leg over the top of the building and sat astride the roof.

'Can I come back down, sir?' George asked plaintively.

'You most certainly can, young man,' said Mr Benson without hesitation. 'It's clear to me that nothing is going to stop you from entering this college.'

6

Saturday, July 1st, 1905

When George told his father he had no intention of visiting the Moulin Rouge, it was the truth. Indeed, the Reverend Mallory had already received a letter from Mr Irving with a detailed itinerary for their visit to the Alps, which did not include stopping off in Paris. But that was before George had saved Mr Irving's life, been arrested for disturbing the peace and spent a night in jail.

George's mother was never able to hide her anxiety whenever her son went off on one of his climbing trips, but she always slipped a five-pound note into his jacket pocket, with a whispered plea not to tell his father.

George joined Guy and Mr Irving at Southampton, where they boarded the ferry for Le Havre. When they disembarked at the French port four hours later, a train was waiting to transport them to Martigny. During the long journey, George spent most of his time staring out of the window.

He was reminded of Mr Irving's passion for punctuality when they stepped off the train to find a horse-drawn charabanc awaiting them. With a crack of the coachman's whip, the little party set off at a brisk pace up into the mountains, allowing George to study even more closely some of the great challenges that lay ahead of him.

It was dark by the time the three of them had booked into

the Hôtel Lion d'Or in Bourg St Pierre, at the foot of the Alps. Over dinner Mr Irving spread a map across the table and went over his plans for the next fortnight, indicating the mountains they would attempt to climb: the Great St Bernard (8,101 feet), Mont Vélan (12,353 feet) and the Grand Combin (14,153 feet). If they succeeded in conquering all three, they would move on to Monte Rosa (15,217 feet).

George studied the map intently, already impatient for the sun to rise the next morning. Guy remained silent. Although it was well known that Mr Irving selected only the most promising climbers among his pupils to accompany him on his annual visit to the Alps, Guy was already having second thoughts about whether he should have signed up.

George, on the other hand, had no such misgivings. But even Mr Irving was taken by surprise the following day when they reached the top of the Great St Bernard Pass in record time. Over dinner that evening George asked him if he could take over as climbing leader when they tackled Mont Vélan.

For some time Mr Irving had realized that George was the most accomplished schoolboy mountaineer he had ever come across, and was more naturally gifted than his seasoned teacher. However, it was the first time a pupil had asked to lead him – and on only the second day of their expedition.

'I will allow you to lead us to the lower slopes of Mont Vélan,' conceded Mr Irving. 'But once we've reached 5,000 feet, I'll take over.'

Mr Irving never took over, because the next day George led the little party with all the assurance and skill of a seasoned alpinist, even introducing Mr Irving to new routes he'd never considered in the past. And when, two days later, they climbed the Grand Combin in a shorter time than Mr Irving had achieved before, the master became the pupil.

All George now seemed to be interested in was when he would be allowed to tackle Mont Blanc.

'Not for some time yet,' said Mr Irving. 'Even I wouldn't attempt it without a professional guide. But when you go up to Cambridge in the autumn, I'll give you a letter of introduction to

Geoffrey Young, the most experienced climber in the land, and he can decide when you're ready to approach that particular lady.'

Mr Irving was confident, however, that they were ready to take on Monte Rosa, and George led them to the summit of the mountain without the slightest mishap, even if Guy had at times found it difficult to keep up. It was on the way down that the accident occurred. Perhaps Mr Irving had become a little too complacent – a climber's worst enemy – believing that nothing would go wrong after the triumphant ascent.

George had begun the descent with his usual confidence, but when they reached a particularly sheer couloir he decided to slow down, remembering that Guy had not found that part of the route easy to negotiate during the ascent. George had almost traversed the couloir when he heard the scream. His immediate reaction undoubtedly saved the lives of all three of them. He thrust his axe into the deep snow and quickly looped the rope around the shaft, securing it firmly against his boot while holding onto the rope with his other hand. He could only watch as Guy careered past him. He assumed that Mr Irving would have carried out the same safety procedure as he had, and that between them they would halt the momentum of Guy's fall, but his housemaster had failed to react quite as quickly, and although he had dug his axe firmly into the snow, he hadn't had time to loop the rope around its shaft. A moment later he too came flying past George. George didn't look down, but kept his boot wedged firmly against the axe head and tried desperately to maintain his balance. There was nothing between him and the valley some six hundred feet below.

He held firm as both of them came to a halt and began swinging in mid-air. George wasn't confident that the rope wouldn't snap under the strain, leaving his companions to fall to their deaths. He didn't have time to pray, and as a second later he was still clinging to the rope his question seemed to have been answered, if only temporarily. The danger hadn't passed because he still had to somehow get both men safely back onto the mountain.

George looked down to see them clinging on to the rope in desperation, their faces as white as the snow. Using a skill he'd developed while endlessly practising on a rope in the school gymnasium, he began to swing his two companions slowly to and fro, until Mr Irving was able to establish a foothold on the side of the mountain. Then, while George held his position, Irving carried out the same process, swinging Guy back and forth until he too was finally secure.

It was some time before any of them felt able to continue the descent, and George did not release his axe until he was convinced that Mr Irving and Guy had fully recovered. Inch by inch, foot by foot, he led the two badly shaken climbers to the safety of a wide ledge, thirty feet below. The three of them rested for nearly an hour before Mr Irving took over and guided them towards safer slopes.

Hardly a word passed between them over dinner that evening, but all three of them knew that if they didn't return to the mountain the following morning, Guy would never climb again. The next day, Mr Irving led his two charges back up Monte Rosa, taking a longer and far less demanding route. By the time George and Guy had returned to the hotel that evening, they were no longer children.

On the previous day, it had only taken a few minutes before all three climbers were safe, but each of those minutes could have been measured in sixty parts, and then not forgotten for a lifetime.

7

It was clear from the moment they entered Paris that Mr Irving was no stranger to the city, and George and Guy were only too happy to allow their housemaster to take the lead, having already agreed to his suggestion that they should spend the final day of their trip in the French capital celebrating their good fortune.

Mr Irving booked them into a small family hotel, located in a picturesque courtyard in the 7th arrondissement. After a light lunch he introduced them to the day life of Paris: the Louvre, Notre Dame, the Arc de Triomphe. But it was the Eiffel Tower, built for the Universal Exhibition of 1889 in celebration of the centenary of the French Revolution, that captured George's imagination.

'Don't even think about it,' said Mr Irving when he caught his charge looking up at the highest point of the steel edifice, some 1,062 feet above them.

Having purchased three tickets for six francs, Mr Irving herded Guy and George into an elevator which transported them on a slow journey to the top of the tower.

'We wouldn't even have reached the foothills of Mont Blanc,' George commented as he looked out over Paris.

Mr Irving smiled, wondering if even conquering Mont Blanc would prove enough for George Mallory.

After they had changed for dinner, Mr Irving took the boys to a little restaurant on the Left Bank where they enjoyed foie gras accompanied by small glasses of chilled Sauternes. This was followed by boeuf bourguignon, better than any beef stew either of them had ever experienced, which then gave way to a ripe brie; quite a change from school food. Both courses were washed down with a rather fine burgundy, and George felt it had already been one of the most exciting days of his life. But it was far from over. After introducing his two charges to the joys of cognac, Mr Irving accompanied them back to the hotel. Just after midnight he bade them goodnight before retiring to his own room.

Guy sat on the end of his bed while George started to undress. 'We'll just hang around for a few more minutes before we slip back out.'

'Slip back out?' mumbled George.

'Yes,' said Guy, happily taking the lead for a change. 'What's the point of coming to Paris if we don't visit the Moulin Rouge?'

George continued to unbutton his shirt. 'I promised my mother . . .'

'I'm sure you did,' mocked Guy. 'And you're now asking me to believe that the man who plans to conquer the heights of Mont Blanc isn't willing to plumb the depths of Parisian night-life?'

George reluctantly rebuttoned his shirt as Guy switched off the light, opened the bedroom door and peeked out. Satisfied that Mr Irving was safely tucked up in bed with his copy of *Three Men in a Boat*, he stepped out into the corridor. George reluctantly followed, closing the door quietly behind him.

Once they had reached the lobby, Guy slipped out onto the street. He'd hailed a hansom cab before George had time for second thoughts.

'The Moulin Rouge,' Guy said with a confidence he hadn't shown on the slopes of any mountain. The driver set off at a brisk pace. 'If only Mr Irving could see us now,' said Guy as he opened a silver cigarette case George had never seen before.

Their journey took them across the Seine to Montmartre, a mountain that hadn't been part of Mr Irving's itinerary. When they came to a halt outside the Moulin Rouge, George wondered if they would even be allowed into the glamorous nightclub when he saw how smartly dressed most of the revellers were – some even wearing dinner jackets. Once again Guy took the lead. After paying the driver, he extracted a ten-franc note from his wallet and handed it to the doorman, who gave the two young men a doubtful look but still pocketed the money and allowed them to enter.

Once they were inside, the maître d' treated the two young men with a similar lack of enthusiasm, despite Guy producing another ten-franc note. A young waiter led them to a tiny table at the back of the room before offering them a menu. While George couldn't take his eyes off the cigarette girl's legs, Guy, aware of his dwindling finances, selected the second cheapest bottle on the wine list. The waiter returned moments later, and poured each of them a glass of Sémillon just as the lights went down.

George sat bolt upright as a dozen girls dressed in flamboyant red costumes revealing layers of white petticoats performed what was described in the programme as the Cancan. Whenever they kicked their black-stockinged legs in the air they were greeted by raucous cheers and cries of 'Magnifique!' from the mainly male audience. Although George had been brought up with two sisters, he had never seen that much bare flesh before, even when they were bathing at St Bees. Guy called for a second bottle of wine, and George began to suspect that this was not his close friend's first experience of a nightclub; but then, Guy had been raised in Chelsea, not Cheshire.

The moment the curtain fell and the lights came up, the waiter reappeared and presented them with a bill that bore no resemblance to the prices on the wine list. Guy emptied his wallet, but it wasn't enough, so George ended up parting with his emergency five-pound note. The waiter frowned when he saw the alien currency, but still pocketed the large white banknote without any suggestion of change – so much for Mr Balfour's *entente cordiale*.

'Oh my God,' said Guy.

'I agree,' said George. 'I had no idea that a couple of bottles of wine could cost that much.'

'No, no,' said Guy, not looking at his friend. 'I wasn't referring to the bill.' He pointed to a table by the stage.

George was just as astonished when he spotted their house-master sitting next to a scantily dressed woman, an arm draped round her shoulder.

'I think the time has come for us to beat a tactical retreat,' said Guy.

'Agreed,' said George. They rose from their places and walked towards the door, not looking back until they were out in the street.

As they stepped onto the pavement, a woman wearing an even shorter skirt than the waitresses selling cigarettes in the Moulin Rouge strolled across to join them.

'Messieurs?' she whispered. 'Besoin de compagnie?'

'Non, merci, madame,' said George.

'Ah, Anglais,' she said. 'Juste prix pour tous les deux?'

'In normal circumstances I would be happy to oblige,' chipped in Guy, 'but unfortunately we've already been fleeced by your countrymen.'

The woman gave him a quizzical look, until George translated his friend's words. She shrugged her shoulders before moving away to offer her wares to other men who were spilling out of the nightclub.

'I hope you know your way back to the hotel,' said Guy, appearing a little unsteady on his feet. 'Because I've no money left for a hansom.'

'Haven't a clue,' said George, 'but when in doubt, identify a landmark you know, and it will act as a pointer to your destination.' He set off at a brisk pace.

'Yes, of course it will,' said Guy as he hurried after him.

George began to sober up as they made their way back across the river, his eyes rarely leaving his chosen point of reference. Guy followed in his wake, and didn't speak until forty minutes later when they came to a halt at the base of a monument many Parisians claimed to detest, and wished to see dismantled bolt by bolt, girder by girder, as soon as its twenty-year permit had expired.

'I think our hotel's somewhere over there,' said Guy, pointing towards a narrow side street. He turned back to see George staring up at the Eiffel Tower, a look of sheer adoration in his eyes.

'So much more of a challenge by night,' George said, not diverting his gaze.

'You can't be serious,' said Guy, as his friend headed off in the direction of one of the four triangular feet at the base of the tower.

Guy ran after him, protesting, but by the time he'd caught up, George had already leapt onto the frame and begun climbing. Although Guy continued to shout at the top of his voice, he could do no more than stand and watch as his friend moved deftly from girder to girder. George never once looked down, but had he done so he would have seen that a small group of night owls had gathered below, eagerly following his every move.

George must have been about halfway up when Guy heard the whistles. He swung round to see a police vehicle drive onto the concourse, coming to a halt at the base of the tower. Half a dozen uniformed officers leapt out and ran towards an official Guy hadn't noticed until then, but who was clearly waiting for them. The official led them quickly to the elevator door and pulled open the iron gates. The crowd watched as the elevator made its slow journey upwards.

Guy looked up to check on George's progress. He was only a couple of hundred feet from the top, and seemed entirely unaware of his pursuers. Moments later the elevator came to a stuttering halt by his side. The gates were pulled open and one of the policemen took a tentative step out onto the nearest girder. After a second step, he thought better of it and quickly leapt back inside. The senior officer began pleading with the miscreant, who pretended not to understand his words.

George was still determined to reach the top, but after ignoring some reasoned words, followed by some harsh expletives that could have been understood in any language, he reluctantly joined the officers in the elevator. Once the police had returned to the ground with their quarry, the watching crowd formed a gangway to the waiting vehicle, applauding the young man all the way.

'Chapeau, jeune homme.'

'Dommage.'

'Bravo!'

'Magnifique!'

It was the second time that night that George had heard a crowd crying, 'Magnifique!'

He spotted Guy just as the police were about to bundle him into the van and drive off to heaven knows where. 'Find Mr Irving,' he shouted. 'He'll know what to do.'

Guy ran all the way back to the hotel and took the lift to the third floor, but when he banged on Mr Irving's door there was no response. Reluctantly he returned to the ground floor and sat on the steps, awaiting the arrival of his housemaster. He even considered making his way back to the Moulin Rouge, but on balance decided that that might cause even more trouble.

The hotel clock had struck six before a carriage bearing Mr Irving pulled up outside the front door. There was no sign of the scantily dressed lady. He was surprised to find Guy sitting on the steps, and even more surprised when he discovered why.

The hotel manager only needed to make a couple of phone calls before he located which police station George had spent the night in. It took all of Mr Irving's diplomatic skills, not to mention emptying his wallet, before the duty officer agreed to release the irresponsible young man, and only then after Mr Irving had assured the inspector that they would leave the country *immédiatement*.

On the ferry back to Southampton, Mr Irving told the two young men that he hadn't yet made up his mind whether to report the incident to their parents.

'And I still haven't made up my mind,' responded Guy, 'whether to tell my father the name of that club you took us to last night.'

8

George was relieved to find that the front door of Magdalene College was open when he arrived for the first day of term.

He strolled into the porter's lodge, placed his suitcase on the floor and said to the familiar figure seated behind the counter, 'My name's—'.

'Mr Mallory,' said the porter, raising his bowler hat. 'As if I'm likely to forget,' he added with a warm smile. He looked down at his clipboard. 'You've been allocated a room on staircase seven, sir, the Pepys Building. I normally escort freshmen on their first day of term, but you seem to be a gentleman who can find his own way.' George laughed. 'Across First Court and through the archway.'

'Thank you,' said George, picking up his suitcase and heading towards the door.

'And sir.' George turned back as the porter rose from his chair. 'I believe this is yours.' He handed George another leather suitcase with the letters 'GLM' printed in black on its side. 'And do try to be on time for your six o'clock appointment, sir.'

'My six o'clock appointment?'

'Yes, sir, you are bidden to join the Master for drinks in the lodgings. He likes to acquaint himself with the new undergraduates on the first day of term.'

'Thank you for reminding me,' said George. 'By the way, has my friend Guy Bullock turned up?'

'He has indeed, sir.' Once again the porter looked down at his list. 'Mr Bullock arrived over two hours ago. You'll find him on the landing above you.'

'That will be a first,' said George without explanation.

As George walked towards First Court, he was careful not to step on the grass, which looked as if it had been cut with a pair of scissors. He passed several undergraduates, some dressed in long gowns to show that they were scholars, others in short gowns to indicate that, like himself, they were exhibitioners, while the rest didn't wear gowns, just mortar boards which they occasionally raised to each other.

No one gave George a second look, and certainly no one raised their mortar board to him as he walked by, which brought back memories of his first day at Winchester. He couldn't suppress a smile when he passed Mr AC Benson's staircase. The senior tutor had telegrammed the day after their meeting, offering George a history exhibition. In a later letter he informed him that he would be tutoring him himself.

George continued on through the archway into Second Court, which housed the Pepys Building, until he came to a narrow corridor marked with a bold '7'. He dragged his cases up the wooden steps to the second floor, where he saw a door with the name 'GL Mallory' painted on it in silver letters. How many names had appeared on that door over the past century, he wondered.

He entered a room not much larger than his study at Winchester, but at least he would not be expected to share the tiny space with Guy. He was still unpacking when there was a knock on the door, and Guy strolled in without waiting for an invitation. The two young men shook hands as if they had never met before, laughed, and then threw their arms around each other.

'I'm on the floor above you,' said Guy.

'I've already made my views clear on that ridiculous notion,' responded George.

Guy smiled when he saw the familiar chart that George had already pinned to the wall above his desk.

Ben Nevis	4,409 ft	✓
Great St Bernard	8,101 ft	✓
Mont Vélan	12,353 ft	✓
Grand Combin	14,153 ft	✓
Monte Rosa	15,217 ft	✓
Mont Blanc	15,774 ft	?

'You seem to have forgotten Montmartre,' he said. 'Not to mention the Eiffel Tower.'

'The Eiffel Tower is only 1,062 feet,' replied George. 'And *you* seem to have forgotten that I didn't reach the top.'

Guy glanced at his watch. 'We'd better get going if we're not to be late for the Master.'

'Agreed,' said George, and quickly slipped on his gown.

As the two young undergraduates strolled across Second Court towards the Master's lodgings, George asked Guy if he knew anything about their head of house.

'Only what Mr Irving told me. Apparently he was our man in Berlin before he retired from the Foreign Office. He had a reputation for being pretty blunt with the Germans. According to Irving, even the Kaiser was wary of him.'

George straightened his tie as they joined a stream of young men who were walking through the Master's garden in the direction of a Victorian Gothic house that dominated one side of the courtyard. They were greeted at the door by a college servant dressed in a white jacket and black trousers, carrying a clipboard.

'I'm Bullock, and this is Mallory,' said Guy.

The man ticked off their names, but not before he'd taken a closer look at George. 'You'll find the Master in the drawing room on the first floor,' he told them.

George ran up the stairs – he always ran up stairs – and entered a large, elegantly furnished room full of undergraduates and dons, with oil paintings of more ancient versions of the latter decorating the walls. Another servant offered them a glass of sherry, and George spotted someone he recognized. He strolled across to join him.

'Good evening, sir,' he said.

'Mallory. I'm delighted you were able to make it,' said the senior tutor, without any suggestion of teasing. 'I was just reminding two of your fellow freshmen that my first tutorial will be at nine o'clock tomorrow morning. As you've now taken up residence in the college, you won't have to climb over the wall to be on time, will you, Mallory?'

'No, sir,' said George, sipping his sherry.

'Though I wouldn't count on it,' said Guy.

'This is my friend, Guy Bullock,' said George. 'You don't have to worry about him, he's always on time.'

The only person in the room not wearing a gown, apart from the college servants, came across to join them.

'Ah, Sir David,' said the senior tutor. 'I don't think you've met Mr Bullock, but I know that you are well acquainted with Mr Mallory, who dropped into your garden earlier in the year.'

George turned to face the head of college. 'Oh Lord,' he said.

Sir David smiled at the new undergraduate. 'No, no, Mr Mallory, "Master" will suffice.'

◄○►

Guy made sure that George was on time for his first tutorial with Mr Benson the following morning, but even so, George still managed to turn up only moments before the appointed hour. The senior tutor opened his remarks by making it clear that weekly essays were to be delivered every Thursday by five o'clock, and if anyone was late for a tutorial, they should not be surprised to find the door locked. George was grateful that his room was a mere hundred yards away from Mr Benson's, and that his mother had supplied him with an alarm clock.

Once the preliminary strictures had been administered, the tutorial went far better than George had dared to hope. His spirits were raised further when he discovered over a sherry that evening that the senior tutor shared his love of Boswell, as well as Byron and Wordsworth, and had been a personal friend of Browning.

However, Mr Benson left George in no doubt what would be

expected of an exhibitioner in his first year, reminding him that although the university term was only eight weeks in length, he would be required to work just as hard during the vacation. As he was leaving, Benson added, 'And do be sure, Mr Mallory, to attend the Freshers' Fair on Sunday, otherwise you will never discover just how many activities this university has to offer. For example,' he said, smiling, 'you might consider joining the dramatic society.'

9

Guy knocked on George's door, but there was no reply. He checked his watch: five past ten. George couldn't be in hall having breakfast, because they finished serving at nine on a Sunday, and he surely wouldn't have gone to the Freshers' Fair without him. He must be either fast asleep or having a bath. Guy knocked again, but still there was no reply. He opened the door and peeked inside. The bed was unmade – nothing unusual about that – an open book lay on the pillow and some papers were strewn across the desk, but there was no sign of George. He must be having a bath.

Guy sat down on the end of the bed and waited. He had long ago stopped complaining about his friend's inability to understand the purpose of a watch. However, it still annoyed many of George's acquaintances, who regularly reminded him of Winchester's motto, *Manners Maketh Man*. Guy was well aware of his friend's shortcomings, but he also recognized that George had exceptional gifts. The accident of fate that had placed them in the same carriage on their way to prep school had changed his whole life. While others sometimes found George tactless, even arrogant, if he allowed them into his confidence they also discovered kindness, generosity and humour in equal measure.

Guy picked up the book from George's pillow. It was a novel by EM Forster, a writer he'd never come across before. He had only managed a few pages of it before George strolled in, a towel around his waist, his hair dripping.

'Is it ten o'clock already?' he asked, taking off his towel and using it to rub his hair.

'Ten past,' said Guy.

'Benson suggested I sign up for the dramatic society. It might give us the chance to meet a few girls.'

'I don't think it's girls that Benson is interested in.'

George swung round. 'You're not suggesting . . .'

'Just in case you haven't noticed,' said Guy to his friend, who was standing naked in front of him, 'it isn't only girls who give you a second look.'

'And which do you prefer?' asked George, giving him a flick of the towel.

'You're quite safe with me,' Guy assured him. 'Now, could you get a move on? Otherwise everyone will have packed up and gone before we even arrive.'

As they crossed the courtyard George set his usual pace, which Guy always found hard to keep up with.

'What clubs are you going to join?' Guy asked, almost running by his side.

'The ones that won't admit you,' said George with a grin. 'Which ought to leave me a wide enough choice.'

Their pace slowed as they joined a teeming horde of under-graduates who were also making their way to the Freshers' Fair. Long before they reached Parker's Piece they could hear bands playing, choirs singing and a thousand exuberant voices all striving to outdo each other.

A large area of the green was occupied by stalls manned by noisy students, all of whom seemed to be hollering like street traders. George and Guy strolled down the first gangway, soaking up the atmosphere. Guy began to show some interest when a man dressed in cricket whites and carrying a bat and ball, which looked somewhat incongruous in autumn, demanded, 'Do either of you play cricket by any chance?'

'I opened the batting for Winchester,' said Guy.

'Then you've come to the right place,' said the man with the bat. 'My name's Dick Young.'

Guy, recognizing the name of a man who had played both cricket and football for England, gave a slight bow.

'What about your friend?' Dick asked.

'You needn't waste your time on him,' said Guy. 'He has his sights on higher things, although he happens to be looking for a man who's also called Young. I'll catch up with you later, George,' said Guy.

George nodded and strolled off through the crowd, ignoring a cry of, 'Do you sing? We're looking for a tenor.'

'But a fiver will do,' quipped another voice.

'Do you play chess? We must beat Oxford this year.'

'Do you play a musical instrument?' asked a desperate voice. 'Even the cymbals?'

George stopped in his tracks when he saw an awning above a stall at the end of the aisle which announced *The Fabian Society, founded 1884*. He walked quickly towards a man who was waving a pamphlet and shouting, 'Equality for all!'

As George came up to him, the man enquired, 'Would you care to join our little band? Or are you one of those hide-bound Tory fellows?'

'Certainly not,' said George. 'I have long believed in the doctrines of Quintus Fabius Maximus. "If you can win a battle without having to fire a shot in anger, you are the true victor."'

'Good fellow,' said the young man, pushing a form across the table. 'Sign up here, and then you can come to our meeting next week, which will be addressed by Mr George Bernard Shaw. By the way, my name's Rupert Brooke,' he added, thrusting out his hand. 'I'm the club's secretary.'

George shook Brooke warmly by the hand before filling in the form and handing it back. Brooke glanced at the signature. 'I say, old chap,' he said, 'are the rumours true?'

'What rumours?' said George.

'That you entered this university by climbing over your college's wall.'

George was about to reply when a voice behind him said, 'And then he was made to climb back out. That's always the most difficult part.'

'And why is that?' enquired Brooke innocently.

'Simple, really,' said Guy, before George had a chance to speak. 'When you're climbing up a rock face, your hands are not more than a few inches from your eyes, but when you're coming down, your feet are never less than five feet below you, which means that when you look down you've far more chance of losing your balance. Got the idea?'

George laughed. 'Ignore my friend,' he said. 'And not just because he's a hide-bound Tory, but he's also a lackey of the capitalist system.'

'True enough,' said Guy without shame.

'So what clubs have you signed up for?' asked Brooke, turning his attention to Guy.

'Apart from cricket, the Union, the Disraeli Society and the Officers' Training Corps,' replied Guy.

'Good heavens,' said Brooke. 'Is there no hope for the man?'

'None whatsoever,' admitted Guy. Turning to George, he added, 'But at least I've found what you've been looking for, so the time has come for you to follow me.'

George raised his mortar board to Brooke, who returned the compliment. Guy led the way to the next row of stalls, where he pointed triumphantly at a white awning that read *CUMC, founded 1904*.

George slapped his friend on the back. He began to study a display of photographs showing past and present undergraduates standing on the Great St Bernard Pass, and on the summits of Mont Vélan and Monte Rosa. Another board on the far side of the table displayed a large photograph of Mont Blanc, on which was written the words *Join us in Italy next year if you want to do it the hard way.*

'How do I join?' George asked a short, stocky fellow standing next to a taller man who was holding an ice axe.

'You can't join the Mountaineering Club, old chap,' he replied. 'You have to be elected.'

'Then how do I get elected?'

'It's quite simple. You sign up for one of our Club meets to Pen-y-Pass, and then we'll decide if you're a mountaineer or just a weekend rambler.'

'I would have you know,' interrupted Guy, 'that my friend—'

'—would be happy to sign up,' said George before Guy could complete the sentence.

Both George and Guy signed up for a weekend trip to Wales, and handed back their application forms to the taller of the two men standing behind the table.

'I'm Somervell,' he said, 'and this is Odell. He's a geologist, so he's more interested in studying rocks than climbing them. The chap at the back,' added Somervell, pointing to an older man, 'is Geoffrey Winthrop Young of the Alpine Club. He's our honorary chairman.'

'The most accomplished climber in the land,' said George.

Young smiled as he studied George's application form. 'Graham Irving has a tendency to exaggerate,' he said. 'However, he's already written to tell me about your recent trip to the Alps. When we're at Pen-y-Pass you'll be given the chance to show if you're as good as he says you are.'

'He's better,' said Guy. 'Irving won't have mentioned our visit to Paris, when . . . ahhh!' he shouted as George's heel collided with his shin.

'Will I be given a chance to join your party for Mont Blanc next summer?' George asked.

'That may not be possible,' said Young. 'There are one or two other fellows already hoping to be selected for that jaunt.'

Somervell and Odell were now taking a far greater interest in the freshman from Magdalene. The two young men couldn't have been more dissimilar. Odell was just a shade over five feet five, with sandy hair, a ruddy complexion and watery blue eyes. He looked too young to be an undergraduate, but the moment he spoke he sounded older than his years. Somervell, in contrast, was over six foot, with dark, unruly hair that looked as if it had rarely been acquainted with a comb. He had the black eyes of a pirate, but when asked a question he bowed his head and spoke softly, not because he was aloof, but simply because he was shy. George knew instinctively that these two disparate men were going to be friends for the rest of his life.

Saturday, June 23rd, 1906

If George had been asked what he had achieved in his first year at Cambridge – and his father did – he would have said that it had been far more than the third class he'd been awarded following his end-of-term exams.

'Is it possible that you have become involved in too many outside activities,' his father remonstrated, 'none of which is likely to assist you when the time comes to consider a profession?' This was something George hadn't given a great deal of thought to. 'Because I don't have to remind you, my boy,' his father added – but he did – 'that I do not have sufficient funds to allow you to spend the rest of your life as a gentleman of leisure' – a sentiment the Reverend Mallory had made all too clear since George's first day at prep school.

George felt confident that this was not a conversation Guy would be having with *his* father, despite the fact that he had also only managed to scrape a third. He concluded that it was not the moment to tell Papa that if he was lucky enough to be among those selected to join Geoffrey Young's climbing party in the Alps, he would be making an excursion to Italy that summer.

Unlike Guy, George had been mortified to be awarded a third. However, Mr Benson had assured him that he had been a borderline case for a second, and added that if he were to work a little harder during the next two years, that would be the class he should attain when he sat his finals – and if he was willing to make sacrifices, he might even secure a first.

George began to consider what sacrifices Mr Benson might have in mind. He had, after all, been elected to the committee of the Fabian Society, where he had dined with George Bernard Shaw and Ramsay MacDonald. He regularly spent evenings with Rupert Brooke, Lytton Strachey, Geoffrey and John Maynard Keynes and Ka Cox, all of whom Mr Benson thoroughly approved of. He'd even played the Pope in Brooke's production of Marlowe's *Doctor Faustus* – although George would have been the first to admit that the reviews had not been all that flattering. He had also begun a thesis on Boswell, which he hoped might in time be published. But all of this had been secondary to his efforts to be elected to the Alpine Club. Did Mr Benson expect him to sacrifice *everything* in order to gain the coveted first?

10

George Mallory had never climbed with anyone he considered his equal. That was until he met George Finch.

During the Michaelmas vacation, George had travelled to Wales to join Geoffrey Young for one of the Cambridge Mountaineering Club meets at Pen-y-Pass. Each day, Young would select the teams for the morning climb, and George quickly came to respect Odell and Somervell, who were not only excellent company, but were able to keep pace with him when they tackled the more demanding climbs.

On the Thursday morning, George was paired with Finch for the ridge climb over Crib Goch, Crib-y-Ddysgl, Snowdon and Lliwedd. As the two men clambered up and down Snowdon, often having to scramble on their hands and knees, George became painfully aware that the young Australian wouldn't rest until everyone else had been left in his wake.

'It's not a competition,' said George, once the rest of the climbers had all fallen behind.

'Oh yes it is,' said Finch, not slackening his pace. 'Haven't you noticed that Young has only invited two people to this meet who aren't at Oxford or Cambridge?' He paused to draw breath before spitting out, 'And the other one is a woman.'

'I hadn't noticed,' admitted George.

'If I'm to have any hope of being invited to join Young in the Alps this summer,' snapped Finch, 'I'll have to leave him in no doubt who's the best climber of all the would-be applicants.'

'Is that right?' said George as he quickened his pace and overtook his first rival.

By the time they swung round the Snowdon Horseshoe, Finch was back by his side. Both men were breathing heavily as they almost jogged down the hill. George slackened his pace, allowing Finch to overtake him just as the Pen-y-Pass hotel came into sight.

'You're good, Mallory, but are you good enough?' said Finch after George had ordered two pints of bitter. They were on their second pint before Odell and Somervell joined them.

In Cornwall a few months later the two rivals honed their rock-climbing skills, and whenever Young was asked to choose who he thought was the better climber, he was unwilling to respond. However, George accepted that once they stepped onto the slopes of the Italian Alps in the summer, Young would have to decide which of them would accompany him in the Courmayeur Valley for the challenging assault on Mont Blanc.

Among the other climbers who regularly attended those trips to Wales and Cornwall was one George wanted to spend more time with. Her name was Cottie Sanders. The daughter of a wealthy industrialist, she could have undoubtedly taken her place at Cambridge had her mother considered it a proper activity for a young lady. George, Guy and Cottie regularly made up a three for the morning climb, but once they'd had lunch together on the lower slopes, Young would insist that George leave them and join Finch, Somervell and Odell for the more demanding after-noon climbs.

Cottie could not have been described as beautiful in the conventional sense, but George had rarely enjoyed a woman's company more. She was just an inch over five feet, and if she possessed a pleasing figure, she disguised it determinedly beneath layers of jumpers and jodhpurs. Her freckled face and curly brown hair gave the impression of a tomboy. But that wasn't what had attracted George to her.

George's father often referred to 'inner beauty' in his morning sermons, and George had just as often silently scoffed at the idea from his place in the front pew. But that was before he met

Cottie. He failed, however, to notice that her eyes always lit up when she was with him. And when Guy asked her if she was in love with George, she simply said, 'Isn't everybody?'

Whenever Guy raised the subject with his friend, George always replied that he did not think of Cottie as anything more than a friend.

—◦—

'What's your opinion of George Finch?' asked Cottie one day when they sat down for lunch on top of a rock.

'Why do you ask?' said George, removing a sandwich from its greaseproof paper wrapping.

'My father once told me that only politicians are expected to answer a question with a question.'

George smiled. 'I admit Finch is a damned fine climber, but he can be a bit much if you have to spend all day with him.'

'Ten minutes was quite enough for me,' said Cottie.

'What do you mean?' asked George as he lit his pipe.

'Once we were out of sight of everybody, he tried to kiss me.'

'Perhaps he's fallen in love with you,' said George, trying to make light of it.

'I don't think so, George,' she said. 'I'm not exactly his type.'

'But he must find you attractive if he wanted to kiss you?'

'Only because I was the one girl within fifty miles.'

'Thirty, my dear,' said George, laughing, as he tapped his pipe on the rock. 'I see our esteemed leader is on his way,' he added as he helped Cottie back on her feet.

George was disappointed when Young chose not to take the party down a rather interesting-looking descent of Lliwedd by way of a sheer rock buttress. When they reached the lower slopes he was irritated to discover that he had left his pipe behind, and would have to return to the summit to retrieve it. Cottie agreed to accompany him, but when they reached the base of the rock George asked her to wait, as he couldn't be bothered to take the long route around the giant obstacle.

She watched in amazement as he began to climb straight up the sheer rock face, showing no sign of fear. Once he had reached the top he grabbed his pipe, put it in his pocket and came straight back down by the same route.

Over dinner that evening, Cottie told the rest of the party what she had witnessed that afternoon. From the looks of incredulity on their faces, it was clear that no one believed her. George Finch even burst out laughing, and whispered to Geoffrey Young, 'She thinks he's Sir Galahad.'

Young didn't laugh. He was beginning to wonder if George Mallory might be the ideal person to accompany him on a climb even the Royal Geographical Society considered impossible.

◄◦►

A month later, Young wrote to seven climbers inviting them to join his party for the Italian Alps during the summer vacation. He made it clear that he wouldn't select the pair who would make the assault on Mont Blanc from the Courmayeur Valley until he had seen which of them acclimatized best to the hazardous conditions.

Guy Bullock and Cottie Sanders did not receive invitations, as Young believed that their presence would be a distraction.

'Distractions,' he pronounced when the team gathered in Southampton, 'are all very well when you're spending a weekend in Wales, but not when you're in Courmayeur attempting to climb some of the most treacherous slopes in Europe.'

11

Like burglars in the night, the two of them slipped out of the hotel unnoticed, carrying the swag under their arms. Silently, they crossed an unlit road and disappeared into the forest, aware that it would be some time before they were missed by their colleagues, who were probably dressing for dinner.

The first few days had gone well. They had pitched up at Courmayeur on the Friday to find that the weather was perfect for climbing. A week later, with the Aiguille du Chardonnet, the Grépon and Mont Maudit 'under their belts', to use one of Geoffrey Young's favourite expressions, they were all prepared for the final challenge – assuming the weather held.

—◇—

When seven o'clock struck on the hotel's grandfather clock, the honorary chairman of the CUMC tapped the side of his glass with a spoon. The rest of the committee fell silent.

'Item number one,' said Geoffrey Young, glancing down at his agenda, 'the election of a new member. Mr George Leigh Mallory has been proposed by Mr Somervell and seconded by Mr Odell.' He looked up. 'Those in favour?' Five hands were raised. 'Carried unanimously,' said Young, and a ripple of applause followed – something he had never experienced before. 'I therefore declare George Leigh Mallory elected as a member of the CUMC.'

'Perhaps someone should go and look for him,' said Odell, 'and tell him the good news?'

'If you're hoping to find Mallory, you'd better put on your climbing boots,' said Young without explanation.

'I know he isn't a Cambridge man,' said Somervell, 'but I propose that we invite George Finch to be an honorary member of the club. After all, he's a fine climber.'

No one seemed willing to second the proposal.

◄○►

George struck a match and lit the little Primus stove. The two men in the tent sat cross-legged, facing each other. They warmed their hands while they waited for the water to boil, a slow process when you're halfway up a mountain. George placed two mugs on the ground while Finch ripped the wrapping off a bar of Kendal Mint Cake, broke it in half and passed a chunk across to his climbing partner.

The previous day, the two of them had stood together on the summit of Mont Maudit and stared up at Mont Blanc, a mere 2,000 feet above them, wondering if they would be looking down from its peak tomorrow.

George checked his watch: 7.35pm. By now Geoffrey Young would be taking the rest of the team through tomorrow's programme, having informed them who would be joining him on the final ascent. The water boiled.

◄○►

'This has been quite a remarkable week for climbing,' continued Young. 'In fact, I would go so far as to say that it has been among the most memorable of my career, which only makes my selection of who will join me for the attack on the summit tomorrow all the more difficult. I am painfully aware that some of you have waited years for this opportunity, but more than one of you has to be disappointed. As you are all well aware, reaching the summit of Mont Blanc is not technically difficult for an experienced climber – unless, of course, he attempts it from the Courmayeur side.' He paused.

'The climbing party will consist of five men: myself, Somervell, Odell, Mallory and Finch. We will set out at four o'clock tomorrow morning, and press on to 15,400 feet, where we will rest for two hours. If that capricious mistress, the weather, allows us, the final team of three will make an attempt on the summit.

'Odell and Somervell will descend to the Grand Mulets hut at 13,400 feet, where Somervell will await the return of the final party.'

'Triumphant return,' said Somervell magnanimously, although he and Odell could barely conceal their frustration at not having been chosen for the assault on the summit.

'Let's hope so,' said Young. 'I know how disappointed some of you must feel not to be selected for the climbing party, but never forget that without a back-up team it wouldn't be possible to conquer any mountain, and every member of the team will have played his part. Should tomorrow's attempt fail for any reason, I shall be inviting Odell and Somervell to join me later in the week when we will make a second attempt on the summit.' The two men smiled slightly ruefully, as if they'd won a silver medal at the Olympic Games. 'There is nothing more for me to say, other than to tell you who I have chosen to join me for the final ascent.'

‑◊‑

George removed a glove, unscrewed the jar of Bovril and dropped a spoonful of the thick brown substance into the mugs. Finch added the hot water and stirred until he was sure there was nothing left on the bottom before he handed George his drink. George broke a second bar of Kendal Mint Cake and passed the larger portion across to Finch. Neither spoke while they savoured their gourmet meal.

It was George who eventually broke the silence. 'I wonder who Young will pick.'

'You're certain to be selected,' said Finch, warming his hands around his mug. 'But I don't know who else he'll choose out of Odell, Somervell and me. If he picks the best climber, then the final place is mine.'

'Why wouldn't he pick the best climber?'

'I'm not an Oxford or Cambridge man, old boy,' said Finch, mimicking his companion's accent.

'Young's no snob,' said George. 'He won't let that influence his decision.'

'We could of course pre-empt that decision,' suggested Finch with a grin.

George looked puzzled. 'What do you have in mind?'

'We could set out for the summit first thing in the morning, and then sit around waiting to see which of them joins us.'

'It would be a pyrrhic victory,' George suggested as he drained his drink.

'A victory's a victory,' said Finch. 'Ask any Epirote how he feels about the word pyrrhic.'

George made no comment as he crawled into his sleeping bag. Finch undid his fly buttons before slipping out of the tent. He looked up at the peak of Mont Blanc glistening in the moonlight, and even wondered if he could manage to climb it alone. When he crawled back into the tent, George was already fast asleep.

—◄○►—

'I can't find either of them,' said Odell as he joined the rest of his colleagues for dinner. 'I've looked everywhere.'

'They've got an important day tomorrow, so they'll be trying to rest,' said Young, as a bowl of hot consommé was placed in front of him. 'But it's never easy to sleep at minus twenty degrees. I will have to make a slight adjustment to tomorrow's plan.' Everyone around the table stopped eating and turned towards him. 'Odell, Somervell and I will be joined by Herford.'

'But what about Mallory and Finch?' asked Odell.

'I have a feeling that the two of them will already be sitting at Grand Mulets, waiting for us to join them.'

12

Mallory and Finch had already finished lunch by the time Young and his party joined them at the Grand Mulets refuge. Neither of them spoke as they waited to see how the expedition's leader would react to their impudence.

'Have you already tried for the top?' asked Young.

'I wanted to,' said Finch as he followed Young into the hut, 'but Mallory advised against it.'

'Shrewd fellow, Mallory,' said Young, before unfolding an old parchment map and laying it out on the table. George and Finch listened intently as he took them all through his proposed route for the last 2,200 feet.

'This will be my seventh attempt from the Courmayeur side,' he said, 'and if we make it, it will only be the third time, so the odds are worse than fifty-fifty.' Young folded the map up and stowed it in his rucksack. He shook hands with Somervell, Herford and Odell. 'Thank you, gentlemen,' he said. 'We'll make every effort to be back with you by five. Half past at the latest. See that you have a cup of Earl Grey on the boil,' he added with a smile. 'We can't risk being any later,' he said as he looked up at the forbidding peak before turning to face his chosen companions. 'Time to rope up. I can assure you, gentlemen, this is one lady you don't want to be out with after dark.'

For the next hour, the three of them worked their way steadily along a narrow ridge that would take them to within a thousand feet of the summit. George was beginning to wonder what all the fuss was about, but that was before they reached the

Barn Door, a vast pinnacle of ice with sheer rock on both sides acting as bookends. There was a simpler, longer route to the summit, but as Young told them, that was for women and children.

Young sat at the foot of the Barn Door and checked his map once again. 'Now you'll begin to understand why we spent all those weekends honing our rock-climbing skills.'

George couldn't take his eyes off the Barn Door, looking for any cracks in the surface, or indentations where other climbers had gone before them. He placed a foot tentatively in a small fissure.

'No,' said Young firmly, as he walked across to take the lead. 'Next year, possibly.'

Young began to slowly traverse the giant overhanging pinnacle, often disappearing from view only to reappear a few moments later. Each of them realized that, roped together as if by an umbilical cord, if one of them made a single mistake they would all come tumbling down.

Finch looked up. Young was out of sight, and all he could see of George were the heels of two hobnail boots disappearing over a ridge. Inch by inch, foot by foot, Mallory and Finch followed slowly behind Young, aware that if they made the slightest error of judgement, the Barn Door would be slammed in their faces and seconds later they would be buried in an unmarked grave.

Inch by inch . . .

◄○►

At Grand Mulets, Odell stood over a wood fire toasting a piece of bread, while Herford boiled a pot of water to make tea.

'I wonder how far they've got,' said Odell.

'Trying to find the key to the Barn Door would be my bet,' said Somervell.

'I ought to be getting back,' said Odell, 'so I can follow their progress through the hotel's telescope. The moment I see that they've joined you, I'll put in our orders for dinner.'

'Along with a bottle of champagne,' suggested Somervell.

◄○►

Young heaved himself up onto the ledge above the Barn Door. He didn't have to wait long before the two Georges joined him. No one spoke for some time, and even Finch didn't pretend he wasn't exhausted. A mere 800 feet above them loomed the summit of Mont Blanc.

'Don't think of it as being 800 feet away,' Young said. 'It's more like a couple of miles, and every foot you take will be into thinner and thinner air.' He checked his watch. 'So don't let's keep the lady waiting.'

Although the stony terrain appeared less demanding than the Barn Door, the climb was still treacherous; crevices, icy stones and uneven rocks covered in only a thin film of snow lay in wait for them should they make the slightest mistake. The summit looked tantalizingly close, but the lady turned out to be a tease. It was another two hours before Young finally placed a foot on the summit.

When Mallory first saw the view from the highest peak in the Alps he was lost for words.

'Magnifique,' he finally managed, as he looked down on Madame Blanc's precocious offspring, which stretched as far as the eye could see.

'It's one of the ironies of mountaineering,' said Young, 'that grown men are happy to spend months preparing for a climb, weeks rehearsing and honing their skills, and at least a day attempting to reach the summit. And then, having achieved their goal, they spend just a few moments enjoying the experience, along with one or two equally certifiable companions who have little in common other than wanting to do it all again, on an even higher mountain.'

George nodded, while Finch said nothing.

'There's one act I have to carry out, gentlemen,' said Young, 'before we begin our descent.' He took a sovereign from his jacket pocket, bent down and placed it in the snow at his feet. Mallory and Finch watched the little ritual with fascination, but said nothing.

'The King of England sends his compliments, ma'am,' said

Young, 'and hopes that you will grant his humble subjects safe passage back to their homeland.'

◄◦►

When Odell arrived back at the hotel a few minutes after four, the first thing he did was order a large flask of hot fruit punch before walking out onto the veranda to take up his post. He peered through the large telescope, and once he'd focused on a rabbit scurrying into the forest, he turned his attention to the mountain. He swung the telescope further up the peak but, although it was a clear day, he knew that the climbing party would be no larger than ants, so searching for them would be pointless.

Odell swung the telescope lower down, and focused on the wooden hut at the Grand Mulets refuge. He thought he could see two figures standing outside it, but he couldn't make out which was Somervell and which was Herford. A waiter in a white jacket appeared by his side and poured him a cup of hot punch. Odell leant back and enjoyed the sensation as the warm liquid slipped down his parched throat. He allowed himself to imagine for a moment what it must feel like to be standing on the peak of Mont Blanc, having unlocked the Barn Door.

He returned to the telescope, although he didn't expect to see much activity at the Grand Mulets before five o'clock. Young was a reliable sort of cove, so he expected him to be on time. Once the climbing team reappeared, he would have that bottle of champagne put on ice to share with those who would be returning in triumph. The grandfather clock in the hall struck once, to indicate that it was 4.30pm. He focused the telescope on the Grand Mulets refuge in case the climbing party was ahead of schedule, but there was still no sign of any activity. He moved the telescope slowly up the mountain, hoping to see three specks appear in the lens.

'Dear God, no,' he exclaimed as the waiter poured him a second glass of punch.

'Una problema, signore?' enquired the waiter.

'An avalanche,' replied Odell.

13

George heard the unmistakable roar behind him, but didn't have time to turn round.

The snow hit him like a giant wave, sweeping all before it. He tried desperately to remain the right way up, making firm breaststrokes with his arms in the hope of keeping a pocket of air in front of his face so that he could buy some time, just as the safety manual recommended. But when the second wave hit him, he knew he was going to die. The third and final wave tossed him like a loose pebble, down and down and down.

His last thoughts were of his mother, who had always dreaded this moment, then of his father who never spoke of it, and finally of his brother and sisters, who would all outlive him. Was this hell? And then he came to a sudden halt. He lay still for a moment, trying to convince himself that he was still alive, and to take in his immediate surroundings. He had landed at the bottom of a crevasse, cast into an Aladdin's cave of ice, the beauty of which he might have appreciated in any other circumstances. What did the manual recommend? Quickly work out which way is up and which is down so that you can at least start heading in the right direction. He spotted a shaft of murky grey light thirty, perhaps forty feet above him.

He recalled the manual's next instruction: find out if anything is broken. He wiggled the fingers and thumb of his right hand; he'd still got five. His left hand was very cold, but at least there was some movement there too. He stretched his right leg, and tentatively raised it off the ground. He had one leg. He raised his left leg – two. He placed his hands by his side and pushed himself up slowly, very slowly. His fingers were beginning to freeze. He looked for his gloves; they were nowhere to be seen. He must have lost them during his fall.

The cave was lined with ridges of ice protruding from every side, making several natural ladders to the roof; but were they safe? He crawled across the soft snow to the far side of his prison, and kicked at the ice with the toe of his hobnailed boot. It made no impression. The ice had taken a hundred years, perhaps even longer, to grow to that thickness, and wasn't going to be budged easily. George became a little more confident, but kept reminding himself to abide by the rules, not to hurry, and not to take any unnecessary risks. He spent some time trying to work out which rungs of the ladder he should mount. It looked as if the best route was on the far side of the cave, so he crawled back on his hands and knees and grabbed at the bottom rung. He prayed. When you're in danger, you need to believe there is a God.

He placed a foot tentatively on a ridge of ice a few inches above the ground, then gripped another above it with his bare fingers, now numb with cold, and pulled himself slowly up. He risked placing his full weight on the lower ridge, because if it broke off, he would only have a short fall into the soft snow. It didn't, which gave him the confidence to climb onto the next rung of his Jacob's ladder, and find out if he was about to join the angels or his fellow humans.

He was about halfway up, feeling more confident with each move, when a piece of ice broke off in his hand. His feet immediately slithered off the ice below, leaving him dangling by one hand, some thirty feet above the floor. George began to sweat in a crevasse that must have been minus forty degrees. He swung slowly backwards and forwards, certain that the Gods above him had simply decided to extend his life by a few minutes, and at any moment the ice he was clinging to would shear off. Then one foot found a toehold, followed by the other. He held his breath, the fingers of his right hand almost glued to the ice above him. His strength was beginning to ebb away. He took some time before selecting the next rung of the ladder. Just three more, and he would be able to push himself through the chink of light. He picked the next rung carefully, and then the next, and at last was able to punch a fist through the little crack above him. He would have cheered, but he couldn't waste the time, as the last rays of sunlight were fast disappearing behind the highest peak.

George pushed his head through the hole, and looked tentatively to his left and right. He didn't need a manual to tell him it made sense to clear the snow around him if he was to have any chance of finding a rock or a hard place.

He swept away with his bare hands until he uncovered a slab of rock that had recently been covered by the avalanche. Gathering all the strength he possessed, he hauled himself out of the hole and clung on to the edge of the rock. He didn't hang around but, like a crab, scurried across its surface, fearful that he might slide back down the icy rock and return to the bottom of the crevasse.

That was when he heard a voice singing 'Waltzing Matilda'. No prizes for guessing who the soloist was. George continued his painful advance across the snow until the source of the voice took shape. Finch was sitting bolt upright repeating the chorus again and again. He clearly didn't know the second verse.

'Is that you, George?' Finch cried out as he peered through the falling snow.

It was the first time Finch had ever called him by his Christian name. 'Yes, it is,' George shouted as he crawled up to his side. 'Are you all right?'

'I'm just fine,' said Finch. 'Apart from a broken leg, and the fact that the toes of my left foot are beginning to freeze up. I must have lost a boot somewhere along the way. What about you?'

'Never better, old chap,' said George.

'Bloody English,' said Finch. 'If we're to have any chance of getting out of here, you'll need to find my torch.'

'Where do I start looking?'

'The last time I saw it, it was some way up the mountain.'

George set off, like a toddler on his hands and knees. He was beginning to despair until he spotted a black object resting in the snow a few yards ahead of him. He cheered. He cursed. It was only Finch's missing boot. He struggled on until he was able to cheer again when he saw the handle of the torch sticking out of the snow. He grabbed at it, and prayed once more before flicking the switch. A beam of light glowed in the dusk. 'Thank God,' he murmured, and returned down the mountain to where Finch was lying.

No sooner had George reached him, than they both heard the moan. 'That must be Young,' said Finch. 'Better go and see if you can help. But for God's sake turn off that torch until the sun's completely disappeared. If Odell spotted the avalanche from the hotel, a rescue party should be on their way by now, but they won't reach us for hours.'

George switched off the torch and began to crawl in the direction of the moan, but it was some time before he came across a body lying motionless in the snow, the right leg buckled under the left thigh.

'Waltzing Matilda, Waltzing Matilda, who'll come a-waltzing, Matilda . . .'

George quickly cleared the snow around Young's mouth, but made no attempt to move him.

'Hold on, old friend,' he whispered in his ear. 'Somervell and Herford should be on their way by now. They're certain to be with us soon.' He only wished he believed his own words. He took Young's hand and began to rub, trying to get some circulation back, all the time having to brush away the falling snow.

'Waltzing Matilda, waltzing Matilda, who'll come a-waltzing, Matilda . . .'

‒◦‒

Odell ran out of the front door of the hotel and onto the driveway. He immediately began to turn the wheel of the ancient klaxon which produced a deafening screeching sound that would alert Somervell and Herford to the danger.

‒◦‒

77

When the sun finally disappeared behind the highest peak, George placed the torch firmly in the snow, facing down the mountain. He switched it on and a beam of light flickered, but how long would it last?

'Waltzing Matilda, waltzing Matilda, who'll come a-waltzing, Matilda, with me? And he sang as he . . .'

There was nothing in the safety manual about what to do about an Australian singing out of tune, thought George as he rested his head in the snow and began to drift off to sleep. Not a bad way to die.

'You'll come a-waltzing, Matilda, with me . . .'

—◇—

When George woke he couldn't be sure where he was, how he'd got there, or how long he'd been there. Then he saw a nurse. He slept.

When he woke again, Somervell was standing by the side of his bed. He gave George a warm smile. 'Welcome back,' he said.

'How long have I been away?'

'Two or three days, give or take. But the doctors are confident they'll have you back on your feet within a week.'

'And Finch?'

'He's got one leg in plaster, but he's eating a hearty breakfast and still singing 'Waltzing Matilda' to any nurse who cares to listen.'

'What about Young?' George asked, fearing the worst.

'He's still unconscious, suffering from hypothermia and a broken arm. The medical chaps are doing everything they can to patch him up, and if they do manage to save his life, he'll have you to thank.'

'Me?' said George.

'If it hadn't been for your torch, we would never have found you.'

'It wasn't my torch,' said George. 'It was Finch's.'

George slept.

14

Tuesday, July 9th, 1907

'Once you've stared death in the face, nothing is ever the same again,' said Young. 'It places you apart from other men.'

George poured his guest a cup of tea.

'I wanted to see you, Mallory, to make sure it wasn't that dreadful experience that has caused you to stop climbing.'

'Of course it wasn't,' said George. 'There's a far better reason. My tutor has warned me that I won't be considered for a doctorate unless I get a first.'

'And what are your chances of that, old fellow?'

'It seems I'm a borderline case. I can't allow myself not to succeed simply because I didn't work hard enough.'

'Understandable,' said Young. 'But all work and no play . . .'

'I'd rather be a dull success than a bright failure,' retorted George.

'But once your exams are over, Mallory, will you consider joining me in the Alps next summer?'

'I certainly will,' said George, smiling. 'If there's one thing I fear even more than failing to get a first, it's the thought of Finch standing on the peaks of higher and higher mountains singing "Waltzing Matilda".'

'He's just had his degree results,' said Young.

'And . . . ?'

◄◇►

Guy was astonished by the amount of work George put in as his finals approached. He didn't take even a day off during the spring vacation to visit Pen-y-Pass or Cornwall, let alone the Alps. His only companions were kings, dictators and potentates, and his only excursions were to battlefields in far-off lands as he studied night and day right up until the morning of the exams.

After five days of continual writing, and eleven different papers, George still couldn't be sure how well he'd done. Only the very clever and the very stupid ever are. Once he'd handed in his final paper, he emerged from the examination room and stepped out into the sunlight to find Guy sitting on the steps of Schools waiting to greet him, a bottle of champagne in one hand, two glasses in the other. George sat down beside him and smiled.

'Don't ask,' he said, as Guy began to remove the wire from around the cork.

For the next ten days a period of limbo followed as the examinees waited for the examiners to tell them the class of degree they had been awarded, and with it, what future had been determined for them.

However much Mr Benson tried to reassure his pupil that it had been a close-run thing, the fact was that George Leigh Mallory had been awarded a second-class honours degree, and therefore would not be returning to Magdalene College in the Michaelmas term to work on a doctorate. And it didn't help when the senior tutor added, 'When you know you're beaten, give in gracefully.'

Despite an invitation from Geoffrey Young to spend a month with him in the Alps that summer, George packed his bags and took the next train back to Birkenhead. If you had asked him, he would have described the next four weeks as a period of reflection, although the word his father continually used was denial, while his mother, in the privacy of the bedroom, described her son's uncharacteristic behaviour as sulking.

'He's not a·child any more,' she said. 'He must make up his mind what he's going to do with the rest of his life.'

Despite his wife's remonstrations, it was another week before the Reverend Mallory got round to tackling head-on the subject of his son's future.

'I'm weighing up my options,' George told him, 'though I'd like to be an author. In fact, I've already begun work on a book on Boswell.'

'Possibly illuminating, but unlikely to be remunerative,' replied his father. 'I assume you have no desire to live in a garret and survive on bread and water.' George was unable to disagree. 'Have you thought about applying for a commission in the army? You'd make a damn fine soldier.'

'I've never been very good at obeying authority,' George replied.

'Have you considered taking up Holy Orders?'

'No, because I fear there's an insurmountable obstacle.'

'And what might that be?'

'I don't believe in God,' said George simply.

'That hasn't prevented some of my most distinguished colleagues from taking the cloth,' said his father.

George laughed. 'You're such an old cynic, Papa.'

The Reverend Mallory ignored his son's comment. 'Perhaps you should consider politics, my boy. I'm sure you could find a constituency that would be delighted to have you as its MP.'

'It might help if I knew which party I supported,' said George. 'And in any case, while MPs remain unpaid politics is nothing more than a rich man's hobby.'

'Not unlike mountaineering,' suggested his father, raising an eyebrow.

'True,' admitted George. 'So I'll have to find a profession which will provide me with sufficient income to allow me to pursue my hobby.'

'Then it's settled,' said the Reverend Mallory. 'You'll have to be a schoolmaster.'

―◦―

Although George hadn't offered any opinion on his father's last suggestion, the moment he returned to his room he sat down and wrote to his former housemaster enquiring if there were any openings at Winchester for a history beak. Mr Irving replied within the week. The college, he informed George, was still considering applications for a classics master, but had recently filled the position of junior history tutor. George was already regretting his month of reflection. *However*, Mr Irving continued, *I hear on the grapevine that Charterhouse are looking for a history master, and should you think of applying for the post, I would be only too happy to act as a referee.*

Ten days later George travelled down to Surrey for an interview with the headmaster of Charterhouse, the Reverend Gerald Rendall. Mr Irving had warned George that almost anything would seem an anticlimax after Winchester and Cambridge, but George was pleasantly surprised by how much he enjoyed his visit. He was both delighted and relieved when the headmaster invited him to join the staff ahead of three other applicants.

What George could not have foretold, when he wrote back to the Reverend Rendall accepting the appointment, was that it would not be the school but one of the governors who would alter the course of his life.

1910

15

'I would need two first-class climbers to join me for the final assault,' Geoffrey Young replied.

'Do you have anyone in mind?' asked the secretary of the Royal Geographical Society.

'Yes,' said Young firmly, not wishing to divulge their names.

'Then perhaps you'd better have a word with both of them,' said Hinks. 'And in the strictest confidence, because unless the Dalai Lama gives his blessing, we won't even be allowed to cross the border into Tibet.'

'I'll write to both of them this evening,' said Young.

'Nothing in writing would be my advice,' said the secretary. Young nodded. 'And I also need you to do me a small favour. When Captain Scott . . .'

◄○►

One of the problems George faced during his first few weeks at Charterhouse was that if he wasn't wearing his mortar board and gown, he was often mistaken for one of the boys.

He enjoyed his first year at the school far more than he'd expected, even if the lower fifth was populated by a group of monsters determined to disrupt his lessons. However, when those same boys returned for their final year in the sixth form, to George's surprise several of them were entirely reformed characters, all their energies directed towards securing a place at the university of their choice. George was happy to spend countless hours helping them to achieve that objective.

However, when his father enquired during the summer vacation what had given him the most satisfaction, he mentioned coaching the Colts football eleven in the winter and the under-fourteen hockey team during the spring, but, most of all, taking a group of boys hill walking in the summer.

'And just occasionally,' he said, 'one comes across an exceptional boy, who displays real talent and curiosity, and is certain to make his name in the world.'

'And have you met such a paragon?' his father enquired.

'Yes,' replied George, without further elucidation.

◄○►

On a warm summer evening, George travelled to London by train and made his way on foot to No.23 Savile Row in Mayfair to join Geoffrey Young for dinner. A porter accompanied him to the members' bar, where George found his host chatting to a group of elderly climbers who were repeating tall stories about even taller mountains. When Young spotted his guest entering the room, he broke away and guided George towards the dining room with the words, 'I fear a bar stool is the highest thing that lot can climb nowadays.'

While they enjoyed a meal of brown Windsor soup and steak and kidney pie followed by vanilla ice cream, Young took George through the programme he had planned for their forthcoming trip to the Alps. But George had a feeling that his host had something more important on his mind, as he had already written to him setting out in great detail which new climbs they would be attempting that summer. It wasn't until they retired to the library for coffee and brandy that George discovered the real purpose behind Young's invitation.

'Mallory,' said Young once they had settled in the far corner of the room, 'I wondered if you'd care to join me as my guest at the RGS next Thursday evening, when Captain Scott will be addressing the Society on his forthcoming expedition to the South Pole.'

George nearly spilt his coffee, he was so excited by the prospect of hearing the intrepid explorer talk about his Voyage of Discovery, not least because he'd recently read in *The Times* that every ticket had been taken up within hours of the Society announcing the speaker for its annual memorial lecture.

'How did you manage to—' began George.

'As a committee member of the Alpine Club, I was able to wangle a couple of extra tickets out of the secretary of the RGS. However, he did request a small favour in return.'

George wanted to ask two questions at once, but it quickly became clear that Young had already anticipated them.

'Of course, you'll be interested to know who my other guest is,' said Young. George nodded. 'Well, it won't come as much of a surprise, because I've invited the only other climber in your class.' Young paused. 'But I must confess that the favour the RGS secretary requested did come as a surprise.'

George put down his coffee cup on a side table, folded his arms and waited.

'It's quite simple really,' said Young. 'Once Captain Scott has finished his lecture and calls for questions, the secretary wants you to raise your hand.'

16

It was one of those rare occasions when George was on time. He had rehearsed his question during the train journey up from Godalming and, although he felt confident that he knew the answer, he was still puzzled why the RGS secretary wanted *him* to ask it.

George had been disappointed when he'd read in *The Times* earlier that year that it was an American, Robert Peary, not an Englishman who had been the first to reach the North Pole. But as the subject of Captain Scott's lecture was 'The South Pole yet unconquered', he assumed that, just as Geoffrey Young had suggested, the great explorer was about to make a second attempt to make amends.

George jumped off the train at Waterloo as it came to a halt, ran along the platform and handed in his ticket before going off in search of a hansom cab. Young had warned him that such was Scott's popularity most of the seats would be taken at least an hour before the lecture was due to begin.

There was already a small queue forming at the entrance to the RGS by the time George presented his invitation card. He joined the chattering crowd as they made their way to the lecture theatre on the ground floor.

When George entered the recently built theatre, he was surprised by how grand it was. The oak-panelled walls were covered with oil paintings of past presidents of the RGS, while the dark parquet floor was covered by what must have been five hundred plush red chairs, perhaps even more. The raised stage at the front of the hall was dominated by a full-length portrait of King George V.

George scanned the rows, searching for Geoffrey Young. He finally spotted him on the far side of the room, seated next to Finch. George quickly made his way across the hall and took the seat next to Young.

'I couldn't have held on to it for much longer,' said Young with a grin.

'Sorry,' said George, as he leant across to shake hands with Finch. He looked around the theatre to see if he knew anyone. Somervell, Herford and Odell were seated near the back. The thing that struck George most was that there were no women in the body of the hall. He knew they could not be elected as fellows of the RGS, but why couldn't they attend as guests? He could only wonder what would have happened if Cottie Sanders had been one of Geoffrey Young's guests. Would they have put her in the front row perhaps, which remained unoccupied? He glanced towards the upper gallery, where several smartly dressed ladies in long gowns and shawls were taking their seats. He frowned before turning his attention back to the stage, where two men were erecting a large silver screen. In the central aisle another man was checking slides in a magic lantern, flicking the shutter backwards and forwards.

The lecture theatre was filling up quickly, and long before the clock below the gallery chimed eight times, a number of members and their guests found themselves having to stand in the aisles and at the back of the room. On the eighth chime, the committee, crocodile-like, entered the room and took their places in the front row, while a short, elegantly dressed gentleman wearing a white tie and tails strode up onto the stage, to be greeted with loud applause. He raised the palms of his hands as if warming himself by a fire, and immediately the applause died down.

'Good evening, ladies and gentlemen,' he began. 'My name is Sir Francis Younghusband. I have the honour of being your chairman this evening, and I believe that tonight's lecture promises to be one of the most exciting in the Society's long history. The RGS prides itself on being a world leader in two different, but not unrelated fields: first, the surveying and drawing up of maps of previously uncharted territories; and second, exploring those distant and dangerous lands where no white man has ever trodden before. One of the Society's statutes allows us to support and encourage those single-minded individuals who are willing to travel the length and breadth of the globe, risking their lives in the service of the British Empire.

'One such man is our lecturer tonight, and I have no doubt,' continued Sir Francis as he glanced up at the portrait of the King, 'that we are about to learn of his plans to make a second attempt to be the first of His Majesty's subjects to reach the South Pole. It is a well-worn phrase to suggest that a speaker needs no introduction, but I suspect there isn't a man, woman or child in our land who does not know the name Captain Robert Falcon Scott RN.'

The audience rose as one as a clean-shaven, stockily built man with fierce blue eyes and in a naval uniform marched out from the wings. He took his place at the centre of the stage, his legs thrust apart, giving the impression that he did not intend to be moved for some time. He smiled down at his audience and, unlike Sir Francis, made no attempt to quell their enthusiasm, ensuring that it was some time before he was able to speak.

George was captivated from Scott's first sentence. He spoke for over an hour, never once referring to notes, while dozens of slides projected on the screen behind him brought dramatically to life his previous expedition to the Antarctic in his ship the *Discovery*. His words were regularly interrupted by spontaneous bursts of applause.

The audience learnt how Captain Scott went about selecting his team, and the qualities he demanded: loyalty, courage and unquestioning discipline were, it seemed to him, prerequisites. He then went on to explain the deprivation and hardship his men would have to take for granted if they hoped to survive for four months in the Antarctic trekking 400 miles across a frozen wasteland on an uncharted journey to the South Pole.

George stared in disbelief at images of men who had been on his previous expedition, some of whom had lost not only fingers and toes to severe frostbite, but ears and in one case even a nose. One of the slides caused a woman in the gallery to faint. Scott paused for a moment before adding, 'Each of the men who accompanies me on this enterprise must be prepared to undergo such suffering if he still hopes to be standing when we eventually reach the South Pole. And never forget, my most important responsibility is to ensure that all my men return home safely.'

George only wished that he could be among those who would be invited to join Scott, but he knew that an inexperienced schoolmaster whose greatest achievement to date was conquering Mont Blanc was an unlikely candidate for Scott's team.

Scott ended his lecture by thanking the RGS, its committee and fellows for their continued support, aware that without their backing he couldn't even consider raising anchor at Tilbury, let alone docking in McMurdo Sound fully equipped and ready to carry out such an ambitious enterprise. When the lights came up, Scott gave a slight bow and the audience rose as one to acknowledge a very British hero. George could only wonder what it must feel like to be standing on that stage receiving such plaudits and, more importantly, what would be expected of him to prove worthy of such adulation.

When the applause eventually died down and the audience resumed their places, Scott thanked them once again before inviting questions from the floor.

A gentleman rose in the front row.

'That's Arthur Hinks,' whispered Geoffrey Young. 'He's just been appointed secretary of the RGS.'

'Sir,' Hinks began, 'rumours abound that the Norwegians, led by Amundsen, are also planning an assault on the South Pole. Does this concern you?'

'No, it does not, Mr Hinks,' replied Scott. 'Let me assure you and the Society's fellows that it will be an Englishman, not a Viking, who will be the first to reach the South Pole.' Once again these sentiments were greeted with loud applause.

From the dozen hands that shot up, Scott next selected a man seated in the third row. The left breast of his dinner jacket was adorned with rows of campaign medals.

'I read in *The Times* this morning, sir, that the Norwegians are willing to use motorized sledges as well as dogs, to make sure they reach the Pole ahead of you.'

Several cries of 'Shame!' emanated from the body of the hall. 'May I ask what your response is to this blatant disregard of the amateur code?' Finch looked at the questioner in disbelief.

'I shall simply ignore them, General,' Scott replied. 'My enterprise remains a challenge of man's superiority over the elements, and I am in no doubt that I have assembled a group of gentlemen who are more than ready to face this challenge.'

Cries of 'Hear, hear!' came from every quarter of the packed hall, although Finch did not join in.

'And allow me to add,' continued Scott, 'that I intend to be the first *human* to reach the South Pole, not the first dog.' He paused. 'Unless, of course, it's a bulldog.'

Laughter followed, before several more hands shot up, George's among them. However, Captain Scott answered three more questions before he pointed in George's direction.

'A young gentleman on the end of the fifth row is showing the sort of determination I look for when selecting my team, so let's hear what he has to say.'

George rose slowly from his place, his legs shaking. He felt five hundred pairs of eyes staring at him.

'Sir,' he said, his voice quivering, 'once you have reached the South Pole, what will there be left for an Englishman to conquer?' He collapsed back onto his chair as some of the audience burst out laughing, while others applauded. A puzzled expression appeared on Finch's face. Why would Mallory ask a question he already knew the answer to?

'The next great challenge for any Englishman,' said Scott without hesitation, 'will undoubtedly be the scaling of the highest mountain on earth, Mount Everest in the Himalaya. It stands at over 29,000 feet above sea level – that's almost five and a half miles high, my boy – and we have no idea how the human body will react to such altitude, as no man has yet been above 22,000 feet. And that's before you consider temperatures that can fall below minus forty degrees Fahrenheit, and winds that will cut your skin to shreds. But of one thing I am certain: dogs and motorized sledges will be of little use up there.' He paused and, looking directly at George, added, 'But whoever succeeds in that magnificent endeavour will be the first man to stand on the roof of the world. I envy him. Let us hope that he will be an Englishman. However,' Scott concluded, turning his attention to a lady seated in the front row of the gallery, 'I have already promised my wife that I will leave that particular challenge to a younger man.' Scott looked back down at George as the audience burst once again into spontaneous applause.

Finch's hand immediately shot up, and Scott nodded in response. 'Do you consider yourself to be an amateur or a professional, sir?'

An audible gasp could be heard around the hall as Finch stared defiantly at the speaker.

Scott took his time before replying, never once taking his eyes off Finch. 'I am an amateur,' he eventually replied, 'but an amateur who surrounds himself with professionals. My doctors, engineers, drivers and even my cooks are all fully qualified, and would be insulted were you to describe them as amateurs. But they would be even more insulted if you were to suggest that their presence on this expedition was motivated by a desire for financial gain.'

This reply was greeted by the loudest applause of the evening, and prevented anyone other than Young and Mallory from hearing Finch say, 'If he really believes that, he has no hope of coming back alive.'

After two or three more questions, Scott once again thanked the RGS for sponsoring the lecture and for their wholehearted backing of his latest enterprise. This was followed by a vote of thanks from Mr Hinks on behalf of the Society, after which the audience stood to attention and lustily sang the National Anthem.

While Young and Finch joined those leaving the theatre, George remained in his place, unable to take his eyes off the stage Scott had occupied; a stage from which one day he intended to address the RGS. Finch grinned when he looked back and saw the immovable Mallory. Turning to Young, he said, 'He'll still be sitting there, listening just as intently, when it's my turn to deliver the annual lecture.'

Young smiled at the presumptuous pup. 'And what, dare I ask, will be the subject of your talk?'

'Everest conquered,' Finch replied. 'Because this lot –' gesturing with a sweeping arm – 'won't let me stand on that stage unless I'm the man who gets there first.'

BOOK TWO

THE OTHER WOMAN

PART TWO

THE OTHER WOMAN

1914

17

Monday, February 9th, 1914

'When Elizabeth ascended the English throne in 1558, neither the court nor the common people welcomed her as their monarch. However, when she died in 1603, forty-five years later, the Virgin Queen was as popular as her father King Henry the Eighth had ever been.'

'Sir, sir,' said a boy in the front row, his hand held high.

'Yes, Carter minor,' said George.

'What's a virgin, sir?'

George ignored the sniggers that followed, and carried on as if he had been asked a serious question. 'A virgin is a female who is *virgo intacta*, Carter minor. I hope your Latin is up to it. Should it not be, you can always look up Luke 1: 27, *To a virgin espoused to a man whose name was Joseph ... and the virgin's name was Mary*. But back to Elizabeth. This was the golden era of Shakespeare and Marlowe, of Drake and Raleigh, a time when the English not only defeated the Spanish Armada, but also put down a civil insurrection led by the Earl of Essex, who some historians have suggested was the Queen's lover.'

Several inevitable hands shot up.

'Wainwright,' said George wearily, only too aware what his question was going to be.

'What's a lover, sir?'

George smiled. 'A lover is a man who lives with a woman, but not in the state of holy matrimony.'

'Then there's no chance of a lover being *virgo intacta*, is there, sir?' said Wainwright with a smirk.

'You are quite right, Wainwright, although I suspect that Elizabeth never took a lover, as it would have called her authority as monarch into question.'

Another hand shot up. 'But wouldn't the court and the common people have preferred to have a man, like the Earl of Essex, on the throne rather than a woman?'

George smiled again. Graves, one of those rare boys who preferred the classroom to the games field, was not one to ask frivolous questions. 'By that time, Graves, even Elizabeth's original detractors would have preferred her to the Earl of Essex. Indeed, over three hundred years later this woman surely ranks as the equal of any man in the pantheon of English monarchs,' he concluded as the chapel bell sounded in the distance.

George looked around to see if there were any more questions. There were none. He sighed. 'That will be all then,' he said. 'But gentlemen,' he added, his voice rising, 'please be sure that your essays on the religious and political significance of Henry the Eighth's marriage to Anne Boleyn are on my desk by midday on Thursday.'

An audible groan went up as the lower fifth gathered their text books and made their way out of the classroom.

George picked up the blackboard duster and began to rub out the names and dates of Henry's six queens. He turned round to see that Graves was still sitting in his place.

'Can you name all six of them, Robert, and the years in which they became Queen?' he asked.

'Catherine of Aragon, 1509, Anne Boleyn, 1533, Jane Seymour, 1536, Anne of Cleves, 1540, Catherine Howard, 1540, and Catherine Parr, 1543.'

'And next week I'll teach you a simple way of recalling their fates.'

'Divorced, beheaded, died, divorced, beheaded, survived. You told us last week, sir.'

'Did I indeed?' said George as he placed the duster back on his desk, seemingly unaware of just how much chalk had ended up on his gown.

George followed Graves out of the classroom and made his way across the quad to the masters' common room to join his colleagues for the mid-morning break. Although he had proved to be a popular master with the majority of staff as well as the boys, he was well aware that not all of his colleagues approved of what they described in hushed tones as his *laissez-faire* attitude, and one or two of them openly voiced the opinion that the lack of discipline in his classes was undermining their own authority, especially when they had to teach the lower fifth on the same day.

When Dr Rendall decided the time had come to take Mallory to one side and have a word with him on the subject, George simply informed him that he believed in self-expression, otherwise how could any boy realize his full potential? As the headmaster had no idea what 'self-expression' meant, he decided not to press the matter. After all, he was due to retire at the end of the school year, when it would become someone else's responsibility.

George had made only one real friend among his colleagues. Andrew O'Sullivan had been a contemporary of his at Cambridge, although they had never met. He had read Geography and won a boxing blue while he was at Fitzwilliam, but despite the fact that he showed no interest in mountaineering, and even less in the beliefs of Quintus Fabius Maximus, he and George had immediately found that they enjoyed each other's company.

When George entered the common room he spotted Andrew slumped in a comfortable leather chair by the window, reading a newspaper. George poured himself a cup of tea and strolled across to join his friend.

'Have you seen *The Times* this morning?' Andrew asked.

'No,' said George, placing his cup and saucer on the table between them. 'I usually catch up with the news after evensong.'

'The paper's correspondent in Delhi,' said Andrew, 'is reporting that Lord Curzon has brokered a deal with the Dalai Lama to allow a select group of climbers to enter—'

George leant forward a little too quickly and knocked over his colleague's tea cup. 'Sorry, Andrew,' he said as he grabbed the newspaper.

Andrew looked faintly amused by his friend's rare lapse of good manners, but said nothing until George had handed the paper back. 'The RGS is inviting interested parties to apply,' continued Andrew. 'Are you by any chance, my dear Mallory, an interested party?'

George didn't want to answer until he'd given the question a little more thought, and was relieved when the bell alerting masters that break would end in five minutes came to his rescue.

'Well,' said Andrew as he rose from his chair, 'if you feel unable to answer that particular question, allow me put a less demanding one to you. Are you doing anything other than reading *The Times* on Thursday evening?'

'Marking the lower fifth's essays on the Armada,' said George. 'I do believe that lot find a sadistic pleasure in rewriting history. Wainwright even appears to think that the Spanish won the battle, and Drake ended up in the Tower.'

Andrew laughed. 'It's just that one of the school governors, a Mr Thackeray Turner, has invited me to join him for dinner that night, and asked if I'd like to bring a friend.'

'It's kind of you to think of me, Andrew,' George said as they walked out of the common room and into the quad, 'but I expect Mr Turner meant a lady friend.'

'I doubt it,' said Andrew. 'At least not while he's still got three unmarried daughters. By the way, George, do you play billiards?'

18

Thursday, February 12th, 1914

George chalked his cue. He liked Thackeray Turner the moment he met him: blunt, open and straightforward, if somewhat old-fashioned, and forever testing your mettle.

Andrew had told George on the journey to Turner's home that he was an architect by profession. When George was driven through a fine pair of wrought-iron gates and down a long avenue of lime trees to see Westbrook for the first time, nestling in the Surrey hills, surrounded by the most magnificent flower beds, lawns and a sunken water garden, he didn't need to be told why Turner had made such a success of his career.

Before they had reached the top step, a butler had opened the front door for them. He guided them silently down a long corridor, where they found Turner waiting in the billiard room. As his dinner jacket was hanging over the back of a nearby chair, George assumed that he was prepared for battle.

'Time for a game before the ladies come down for dinner,' were Turner's first words to his guests. George admired a full-length portrait of his host by Lavery above the fireplace, and other nineteenth-century watercolours that adorned the walls – including one by his host's namesake – before he removed his jacket and rolled up his sleeves.

Once the three balls had been placed in position on the green baize, George was quickly introduced to another side of his host's character. Mr Turner liked winning, and even expected to win. What he hadn't anticipated was that George didn't like losing. George wasn't sure if Andrew was simply happy to humour the old man, or just wasn't that good a player. Either way, George wasn't quite so willing to fall in with his host's expectations.

'Your turn, old fellow,' said Turner, after he had posted a break of eleven.

George took some time considering his shot, and when he handed his cue to Andrew he'd amassed a break of fourteen. It soon became clear that Turner had met his match, so he decided to try a different tactic.

'O'Sullivan tells me that you're a bit of a radical, Mallory.'

George smiled. He wasn't going to let Turner get the better of him, on or off the table. 'If you are alluding to my support for universal suffrage, you would be correct, sir.'

Andrew frowned. 'Only three points,' he said before adding that sum to his meagre total.

Turner returned to the table, and didn't speak again until he had posted another twelve to his name, but just as George bent down to line up his next shot, Turner asked, 'So you would give women the vote?'

George stood back up and chalked his cue. 'I most certainly would, sir,' he replied before lining up the balls once again.

'But they haven't been sufficiently educated to take on such a responsibility,' said Turner. 'And in any case, how can one ever expect a woman to make a rational judgement?'

George bent over the table again, and this time he had scored another twenty-one points before he handed over his cue to Andrew, who failed to score.

'There's a simple way to remedy that,' said George.

'And what might that be?' asked Turner as he surveyed the table and considered his options.

'Allow women to be properly educated in the first place, so that they can go to university and study for the same degrees as men.'

'Presumably this would not apply to Oxford and Cambridge?'

'On the contrary,' said George. 'Oxford and Cambridge must lead the way, because then the rest will surely follow.'

'Women with degrees,' snorted Turner. 'It's unthinkable.' He bent down to take his next shot, but miscued, and the white ball careered into the nearest pocket. George had to make a supreme effort not to burst out laughing. 'Let me be sure I understand exactly what you are proposing, Mallory,' said Turner as he handed the cue to his guest. 'You are of the opinion that clever women, the ones with degrees from Oxford and Cambridge, should be given the vote?'

'No, sir, that is not what I was proposing,' said George. 'I believe that the same rule should apply to women as it does to men. The stupid ones should get a vote as well.'

A smile appeared on Turner's lips for the first time since the game had begun. 'I can't see Parliament agreeing to that. After all, turkeys don't usually vote for Christmas.'

'Until one of the turkeys works out that it might just win them the next election,' George suggested as he successfully executed a cannon and pocketed the red. He stood up and smiled. 'My game, I believe, sir.'

Turner nodded reluctantly. As he was putting his jacket on, there was a gentle tap on the door. The butler entered. 'Dinner is served, sir.'

'Thank you, Atkins,' said their host. Once he'd left the room, Turner whispered, 'I'd wager a year's income that Atkins wouldn't give women the vote.'

'And I'd wager a year's income that you've never asked him,' said George, regretting his words the moment he uttered them. Andrew looked embarrassed, but said nothing.

'I do apologize, sir,' said George. 'That remark was unforgivable, and—'

'Not at all, dear boy,' said Turner. 'I fear that since my wife died I have become something of – what's the modern expression? – an old fuddy-duddy. Perhaps we should join the ladies for dinner.' As they crossed the hall he added, 'Well played, Mallory. I look forward to a return match, when no doubt you'll enlighten us with your views on workers' rights.'

The butler held open the door to allow Turner and his guests to enter the dining room. A large oak table that looked more Elizabethan than Victorian dominated the centre of the oak-panelled room. Six places had been laid, with the finest cutlery, linen and china.

As George walked in, he caught his breath, which he rarely did even when he stood on the top of a mountain. Although all three of Mr Turner's daughters, Marjorie, Ruth and Mildred, were waiting to be introduced, George's gaze remained fixed on Ruth, causing her to blush and look away.

'Don't just stand there, Mallory,' said Turner, noticing that George was still hovering in the doorway. 'They won't bite you. In fact, you're far more likely to find them in sympathy with your views than mine.'

George stepped forward and shook hands with the three young women, and tried not to show his disappointment when his host placed him between Marjorie and Mildred. Two maids served the first course, a plate of cold salmon and dill, while the butler poured half a glass of Sancerre for Turner to taste. George ignored the most appetizing dish he'd seen in weeks as he tried to steal the occasional glance at Ruth, who was seated at the other end of the table. She seemed quite unaware of her own beauty. *Botticellian*, he whispered to himself as he contemplated her fair skin, china blue eyes and luxuriant reddish brown hair. *Botticellian*, he repeated, as he picked up his knife and fork.

'Is is true, Mr Mallory,' asked Marjorie, the eldest of the three sisters, interrupting his thoughts, 'that you have met Mr George Bernard Shaw?'

'Yes, Miss Turner, I had the honour of dining with the great man after he addressed the Fabian Society at Cambridge.'

'Great man be damned,' said Turner. 'He's just another socialist who delights in telling us all how we should conduct our lives. The fellow isn't even an Englishman.'

Marjorie smiled benignly at her father. 'The theatre critic of *The Times*,' she continued, still addressing George, 'felt that *Pygmalion* was both witty and thought-provoking.'

'He's probably a socialist as well,' said Turner between mouthfuls.

'Have you seen the play, Miss Turner?' asked George, turning to Ruth.

'No, Mr Mallory, I haven't,' Ruth replied. 'The last theatre production we attended was *Charley's Aunt* in the village hall, and that was only after the vicar had banned a reading of *The Importance of Being Earnest.*'

'Written by another Irishman,' said Turner, 'whose name should not be mentioned in respectable society. Don't you agree with me, Mallory?' he asked as the first course was removed. George's untouched salmon looked as if it was still capable of swimming.

'If respectable society is unable to discuss the two most gifted playwrights of their generation, then yes, sir, I agree with you.'

Mildred, who had not spoken until that moment, leant across and whispered, 'I do so agree with you, Mr Mallory.'

'What about you, O'Sullivan,' asked Turner. 'Are you of the same opinion as Mallory?'

'I rarely agree with anything George says,' replied Andrew, 'which is why we remain on such good terms.' Everyone burst out laughing as the butler placed a baron of beef on the sideboard and, having presented it to his master for approval, began to carve.

George took advantage of the distraction to glance once again towards the other end of the table, only to find that Ruth was smiling at Andrew.

'I must confess,' Andrew said, 'that I have never attended a play by either gentleman.'

'I can assure you, O'Sullivan,' said Turner after sampling a glass of red wine, 'that neither of them is a gentleman.'

George was about to respond when Mildred jumped in. 'Ignore him, Mr Mallory. It's the one thing our father can't abide.'

George smiled, and indulged himself in a more genteel conversation with Marjorie about basket weaving until the plates had been cleared away, although he did steal a glance towards the other end of the table from time to time. Ruth didn't appear to notice.

'Well, gentlemen,' said Mr Turner as he folded his napkin, 'let us hope that you've learnt one lesson from this evening.'

'And what might that be, sir?' asked Andrew.

'To make sure that you don't end up with three daughters. Not least because Mallory won't rest until they've all gone to university and been awarded degrees.'

'A capital suggestion, Mr Mallory,' said Mildred. 'Had I been given the opportunity to follow my father's example and become an architect, I would have happily done so.'

For the first time that evening, Mr Turner was struck dumb. It was some time before he recovered sufficiently to suggest, 'Perhaps we should all go through to the drawing room for coffee?'

This time it was the girls who were unable to hide their surprise at Papa's break with traditional routine. Usually he enjoyed a brandy and cigar with his male guests before he even considered joining the ladies.

'A memorable victory, Mr Mallory,' whispered Marjorie as George held back her chair. George waited until all three sisters had left the dining room before he made his move. He was pleased to see that Andrew was deep in conversation with the old man.

Once Ruth had taken her place on the sofa in the drawing room, George casually strolled across and sat down beside her. Ruth said nothing, and appeared to be looking across at Andrew, who had joined Marjorie on the chaise-longue. Having achieved his objective, George was suddenly lost for words. It was some time before Ruth came to his rescue.

'Did you defeat my father at billiards, by any chance, Mr Mallory?' she eventually offered.

'Yes, I did, Miss Turner,' said George as Atkins placed a cup of coffee by her side.

'That would explain why he was so argumentative during dinner.' She took a sip of her coffee before adding, 'Should he invite you again, Mr Mallory, perhaps it might be more diplomatic to let him win.'

'I'm afraid I could never agree to that, Miss Turner.'

'But why not, Mr Mallory?'

'Because it would reveal a weakness in my character that she might find out about.'

'She?' repeated Ruth, genuinely puzzled.

'Chomolungma, Goddess Mother of the Earth.'

'But my father told me that it was Everest that you were hoping to conquer.'

'"Everest" is the name the English have labelled her with, but it's not the one she answers to.'

'Your coffee will be getting cold, Mr Mallory,' said Ruth as she glanced across the room.

'Thank you, Miss Turner,' he said, taking a sip.

'And are you hoping to become better acquainted with this goddess?' she enquired.

'In time, perhaps, Miss Turner. But not before one or two other ladies have fallen under my spell.'

She looked at him more quizzically. 'Anyone in particular?'

'Madame Matterhorn,' he replied. 'It's my intention to leave a calling card during the Easter vacation.' He took another sip of his cold coffee before asking, 'And where will you be spending Easter, Miss Turner?'

'Father is taking us to Venice in April. A city that I suspect would not meet with your approval, Mr Mallory, as it languishes only a few feet above sea level.'

'It's not only elevation that matters, Miss Turner. "Underneath day's azure eyes, ocean's nursling, Venice lies, a peopled labyrinth of walls, Amphitrite's destined halls."'

'So you admire Shelley,' said Ruth as she placed her empty cup back on a side table.

George was about to reply when the clock on the mantelpiece struck once to indicate that it was half past the hour. Andrew rose from his place and, turning to his host, said, 'It's been a delightful evening, sir, but perhaps the time has come for us to take our leave.'

George glanced at his watch: 10.30. The last thing he wanted to do was take his leave, but Turner was already on his feet, and

Marjorie was heading towards him. She gave him a warm smile. 'I do hope that you'll come and see us again soon, Mr Mallory.'

'I hope so too,' said George, still looking in Ruth's direction.

Mr Turner smiled. He might not have defeated Mallory, but one of his daughters certainly had the measure of him.

19

Friday, February 13th, 1914

George didn't want Andrew to discover what he was up to.

He couldn't get Ruth out of his mind. He had never come across such serene beauty, such delightful company, and all he had managed to do, when left alone with her, was stare into those blue eyes and make a complete fool of himself. And the more she smiled at Andrew, the more desperate he had become, quite unable to come up with a witty comment, or even to manage polite conversation.

How much he had wanted to hold her hand, but Mildred had kept distracting him, allowing Andrew to retain Ruth's attention. Did she have any interest in him at all, or had Andrew already spoken to her father? During dinner he had watched the two of them deep in conversation. He had to find out what they had talked about. He had never felt so pathetic in his life.

George had observed smitten men in the past, and had simply dismissed them as deluded fools. But now he had joined their number and, even worse, his goddess appeared to favour another creature. Andrew isn't worthy of her, George said out loud before he fell asleep. But then he realized that neither was he.

When he woke the following morning – if he had ever slept – he tried to dismiss her from his thoughts and prepare for the day's lessons. He dreaded the thought of forty minutes with the lower fifth, having to listen to their opinions of Walter Raleigh and the significance of his importing tobacco from Virginia. If only Guy wasn't serving as a diplomat on the other side of the world, he could ask his advice about what to do next.

To George, the first lesson that morning felt like the longest forty minutes in history. Wainwright almost made him lose his temper, and for the first time Carter minor got the better of him, but then thankfully the bell tolled. But for whom, he wondered? Not that any of them would have heard of Donne – except perhaps Robert Graves.

As George made his way slowly across the quad to the common room, he rehearsed the lines he'd gone over again and again during the night. He must stick to the script until every one of his questions had been answered, otherwise Andrew would work out what he was up to, and mock him. A hundred years ago George would have challenged him to a duel. Then he remembered which one of them had a boxing blue.

George strode into the main block trying to look confident and relaxed, as if he didn't have a care in the world. As he opened the common room door, he could hear his heart thumping. But what if Andrew wasn't there? He didn't think he could go through another lesson with the lower fifth until at least some of his questions had been answered.

Andrew was sitting in his usual place by the window, reading the morning paper. He smiled when he saw George, who poured himself a cup of tea and strolled across to join him. He was annoyed to find that a colleague had just taken the chair next to Andrew, and was busily discussing the iniquities of the school timetable.

George perched himself on the radiator between them. He tried to remember his first question. Ah, yes . . .

'Good show last night,' said Andrew as he folded his newspaper and turned his attention to George.

'Yes, good show,' George repeated lamely, even though it wasn't in his script.

'You seemed to be enjoying yourself.'

'Had a splendid time,' said George. 'Turner's quite a character.'

'He obviously took a shine to you.'

'Oh, do you think so?'

'Certain of it. I've never seen him so animated.'

'Then you've known him for some time?' ventured George.

'No, I've only been to Westbrook a couple of times, and he hardly opened his mouth.'

'Oh, really?' said George, his first question answered.

'So what did you think of the girls?' asked Andrew.

'The girls?' repeated George, annoyed that Andrew seemed to be asking him all his own questions.

'Yes. Did you take a fancy to any of them? Marjorie clearly couldn't take her eyes off you.'

'I didn't notice,' said George. 'What about you?'

'Well, it all came as a bit of a surprise, to be frank with you, old chap,' admitted Andrew.

'A bit of a surprise?' said George, hoping he didn't sound desperate.

'Yes. You see, I didn't think she had the slightest interest in me.'

'She?'

'Ruth.'

'Ruth?'

'Yes. On my two previous visits, she didn't give me a second look, but last night she never stopped chatting. I think I might be in with a chance.'

'In with a chance?' George bobbed up.

'Are you all right, Mallory?'

'Of course I am. Why do you ask?'

'Well, it's just that you keep repeating everything I say.'

'Everything you say? Do I?' said George, sitting back down on the radiator. 'Then you'll be hoping to see Ruth again, will you?' he ventured, at last getting in one of his questions.

'Well, that's the funny thing,' said Andrew. 'Just after dinner, the old man took me to one side and invited me to join the family in Venice over Easter.'

'And did you accept?' asked George, horrified by the very idea.

'Well, I'd like to, but there's a slight complication.'

'A slight complication?'

'You're at it again,' said Andrew.

'Sorry,' replied George. 'What's the complication?'

'I've already committed myself to a hockey tour of the West Country at Easter, and as I'm the only goalkeeper available, I don't feel I can let the team down.'

'Certainly not,' said George, having to jump up again. 'That would be damn bad form.'

'Quite,' said Andrew. 'But I think I may have come up with a compromise.'

'A compromise?'

'Yes. If I were to miss the last match, I could take the boat train from Southampton on the Friday evening and be in Venice by Sunday morning, which would mean I could still spend a whole week with the Turners.'

'A whole week?' said George.

'I put the idea to the old man, and he seemed quite agreeable, so I'll be joining them during the last week of March.'

That was all George needed to know. He jumped off the radiator, the seat of his trousers scorched.

'Are you sure you're all right, Mallory? You seem quite distracted this morning.'

'Blame it on Wainwright,' said George, glad of the chance to change the subject.

'Wainwright?' said Andrew.

'I nearly lost my temper with him this morning when he suggested that it was the Earl of Essex who defeated the Spanish Armada, and Drake wasn't even there.'

'Playing bowls on Plymouth Hoe, no doubt.'

'No, Wainwright has a theory that Drake was at Hampton Court at the time, having a protracted affair with Elizabeth, and that he'd sent Essex off to Devon to keep him out of the way.'

'I thought it was meant to be the other way round,' said Andrew.

'Let's hope so,' said George.

20

Tuesday, March 24th, 1914

The first couple of days' climbing had gone well, even if Finch seemed a little preoccupied and not his usual forthright self. It wasn't until the third day, when they were both stuck on a ledge halfway up the Zmutt Ridge, that George found out why.

'Do you begin to understand women?' asked Finch, as if this was something they discussed every day.

'Can't say I have a great deal of experience in that particular field,' admitted George, his thoughts turning to Ruth.

'Join the club,' responded Finch.

'But I always thought you were considered to be a bit of an authority on the subject?'

'Women don't allow any man to be an authority on the subject,' said Finch bitterly.

'Fallen in love with someone, have you?' asked George, wondering if Finch was suffering from the same problem as he was.

'Out of love,' said Finch. 'Which is far more complicated.'

'I feel sure it won't be too long before you find a replacement.'

'It's not a replacement I'm worried about,' said Finch. 'I've just found out that she's pregnant.'

'Then you'll have to marry her,' said George matter-of-factly.

'That's the problem,' Finch said. 'We're already married.'

That was the nearest George had come to falling off a mountain since the avalanche on Mont Blanc.

A head appeared over the ledge. 'Let's keep moving,' said Young. 'Or can't you two see a way out of the problem?'

As neither of them replied, Young simply said, 'Follow me.'

For the next hour, all three men struggled gamely up the last thousand feet, and it wasn't until George had joined Young and Finch at the top of the mountain that Finch spoke again.

'Is there any news about the one mountain we all want to stand on top of?' he asked Young.

Although George didn't approve of Finch's blunt approach, he hoped that Young would answer the question, as one thing was certain: no one was going to overhear them at 14,686 feet on the summit of the Matterhorn.

Young looked out across the valley, wondering how much information he should divulge. 'Anything I have to say on this subject must remain between the three of us,' he said eventually. 'I'm not expecting an official announcement from the Foreign Office for at least another couple of months.' He didn't speak again for a few moments, and for once even Finch remained silent. 'However, I can tell you,' he continued at last, 'that the Alpine Club has come to a provisional agreement with the Royal Geographical Society to set up a joint body which will be known as the Everest Committee.'

'And who will be sitting on that committee?' asked Finch.

Once again Young took his time before responding. 'Sir Francis Younghusband will be chairman, I will be deputy chairman, and Mr Hinks will be secretary.'

'No one can object to Younghusband as chairman,' said George, choosing his words carefully. 'After all, he was instrumental in getting an Everest expedition off the ground.'

'But that doesn't apply to Hinks,' responded Finch, not choosing his words carefully. 'There's a man who's managed to turn snobbery into an art form.'

'Isn't that a little rough, old boy?' suggested George, who had thought he could no longer be shocked by anything Finch came out with.

'Perhaps you failed to notice that at Scott's RGS lecture the women, including Hinks's and Scott's wives, were relegated to the gallery like cattle on a goods train.'

'Traditions die hard in such institutions,' suggested Young calmly.

'Don't let's excuse snobbery by passing it off as tradition,' said Finch. 'Mind you, George,' he added, 'Hinks will be delighted if you're chosen as one of the climbing party. After all, you went to Winchester and Cambridge.'

'That was uncalled for,' said Young sharply.

'We'll find out if I'm right soon enough,' said Finch, standing his ground.

'You need have no fear on that front,' said Young. 'I can assure you that it will be the Alpine Club that selects the climbing team, not Hinks.'

'That may be,' said Finch, unwilling to let go of his bone, 'but what really matters is who sits on that committee.'

'It will have seven members,' said Young. 'Three of them will be from the Alpine Club. Before you ask, I shall be inviting Somervell and Herford to join me.'

'Couldn't say fairer than that,' said George.

'Possibly,' said Finch. 'But who are the RGS's candidates?'

'Hinks, a fellow called Raeburn, and a General Bruce, so our numbers will be equal.'

'That leaves Younghusband with the casting vote.'

'I have no problem with that,' said Young. 'Younghusband's been an excellent president of the RGS, and his integrity has never been in question.'

'How very British of you,' remarked Finch.

Young pursed his lips before adding, 'Perhaps I should point out that the RGS will only be selecting those members of the party who will be responsible for drawing up detailed maps of the outlying district and collecting geological specimens, as well as flora and fauna that are unique to the Himalaya. It will be up to the Alpine Club to choose the climbing party, and it will also be our task to identify a route to the summit of Everest.'

'And who's likely to lead the expedition?' asked Finch, still not giving an inch.

'I expect it will be General Bruce. He's served in India for years, and is one of the few Englishmen who is familiar with the Himalaya as well as being a personal friend of the Dalai Lama's. He would be the ideal choice to take us across the border into Tibet. Once we reach the foothills of Everest and have established base camp, I will take over as climbing leader, with the sole responsibility of ensuring that it's an Englishman who is the first man to stand on the roof of the world.'

'I'm an Australian,' Finch reminded him.

'How appropriate that another member of the Commonwealth will be standing by my side,' said Young with a smile, before adding, 'Perhaps it might be wise for us to begin our descent, gentlemen. Unless you were planning to spend the night on top of this mountain?'

George put his goggles back on, excited by Young's news, although he suspected that Finch had provoked him to reveal far more than he had originally intended.

Young placed a sovereign on the highest point of the Matterhorn, bowed and said, 'His Majesty pays his compliments, ma'am, and hopes you will allow his subjects a safe journey home.'

'One more question,' said Finch.

'And only one,' said Young.

'Do you have any idea when this expedition plans to leave for Tibet?'

'Yes,' replied Young. 'It can't leave any later than February next year. We'll have to establish base camp by May if we're to have time to reach the summit before the monsoon season sets in.'

Finch seemed satisfied with this reply, but George could only wonder how Mr Fletcher, the newly appointed headmaster of Charterhouse, would react to one of his staff requesting a six-month leave of absence.

Young led them slowly back down the mountain, not wasting

any words on small talk until they were on safer ground. When their hotel came into sight, he uttered his last words on the subject. 'I would be obliged, gentlemen, if this matter was not referred to again, even between ourselves, until the Foreign Office has made an official announcement.'

Both men nodded. 'However,' Young added, 'I hope you don't have anything else planned for 1915.'

-◄◦►-

Finch was on his way down to dinner, dressed in an open-necked shirt, flannel trousers and a sports jacket, when he spotted Mallory at the reception desk writing out a cheque.

'Off on another little adventure, are we?' enquired Finch, looking down at the suitcase by Mallory's feet.

Mallory smiled. 'Yes. I have to admit that you're not the only man I'm trying to stay a yard ahead of.'

Finch glanced at the label attached to the suitcase. 'As there are no mountains that I'm aware of in Venice, I can only assume that another woman must be involved.'

George didn't reply as he handed his cheque to the clerk standing behind the counter.

'Just as I thought,' said Finch. 'And as you've already implied that I'm something of an expert when it comes to the fairer sex, allow me to warn you that trying to juggle two women at once, even if they do live on different continents, is never easy.'

George grinned as he folded his receipt and placed it in an inside pocket. 'My dear Finch,' he said, 'allow me to point out that there has to be a first woman before there can be a second.' Without another word he picked up his suitcase, gave Finch a thin smile and headed towards the front door.

'I wouldn't repeat that when you come face to face with Chomolungma for the first time,' said Finch quietly. 'I have a feeling that particular lady might well turn out to be an unforgiving mistress.'

George didn't look back.

21

Thursday, March 26th, 1914

Ever since he had set eyes on her at Westbrook, George hadn't been able to get Ruth out of his mind, even when he was climbing. Was that the reason Finch had reached the top of the Matterhorn before him, and Young had chosen Somervell and Herford to join him on the Everest Committee? Was Finch right when he had suggested that at some time George would have to decide between them? No choice was necessary at the moment, thought George, as both the ladies in question were studiously ignoring him.

George had slipped away from Zermatt on the Tuesday night, leaving his colleagues to settle their differences with one or two of the lesser peaks. He boarded the train for Lausanne, changing at Visp, where he spent most of his time planning how they might casually bump into each other – that was, assuming he managed to find her.

As the train rattled along, George couldn't help thinking that although mountains were not to be depended on, at least they remained in one place. Wouldn't it be all too obvious that he'd travelled from Switzerland to Italy specially to see her? He knew one person who would work it out immediately.

When George disembarked at Lausanne, he purchased a third-class ticket on the Cisalpino to Verona, from where he would join the express for Venice. There was no need to waste money on a more expensive ticket when all he intended to do was sleep. And he would have slept if he hadn't been seated next to a Frenchman who clearly felt that every dish he ate should be liberally laced with garlic, and whose snoring rivalled the engine for noise.

George was able to grab only a few moments' sleep before the train reached its destination. He had never visited Venice before, but Baedeker's guide had been his constant companion for the past month, so by the time he stepped out onto the platform at Santa Lucia, he knew the exact location of every five-star hotel in the city. He even knew that the Firenze was the first hotel in Europe to offer what they described as an en-suite bathroom.

Once the waterbus had dropped him off at the Piazza San Marco, George went in search of the one hotel he could afford that wasn't miles from the city centre. He checked into the smallest room on the top floor, a proper place for a mountaineer, and settled down, desperate for a good night's sleep. He would, like all well-prepared climbers, have to rise before the sun if he hoped to carry out his little subterfuge. He was confident that the Turners wouldn't be setting foot outside whichever hotel they were staying at much before ten o'clock.

George spent another sleepless night, and this time he couldn't blame garlic or a rattling train, but rather a mattress with no springs and a pillow that had never been introduced to more than a handful of feathers; even his young charges at Charterhouse would have complained.

He rose before six, and was crossing the Rialto Bridge half an hour later, accompanied by late revellers and a few early morning workers. He took a list of hotels from the inside pocket of his jacket, and set about his quest methodically.

The first establishment he entered was the Hotel Bauer, where he asked at the reception desk if the Turner family – one elderly gentleman and his three daughters – were guests. The night porter ran a finger down a long list before shaking his head. At the nearby Hotel Europa e Regina, George received the same response. The Hotel Baglione had a Thompson and a Taylor, but no Turner, while the night manager of the Gritti Palace waited for a tip before he even considered answering George's question, but then gave him the same response. The next hotel refused to divulge the names of its guests, even after George claimed to be a close friend of the family.

He was beginning to wonder if the Turners had changed their holiday plans until the head porter of the San Clemente, an Englishman, gave a smile of recognition when he heard the name, although he didn't smile again until George had passed over a large-denomination note. The Turners' party, he told him, were not staying at the San Clemente, but they occasionally dined there, and he had once been asked to book a vaporetto to take them back to . . . He didn't finish the sentence until a second note of the same denomination had joined the first . . . back to their hotel. A third note secured the hotel's name, the Cipriani, as well as the dock where its private water taxi always dropped off its guests.

George placed a thinner wallet back in his jacket pocket and made his way quickly to Piazza San Marco, from where he could see the island of Giudecca, on which the Cipriani hotel proudly stood. Every twenty minutes a water taxi docked with the name *Cipriani* on its bow. He stepped into the shadows of a large archway from where he could observe every boat as it disgorged its customers, confident that an elderly gentleman accompanied by three young ladies would be easy enough to identify, especially when the vision of one of those ladies had rarely left his mind for the past six weeks.

For the next two hours George checked every customer coming by water taxi from Giudecca. After another hour he began to wonder if the Turners had moved to a different hotel; perhaps the one that had refused to divulge its guest list. He watched as the cafés all around him began to fill up. The pervading aroma of freshly baked panini, crostini and piping hot coffee reminded him he hadn't had any breakfast. But he dared not desert his post, for fear that if he did so, that would be the moment the Turner family set foot on the shore. George decided that if they hadn't appeared by midday, he might have to risk taking the taxi across to the island, and even entering their hotel. But if he were to bump into them, how would he explain what he was doing there? Mr Turner would have known that a night at the Cipriani would barely have been covered by George's monthly salary, however small the room was.

And then George saw her. His first thought was that she was even more beautiful than he'd remembered. She was wearing a long, empire-line yellow silk dress with a wide red ribbon tied just below the bust. Her wavy auburn hair fell to her shoulders, and she shaded herself from the morning sun with a white parasol. If you'd asked him what Marjorie and Mildred were wearing, he wouldn't have been able to tell you.

Mr Turner was the first to step onto the quay. He was dressed in a smart cream suit, white shirt and striped tie. He raised an arm to assist his daughters as they stepped off the boat. George was relieved to see no sign of Andrew, who he hoped was defending a goal in Taunton.

The Turners strolled off in the direction of Piazza San Marco with an air of knowing exactly where they were heading, as indeed they clearly did, because when they walked into a crowded café, the head waiter immediately guided them to the only unoccupied table. Once they had ordered, Turner settled down to read the previous day's *Times* while Ruth leafed through a book that must have been a guide to Venice, because she kept sharing the contents with her sisters while occasionally pointing out landmarks.

At one point Ruth looked in his direction, and for a moment George wondered if she had seen him, although you rarely notice someone you're not looking for, especially if they're obscured by shadows. He waited patiently until Mr Turner called for the bill, realizing that the next part of his plan could not be put off for much longer.

The moment the Turners left the café, George stepped out of the shadows and headed towards the centre of the square. His eyes never left Ruth, the guidebook still open in her hand. She was now reading passages out from it while the rest of the family listened intently. George began to wish he was back on top of a mountain, even if it had meant that Finch was his only companion. Surely the moment they saw him they would twig. There was only one way he was going to find out.

He emerged from behind a group of ambling tourists, and when he was just a few paces away, came to a halt in front of Mr Turner.

'Good morning, sir,' said George, raising his boater and trying to look astonished. 'What a pleasant surprise.'

'Well, it's certainly a surprise for me, Mr Mallory,' said Turner.

'And a most pleasing one,' said Marjorie.

'Good morning, Miss Turner,' said George, once again raising his hat. Although Mildred rewarded him with a shy smile, Ruth continued to read her guidebook, as if George's unexpected appearance was nothing more than an irritating distraction.

'Before the five arched portals of the Basilica,' she declared, her voice rising, 'rests the Piazza San Marco, a vast, paved, arcaded square once described by Napoleon as the drawing room of Europe.'

George continued to smile at her, feeling like Malvolio because like Olivia, she didn't return the compliment. He was beginning to feel that he had embarked on a wasted journey, and should never have allowed himself to imagine, even for a moment . . . He would slip away, and they would soon forget he'd ever been there.

'The bell tower,' continued Ruth, looking up, 'rises to a height of three hundred and twenty-five feet, and visitors can reach the parapet by ascending its four hundred and twenty-one steps.'

George raised his hat to Mr Turner, and turned to leave.

'Do you think you could manage that, Mr Mallory?' asked Ruth.

George hesitated. 'Possibly,' he said, turning back. 'But the weather conditions would have to be taken into consideration. A high wind might make it difficult.'

'I can't imagine why a high wind would make it difficult if you were safely inside, Mr Mallory.'

'And then one must always remember, Miss Turner,' continued George, 'that the most important decision when considering any climb is the route you select. You rarely end up going in a straight line, and if you make the wrong choice, you might have to turn back unrewarded.'

'How interesting, Mr Mallory,' said Ruth.

'But if a more direct route does present itself, you should always be prepared to consider it.'

'I can find nothing in Baedeker to suggest that there might be a more direct route,' said Ruth.

That was the moment George decided that if he was going to leave them, he might as well do it in style.

'Then perhaps the time has come to write a new chapter for your guidebook, Miss Turner.' Without another word, George took off his hat and jacket, and handed them to Ruth. He took one more look at the tower, then walked towards the public entrance, where he joined the line of tourists waiting to go inside.

When he got to the front of the queue, he leapt onto the turnstile and reached up to grasp the archway above the entrance. He pulled himself up and stood on the ledge. Moments later, with a line of startled onlookers following his progress, he was hanging from the first parapet. He paused for a moment to consider his next move. It was to place his right foot on the statue of a saint – Saint Thomas, Mildred noted – who looked doubtful.

Mr Turner turned his attention away from George for a moment, as he progressed from ledge to ledge, buttress to buttress, to observe his daughters. Mildred appeared fascinated by George's skill, while Marjorie had a look of awe on her face, but it was Ruth's reaction that took him most by surprise. Her face had gone deathly pale, and her whole body seemed to be trembling. When George appeared to lose his footing only a few feet from the top, Mr Turner thought his favourite daughter was going to faint.

George looked down into the crowded square, no longer able to identify Ruth among the patchwork quilt of speckled colours below. He placed both hands firmly on the wide balustrade, pulled himself up onto the top parapet, and joined the visitors who had made the ascent by a more orthodox route.

A small group of mesmerized tourists took a step back, hardly able to believe what they were witnessing. One or two of them had taken photographs so they could prove to the folks back home that they hadn't made it up. George leant over the balustrade and began to consider his route back down – that was until he spotted two members of the Carabinieri running into the square.

George could not risk returning by the same route if there was a possibility of adding an Italian prison to his French experience. He bolted towards the main exit at the top of the stairs and joined the sightseers who were beginning to make their slow progress down the winding stone staircase back to the square. He brushed past several of them, finally slowing his pace to join a party of Americans who had clearly not witnessed his efforts. Their only topic of conversation was where they would be having lunch.

As they spilled out of the tower and back into the square, George linked arms with an elderly American matron from Illinois, who didn't protest. She smiled up at him. 'Have I ever told you I had a relative who was on the *Titanic*?'

'No,' said George. 'How fascinating,' he added, as the group passed two Carabinieri who were searching for an unaccompanied man.

'Yes, it was my sister's child, Roderick. You know, he wasn't even meant . . .' but George had already disappeared.

Once he had escaped from the crowded square, he made his way swiftly back to his hotel, but never once broke into a run for fear of attracting attention. It only took him fifteen minutes to pack, settle the bill – a surcharge was added for checking out after midday – and leave.

He walked briskly in the direction of the Rialto Bridge, where he knew there would be a vaporetto to take him to the railway station. As the motor launch glided slowly past Piazza San Marco, he spotted an officer questioning a young man who must have been about his own age.

When he was dropped off at Santa Lucia station he headed straight for the booking office and asked the clerk what time was the next train to London Victoria.

'Three o'clock, sir,' he replied, 'but I'm afraid I have no more first-class tickets available.'

'Then I'll have to settle for third class,' said George, emptying his wallet.

George nipped into the shadows whenever he spotted a policeman, and it seemed an eternity before the platform bell was rung and a guard, at the top of his voice, invited all first-class passengers to board the express. George joined the select group as they strolled towards the train, suspecting that they were the last people the police would be taking any interest in. He even thought about climbing onto the roof of the train, but decided that it would leave him even more exposed.

Once George was on board he hung around in a corridor, keeping a wary eye out for any ticket collectors. He was just wondering whether he should lock himself in a lavatory and wait there until the train had moved off, when a voice behind him said, 'Il vostro biglietto, signore, per favore.'

George swung round to see a man dressed in a long blue jacket with thick gold piping on the lapels and holding a leather book. He looked out of the window, and spotted a policeman walking down the platform and peering in the carriage windows. He began to make a pretence of searching for his ticket, when the policeman boarded the carriage.

'I must have mislaid it,' said George. 'I'll just go back to the booking office, and—'

'No need to do that, sir,' said the ticket collector, switching languages effortlessly. 'All I require is your name.'

'Mallory,' George said with resignation, as the policeman headed towards him.

'Ah, yes,' said the ticket collector. 'You're in carriage B, stateroom eleven. Your wife has already arrived, sir. Would you care to follow me?'

'My wife?' said George, before following the ticket collector through the dining car and into the next carriage, trying to think up some plausible excuse before the ticket collector realized his mistake. When they reached cabin number 11, the concierge pulled open a door marked *Riservato*. George peered inside to see his jacket and boater on the seat opposite her.

'Ah, there you are, darling,' said Ruth. 'I was beginning to wonder if you'd make it in time.'

'I thought you weren't going back to England for another week,' George spluttered, taking the seat by her side.

'So did I,' replied Ruth. 'But someone once told me that if a more direct route presents itself, you should be prepared to consider it, unless of course there's a high wind.'

George laughed, and wanted to leap in the air with joy, until he remembered an encumbrance every bit as terrifying as the Italian police. 'Does your father know you're here?'

'I managed to convince him that, on balance, it wouldn't be a good thing for the school's reputation to have one of its masters languishing in an Italian jail just before the new term begins.'

'What about Andrew? Weren't you meant—'

Ruth threw her arms around him.

George heard the door of the compartment sliding open. He didn't dare look round.

'Of course the answer's yes, my darling,' said Ruth before kissing him.

'Scusi.' The policeman saluted before adding, 'Mille congratulazioni, signore!'

22

Friday, May 1st, 1914

'Your shot, I believe,' said Turner.

George lined up the tip of his cue on the white. He could feel his legs shaking as he made the shot. He miscued and the ball careered wildly up and down the table, bouncing off a side cushion before coming to rest several inches from the red.

'Foul,' said Turner. 'And four more points for me.'

'Agreed,' sighed George, as his host returned to the table. Turner didn't speak again until he had amassed another sixteen points.

◄○►

The past month had been the happiest of George's life. In fact, he had had no idea that such happiness could exist. As each day went by, he fell more and more in love with Ruth. She was so bright, so gay, such fun to be with.

The journey back to England had been idyllic. They had spent every minute getting to know each other, although George did have a flash of anxiety when the train stopped at the Italian border and a customs official took a close look at his passport. When they finally crossed the border into France, George relaxed for the first time, and even spent a moment thinking about Young and Finch climbing in Zermatt. But only a moment.

He told Ruth over dinner why he'd ordered all five courses on the menu, explaining that he hadn't eaten for three days. She laughed when he described the last person he'd spent a night with on a train, a man who belched garlic when he was awake and snored fumes while he was asleep.

'So you haven't slept for the past three nights,' she said.

'And it doesn't look as if I will tonight either, my darling,' said George.

'I can't pretend that this was how I expected to spend my first night with the man I love,' said Ruth. 'But why don't we . . .' she leant across the table and whispered in George's ear. He thought about her proposal for a moment, and then happily agreed.

A few minutes later, Ruth left the table. In their compartment she found that the seats had been converted into single beds. She undressed, hung up her clothes, washed her face in the little hand basin, climbed into bed and switched off the light. George remained in the dining car, drinking black coffee. Only after the last remaining customer had departed did he return to the compartment.

He slid the door open quietly and slipped inside, then stood still for a moment, waiting for his eyes to become accustomed to the dark. He could see the outline of Ruth's slim body under the sheet, and wanted to touch her. He took off his jacket, tie, trousers, shirt and socks, and left them on the floor before climbing into bed. He wondered if Ruth was still awake.

'Good night, Mr Mallory,' she said.

'Good night, Mrs Mallory,' he replied. George slept soundly for the first time in three nights.

◄○►

As George bent down to take his next shot, Turner said, 'You wrote earlier in the week, Mallory, to say there was something of importance you wished to discuss with me.'

'Yes, indeed,' said George, as his cue ball disappeared into the nearest pocket.

'Another foul,' said Turner. He returned to the table and took his time piling up even more points, which only made George feel more and more inadequate.

'Yes, sir,' he finally managed, and then paused before adding, 'I'm sure you must have noticed that I've been spending a lot of time with your daughter.'

'Which one?' asked Turner as George missed another shot. 'Another foul. Are you hoping to score anything this evening, young man?'

'It was just, sir, just that . . .'

'You would like my blessing before you ask Ruth for her hand in marriage.'

'I've already asked her,' admitted George.

'I would hope so, Mallory. After all, you have already spent a night with her.'

◄◦►

When George had woken after that night it was pitch dark. He leant forward and pushed the blind to one side to observe the first rays of sunlight creeping over the horizon: a joyful sight for any mountaineer.

He slipped quietly out of bed, felt around on the floor for his pants and slipped them on. Next he located the rest of his clothes. Not too difficult an exercise when you're used to sleeping in a small tent with only a candle to see by. George quietly slid open the compartment door and stepped outside. He looked up and down the corridor, thankful that no one was in sight. He quickly did up his shirt, pulled on his trousers and socks, tied his tie and slipped on his jacket. When he strolled into the dining car, the attendants laying the tables for breakfast were surprised to see a first-class passenger so early in the morning.

'Good morning, sir,' said a waiter who was staring at Mallory's trousers, looking slightly embarrassed.

'Good morning,' said George, and two paces later realized his fly buttons were undone. He laughed, did them up and hurried through the dining car in search of a morning paper.

It wasn't until he reached carriage K that he came across the newspaper kiosk. The sign in the window read *Chiuso*, but

George could see a young man standing behind the counter undoing the thick string from around a pile of newspapers. He stared at the front page in disbelief. He could only just recognize himself in the blurred photograph, but even with his limited command of Italian he could translate the headline: *Police seek mystery climber of St Mark's Campanile*.

He pointed to the pile of newspapers, and the assistant reluctantly unlocked the door.

'How many copies of that paper do you have?'

'Twenty, sir,' he replied.

'I'll take all of them,' said George.

The assistant looked uncertain, but when George handed over the cash, he shrugged his shoulders and deposited the money in the till.

George was admiring a piece of jewellery in the display cabinet when the assistant handed back his change. 'How much is that?' he asked, pointing to one of the velvet stands.

'Which currency, sir?'

'Pounds,' replied George, taking out his cheque book.

The young man ran his finger down a line of figures on a card attached to the back wall. 'Thirty-two pounds, sir.'

George wrote out a cheque for next month's salary, while the assistant wrapped the tiny gift.

George made his way back to the dining car with the papers under one arm, having put the gift in his jacket pocket. As he entered the next carriage, he glanced up and down the corridor again. Still no one around. He slipped into the nearest lavatory and spent the next few minutes tearing off the front page of every paper, except one, and considerably longer flushing them down the lavatory. The moment he'd seen the last headline disappear, he unlocked the door and stepped back into the corridor. As George continued on towards the dining car, he dropped a copy of the morning paper on the floor outside each stateroom.

—◁◦▷—

'But, sir, I can explain how that happened,' protested George as the object ball bounced off the table and ran along the floor.

'Another foul,' said Turner, picking up the ball and placing it back on the baize. 'I don't require an explanation, Mallory, but what are your prospects?'

'As you know, sir, I'm on the teaching staff at Charterhouse, where my current salary is three hundred and seventy-five pounds a year.'

'That's certainly not enough to keep one of my daughters in the style they've grown accustomed to,' said Turner. 'Do you by any chance have a private income?'

'No, sir, I do not. My father is a parish priest who had four children to bring up.'

'Then I shall settle seven hundred and fifty pounds a year on Ruth, and give her a house as a wedding present. Should there be any offspring, I shall pay for their education.'

'I could never marry a girl who had a private income,' said George haughtily.

'You couldn't marry Ruth if she *didn't* have one,' said Turner as he cannoned successfully off the red.

—◦—

George sat alone and sipped his coffee while he waited for Ruth to join him. Was there really a beautiful woman asleep in compartment B11, or was he about to wake from his dream and find himself locked up in an Italian jail, with no Mr Irving to rescue him?

Several other passengers had appeared and were enjoying their breakfast, although the waiters were unable to explain why their morning papers didn't have a front page. When Ruth walked into the dining car, George had only one thought: I'm going to have breakfast with this woman every morning for the rest of my life.

'Good morning, Mrs Mallory,' he said as he rose from his side of the table and took her in his arms. 'Do you begin to know how much I love you?' he added before kissing her.

Ruth blushed at the disapproving stares from a few of the older passengers.

'Perhaps we shouldn't kiss in public, George.'

'You were happy enough to kiss me yesterday in front of a policeman,' George reminded her as he sat back down.

'But only because I was trying to stop you being arrested.'

The waiter joined them and smiled ingratiatingly. After all, they were used to honeymoon couples on the Orient Express.

After the two of them had given their breakfast orders, George slid the front page of the morning paper across the table.

'Nice photograph, Mr Mallory,' Ruth whispered once she'd read the headline. 'And if it isn't bad enough for a girl to be compromised on her first date, I now seem to be harbouring a fugitive. So the first thing my father will want to know is whether your intentions are honourable, or can I only hope to be a criminal's moll?'

'I'm surprised you need to ask, Mrs Mallory.'

'It's just that my father told me that you already have a mistress who resides in very high places.'

'Your father is correct, and I explained to him that I have been promised to the lady in question since my coming of age, and several people have already borne witness to the engagement. It's what they call in Tibet an arranged marriage – where neither party sees the other before the wedding day.'

'Then you must visit this little hussy as soon as possible,' said Ruth, 'and tell her in no uncertain terms that you are spoken for.'

'I fear she's not that little,' said George with a grin. 'But once the diplomatic niceties have been sorted out, I hope to pay her a visit early in the new year, when I will explain why it's no longer possible for us to go on seeing each other.'

'No woman ever wants to be told that,' said Ruth, sounding serious for the first time. 'You can tell her that I'll agree to a compromise.'

George smiled. 'A compromise?'

'It's possible,' said Ruth, 'that this goddess may not agree to see you when you make your first approach, because like any woman, she will want to confirm that you are constant and will return to woo her again. All I ask, George, is that once you have seduced your goddess, you will return to me, and never court her again.'

'Why so serious, my darling?' asked George, taking her hand.

'Because when I saw you climb St Mark's you convinced me of your love, but I also saw the risks you're willing to take if you believe in something passionately enough – whatever dangers are placed in your path. I want you to promise me that once you've stood on the summit of that infernal mountain, it will be for the first and last time.'

'I agree, and shall now prove it,' said George, letting go of her hand. He took the little package out of his pocket, removed the wrapping and placed the small leather box in front of her. Ruth opened the lid to reveal a slim gold ring set with a single diamond.

'Will you marry me, my darling?'

Ruth smiled. 'I thought we'd agreed on that yesterday,' she said as she slipped on the ring, leant across the table and gave her fiancé a kiss.

'But I thought we also agreed that . . .'

◄○►

George considered Mr Turner's offer for a moment before he said, 'Thank you, sir.' After managing to score three points, his first of the evening, he added, 'That's most generous of you.'

'It's no more, and certainly no less, than I decided when you came to see Ruth in Venice.' George laughed for the first time that evening. 'Despite the fact,' added Turner, 'that you only escaped being thrown in jail by a matter of minutes.'

'By a matter of minutes?'

'Yes,' Turner replied after he'd potted another red. 'I had a visit from the Italian police later that afternoon. They wanted to know if I'd come across an Englishman called Mallory who had at some time in the past been arrested in Paris for climbing the Eiffel Tower.'

'That wasn't me, sir,' said George.

'The description of this vagabond bore a striking resemblance to you, Mallory.'

'It's still not true, sir. I had at least a hundred feet to go when they arrested me.'

Turner burst out laughing. 'All I can say, Mallory, is that you'd better not plan to spend your honeymoon in France or Italy, unless you wish to spend your first night of married life in a prison cell. Mind you, when I looked into your criminal activities in Venice, it seems that you only broke a by-law.'

'A by-law?'

'Failure to pay an entrance fee when entering a public monument.' Turner paused, 'Maximum fine one thousand lira.' He smiled at his future son-in-law. 'On a more serious matter, dear boy – my game, I think.'

23

Tuesday, June 2nd, 1914

'Do you think we'll have to go to war, sir?' asked Wainwright on the first day of term.

'Let's hope not, Wainwright,' George replied.

'Why not, sir, if it's a just cause? After all, we should stand up for what we believe in; the English always have in the past.'

'But if it were possible to negotiate an honourable agreement with the Germans,' said George, 'wouldn't that be a better solution?'

'You can't negotiate an honourable agreement with the Hun, sir. They never keep to their side of the bargain.'

'Perhaps history will prove you wrong on this occasion,' said George.

'You've always taught us, sir, to study the past carefully if you want to predict the most likely outcome in the future, and the Hun—'

'The Germans, Wainwright.'

'The Germans, sir, have throughout history proved to be a warlike nation.'

'Some might say the same of the English, whenever it's been in our interests.'

'Not true, sir,' said Wainwright. 'England only goes to war when there's a just cause.'

'As seen by the English,' suggested George, which silenced Wainwright for a moment.

'But if we did have to go to war,' jumped in Carter minor, 'would you enlist?'

Before George could reply, Wainwright interjected, 'Mr Asquith has said that should we go to war, schoolmasters would be exempt from serving in the armed forces.'

'You seem unusually well informed on this subject, Wainwright,' said George.

'My father's a general, sir.'

'Views overheard in the nursery are always harder to dislodge than those taught in the classroom,' replied George.

'Who said that?' asked Graves.

'Bertrand Russell,' George replied.

'And everyone knows he's a conchie,' chipped in Wainwright.

'What's a conchie?' asked Carter minor.

'A conscientious objector. Someone who will use any excuse not to fight for his country,' said Wainwright.

'Everyone should be allowed to follow their own conscience, Wainwright, when it comes to facing a moral dilemma.'

'Bertrand Russell, no doubt,' said Wainwright.

'Jesus Christ, actually,' said George.

Wainwright fell silent, but Carter minor came back, 'If we were to go to war, sir, wouldn't that rather scupper your chances of climbing Everest?'

Out of the mouths of babes ... Ruth had put the same question to him over breakfast, as well as the more important one of whether he would feel it was his duty to enlist or, as her father had crudely put it, would hide behind the shield of a schoolmaster's gown.

'My personal belief—' began George just as the bell sounded. The class, in their eagerness not to miss morning break, didn't seem all that interested in his personal beliefs.

As George walked across to the common room, he dismissed any thoughts of war in the hope of coming to a peaceful settlement with Andrew, whom he hadn't seen since he'd returned from Venice. When he opened the common room door he spotted his chum sitting in his usual seat reading *The Times*. He didn't look up. George poured himself a cup of tea and walked slowly across to join him, quite ready for a bout of mental fisticuffs.

'Good morning, George,' Andrew said, still not looking up.

'Good morning, Andrew,' George replied, slipping into the seat beside him.

'I hope you had decent hols,' Andrew added as he abandoned his newspaper.

'Pleasant enough,' replied George cautiously.

'Can't say I did, old boy.'

George sat back and waited for the onslaught.

'I suppose you've heard about Ruth and me,' said Andrew.

'Of course I have,' said George.

'So what would you advise me to do about it, old boy?'

'Be magnanimous?' suggested George hopefully.

'Easy enough for you to say, old boy, but what about Ruth? I can't see her being magnanimous.'

'Why not?' asked George.

'Would you be if I let you down at the last moment?'

George couldn't think of a suitable reply.

'I really did mean to go to Venice, don't you know,' continued Andrew, 'but that was before we reached the semi-final of the Taunton Cup.'

'Congratulations,' said George, beginning to understand.

'And the lads prevailed on me, said I couldn't let the side down, especially as they didn't have another goalkeeper.'

'So you never went to Venice?'

'That's what I've been trying to tell you, old boy. And worse, we didn't even win the cup, so I lost out both ways.'

'Bad luck, old chap,' said George, trying to hide a smirk.

'Do you think she'll ever speak to me again?' asked Andrew.

'Well, you'll be able to find out soon enough,' said George.

Andrew raised an eyebrow. 'How come, old chap?'

'We've just sent you an invitation to our wedding.'

24

'Have you met this paragon of virtue?' asked Odell as he folded his copy of the *Manchester Guardian* and placed it on the seat beside him.

'No,' said Finch, 'but I should have guessed something was up when Mallory left us early and disappeared off to Venice.'

'I think it's what female novelists describe as a whirlwind romance,' said Young. 'They've only known each other a few months.'

'That would have been quite long enough for me,' chipped in Guy Bullock, who had returned to England. 'I can tell you chaps, she's ravishing, and anyone who might have been envious of George in the past will turn into a green-eyed monster the moment they set eyes on her.'

'I can't wait to meet the girl George fell for,' said Somervell with a grin.

'It's time to call this meeting to order,' said Young when the guard shouted, 'Next stop, Godalming.'

'To start with,' continued Young, 'I hope you all remembered to bring your ice axes . . .'

—◇—

'Wilt thou have this Woman to thy wedded wife, to live together after God's ordinance in the holy estate of Matrimony? Wilt thou love her, comfort her, honour, and keep her in sickness and in health; and, forsaking all other, keep thee only unto her, so long as ye both shall live?'

George never took his eyes off Ruth while his father was addressing him. 'I will,' he responded firmly.

The Reverend Mallory turned his attention to the bride, and smiled. 'Wilt thou have this Man to thy wedded husband, to live together after God's ordinance in the holy estate of Matrimony? Wilt thou obey him, and serve him, love, honour and keep him in sickness and in health; and forsaking all other, keep thee only unto him, so long as ye both shall live?'

'I will,' said Ruth, although few beyond the front pew would have heard her response.

'Who giveth this Woman to be married to this Man?' asked the Reverend Mallory.

Mr Thackeray Turner stepped forward.

Geoffrey Young, who was George's best man, handed the Reverend Mallory a simple gold ring. George slipped it onto the fourth finger of Ruth's left hand and said, 'With this Ring, I thee wed, with my body I thee worship, and with all my worldly goods I thee endow.'

Mr Turner smiled to himself.

The Reverend Mallory once more joined the couple's right hands, and addressed the congregation joyfully. 'I pronounce that they be Man and Wife together. In the name of the Father, and of the Son, and of the Holy Ghost. Amen.'

As the first strains of Mendelssohn's Wedding March sounded, George kissed his wife for the first time.

Mr and Mrs Mallory walked slowly down the aisle together, and George was delighted to see how many of his friends had taken the trouble to make the journey to Godalming. He spotted Rupert Brooke and Lytton Strachey, both Maynard and Geoffrey Keynes, as well as Ka Cox, who was sitting next to Cottie Sanders, who gave him a sad smile. But the real surprise came when they walked out of the church and into the warm sunshine, because waiting to greet them was a guard of honour made up of Young, Bullock, Herford, Somervell, Odell and of course George Finch, their shining ice axes held aloft to form an archway under which the bride and groom walked, confetti appearing like falling snow.

After a reception at which George and Ruth managed to speak to every one of their guests, the newlyweds left in Mr Turner's brand new bull-nose Morris, for a ten-day walking holiday in the Quantocks.

'So what did you make of the chaperons who will accompany me when I leave you to pay homage to the other woman in my life?' George asked as he drove down an empty, winding road.

'I can see why you're so willing to follow Geoffrey Young,' Ruth replied, studying the map resting in her lap. 'Especially after his thoughtful speech on behalf of the bridesmaids. Odell and Somervell looked as if, like Horatius, they'd stand by your side on the bridge, while I suspect Herford will match you step for step if he's chosen for the final climb.'

'And Finch?' said George, glancing at his bride.

Ruth hesitated. The tone of her voice changed. 'He'll do anything, George, and I mean anything, to reach the top of that mountain ahead of you.'

'What makes you feel so sure of that, my darling?' asked George, sounding surprised.

'When I came out of the church on your arm, he looked at me as if I was still a single woman.'

'As many of the bachelors in the congregation might have done,' suggested George. 'Including Andrew O'Sullivan.'

'No. Andrew looked at me as if he *wished* I was still a single woman. There's a world of difference.'

'You may be right about Finch,' admitted George, 'but there's no climber I'd rather have by my side when it comes to tackling the last thousand feet of any mountain.'

'Including Everest?'

'Especially Chomolungma.'

—◦—

The Mallorys pulled up outside their small hotel in Crewkerne just after seven o'clock that evening. The manager was standing at the entrance waiting to greet them, and once they had completed the guest register – signing as 'Mr and Mrs Mallory' for only the second time – he accompanied them to the bridal suite.

They unpacked their suitcases, thinking about, but not mentioning, the one subject that was on their minds. When they had completed this simple task, George took his wife by the hand and accompanied her down to the dining room. A waiter handed them a large menu, which they studied in silence before ordering.

'George, I was wondering,' began Ruth, 'if you had—'

'Yes, my darling?'

Ruth would have completed the sentence if the waiter hadn't returned carrying two bowls of piping hot tomato soup which he placed in front of them. She waited until he was out of earshot before she tried again.

'Do you have any idea just how nervous I am, my darling?'

'Not half as nervous as me,' admitted George, not lifting his spoon.

Ruth bowed her head. 'George, I think you ought to know—'

'Yes, my darling?' said George, taking her hand.

'I've never seen a naked man, let alone—'

'Have I ever told you about my visit to the Moulin Rouge?' asked George, trying to ease the tension.

'Many times,' said Ruth with a smile. 'And the only woman you showed any interest in on that occasion was Madame Eiffel, and even she spurned you.'

George laughed, and without another word rose from his place and took his wife by the hand. Ruth smiled as they left the dining room, just hoping that no one would ask why they hadn't even tasted their soup.

They walked quickly up the three flights of stairs without another word. When they arrived outside their bedroom, George fumbled with the key and finally managed to open the door. As soon as they were inside, he took his wife in his arms. Eventually he released her, took a step back and smiled. He slowly took off his jacket and tie, his eyes never leaving her. Ruth returned his smile, and unbuttoned her dress, allowing it to fall to the floor, revealing a long silk petticoat that fell just below the knees. She pulled it slowly over her head, and once it had joined the dress on the floor, George took her in his arms and kissed her. While she tried to pull off his trousers, he fumbled with the strap of her bra. Once they were both naked, they just stood and stared at each other for a moment before they fell onto the bed. George stroked her long auburn hair while Ruth kissed him gently as they began to explore each other's bodies. They quickly became aware that there wasn't anything to be nervous about.

After they had made love, Ruth fell back on the pillow and said, 'Now tell me, Mr Mallory, who you'd rather spend the night with, Chomolungma or me?'

George laughed so loud that Ruth had to place a hand over his mouth for fear they might be heard in the next room. He held her in his arms until she finally fell into a deep sleep.

George was the first to wake the next morning, and began to kiss Ruth's breasts until her eyes blinked open. She smiled up at him as he took her in his arms, his hands moving freely over her body. George could only wonder what had happened to the shy girl who couldn't take a single spoonful of soup the previous evening. After they had made love a second time, they padded furtively down the corridor to the bathroom where Ruth joined George in the largest bath they'd ever seen. Afterwards he sat on the end of the bed, a towel wrapped around his waist, and watched his beautiful wife as she dressed.

Ruth blushed. 'You'd better hurry up, George, or we'll miss breakfast as well.'

'Suits me,' said George.

Ruth smiled, and slowly unbuttoned her dress.

◄○►

For the next ten days George and Ruth roamed around the Quantocks, often returning to their hotel long after the sun had set. Each day, Ruth continued to quiz George about her rival, trying to understand why Chomolungma had such a hold over him. He was still planning to leave for Tibet early in the new year, which would mean they'd be apart for at least six months.

'How many days and nights do you think it will take you to reach the summit?' she asked as they stood on the top of Lydeard Hill.

'We have no way of knowing,' George admitted. 'But Finch is convinced that we'll have to sleep in smaller and smaller tents as our altitude increases. We might even have to spend the last night at 27,000 feet before we attempt the final assault.'

'But how can you begin to prepare for such an ordeal?' asked Ruth as she looked down from 2,700 feet.

'I have no idea,' said George as they began to stroll back down the hill, hand in hand. 'No one knows how the human body will react to altitudes above 22,000 feet, let alone 29,000, where the temperature can be minus forty, and if the wind's in your face, you have to take ten steps just to advance a few feet. Finch and I once spent three days in a small tent at 15,000 feet, and at one point it became so cold that we ended up in the same sleeping bag, having to cling to each other all night.'

'I'd like to cling to you all night,' Ruth said with a grin, 'so that when you leave me, I'll have a better understanding of what you're going through.'

'I don't think you're quite ready for 29,000 feet, my darling. Even a couple of nights in a small tent on a beach could prove quite a baptism.'

'Are you sure you're up to it, Mr Mallory?'

'The last time you asked me that, Mrs Mallory, I nearly ended up in jail.'

In the nearest town they found a shop that sold camping supplies, and George bought a small canvas tent and a single sleeping bag. After a hearty dinner back at their hotel, they slipped out into the night and drove to the nearest beach. George selected an isolated spot facing the ocean which offered them little protection from the fierce wind. They began to hammer enough pegs into the sand to be sure that their first home wouldn't be blown away.

Once they'd secured the tent, anchoring the pegs with stones, Ruth crawled inside while George remained on the beach. Once he'd taken his clothes off, he joined Ruth in the tent and climbed into the sleeping bag, wrapping his arms around his shivering wife. After they'd made love, Ruth didn't let go of her husband.

'You'd leave home to sleep like this, night after night?' she asked in disbelief.

'At minus forty degrees, with air so thin that you may hardly be able to breathe.'

'While hugging another man, Mr Mallory. You've still got a few months to change your mind,' she added wistfully.

Neither of them could remember when they fell asleep, but they would never forget when they woke. George blinked as a flashlight beamed in his eyes. He sat up to find Ruth, her skin now covered in midge bites, still clinging to him.

'If you'd be kind enough to step outside, sir,' said an authoritative voice.

George had to decide whether to be gallant, or leave his wife freezing in the nude. He decided on Sir Galahad, and slowly, so as not to wake Ruth, crawled out of the tent to find two officers from the local constabulary shining their torches directly at his naked body.

'May I ask exactly what you're up to, sir?' asked the first officer.

George thought about telling them that his wife wanted to know what it would be like to spend a night on Mount Everest, but he settled for, 'We're on our honeymoon, sergeant, and just wanted to spend a night on the beach.'

'I think you'd better both come down to the station, sir,' said a voice from behind the other torch. 'But perhaps you and your wife ought to get dressed first.'

George crawled back into the tent to find Ruth laughing.

'What's so funny?' he demanded as he slipped his trousers on.

'I did warn you that you'd get arrested.'

A chief inspector who had been woken in the middle of the night and asked to come down to the station to interview the two suspects, soon found himself apologizing.

'What made you think we were spies?' George asked him.

'You pitched your tent less than a hundred yards from a top secret naval depot,' said the chief inspector. 'I'm sure I don't have to remind you, sir, that the Prime Minister has asked everyone to be vigilant while we prepare for war.'

25

October 1914

The received wisdom had been that the war would be all over by Christmas.

George and Ruth had returned to Godalming after their honeymoon to settle in the house Mr Turner had given his daughter as a wedding present. The Holt was more than either of them could have asked for, and certainly more than George had expected. Set in ten acres of land, it was a magnificent house with a garden in which Ruth knew she would be spending many happy hours pottering about.

No one could have been in any doubt how much George loved his wife, and Ruth had the glow of a woman who knows she's cherished. They wanted for nothing, and anyone who saw them together must have considered them a charmed couple, living an idyllic existence. But it was a façade, because George had a conscience.

During the next few months George could only stand by as many of his friends and contemporaries from Cambridge, and even some of the young men he'd taught at Charterhouse, left for the Western Front, never to return, while the only sacrifice he'd made was to put off his proposed trip to Tibet until after the hostilities had ceased. It didn't help that the friends who visited him at The Holt always seemed to be in uniform. Brooke, Young, Somervell, Odell, Herford and even Finch dropped in to spend the night before travelling on to France. George often wondered if any of them thought he'd found an easy way out. But even though they never once raised the subject, indeed went out of their way to stress the importance of the work he was doing, he could never be sure. And whenever the headmaster, Mr Fletcher, read out the names of those Old Carthusians who had sacrificed their lives in the service of their country, it only made him feel more guilty.

George decided to discuss his misgivings with his oldest friend, Guy Bullock, who had returned to London to take up a post at the War Office. Guy tried to reassure him that there could be no greater calling than to teach the next generation of children, who would have to take the place of those who had fallen.

George next sought the counsel of Geoffrey Young, who reminded him that if he did decide to join up, someone else would have to take his place. He also mulled over the never-ending debate with Andrew O'Sullivan, who wasn't in any doubt that they were doing the right thing by remaining at their posts. Mr Fletcher was even more adamant, saying that he couldn't afford to lose someone with George's experience.

Whenever he raised the subject with Ruth, she left him in no doubt about how she felt. It finally caused their first argument since they'd been married.

George was finding it more and more difficult to sleep at night as he wrestled with his conscience, and Ruth often lay awake too, aware of the dilemma he was going through.

'Are you still awake, my darling?' she whispered one night.

He leant over and kissed her gently on the lips, before placing an arm around her as she rested her head on his shoulder.

'I've been thinking about our future,' George said.

'Bored with me already are you, Mr Mallory?' she teased. 'And to think we've only been married for a few months.'

'Terrified of losing you would be nearer the truth,' George said quietly. He felt her body stiffen. 'No one knows better than you, my darling, just how guilty I feel about not joining my friends in France.'

'Have any of those friends said anything to make you feel guilty?' she asked.

'No, not one of them,' admitted George. 'Which only makes it more telling.'

'But they know you're serving your country in a different way.'

'No one, my darling, can exempt themselves from their conscience.'

'If you were killed, what would that achieve?'

'Nothing, other than that you'd know I'd done the honourable thing.'

'And I'd be a widow.'

'Along with so many other women married to honourable men.'

'Have any of the staff at Charterhouse joined up?'

'I can't speak for my colleagues,' replied George, 'but I can speak for Brooke, Young, Bullock, Herford, Somervell and Finch, who are among the finest men of my generation, and who haven't hesitated to serve their country.'

'They've also made it clear that they understand your position.'

'Perhaps, but *they* haven't taken the easy way out.'

'The man who climbed St Mark's Campanile could never be accused of taking the easy way out,' protested Ruth.

'But what if that same man failed to join his comrades at the Front when his country was at war?' George took his wife in his arms. 'I understand how you feel, my darling, but perhaps—'

'Perhaps it would make a difference, George,' she interrupted, 'if I told you I was pregnant?'

—◇—

This joyful piece of news did delay George from making a decision, but soon after the birth of his daughter, Clare, the feelings of guilt resurfaced. Having a child of his own made him feel an even greater responsibility to the next generation.

George continued to teach as the war dragged on, but it didn't help that every day he had to pass a recruitment poster on his walk to school, showing a young girl seated on her father's lap, asking, *Daddy, what did YOU do in the Great War?*

What would he tell Clare?

With each friend George lost, the nightmare revisited him. He had read that even the bravest of men could snap when going over the top and facing gunfire for the first time. George was sitting peacefully in his usual pew in the school chapel when he snapped.

The headmaster rose from his place to lead the morning service. 'Let us pray,' he began, 'for those Old Carthusians who have made the ultimate sacrifice by laying down their lives for the greater cause. Sadly,' he continued, 'I must add two new names to that growing list. Lieutenant Peter Wainwright of the Royal Fusiliers, who died at Loos while leading an attack on an enemy post. Let us remember him.'

'Let us remember him,' repeated the congregation.

George buried his head in his hands and wept silently before the headmaster added the second name.

'Second Lieutenant Simon Carter, who many of us will fondly remember as Carter minor, was killed while serving his country in Mesopotamia. Let us remember him.'

While the rest of the congregation lowered their heads and repeated, 'Let us remember him,' George rose from his place, bowed before the altar and marched out of the chapel. He didn't stop walking until he'd reached Godalming High Street, where he joined a queue of young men standing in line outside the local recruitment office.

'Name?' said the recruiting sergeant when George reached the front of the queue.

'Mallory.'

The sergeant looked him up and down. 'You do realize, sir, that under the terms of the new Conscription Act, schoolmasters are exempt from military service?'

George took off his long black gown and mortar board, and threw them in the nearest wastepaper basket.

BOOK THREE

NO MAN'S LAND

1916

26

My darling Ruth,

It was one of the unhappiest days of my life when we parted on that cold, desolate railway station in Godalming. Only being allowed a weekend together after I'd completed my basic training was cruel indeed, but I promise, I will write to you every day.

It was kind of you to leave me with the assurance that you believe I'm doing the right thing, even though your eyes revealed your true feelings.

I joined my regiment at Dover, and bumped into a few old friends. Do you remember Siegfried Herford? What a difficult decision he had to make, having a German father and an English mother.

The following day we set off for ▇▇▇▇▇▇ in a boat that leaked like a colander and bobbed up and down like a rubber duck. One of the lads suggested it must have been a personal gift from the Kaiser. We spent most of the crossing using our billycans to return gallons of water to the ocean. You will recall from our last trip across the Channel that I've never been much of a sailor, but I somehow managed not to be sick in front of the men.

We docked at ▇▇▇▇▇▇ at first light, without much sign of the French taking any part in this war. I joined a couple of brother officers in a café for a hot croissant and some coffee. We met up with some other officers returning from

*the Front, who advised us to enjoy our last meal on a table
cloth (let alone the luxury of a china plate) for several
months, and reminded us that we would be sitting in a
different sort of dining room in 24 hours' time.*

*As usual I can be relied on to forget something, and this
time it was your photograph. I'm desperate to see your face
again, even if it's only in black and white, so please send me
the snap I took of you on Derden Heights the day before we
were arrested. I want to carry it with me all the time.*

*God knows I miss you, and I don't begin to understand
how one can be surrounded by so many people, so much
furious activity and so much deafening noise, and still feel so
very lonely. I'm just trying to find another way of saying that
I love you, although I know you'd tease me if I were to
suggest that you are the only woman in my life. But I
already look upon Chomolungma as just an old flame.*

Your loving husband,
George

Once George had handed the letter to his regiment's postal clerk,
he hung around waiting for the convoy of trucks to begin its one-
way journey to the front line.

In the space of a few miles, the beautiful French countryside
of Millet and Monet, with its dappled greens and bright yellows,
and sheep and cows grazing in the fields, had been replaced by a
far uglier canvas of burnt and withered trees, slaughtered horses,
roofless houses and desolate civilians who had become pawns on
the chessboard of war.

The convoy rolled relentlessly on, but before George was
given the chance to be deafened by the noise, he watched as
angry grey and black clouds of sulphurous fumes gathered until
they completely masked the sun. They finally came to a halt at a
camp three miles behind the front line, which didn't have a
signpost and where the days had been turned into perpetual
night. Here, George met a group of men in uniform who
wondered if they would be alive in twenty-four hours.

After a billycan of bully beef with a plate of stuck-together beans and maggot-riddled potatoes, George was billeted in a tent with three fellow officers, all younger than himself. They had experienced varying lengths of service – one month, nine weeks and seven months: the last, a Lieutenant Evans, considered himself something of a veteran.

The following morning, after George had devoured breakfast served on a tin plate, he was driven forward to an artillery post some four hundred yards behind the front line, where he was to relieve Evans, who was long overdue a fortnight's furlough.

'It's not all bad, old fellow,' Evans assured him. 'It's a damn sight less dangerous than the front line. Think of those poor bastards just a quarter of a mile in front of you, waiting for the sound of the lone bugle that will send them over the top, having spent months being stalked by death. Our job's simple in comparison. You have a detail of thirty-seven soldiers under your command, and twelve howitzers which are hardly ever out of action, unless they break down. The senior NCO is Sergeant Davies. He's been out here for over a year, and before that he served fifteen years with the colours. He began army life as a private in the Boer War, so don't even think about making any sort of move until you've consulted him. Then there's Corporal Perkins. The damn man never stops complaining, but at least his sick sense of humour keeps the lads' minds off the Hun. You'll get to know the rest of the squad soon enough. They're a good bunch of fellows and won't let you down when it comes to the crunch.' George nodded, but didn't interrupt. 'The hardest decision you'll have to make,' Evans continued, 'comes every Sunday afternoon, when you have to send three lads to our forward look-out post for the next seven days. I've never known all three of them to return alive. It's their job to keep us informed of what the enemy's up to, so we can range our guns on them rather than our own troops.'

'Good luck, Mallory,' the young lieutenant had said as he shook hands with George later that morning. 'I'll say goodbye, in case we never meet again.'

September 5th, 1916

My dearest Ruth,

*I am stationed a long way behind the front line, so there's no need to feel at all anxious about me. I've inherited 37 men who seem to be good chaps, in fact one of them you may even remember – Private Rodgers. He used to be our postman before he joined up. Perhaps you could let his family know that he's alive and well, and actually doing rather well out here. He says he'll stay on in the army once this war is over. The rest of the lads have made me feel very welcome, which is good of them, as they're only too aware I joined up so recently. I understood for the first time this morning what my training officer back at *████████ *meant when he said a week in the field will serve you better than a three-month training course.*

I never stop thinking about you and Clare, my darling, and the world we are bringing our children into. Let's hope the politicians are right when they call this the war to end all wars, because I wouldn't want my children ever to experience this madness.

No man is expected to serve at the Front for more than three months at a time, so it's possible I'll be home in time for the birth of Clare's little brother or sister.

George stopped writing, and thought about his words. He knew all too well that King's regulations were regularly ignored when it came to granting leave, but he needed Ruth to stay optimistic. As for the reality of life on the Somme, he'd rather she didn't discover the truth about that until he was able to tell her face to face. He knew the anxiety she must have been suffering, when every day could bring the telegram that began, *It is with deep regret that the Secretary for War has to inform you . . .*

My darling, our two years together have been the happiest time of my life, and I know that I always close my letters by telling you just how much I miss you, perhaps because never a minute goes by when you are not in my

*thoughts. I've received several letters from you in the past
month, and thank you for all the news about Clare and
what's happening at The Holt – but there's still no
photograph. Perhaps it will turn up in the next post. Even
more than your image, I look forward to the day when I will
see you in person and hold you in my arms, because then
you'll truly realize just how much I've missed you.*

 Your loving husband,
 George

—◦—

''Ave you got some sort of problem, Perkins?'

'Don't think so, Sarge.'

'Then why is your unit taking ninety seconds to reload when
the rest of the battery's taking less than a minute?'

'We're doing our best, Sarge.'

'Your best isn't good enough, Perkins, do I make myself clear?'

'Yes, Sarge.'

'Don't "Yes, Sarge" me, Perkins, just do something about it.'

'Yes, Sarge.'

'And, Matthews.'

'Yes, Sarge.'

'I'll be inspecting your gun at twelve hundred hours, and if it
doesn't shine like the sun coming out of my arse, I'll personally
ram you down the barrel and fire you at the Hun. Do I make
myself abundantly clear, lad?'

'Abundantly clear, Sarge.'

The buzzer sounded on the field telephone. George grabbed
the receiver.

'There's a heavy barrage coming from about a mile away, sir,
eleven o'clock,' said one of the men manning the forward look-
out post. Could mean the Germans are planning an attack.' The
line went dead.

'Sergeant Davies,' hollered George, struggling to make himself heard above the sound of gunfire.

'Sir!'

'One mile, eleven o'clock, Germans advancing.'

'Sir! Look lively, lads, we want to be sure to give the Hun a warm welcome. Let's see who can be the first to land one right on top of Jerry's tin helmet.'

George smiled as he walked up and down the line, checking on each gun, grateful that Sergeant Davies had been born in Swansea, and not on the other side of the Siegfried Line.

'Well done, Rodgers,' said Davies. 'First into action again. Keep this up and you'll be a lance corporal in no time.'

Even George couldn't miss the less than subtle hint as to who he should be considering for the next promotion.

'Well done, Perkins, that's more like it,' said Davies a few moments later. 'Needn't start unpicking your stripes just yet.'

'Thanks, Sarge.'

'And don't ever thank me, Corporal. Wouldn't want you to think I'm going soft.'

'No, Sarge.'

'Matthews, don't tell me you're going to be last again.'

'My loading spring's busted, sarge.'

'Oh I am so sorry to hear that, Matthews. Well then, why don't you run along to the ammunition store and see if you can get yourself a nice shiny new one – sharpish, you bleedin' halfwit.'

'But the depot's three miles behind the line, Sarge. Can't I wait for the supply truck in the morning?'

'No you can't, Matthews, because if you don't get moving, by the time you get back the fuckin' Germans – excuse my French – will have joined us for breakfast. Do I make myself clear?'

'Yes, Sarge.'

'On the double, then.'

'Yes, Sarge.'

◄○►

October 14th, 1916

My darling Ruth,

It's been another one of those endless days, with both sides pounding away at each other, while we have no way of knowing who's getting the better of this war. A field officer occasionally turns up to assure us that we're doing a first-

class job and the Germans are on the retreat – which raises
the question, then why aren't we advancing? No doubt some
German field officer is telling his men exactly the same thing.
Only one thing is certain, they can't both be right.

By the way, tell your father that if he wants to make a
second fortune, he should open a factory that makes ear
trumpets, because once this war is over they're certain to be
in great demand.

I'm sorry, my darling, if these letters are becoming a little
repetitive, but only two things remain constant, my love for
you and my desire to hold you in my arms.

Your loving husband,
George

George looked up to see that one of his corporals was also
scribbling away.

'A letter to your wife, Perkins?'

'No, sir, it's my will.'

'Isn't that a little pessimistic?'

'I don't think so, sir,' Perkins replied. 'Back on civvy street
I'm a bookie, so I'm used to havin' to weigh up the odds. Men
on the front line survive an average of sixteen days, and I've
already been out here for over three months, so I can't expect to
buck the odds for much longer.'

'But you're in far less danger back here than those poor devils
on the front line, Perkins,' George tried to reassure him.

'You're the third officer to tell me that, sir, and the other two
went home in wooden boxes.'

George was still horrified by such casual references to death,
and wondered how long it would be before he became just as
hardened.

'The way I see it, sir,' continued Perkins, 'is war's like the
Grand National. There's lots of runners and riders at the start,
but there's no way of knowing which of them will finish the
course. And in the end there's only one winner. To be honest,
sir, it's not a racing certainty that the winner's going to be an
English nag.'

George noticed that Private Matthews was nodding his agree-ment, while Private Rodgers kept his head down as he cleaned the barrel of his rifle with an oily rag.

'Well, at least you'll be getting some leave soon, Matthews,' said George, trying to steer the conversation away from a subject that was never far from their minds.

'Can't wait for the day, sir,' Matthews said as he began to roll a cigarette.

'What's the first thing you'll do when you get home?' asked George.

'Bang the missus,' said Matthews.

Perkins and Rodgers burst out laughing. 'All right, Matthews,' said George. 'And the second thing?'

'Take my boots off, sir.'

—◦—

December 7th, 1916

My dearest Ruth,

Your photograph has just arrived in this morning's post, and as I write this letter from a trench just outside ███████ ████████████*, it's balanced on my knee. 'Quite a looker,' I heard one of the lads say, and I agree with him. It won't be long before our second child is born, and I've been promised compassionate leave some time in the next three months. If I can't make it home for the birth don't imagine, even for a moment, that you are ever out of my thoughts.*

I've been at the Front now for four months, and the new second lieutenants arriving from Blighty look younger by the day. Some of them treat me as if I'm an old soldier. Once this war is over, I'll spend the rest of my days with you at The Holt.

By the way, if it's a boy, let's call him John . . .

'Sorry to disturb you, sir,' said Sergeant Davies, 'but we've got a bit of a problem.'

George immediately leapt to his feet, because he'd never heard Davies utter that particular word. 'What kind of problem?'

'We've lost communication with the lads at the forward look-out post.'

George knew that *lost communication* was Davies's way of saying that all three of the men had been killed. 'What do you recommend, Sergeant?' he asked, recalling Evans's advice.

'Someone's got to get up there, sir, and sharpish, so we can restore contact before the bloody Hun trample all over us. If I may suggest, sir . . .'

'Please do, Sergeant.'

'I could take Matthews and Perkins, and see what can be done, then we'll report back to you.'

'No, Sergeant,' said George. 'Not Matthews. He's due to go on leave tomorrow.' He looked across at Perkins, who had turned ice white and was trembling. George had no need to consult him about the odds of any of them reporting back. 'I think I'll join you for this one, Sergeant.'

When George had been at Winchester, on sports day he'd covered a quarter of a mile in under a minute, and at the end of the race he wasn't even out of breath. He never knew how long it took him, Davies and Perkins to reach the front line, but when he threw himself into the trench he was exhausted and terrified, and all too aware what the men at the Front were being asked to endure every minute of the day and night.

'Keep your head down, sir,' said Davies as he studied the battlefield through a pair of field binoculars. 'The look-out post is about a hundred yards away, sir, one o'clock.' He passed the binoculars across to George.

George refocused the lenses, and once he'd located the post he could see exactly why communications had broken down. 'Right, let's get on with it,' he said before he had time to think what it was that he was meant to be getting on with. He leapt out of the trench and ran as he had never run before, zigzagging through waterlogged potholes and treacle black mud as he charged towards the forward look-out post. He never looked back, because he was sure that Davies and Perkins would only be a stride behind. He was wrong. Perkins had been brought down by a bullet after only a dozen paces and lay dying in the mud, while Davies had managed almost sixty yards before he was killed.

The look-out post was only twenty yards ahead of George. He had covered fifteen of those yards when the mortar shell exploded at his feet. It was the first and last time in his life that he said *fuck*. He fell on his knees, thought of Ruth, and then collapsed face down in the mud. Just another statistic.

27

The regular flow of letters suddenly dried up; always the first sign, all too often followed by an unwelcome telegram.

Ruth had taken to sitting in the alcove by the drawing room window every morning, hands clasped over her ever-growing belly, thirty minutes before old Mr Rodgers cycled up the drive. When he came into view she would try to fathom the expression on his face. Was it a letter face, or a telegram face? She reckoned she would know the truth long before he reached the door.

Just as she spotted Mr Rodgers coming through the gates, Clare began to cry. Did she still have a father? Or had George died before his second child was born?

Ruth was standing by the door when Mr Rodgers stopped pedalling, put on his brakes and came to a halt by the bottom step. Always the same routine: dismount, rummage around in his post bag, extract the relevant letters, and finally walk up the steps and hand them to Mrs Mallory. It was no different today. Or was it? As Mr Rodgers mounted the steps he looked up at her and smiled. This wasn't a telegram day.

'Two letters today, Mrs Mallory, and if I'm not mistaken, one of them's from your husband,' he added, passing over an envelope that bore George's familiar handwriting.

'Thank you,' said Ruth, almost unable to hide her relief. Then she remembered that she wasn't the only person having to suffer like this every day. 'Any news of your son, Mr Rodgers?' she asked.

''Fraid not,' replied the postman. 'Mind you, our Donald

167

never was much of a letter writer, so we live in hope.' He climbed back on his bicycle and pedalled away.

Ruth had opened George's letter long before she'd reached the drawing room. She returned to her seat by the window, sank back and began to read, first quickly and then very slowly.

January 12th, 1917

My dearest one,

 I'm alive, even if I'm not kicking. Don't fret. All I've ended up with is a broken ankle. It could have been much worse. The doc tells me that in time I'll be right as rain, and even able to climb again, but in the meantime they're sending me home to recuperate.

Ruth stared out of the window at the Surrey hills in the distance, not sure whether to laugh or cry. It was some time before she returned to George's letter.

 Sadly, Sergeant Davies and Corporal Perkins were struck down in the same action. Two fine men, like so many of their comrades. I hope you'll forgive me, my darling, but I felt I had to drop a line to their wives before I got down to writing to you.

 It all began when Sgt Davies told me that we had a problem . . .

—◇—

'I'm going to recommend that you are discharged in the next few days, Mallory, and sent back to Blighty until you're fully recovered.'

'Thanks, doc,' said George cheerfully.

'Don't thank me, old fellow, frankly I need the bed. By the time you're ready to come back, with a bit of luck this damn war will be over.'

'Let's hope so,' said George, looking around the field tent, full of brave men whose lives would never be the same again.

'By the way,' the doctor added, 'a Private Rodgers dropped by this morning. Thought this might be yours.'

'It certainly is,' said George, taking the photograph of Ruth he'd thought he'd never see again.

'She's quite a looker,' mused the doctor.

'Not you as well,' said George with a grin.

'Oh, and you've got a visitor. Do you feel up to it?'

'Yes, I'd be delighted to see Rodgers,' said George.

'No, it's not Rodgers, it's a Captain Geoffrey Young.'

'Oh, I'm not sure I'm up to that,' said George, a huge smile appearing on his face.

A nurse plumped up George's pillow and placed it behind his back as he waited for his climbing leader. He could never think of Geoffrey Young as anything else. But the welcoming smile on his lips turned to a frown as Young limped into the tent.

'My dear George,' Young said, 'I came the moment I heard. One of the advantages of being in the Ambulance Auxiliary Service is that you get to know where everyone is and what they're up to.' Young pulled up a small wooden chair that must have previously been used in a French classroom and sat down beside George's bed. 'So much news, I don't know where to begin.'

'Why not start with Ruth. Did you get the chance to visit her when you were last on leave?'

'Yes. I dropped in to The Holt on my way back to Dover.'

'And how is she?' asked George, trying not to sound impatient.

'As beautiful as ever, and seems to have fully recovered.'

'Fully recovered?' said George anxiously.

'Following the birth of your second child,' said Young.

'My second child?' said George.

'You mean to say that nobody's told you that you're the proud father of . . .' He paused. 'I think it was a girl.'

George offered up a silent prayer to a God he didn't believe in. 'And how is she?' he demanded.

'Seemed fine to me,' said Young. 'But then, to be honest, I can never tell one baby from another.'

'What colour are her eyes?'

'I've no idea, old chap.'

'And is her hair fair or dark?'

'Sort of in between, I think, although I could be wrong.'

'You're hopeless. Has Ruth decided on a name?'

'I had a ghastly feeling you might ask me that.'

'Could it be Elizabeth?'

'I don't think so. More unusual than that. It will come to me in a moment.'

George burst out laughing. 'Spoken like a true bachelor.'

'Well, you'll find out for yourself soon enough,' said Young, 'because the doc tells me he's sending you home. Just make sure you don't come back. You've done more than enough to salve your conscience, and there's certainly no need to shorten the odds against you.'

George thought about a dead corporal who would have agreed with Young.

'What other news?' asked George.

'Some good, some bad – mostly bad I'm afraid.' George remained silent while Young tried to compose himself. 'Rupert Brooke died at Lemnos while on his way to Gallipoli – even before he reached some foreign field.'

George pursed his lips. He'd kept a book of Brooke's poetry in his knapsack, and had assumed that once the war was over he must surely produce some memorable verse. George didn't interrupt as he waited for other names to be added to the inevitable list of dead. One he dreaded most.

'Siegfried Herford bought it at Ypres, poor devil; it took him three days to die.' Young sighed. 'If a man like that has to die before his time, it shouldn't be on some muddy field in no man's land, but on the summit of a great mountain he's just conquered.'

'And Somervell?' George dared to ask.

'He's had to witness some of the worst atrocities this war could throw at a man, poor fellow. Being a front-line surgeon can't be much fun, but he never complains.'

'Odell?'

'Wounded three times. The War Office finally got the message and sent him back to Cambridge, but only after his old college had offered him a fellowship. Someone up there has at last worked out that we're going to need our finest minds once this mess has been sorted out.'

'And Finch? I'll bet he found himself some cushy number taking care of nurses.'

'Far from it,' said Young. 'He volunteered to head up a bomb disposal unit, so his chances of survival are even less than the boys at the Front. He's had several offers of a safe job in Whitehall, but he always turns them down – it's almost as if he wants to die.'

'No,' said George, 'he doesn't want to die. Finch is one of those rare individuals who doesn't believe anyone or anything can kill him. Remember him singing "Waltzing Matilda" on Mont Blanc?'

Young chuckled. 'And to cap it all, they're going to give him an MBE.'

'Good heavens,' laughed George, 'nothing will stop him now.'

'Unless you do,' said Young quietly, 'once that ankle of yours is healed. My bet is that you two will still be the first to stand on the top of the world.'

'After you've led the way.'

'I'm afraid that will no longer be possible, old boy.'

'Why not? You're still a young man.'

'True,' said Young. 'But it might not prove quite that easy, with one of these.' He pulled up his left trouser leg to reveal an artificial limb.

'I'm so sorry,' said George, shocked. 'I had no idea.'

'Don't worry about it, old fellow,' said Young. 'I'm just thankful to be alive. However, once this war is over I'll be recommending to the Everest Committee that you take my place as climbing leader.'

─◄○►─

Ruth was sitting by the window in the drawing room when a khaki-coloured car drove through the front gates. She couldn't make out who was behind the wheel, apart from the fact that he or she was in uniform.

Ruth was already outside by the time the young woman driver stepped out of the car and opened the back door. The first thing to emerge was a pair of crutches, followed by a pair of legs, followed by her husband. Ruth dashed down the steps and threw her arms around him. She kissed him as if it were the first time, which brought back memories of a sleeping compartment on the train home from Venice. The driver stood to attention, looking slightly embarrassed.

'Thank you, Corporal,' said George with a grin. She saluted, climbed back into the car and drove off.

Ruth eventually let go of George, but only because he refused to allow her to help him up the steps and into the house. As she walked beside him into the drawing room, George demanded, 'Where's my little girl?'

'She's in the nursery with Clare and nanny. I'll go and fetch them.'

'What's her name?' George called after her, but Ruth was already halfway up the stairs.

George propelled himself into the drawing room and fell into a chair by the window. He didn't remember a chair being there before, and wondered why it was facing outwards. He looked at the English countryside that he loved so much, reminded once again of just how lucky he was to be alive. Brooke, Herford, Wainwright, Carter minor, Davies, Perkins . . .

His thoughts were interrupted by cries that he heard long before he set eyes on his second daughter. George heaved himself up as Ruth and Nanny Mallory entered the room with his two daughters. He hugged Clare for some time before taking the little bundle in his arms.

'Fair hair and blue eyes,' he said.

'I thought you already knew that,' said Ruth. 'Didn't you get my letters?'

'Sadly not. Only your messenger, Geoffrey Young, who just about remembered that it was a girl, and certainly couldn't recall her name.'

'That's funny,' said Ruth, 'because I asked him if he'd be godfather, and he agreed.'

'So you don't know her name, Daddy?' said Clare, jumping up and down.

'No, I don't,' said George. 'Is it Elizabeth?'

'No, Daddy, don't be silly. It's Beridge,' said Clare, laughing.

More unusual than that, said George to himself, recalling Geoffrey Young's words.

After only a few moments in George's arms, Beridge began howling, and nanny quickly took charge of her. The child obviously didn't appreciate being held by a strange man.

'Let's have half a dozen more,' said George, taking Ruth in his arms once nanny had taken Clare and Beridge back to the nursery.

'Behave yourself, George,' teased Ruth. 'Try to remember that you're no longer on the front line with your troops.'

'Some of the finest men I've ever known,' said George sadly.

Ruth smiled. 'Will you miss them?'

'Not half as much as I've missed you.'

'So now you're back, my darling, what's the first thing you'd like to do?'

George thought about Private Matthews's response when he'd been asked the same question. He smiled to himself, realizing that there wasn't a great deal of difference between an officer and a private soldier.

He bent down and began to untie his shoe lace.

BOOK FOUR

SELECTING THE TEAM

1921

28

Wednesday, June 22nd, 1921

When George came down to breakfast that morning, nobody spoke.

'What's going on?' he asked as he took his place at the head of the table between his two daughters.

'I know,' said Clare, 'but Mummy told me not to tell you.'

'What about Beridge?' said George.

'Don't be silly, Daddy, you know Beridge can't read.'

'Read?' said George, looking at Clare more closely. 'Sherlock Holmes would have told us that *read* was the first clue.'

'Who's Sherlock Holmes?' demanded Clare.

'A great detective,' said George. 'He would have looked around the room to see what there was to read. Now, could this secret possibly be in the newspaper?'

'Yes,' said Clare, clapping her hands. 'And Mummy says it's something you've wanted all your life.'

'Another clue,' said George, picking up that morning's *Times*, which was open at page eleven. He smiled the moment he saw the headline. 'Your mother is quite right.'

'Read the story, Daddy, read the story.'

'MP Nancy Astor has made a speech in the House of Commons on women's rights.' George looked up at Ruth and said, 'I only wish I was having breakfast with your father this morning.'

'Perhaps,' said Ruth, 'but Sherlock Holmes would tell you that you're wasting your time. Mrs Astor's speech is nothing more than a red herring.'

George began to turn the pages. Ruth smiled when she saw his hand begin to tremble. She hadn't seen that look on his face since . . .

'Read the story, Daddy.'

George dutifully obeyed. 'Sir Francis Younghusband,' he began, 'announced last night that the Royal Geographical Society will be joining forces with the Alpine Club to form an Everest Committee, of which he will be the chairman, with Mr Geoffrey Young as his deputy.' He looked up to see Ruth smiling at him.

'Keep on reading, Daddy, keep on reading.'

'The committee's first task will be to select a party of climbers who will make the first assault on Mount Everest.'

George looked up again. Ruth was still smiling. He quickly returned to the article before Clare could admonish him again. 'Our correspondent understands that among the names being canvassed for climbing leader are Mr George Mallory, a school-master at Charterhouse, and Mr George Finch, an Australian scientist, currently lecturing at Imperial College, London.'

'But no one's been in touch with me,' said George.

Ruth was still smiling as she handed him an envelope that had arrived in the morning post, bearing the Royal Geographical Society's crest on the back. 'Elementary, my dear Watson,' she said.

'Who's Watson?' demanded Clare.

29

None of the five men seated around the table particularly liked each other, but that was not their purpose. They had all been chosen as members of the Everest Committee for different reasons.

The chairman, Sir Francis Younghusband, had been closer to Everest than any of them, forty miles, when he had been entrusted to negotiate terms with the Dalai Lama for the expedition's safe crossing of the border into Tibet; the exact words had been spelt out in a treaty signed earlier that year by Lord Curzon, the Foreign Secretary. Sir Francis sat bolt upright at the head of the table, his feet not quite touching the floor, as he stood barely five foot one. His thick, wavy grey hair and lined forehead give him an air of authority that was rarely questioned.

On his left sat Arthur Hinks, the secretary of the committee, whose primary purpose was to protect the reputation of the RGS, which he represented and which paid his annual stipend. His forehead was not yet lined, and the few tufts of hair left on his otherwise bald head were not yet grey. On the table in front of him were several files, and a newly acquired minute book. Some wags claimed that he wrote up the minutes of a meeting the day before it took place, so he could be certain that everything went as planned. No one would have suggested as much to his face.

On Hinks's left sat Mr Raeburn, who had once been considered a fine alpinist. But the cigar he held permanently in one hand, and the paunch pressed against the edge of the table, meant that only those with good memories could recall his climbing days.

Opposite him sat Commander Ashcroft, a retired naval officer who always had a snifter with Hinks just before a meeting opened, so that he could be instructed how to cast his vote. He'd reached the rank of commander by never disobeying orders. His weatherbeaten face and white beard would have left even a casual observer in no doubt where he'd spent the majority of his days. On his left, and the chairman's right, sat a man who had hoped to be the first person to stand on top of the world, until the Germans had put a stop to that.

The grandfather clock at one end of the room chimed six and it pleased Sir Francis that he didn't have to call for order. After all, the men seated around the table were used to giving and taking orders. 'Gentlemen,' he said, 'it is an honour for me to open this inaugural meeting of the Everest Committee. Following the success of the expedition that surveyed the outlying regions of the Himalaya last year, our purpose is now to identify a group of climbers who are capable of planting the Union Jack at the summit of the highest mountain on earth. I was recently granted an audience with His Majesty –' Sir Francis glanced up at the portrait of their patron hanging on the wall – 'and I assured him that one of his subjects would be the first man to stand on the summit of Everest.'

'Hear, hear,' mumbled Raeburn and Ashcroft in unison.

Sir Francis paused, and looked down at the notes prepared for him by Hinks. 'Our first task this evening will be to appoint a leader to take the team we select as far as the foothills of the Himalaya, where he will set up a base camp, probably at around 17,000 feet. Our second duty will be to choose a climbing leader. For some years, gentlemen, I had anticipated that that man would be Mr Geoffrey Winthrop Young, but due to an injury he sustained in the war, that will sadly not be possible. However, we are still able to call upon his vast experience of and expertise in climbing matters, and warmly welcome him to this committee as deputy chairman.' Young gave a slight bow. 'I will now call upon Mr Hinks to guide us through the agenda for this meeting.'

'Thank you, Mr Chairman,' said Hinks, touching his moustache. 'As you have reminded us, our first duty is to select a leader for the expedition. This must be a man of resolute character and proven leadership ability, preferably with some experience of the Himalaya. He must also be skilled in diplomacy, in case there should be any trouble with the natives.'

'Hear, hear,' said a member of the committee, sounding to Young as if he was coming in on cue.

'Gentlemen,' continued Hinks, 'I am in no doubt that we have identified the one man who embodies all these characteristics, namely General Charles Granville Bruce, late of the Fifth Royal Gurkha Rifles. The committee may be interested to know that the General is the youngest son of Lord Aberdare, and was educated at Harrow and Sandhurst.'

Raeburn and Ashcroft immediately responded again with 'Hear, hear.'

'I have no hesitation, therefore, in recommending to the committee that we appoint General Bruce as campaign leader, and invite him to join us as a member.'

'That all sounds very satisfactory,' said Younghusband. 'Can I assume that the committee is in agreement, and that Bruce is the obvious man for the job?' He glanced around the table, to find that all but one of the committee members were nodding.

'Mr Chairman,' said Young, 'this decision as to who should lead the expedition has been taken by the RGS, and rightly so. However, as I was not privy to the selection process, I am curious to know if any other candidate was considered for the post.'

'Perhaps you would care to answer that query, Mr Hinks,' said Younghusband.

'Of course, Mr Chairman,' responded Hinks, placing a pair of half-moon spectacles on the end of his nose. 'Several names were put forward for our consideration, but frankly, Young, it quickly became clear that General Bruce was head and shoulders above the rest.'

'I hope that answers your question, Young,' said Sir Francis.

'I hope so too, Mr Chairman,' said Young.

'Then perhaps the time has come to invite the General to join us,' said Sir Francis.

Hinks coughed.

'Yes, Mr Hinks?' said Sir Francis. 'Have I forgotten something?'

'No, Mr Chairman,' said Hinks, peering over the top of his spectacles. 'But perhaps we should put the matter to a vote before General Bruce is elected as a member of the committee?'

'Yes, of course,' said Sir Francis. 'I propose that General Bruce be appointed as leader of the expedition, and be co-opted onto this committee. Will someone please second that motion?'

Hinks immediately raised his hand.

'Those in favour?' said Sir Francis.

Four hands shot up.

'Those against?'

No hands were raised.

'Are there any abstentions?'

Young raised his hand.

'Before you make a note in the minutes, Mr Hinks,' said Younghusband, 'don't you think, Young, that it would be helpful if we were to give General Bruce our unanimous support?'

'In normal circumstances I would agree with you, Mr Chairman,' said Young. Sir Francis smiled. 'However, I feel it would be irresponsible of me to vote for a man I've never met, however well qualified he appears to be.'

'So be it,' said Sir Francis. 'I declare the motion carried by four votes to none, with one abstention.'

'Shall I ask General Bruce to join us?' said Hinks.

'Yes, please do,' replied Sir Francis.

Hinks rose from his place and a porter immediately jumped up, opened the door at the far end of the room and stood aside to allow him to enter an ante-room where three men were seated, waiting to be called before the committee.

'General Bruce, if you would be kind enough to join us?' said Hinks, without giving the other two men so much as a glance.

'Thank you, Hinks,' said the General, heaving himself up from his chair and following the secretary slowly back into the committee room.

'Welcome, General Bruce,' said Sir Francis. 'Do come and join us,' he added, ushering Bruce towards an empty chair.

'I am delighted to tell you,' said Sir Francis after Bruce had taken his seat, 'that the committee has voted to invite you to oversee this great adventure, and also to join us as a member of the executive board.'

'My thanks, Mr Chairman, to you and the committee for its confidence,' said the General, toying with his monocle before pouring himself a large whisky. 'Be assured I will do my damnedest to prove worthy of it.'

'I believe you're acquainted with everyone on the committee, General, except our deputy chairman, Mr Young.'

Young took a closer look at the General, and doubted if he was a day under sixty. If he was to make the arduous journey to the foothills of the Himalaya, a very sturdy beast would be needed to transport him.

'Our next duty, gentlemen,' said Sir Francis, 'is to select a climbing leader, who will take over from General Bruce once he has led the expedition across the border into Tibet where he will set up base camp. The person we choose will have the responsibility of identifying the route by which the final party, possibly including himself, will make the first assault on the summit of Everest.' Sir Francis paused. 'Let us pray that whomever we select will succeed in this noble enterprise.'

Young bowed his head, and wondered if any of the men seated around the table had the slightest idea what they were asking these brave young men to do in God's name.

Sir Francis paused again before adding, 'The Alpine Club has put forward two names for our consideration. Perhaps this would be the appropriate moment to ask our deputy chairman if he would like to say a few words by way of introduction.'

'Thank you, Mr Chairman,' said Young. 'I can tell the committee that in the opinion of the Alpine Club, these two candidates are unquestionably the finest climbers in the British Isles. The only other man in their class was Siegfried Herford, who was sadly cut down at Ypres.'

'Thank you,' said the chairman. 'I should point out once again that had Captain Young not been wounded on the Western Front, there would be no need for this interview to take place.'

'It's kind of you to say so, Mr Chairman, but I can assure the committee that both of these young men are capable of carrying out the task.'

'And which of the two gentlemen should we see first?' asked Sir Francis.

'Mr Leigh Mallory,' said Hinks, before anyone else could offer an opinion.

'It's George Mallory, actually,' said Young.

'Very well, perhaps we should invite Mr Mallory to join us,' suggested the chairman.

Once again Hinks rose from his place, and the porter opened the door that led into the ante-room. Hinks peered at the two men who were seated below a portrait of Queen Mary, and without having the slightest idea which was which, said, 'Mr Mallory, please follow me.' George stood up.

'Good luck, Mallory,' said Finch. 'Don't forget that you've only got one friend in there.'

Hinks stopped in his tracks, and for a moment looked as if he was going to respond, but evidently thought better of it and walked back into the committee room without another word.

'Mr Mallory,' said Sir Francis as George entered the room. 'It's good of you to spare us your time.' He rose from his chair and shook hands with the candidate. 'I do apologize for keeping you waiting.' George smiled. 'I know that Mr Young has informed you why you're here this evening, so perhaps you'd be kind enough to take a seat at the top of the table. The committee have one or two questions for you.'

'Of course, Sir Francis,' said George a little nervously.

'May I begin,' said Sir Francis once George was seated, 'by asking if you are in any doubt that we can succeed in this massive endeavour, and by that I mean conquering Everest.'

'No one can possibly answer that question with any authority, Sir Francis,' said George, 'as only a handful of mountaineers have ever climbed higher than 20,000 feet. My brother Trafford, a pilot with the RAF, tells me that even an aeroplane hasn't yet reached 29,000 feet, which is the height of Everest.'

'But you'd still be willing to give it a go, wouldn't you?' asked Raeburn who was puffing away on a cigar, and looked as if his idea of a challenging climb would be the steps to his club.

'Of course I would,' said George enthusiastically. 'But as no one has ever attempted to scale Everest, we have no way of knowing what difficulties it might present. For example—'

'Are you a married man, Mr Mallory?' asked Commander Ashcroft, reading from the piece of paper in front of him.

'Yes, I am, sir.'

'Any family?'

'Two daughters,' George replied, slightly puzzled by the question. He couldn't see how Clare and Beridge could possibly help him to climb a 29,000-foot mountain.

'Are there any more questions for Mr Mallory?' asked Sir Francis as he checked his half-hunter pocket watch.

Was that it? thought George in disbelief. Was this bunch of old buffers going to decide between Finch and himself on the basis of such irrelevant questions? It looked as if Finch had been right about Hinks and his cronies.

'I have a question for Mr Mallory,' said Hinks.

George smiled. Perhaps he'd misjudged the man.

'Can I confirm,' said Hinks, 'that you were educated at Winchester?'

'Yes, I was,' said George, wondering once again what possible relevance the question might have.

'And from there you went up to Magdalene College, Cambridge, to read history?'

'Yes,' repeated George. He was tempted to add, 'But I had to climb the college wall to make sure they offered me a place,' but somehow he managed to hold his tongue.

'And you graduated with an honours degree before taking up a teaching post at Charterhouse?'

'That is correct,' said George, still unsure where this could possibly be leading.

'And although as a schoolmaster you were exempt from serving in the armed forces, you nevertheless volunteered and were commissioned as an officer in the Royal Artillery, seeing action on the Western Front?'

'Yes,' said George. He glanced at Young in the hope of guidance, only to find that he looked equally bemused.

'And after the war you returned to Charterhouse to become the senior history master.'

George nodded, but said nothing.

'That's all I needed to know. Thank you, Mr Chairman.'

George once again glanced at Young, but he just shrugged his shoulders.

'Are there any more questions for Mr Mallory,' asked Sir Francis. 'Or can we let him go?'

The man with the cigar raised his hand. 'Yes, Mr Raeburn?' said Younghusband.

'If you were selected as climbing leader for this expedition, Mallory, would you be willing to purchase your own equipment?'

'I'm sure I could manage that,' said George after a moment's hesitation.

'And would you also be able to pay for your passage to India?' enquired Ashcroft.

George hesitated, because he couldn't be sure to what extent his father-in-law would be willing to assist him. He eventually said, 'I would hope so.'

'Good show, Mallory,' said Sir Francis. 'Now, all that's left for me to do is thank you on behalf of the . . .' Hinks furiously scribbled a note, which he thrust under Younghusband's nose. 'Ah, yes,' Sir Francis said. 'If you were to be selected, would you be prepared to undergo a medical examination?'

'Of course, Sir Francis,' said George.

'Capital,' said the chairman. 'The committee will be in touch with you in the near future, to let you know our decision.'

George rose from his place, still slightly bemused, and left the room without another word. When the porter had closed the door behind him George said, 'It was even worse than you predicted.'

'I did warn you,' said Finch.

'Just be sure you don't say anything you'll regret, George.'

Finch always knew Mallory was serious when he addressed him by his Christian name.

'What can you possibly mean, old chap?' he asked.

'Humour them, don't lose your temper. Try to remember that it's going to be you and me standing at 27,000 feet preparing for the final climb, while that lot will be back in their clubs, sitting in front of a log fire and enjoying a glass of brandy.'

◄○►

'What a splendid fellow,' Hinks said.

'I agree,' said Raeburn. 'Exactly the sort of chap we're looking for. Wouldn't you agree, General?'

'I certainly liked the cut of his jib,' said Bruce. 'But I think we need to see the other chap before we come to a decision.'

Geoffrey Young smiled for the first time.

'The other fellow doesn't look in the same class on paper,' said Ashcroft.

'You won't find many mountains on paper, Commander,' said Young, trying not to sound exasperated.

'That may well be the case,' said Hinks, 'but I feel I should point out to the committee that Mr Finch is an Australian.'

'I was given to understand,' said Raeburn, 'that we were only considering chaps from the British Isles.'

'I think you'll find, Mr Chairman,' said Young, 'that Australia is still part of His Majesty's far-flung Empire.'

'Quite so,' said Sir Francis. 'Perhaps we should see the fellow before we jump to conclusions.'

Hinks made no effort to rise from his seat. He simply folded his arms and nodded at the porter, who bowed deferentially, opened the door and announced, 'Mr Finch.'

30

'Mr Finch,' the porter repeated, a little more firmly.

'Got to leave you, old chap,' said Finch, and added with a grin, 'which is exactly what I'll be saying when we're a couple of hundred feet from the summit.'

Finch strolled into the committee room and sat down in the chair at the end of the table before Sir Francis had an opportunity to welcome him. Young could only smile when he saw how Finch had dressed for the interview. It was almost as if he'd set out to provoke the committee: a casual corduroy jacket, a pair of baggy cream flannels, an open-necked shirt and no tie.

When Young had briefed Mallory and Finch, it hadn't crossed his mind to mention a dress code. But to this committee the candidates' appearance would be every bit as important as their climbing record. They were now all staring at Finch in disbelief. Ashcroft even had his mouth open. Young leant back and waited for the fireworks to be ignited.

'Well, Mr Finch,' said Sir Francis once he'd recovered, 'let me welcome you on behalf of the committee, and ask if you are prepared to answer a few questions.'

'Of course I am,' said Finch. 'That's why I'm here.'

'Capital,' said Sir Francis. 'Then I'll get the ball rolling by asking if you're in any doubt that this great enterprise can be achieved. By that I mean, do you believe you are capable of leading a team to the summit of Everest?'

'Yes, I can do that,' said Finch. 'But nobody has any idea how the human body will react to such altitude. One scientist has even suggested we might explode, and although I think that's a fatuous notion, it does indicate that we haven't a clue what we'll be up against.'

'I'm not sure I follow you, old chap,' said Raeburn.

'Then allow me to elucidate, Mr Raeburn.' The elderly gentleman looked surprised that Finch knew his name. 'What we do know is that the higher you climb, the thinner the air becomes, meaning that every movement a mountaineer makes at altitude will be more difficult than the last. That may result in some falling by the wayside.'

'Yourself included, perhaps?' said Hinks, not looking directly at him.

'Yes indeed, Mr Hinks,' Finch said, looking back at the secretary.

'But despite all that,' said Raeburn, 'you would still be willing to give it a go.'

'Yes, I would,' Finch replied firmly. 'But I should warn the committee that the success or failure of this project may depend on the use of oxygen during the last two thousand feet.'

'I'm not altogether sure I follow your drift,' said Sir Francis.

'I reckon that above 24,000 feet,' replied Finch, 'we will find it almost impossible to breathe. I've carried out some experiments at 15,000 feet which showed that with the assistance of bottled oxygen, it's possible to continue climbing at almost the same rate as at a much lower altitude.'

'But wouldn't that be cheating, old chap?' asked Ashcroft. 'It's always been our aim to test man's ability against the elements without having to resort to mechanical aids.'

'The last time I heard a similar opinion expressed publicly was at a lecture given by the late Captain Scott in this very building. I'm sure, gentlemen, that you don't need reminding how that sad adventure ended.'

Everyone on the committee was now staring at Finch as if he was the subject of a Bateman cartoon, but he continued unabashed.

'Scott not only failed to be first to reach the South Pole,' Finch reminded them, 'but as you all know only too well, he

and the rest of his party perished. Amundsen not only reached
the Pole ahead of Scott, but is continuing to lead expeditions
to the uncharted places around the globe. Yes, I would like to
be the first person to stand on the top of the world, but I would
also like to return to London to deliver a lecture on the subject
to the Royal Geographical Society.'

It was some time before the next question was asked.

'Allow me to ask you, Mr Finch,' said Hinks, choosing his
words carefully, 'does Mr Mallory agree with you on the use of
oxygen?'

'No, he doesn't,' admitted Finch. 'He thinks he can climb
Everest without it. But then, he's a historian, Mr Hinks, not a
scientist.'

'Are there any more questions for this candidate?' asked Sir
Francis, looking as if he had already made up his mind on who
the committee should select as climbing leader for the expedition.

'Yes, Mr Chairman,' said Hinks. 'There are just one or two
matters I'd like to clear up, simply for the record, you understand.' Sir Francis nodded. 'Mr Finch, could you tell the committee where you were born and where you were educated?'

'I don't see how that's relevant,' replied Finch. 'I have no
idea where Mr Alcock or Mr Brown was educated, but I do know
that they were the first men to fly across the Atlantic, and that
they were only able to achieve that, Mr Hinks, with the help of a
mechanical aid known as an aeroplane.'

Young tried not to smile, although he was no longer in any
doubt who the committee would select as climbing leader.

'Be that as it may,' said Hinks, 'we at the RGS—'

'Forgive me for interrupting you, Mr Hinks, but I was under
the impression that I was being interviewed by the Everest
Committee,' said Finch. 'As the Society's secretary, you signed a
minute to that effect.'

'Be that as it may,' repeated Hinks, trying to compose himself,
'perhaps you would be kind enough to answer my question.'

Young considered intervening, but remained silent, confident
that Finch could handle himself just as well in a committee room
as he did on a mountain.

'I was born in Australia, but I was educated in Zurich,' said Finch, 'and graduated from the University of Geneva.'

Ashcroft leant across the table and whispered to Raeburn, 'I had no idea that Geneva had a university. I thought it was just full of banks.'

'And cuckoo clocks,' said Raeburn.

'And what is your profession?' asked Hinks.

'I'm a chemist,' replied Finch. 'Which is how I know about the significance of oxygen at high altitude.'

'I always thought chemistry was a hobby,' said Ashcroft, this time loud enough to be heard, 'not a profession.'

'Only for children, Commander Ashcroft,' said Finch, looking him straight in the eye.

'And are you a married man, Finch?' asked Raeburn, flicking some ash off the end of his cigar.

'I am a widower,' said Finch, a reply which took Young by surprise.

Hinks scribbled a question mark against *marital status*.

'And do you have any children?' asked Ashcroft.

'Yes, one son, Peter.'

'Tell me, Finch,' said Raeburn, clipping the end off another cigar, 'if you were selected for this important role, would you be willing to pay for your own equipment?'

'Only if I had to,' said Finch. 'I am aware that the committee has launched an appeal to raise funds for this expedition, and I assumed that some of that money would be used to equip the climbers.'

'And what about your travel expenses?' pressed Ashcroft.

'Out of the question,' replied Finch. 'If I were to take part in the expedition I would be out of work for at least six months, and although I don't expect any financial recompense for loss of earnings, I see no reason why I should also have to cover my own expenses.'

'So you wouldn't describe yourself as an amateur, old chap?' said Ashcroft.

'No, sir, I would not. I'm a professional in everything I do.'

'Are you indeed?' said Ashcroft.

'I don't think we need detain Mr Finch any longer, gentlemen?' suggested Sir Francis, looking around the table.

'I have some further questions for Mr Finch,' said Young, unable to maintain his silence any longer.

'But surely you know everything you need to know about Mr Finch,' said Hinks. 'You've known this candidate for years.'

'I have indeed, but the rest of the committee has not, and I suspect they might find Mr Finch's answers to my questions illuminating. Mr Finch,' said Young, turning to face the candidate, 'have you ever climbed Mont Blanc, the highest mountain in Europe?'

'On seven occasions,' replied Finch.

'And the Matterhorn?'

'Three times.'

'And any of the other major peaks in the Alps?'

'All of them. I climb in the Alps every year.'

'And what about the highest mountains in the British Isles?'

'I gave them up before I was out of short trousers.'

'This is all on the record, Mr Chairman,' said Hinks.

'For those who've taken the trouble to read it,' retorted Young, unperturbed. 'Can I confirm, Mr Finch, that after completing your education in Geneva, you took up a place as an undergraduate at Imperial College, London?'

'That is correct,' confirmed Finch.

'And what subject did you read?'

'Chemistry,' replied Finch, having decided to play along with Young's little ruse.

'What class of degree did that august establishment award you?'

'A first-class honours degree,' said Finch, smiling for the first time.

'And did you remain at London University after you had graduated?' asked Young.

'Yes, I did,' said Finch. 'I joined the staff as a lecturer in chemistry.'

'And did you remain in that position after the war broke out,

Mr Finch, or did you, like Mr Mallory, enlist in the armed forces?'

'I enlisted in the army in August 1914, a few days after war was declared.'

'And in which branch of the army did you serve?' asked Young.

'As a chemist,' replied Finch, looking directly at Ashcroft, 'I felt my expertise could be put to good use by volunteering for the bomb disposal squad.'

'Bomb disposal squad,' said Young, emphasizing all three words. 'Can you elaborate?'

'Certainly, Mr Young. The War Office was looking for men to defuse unexploded bombs. Quite fun, really.'

'So you never saw action on the front line?' said Hinks.

'No, Mr Hinks, I did not. I found that German bombs had a tendency to fall on our side of the line, not theirs.'

'And were you ever decorated?' asked Hinks, leafing through his notes.

Young smiled. The first mistake Hinks had made.

'I was awarded the MBE,' said Finch matter-of-factly.

'Good show,' said Bruce. 'That's not something they give out with the rations.'

'I see no mention of this decoration in your records,' blustered Hinks, trying to recover.

'Perhaps that's because I didn't feel one's place of birth, educational qualifications and marital status had much to do with attempting to climb the highest mountain on earth.'

Hinks was silenced for the first time.

'Well, if there are no more questions,' said Sir Francis, 'allow me to thank Mr Finch for attending this meeting.' He hesitated before adding, 'Someone will be in touch with you in the near future.'

Finch rose from his place, nodded to Young, and was just about to leave when Hinks said, 'Just one more question. Can I confirm that, like Mr Mallory, you would be willing to undergo a medical examination?'

'Of course I would,' said Finch, and left the room without another word.

'Rum sort of fellow, don't you think?' said Raeburn once the porter had closed the door.

'But surely there can be no doubting his ability as an alpine climber,' said Young.

Hinks smiled. 'No doubt you're right, Young, but we at the RGS have always been wary of *social* climbers.'

'Don't you think that's a little rough, Hinks?' said Sir Francis. 'Considering the chap's war record.' Turning to Bruce, he asked, 'You've led men into battle, General. What did you make of the fellow?'

'I'd prefer to have him on my side rather than the enemy's, that's for sure,' said Bruce. 'Given a fair wind, I think I could knock him into shape.'

'What do we do next?' asked Sir Francis, turning back to Hinks for guidance.

'The members should now proceed to vote on their choice for climbing leader, Mr Chairman. For the convenience of the committee I've had ballot papers prepared, on which members may place a cross beside the name of their preferred candidate.' Hinks handed a slip of paper to each member of the committee. 'Once you've made your choice, please return your ballot papers to me.'

The process took only a few moments, and as Hinks counted the votes, a thin smile appeared on his face that grew wider every time he opened another ballot paper. He finally passed the result across to the chairman, so that he could officially announce the outcome.

'Five votes for Mallory. And there's one abstention,' said Younghusband, unable to hide his surprise.

'It was me again,' announced Young.

'But you know both the candidates well,' said Sir Francis. 'After all, it was you who placed their names in front of the committee.'

'Perhaps I know them too well,' replied Young. 'They are both fine young men in their different ways, but after all these years I still can't make up my mind which one of them is more likely to accomplish the feat of being the first man to stand on top of the world.'

'I am in no doubt which man I'd prefer to see representing this country,' said Hinks.

There were mutterings of 'Hear, hear,' but not from all quarters.

'Any other business?' asked Younghusband.

'We should simply confirm for the official record,' said Hinks, 'that now that we have appointed a climbing leader, we willingly accept *nem. con.* Mr Young's recommendations for the remaining eight places in the climbing team.'

'Yes, of course,' said Sir Francis. 'After all, that is no more than I agreed with the Alpine Club prior to this committee being set up.'

'I hope,' remarked Ashcroft, 'that not too many of them are cut from the same cloth as that fellow Finch.'

'No fear of that,' said Hinks, looking down at the list. 'Apart from Finch, they're all Oxford or Cambridge men.'

'Well, that must just about wrap it up,' said Sir Francis.

A smile returned to Hinks's lips. 'Mr Chairman, there's still the small matter of the medical examinations that all the prospective members of the climbing team have agreed to undergo. Presumably you'd like that to be out of the way before the committee reconvenes next month.'

'That makes sense to me,' said Sir Francis. 'No doubt you will handle all the details, Mr Hinks.'

'Of course, Mr Chairman.'

31

Hinks sat alone in his club, nursing a glass of brandy while he waited for his guest. He knew that Lampton wouldn't be late, but he needed a little time to compose his thoughts before the good doctor arrived.

Lampton had carried out several delicate commissions for the RGS in the past, but his next undertaking would have to be handled most carefully if no one was to suspect Hinks of being personally involved. Hinks smiled as he recalled Machiavelli's words, *Once you know a man's ambition, if you can assist it, he becomes beholden to you.* He was well aware of one of Lampton's ambitions.

Hinks rose from his seat as a porter led Dr Lampton into the library. Once they'd settled in a secluded corner of the room and dispensed with the usual small talk, Hinks made his well-prepared opening.

'I see your name is up for membership of the club, Lampton,' he said as a waiter placed two glasses of brandy on the table between them.

'It is indeed, Mr Hinks,' Lampton replied, nervously picking up and toying with his glass. 'But then, who wouldn't want to be a member of Boodle's?'

'And you shall be a member, dear boy,' said Hinks. 'In fact I can tell you that I've added my name to your list of supporters.'

'Thank you, Mr Hinks.'

'I think we can dispense with the Mr. After all, you'll soon be a member of this club. Do call me Hinks.'

'Thank you, Hinks.'

Hinks glanced around the room, to check that he could not be overheard. 'As you know, old boy, one of the club rules is that you can't discuss business matters over dinner.'

'Damned fine rule,' said Lampton. 'I only wish it applied at St Thomas's. I often feel like telling my colleagues that the last thing I want to talk about over lunch is what's going on in the hospital.'

'Quite so,' said Hinks. 'Mind you, the rule doesn't apply here in the library, so let me tell you, in the strictest confidence, that the Society wishes to instruct you to carry out a most important piece of scientific research on its behalf. I must emphasize, this is in the strictest confidence.'

'You can rely on me, Hinks.'

'Excellent, but first a little background. You may have read in *The Times* that the Society is planning to send a select team of climbers to Tibet for the purpose of making an attempt on the summit of Mount Everest.'

'Good heavens.'

'Rather appropriate,' said Hinks, and both men laughed. 'With that in mind, we would like to appoint you to conduct a series of tests on the twelve men who are under consideration for the nine places in that team. Clearly, the most important matter will be your professional opinion as to how well equipped they are to survive at an altitude of 29,000 feet.'

'Is that the height of Everest?'

'Twenty-nine thousand and two feet, to be exact,' said Hinks. 'Now, of course it goes without saying that the RGS cannot risk sending a chap all that way if he's going to break down the moment he reaches a certain altitude. That would be a waste of the Society's time and money.'

'Quite so,' agreed Lampton. 'How much time do I have to conduct these tests?'

'I have to report back to the committee in three weeks' time,' said Hinks, removing a piece of paper from an inside pocket. 'Here are the twelve names that have been put forward by the Alpine Club. Only nine of them will travel as part of the climbing team, so feel free to eliminate any three who fall short of the mark.' He passed the slip of paper to his guest so that he could study the names more carefully.

Lampton glanced at the list. 'I see no reason why my report shouldn't be on your desk within a fortnight. That's assuming all the climbers will be available.'

'They'll be available,' said Hinks. He paused and once again looked around the room. 'I wonder, Lampton, if I may speak to you on a confidential matter?'

'Feel free to do so, old fellow.'

'You should know that the committee would not be displeased if you were to find that one particular applicant did not possess the physical attributes necessary for such a demanding expedition.'

'I fully understand,' said Lampton.

Hinks leant across and placed a finger next to the second name on the list.

32

'. . . One hundred and twelve . . . one hundred and thirteen . . . one hundred and fourteen.' Finch finally collapsed on the ground. George kept going, but he only managed another seven press-ups before he also gave up: 121, a personal record. He lay flat on the floor, raised his head and grinned at Finch, who always managed to bring out the best in him. Or was it the worst?

Dr Lampton made an entry on his clipboard of the totals achieved by each of the twelve men, and noted that Mallory and Finch had been in the top five for every test, with very little to choose between them. He was already beginning to wonder what possible reason he could come up with to disqualify Finch, who clearly only had one rival as the fittest member of the group.

Lampton stood in the centre of the gymnasium and asked the twelve men to gather around him. 'I congratulate all of you,' he said, 'on having come through the first part of the test unscathed, which means that you're qualified to enter my torture chamber.' They all laughed. Lampton wondered how many of them would be laughing in an hour's time. 'Please follow me, gentlemen,' he said, and led them down a long brick corridor until he came to an unmarked door. He unlocked it and stepped into a large, square room, the like of which George had never seen.

'Gentlemen,' said Lampton, 'you are now standing in a decompression chamber that was commissioned by the Admiralty during the war to test submariners' ability to endure long periods of time below the surface of the ocean. The chamber has been modified to reproduce the conditions we believe you are likely to encounter when climbing Everest.

'Let me tell you about some of the equipment you see before you. The moving staircase in the centre of the room is not unlike those you will be familiar with from travelling on the London Underground.' One or two of those present were loath to admit they had never travelled on the Underground, and remained silent. 'There is, however, one significant difference,' continued Lampton. 'Our moving staircase is not intended to assist you; on the contrary, it is there to resist you. While it is moving downwards, you will be climbing upwards, a motion that will take you a few moments to become accustomed to. It is important to remember that this is not a race, but an endurance test. The staircase will move at approximately five miles an hour, and you will attempt to remain on it for sixty minutes.

'I can see from the expressions on one or two of your faces that you are beginning to wonder what all the fuss is about,' continued Lampton. 'After all, it would not be uncommon for men of your experience and ability to climb for many hours without a break. However, there are one or two other things you will have to contend with during the next sixty minutes. The chamber is currently at room temperature, and its atmosphere is set to closely approximate that found at sea level. By the end of the hour, any of you who are still able to move at that pace will be experiencing the conditions they might expect to encounter at 29,000 feet, as the temperature in the room will have fallen to minus forty degrees. That is the reason I asked you to dress exactly as you would for a climb.

'I shall also be introducing another little challenge. If you look at the far wall, you will see two large industrial fans: my wind machines. And let me assure you, gentlemen, it will not be a following wind.' One or two of the twelve laughed nervously. 'Once I set them in motion they will do everything in their power to blow you off the escalator.

'Finally, you will notice several rubber mats, blankets and buckets placed around the room. Once you have been forced off the moving staircase, you will be able to rest and warm yourself.

I'm sure I don't have to explain why the buckets are placed by the bottom of the escalator.' This time no one laughed. 'On the wall to your left are a clock, a gauge showing the temperature in the chamber, and an altimeter to indicate the atmospheric pressure. I will now give you a few moments to familiarize yourself with how the moving staircase works. I suggest that you position yourselves two steps apart. Should you find yourself having difficulty in maintaining your pace, move to the right and allow the man behind to overtake you. Are there any questions?'

'What's on the other side of that window?' asked Norton, the only candidate George hadn't come across before; a soldier who had been recommended by General Bruce.

'That's where the control room is located. It's from there that my staff will observe your progress. We can see you, but you can't see us. When the hour is up, the escalator will come to a halt, the wind machines will be turned off and the temperature will return to normal. At that point, you will be joined by several doctors and nurses who will carry out tests to assess your rate of recovery. Now, gentlemen, would you be so kind as to take your places on the escalator.'

Finch immediately ran up to the top step, while George took his place two steps below him, with Somervell a further two steps behind.

'The staircase will start to move the moment the buzzer sounds,' said Lampton. 'It will sound again ten minutes later, by which time the atmosphere in the chamber will be equivalent to that found at an altitude of five thousand feet and the temperature will have fallen to zero. The buzzer will continue to sound at ten-minute intervals throughout the test. The wind machines will be turned on after forty minutes. If anyone is still on their feet at the end of one hour, they will, I repeat, be experiencing a temperature of minus forty degrees and the atmosphere found at 29,000 feet. Good luck, gentlemen.' Lampton left the room and closed the door behind him. They all heard a key turning in the lock.

The twelve men stood nervously on the staircase, waiting for the buzzer to sound. George took a deep breath through his nose, filling his lungs with air. He avoided looking at Finch, two steps above him, or at Somervell two steps below.

'Are you ready, gentlemen?' said the voice of Dr Lampton over a loudspeaker. The buzzer sounded, and the staircase began to move at what seemed to George a fairly gentle pace. For ten minutes the twelve climbers all maintained their positions, and George didn't sense much of a change when the buzzer sounded a second time. The staircase continued to move at the same speed, although the indicators on the wall showed that the temperature had fallen to zero and the atmospheric conditions were those of 5,000 feet.

Everyone was still in place after twenty minutes, when the buzzer sounded a third time. By thirty minutes they had reached 15,000 feet, and the temperature was ten degrees below zero. Still no one had fallen by the wayside. Kenwright was the first to take a step to the right, and slowly drift down past his colleagues before finally ending up at the foot of the staircase. He struggled gamely to reach the nearest mat, where he collapsed in a heap. It was some minutes before he had the strength even to pull a blanket over his body. Lampton drew a line through his name. He would not be part of the team travelling to Tibet.

Finch and Mallory were maintaining the pace at the top of the escalator, with Somervell, Bullock and Odell on their heels. George had almost forgotten about the wind machines, until the buzzer sounded for the fifth time and a blast of cold air hit him in the face. He wanted to rub his eyes, but knew that if he removed his goggles on a real mountain at 29,000 feet, he risked snow blindness. He thought he saw Finch stumble in front of him, but he quickly recovered.

George didn't see the poor fellow a few steps below him who had removed his goggles and reeled backwards as he took the full blast of cold wind in his face. Moments later he was on his hands and knees on the floor at the base of the staircase, covering his eyes and vomiting. Lampton drew a line through the name of another man who wouldn't be making the passage to India.

When the buzzer sounded at fifty minutes, they had reached 24,000 feet, with temperatures of minus 25 degrees. Only Mallory, Finch, Odell, Somervell, Bullock and Norton were still on their feet. By the time they had reached 25,000 feet, Bullock and Odell had joined the others on the mats, so exhausted they didn't have the strength to follow the progress of the four survivors. Dr Lampton checked the clock and put a tick beside Odell's and Bullock's names.

Somervell managed just over fifty-three minutes before he fell off the staircase and collapsed to his hands and knees. He tried valiantly to step back on, but was immediately thrown off again. Norton was kneeling by his side a moment later. Lampton wrote *53 minutes* and *54 minutes* next to their names. He then turned his attention to the two men who appeared to be immovable.

Lampton lowered the temperature to minus 40 degrees and raised the atmospheric pressure to that at 29,000 feet, but the two survivors still refused to be budged. He turned the wind machine up to forty miles an hour. Finch stumbled, regretting that he had bagged the top step, as he was now shielding George from the full force of the wind. But just as it looked as if he was beaten, he somehow managed to recover and find enough strength to keep pace with the relentlessly moving escalator.

The clock showed both climbers that they only had three more minutes to go. That was when George decided he would have to give up. His legs felt like lumps of jelly, he was frozen and gasping for breath, and he was beginning to fall back. He accepted that the victory would be Finch's. Then, without warning, Finch fell back a step, and then another, followed by a third, which only made George more determined to hold on for the last ninety seconds until the final buzzer sounded. When the staircase at last came to a halt, he and Finch fell into each other's arms like a pair of legless drunks.

Odell hauled himself up from his mat and staggered across to congratulate them. Somervell and Norton joined them a moment later. If Bullock could have crawled across, he would have done so, but he remained spread-eagled on the mat, still gasping for breath.

Once the wind machine had been turned off, the altitude returned to sea level and the temperature raised to normal, the door of the chamber was unlocked and a dozen doctors and nurses rushed into the room and began to carry out tests on the participants to gauge their rates of recovery. In less than five minutes, George's heartbeat was back down to forty-eight, by which time Finch was strolling round the room chatting to those colleagues who were still standing.

Dr Lampton remained in the control room. He knew he was going to have to tell Hinks that Mallory and Finch were by far the most impressive candidates, and frankly there was nothing to choose between them. He was convinced that if anyone was likely to reach 29,000 feet and stand on top of the world, it was going to be one of those two.

33

When Ruth picked up the phone, she immediately recognized the voice on the other end of the line.

'Good morning, headmaster,' she said. '– Yes, he left a few moments ago – no, he never drives to school, headmaster, he always walks – it's just under five miles, and it usually takes him around fifty minutes. Goodbye, headmaster.'

George raised his ancient umbrella when he felt a few drops of rain land on his forehead. He tried to think about his morning lesson with the lower fifth – not that he had anything new to tell them about the Elizabethans. He wondered how Francis Drake would have handled the problem that had been nagging away at him for the past decade.

He had not yet heard from the Everest Committee following last week's medical tests. Still, there could be a letter waiting for him when he returned home that evening. There might even be a mention of the team selection in *The Times* – if so, Andrew O'Sullivan would be certain to bring it to his attention during the mid-morning break. However, after Finch's stalwart effort at the medical, George would have no complaint if he turned out to be the committee's choice as climbing leader. He'd laughed out loud when Young had reported verbatim the exchange between Finch and Hinks that had taken place at the committee meeting. He only wished he had been able to witness the encounter himself.

Although he didn't agree with Finch about the use of oxygen at high altitude, he did accept that if they were to have any chance of making a good fist of it, they would have to approach

the whole exercise in a more professional manner than in the
past, and to learn from the mistakes made during the South Pole
debacle.

His thoughts turned to Ruth, and how supportive she had
been. The past year had been idyllic. They were blessed with two
lovely daughters and a lifestyle that would have been the envy of
most men. Did he really want to travel to the other side of the
earth, and have to watch his children growing up by letter and
photograph? But it was Ruth who had cruelly summed up his
innermost dilemma when she had casually asked him how he
would feel if Andrew pointed out a photograph in *The Times* of
George Finch standing on top of the world, while he had just
come from teaching the lower fifth?

George checked his watch as he passed a signpost that told
him he still had three miles to walk, and smiled. He was a couple
of minutes ahead of schedule for a change. He disliked being
late for morning assembly, and Ruth always did everything in her
power to make sure he left home each morning well in time. The
headmaster always entered Great Hall as the clock chimed nine,
and if George was so much as thirty seconds late, he had to slip
in at the back during prayers, while heads were bowed. The
problem was that the headmaster's head was never bowed – nor
were the lower fifth's for that matter.

As he walked into School Lane, George was surprised to
notice how few boys and masters were about. Even more puz-
zling, when he reached the school gates there was nobody in
sight. Was it half term? A Sunday, perhaps? No, Ruth would
have remembered and reminded him to put on his best suit.

He walked across the empty quad towards the main hall, but
not a sound was coming from inside. No headmaster, no music,
not even a cough. Perhaps their heads were bowed in prayer?
He turned the large wrought-iron handle slowly, and, not wishing
to make a sound, pushed open the door and peered inside. The
hall was packed, with every pupil in his place. On the stage stood
the headmaster, with the rest of the staff seated behind him.
George was more mystified than ever – after all, nine o'clock
hadn't yet chimed.

And then one of the boys shouted, 'There he is!' and everyone in the hall rose as one and began clapping and cheering.

'Well done, sir.'

'What a triumph.'

'You'll be first to reach the top!' someone shouted at him as he made his way down the centre aisle towards the stage.

The headmaster shook George warmly by the hand and said, 'We are all so very proud of you, Mallory,' then waited for the boys to resume their seats before announcing, 'I will now call upon David Elkington to address assembly.'

The head boy rose from his place in the front row and walked up onto the stage. He unrolled a scroll and began to read.

'Nos, scholae Carthusianae et pueri et magistri, te Georgium Leigh Mallory salutamus. Dilectus ad ducendum agmen Britannicum super Everest, tantos honores ad omnes Carthusianos iam tribuisti. Sine dubio, O virum optime, et maiorem gloriam et honorem in scholam tuam, in universitatem tuam et ad patriam.' *We, the boys and masters of Charterhouse, salute George Leigh Mallory. You have honoured all Carthusians by being chosen to lead the British assault on Everest. We are in no doubt, Sir, that you will bring further glory and honour to your school, your university and your country.*

The head boy bowed before presenting the scroll to George. Once again, the whole school rose to their feet and let the senior history master know exactly how they felt.

George bowed his head. He preferred the lower fifth not to see him in tears.

34

'Allow me to welcome you as a member of the committee, Mallory,' said Sir Francis warmly. 'And may I add that we are delighted you felt able to accept the role of climbing leader.'

'Hear, hear! Hear, hear!'

'Thank you, Sir Francis,' said George. 'It's a great honour to be invited to lead such a fine bunch of chaps,' he added as he took his place between Geoffrey Young and General Bruce.

'You will have read General Bruce's report,' said Younghusband, 'describing how the party will travel from Liverpool to the foothills of Everest. Perhaps you could advise the committee how you see matters proceeding once you've set up a base camp.'

'I've read General Bruce's report with great interest, Mr Chairman,' said George, 'and I agree with his assessment that it will be thorough and detailed preparation that will determine the success or failure of this whole expedition. We must not forget that no Englishman has ever been within forty miles of Everest, let alone set up a base camp on its lower slopes.'

'Fair point,' admitted Bruce, his monocle falling from his eye, 'but I am able to inform the committee that since writing my report I have had a meeting with Lord Curzon at the Foreign Office and he has assured me that he will do everything in his power to ensure a safe and swift passage across the border and into Tibet.'

'Jolly good show,' said Raeburn, flicking some ash off the end of his cigar.

'But even if we are able to cross the border without incident,' said George, 'the committee must understand that no human being has ever climbed above 25,000 feet. We don't even know if it's possible to survive at such heights.'

'I'm bound to say, Mr Chairman,' said Ashcroft, 'that I can't see a great deal of difference between 25,000 and 29,000 feet, don't you know.'

'Speaking for myself, I don't know,' said George, 'because I've never stood at 25,000 feet, let alone 29,000. But if I ever do, commander, I'll let you know.'

'Now, Mallory,' said Sir Francis, 'as no one knows the climbing team better than you, we'd be interested to hear who you think will accompany you on the final assault.'

'I won't be able to answer that question, Mr Chairman, until I know who has acclimatized best to the conditions. But if I were to make a calculated guess, I've pencilled in Odell and Somervell –' Hinks allowed a smile to cross his face – 'as the back-up team. However, I have only ever considered one man to be the obvious choice for the final climb, and that's Finch.'

No one around the table spoke. Raeburn lit another cigar, and Ashcroft stared at his agenda. It was left to Sir Francis to break the embarrassing silence. He turned to Hinks and said, 'But I thought—'

'Yes, Mr Chairman,' said Hinks. Looking across the table at George, the secretary said, 'I'm afraid that's not going to be possible, Mallory.'

'And why not?' asked George.

'Because Finch will not be a member of the climbing party. Two of the Alpine Club's recommendations failed the medical. One of them was Kenwright, the other was Finch.'

'But there must be some mistake,' said George. 'I've rarely come across a fitter man in all my years of climbing.'

'I can assure you, Mallory, there is no mistake,' said Hinks, extracting a sheet of paper from his file. 'I have Dr Lampton's report to hand, and it would appear that Finch has a perforated eardrum, which Lampton believes could cause dizziness and vomiting, and would prevent him from climbing for sustained periods at very high altitude.'

'It's a pity that Dr Lampton hasn't stood by Finch's side on the top of Mont Blanc or the Matterhorn,' said Young. 'If he had, he would have been able to record that he didn't have as much as a nosebleed.'

'That may well be,' said Hinks. 'However—'

'Don't forget, Mr Hinks,' said George, 'that Finch is the only member of the team who has extensive knowledge of the use of oxygen.'

'But – correct me if I am wrong, Mallory – when we last met you were opposed to the very idea of using oxygen,' said Hinks.

'You're right, and I still am,' said George. 'But if I were to discover, having reached 27,000 feet, that not one member of my team was able to place one foot in front of the other, I might be willing to reconsider my position.'

'Norton and Odell have also stated that they do not believe oxygen will prove necessary for the final climb.'

'Norton and Odell have never been higher than 15,000 feet,' said Young. 'They might also be forced to change their minds.'

'Perhaps I should point out to you, Mallory,' said Hinks, 'that Finch's medical condition was not the only factor that influenced the Society's decision.'

'It wasn't the Society's decision to make,' said Young angrily. 'Sir Francis and I agreed that the Alpine Club would submit the names of the climbing party, and the committee would not question its recommendations.'

'That may well have been the case,' said Hinks. 'However, we have since discovered that when we interviewed Finch for the position of climbing leader, he lied to this committee.'

Both Mallory and Young were momentarily silenced, which allowed Hinks to continue uninterrupted.

'When Mr Raeburn asked Finch if he was a married man, he informed this committee that he was a widower.' Young bowed his head. 'That turns out not to be the case, as I found to my dismay when Mrs Finch wrote to assure me that she is alive and well.' Hinks extracted a letter from his file. 'The committee may wish to place on record the final paragraph of her letter,' he added solemnly.

Mallory pursed his lips. Young, however, did not appear to be surprised.

'*George and I were divorced some two years ago,*' read Hinks, '*and I'm sorry to have to inform your committee that a third party was involved.*'

'The rotter,' said Ashcroft.

'Not a man to be trusted,' said Raeburn.

'Frankly,' said George, ignoring both of them, 'if we do manage to reach 27,000 feet, it isn't going to matter much if my climbing partner is a divorcee, a widower or even a bigamist, because I can assure you, Mr Hinks, no one will notice whether he is wearing a wedding ring.'

'Let me try to understand what you're saying, Mallory,' said Hinks, going red in the face. 'Are you telling this committee that you would climb the last 2,000 feet of Mount Everest with anyone, provided that you were able to reach the summit?'

'Anyone,' said George without hesitation.

'Even a German?' said Hinks quietly.

'Even the devil,' replied George.

'I say, old chap,' said Ashcroft, 'don't you think that was uncalled for?'

'Not as uncalled for as dying an unnecessary death five thousand miles from home because I didn't have the right climbing partner,' said George.

'I am quite happy to record your strongly held feelings in the minutes, Mallory,' said Hinks, 'but our decision on Finch is final.'

George was silent for a moment. 'Then you can also record in the minutes, Mr Hinks, my resignation as climbing leader and as a member of this committee.' Several of those around the table began to speak at once, but George ignored them, and added, 'I am not willing to leave my wife and children for at least six months to take part in a mission that failed simply because it left its finest climber behind.'

Sir Francis had to raise his voice to make himself heard above the tumult that followed. 'Gentlemen, gentlemen,' he said, tapping the side of his brandy glass with a pencil. 'It is clear that we have reached an impasse that can be resolved in only one way.'

'What do you have in mind, Mr Chairman?' asked Hinks suspiciously.

'We shall have to take a vote.'

'But I haven't had time to prepare the necessary ballot papers,' blustered Hinks.

'Ballot papers won't be necessary,' said Sir Francis. 'After all, it's a simple enough decision. Is Finch to be included in the climbing party or not?' Hinks sank back in his chair, struggling to conceal a smile.

'Very well,' said Sir Francis. 'Will those members in favour of Finch being included in the climbing party please raise their hands.'

Mallory and Young immediately put up their hands, and to everyone's surprise General Bruce joined them.

'Those against?' said the chairman.

Hinks, Raeburn and Ashcroft raised their hands without hesitation.

'That's three votes each,' said Hinks, recording the decision in his minute book. 'Which leaves you, Mr Chairman, with the casting vote.'

Everyone around the table turned towards Sir Francis. He considered his position for a few moments before saying, 'I cast my vote in favour of Finch.'

Hinks held his pen poised above the minute book, seemingly unable to record the chairman's vote. 'Mr Chairman,' he said, 'for the record, may we know what caused you to reach this decision?'

'Most certainly,' said Sir Francis. 'It won't be me being asked to risk my life when Mallory reaches 27,000 feet.'

35

The little brass bell above the door rang.

'Good morning, Mr Pink,' said George as he entered Ede & Ravenscroft.

'Good morning, Mr Mallory. How may I assist you on this occasion, sir?'

George leant across the counter. 'I've just been selected as a member of the climbing party for the expedition to Everest,' he whispered.

'How very interesting, Mr Mallory,' said the manager. 'We haven't had any other customers planning a holiday in that part of the world, so may I be so bold as to ask what sort of weather conditions you might be expecting?'

'Well, I'm not altogether certain,' admitted George. 'But as far as I can make out, once we've reached 27,000 feet, we can expect gale-force winds, a temperature of forty degrees below zero and so little oxygen that it may be almost impossible to breathe.'

'Then you'll certainly be needing a woollen scarf and some warm gloves, not to mention the appropriate headgear,' said Mr Pink, coming out from behind the counter.

The manager's first suggestion was a cashmere Burberry scarf, followed by a pair of fleece-lined black leather gloves. George followed Mr Pink around the shop as he selected three pairs of thick grey woollen socks, two navy blue jumpers, a Shackleton windcheater, several silk shirts and the latest pair of fur-lined camping boots.

'And may I enquire, sir, do you anticipate any snow during this trip?'

'Most of the time, I suspect,' said George.

'Then you'll be needing an umbrella,' suggested Mr Pink. 'And what about headgear, sir?'

'I thought I'd take my brother's leather flying helmet and goggles,' said George.

'I don't think you'll find that's what fashionable gentlemen will be wearing climbing this year,' said Mr Pink, handing him the latest deerstalker.

'Which is why it won't be a fashionable gentleman who'll be the first to set foot on the summit of Everest.'

George smiled when he saw Finch approaching the counter, his arms laden with goods.

'We at Ede and Ravenscroft,' ventured Mr Pink, 'believe that it matters how a gentleman looks when he attains the summit of any mountain.'

'I can't imagine why,' said Finch, as he placed his purchases on the counter. 'There won't be any girls up there waiting for us.'

'Will there be anything else, Mr Finch?' asked the manager, trying not to show his disapproval.

'Not at these prices, there won't,' George said after checking his bill.

Mr Pink bowed politely and began to wrap up his customer's purchases.

'I'm glad we bumped into each other, Finch,' said George. 'There's something I need to discuss with you.'

'Don't tell me you've seen the light,' said Finch, 'and are at last considering the use of oxygen.'

'Perhaps,' said George. 'But I still need to be convinced.'

'Then I need at least a couple of hours of your time, as well as the proper equipment to hand, so I can demonstrate why oxygen will make all the difference.'

'Let's discuss it while we're on the boat to Bombay, when you'll have more than enough time to convince me.'

'That's assuming I'll be on the boat.'

'But you've already been selected for the team.'

'Only thanks to your intervention,' said Finch, scowling. 'And I'm grateful, because I suspect the nearest that Hinks has been to a mountain is a Christmas card.'

'That will be thirty-three pounds and eleven shillings, Mr Finch,' said Mr Pink. 'May I enquire how you intend to settle your bill on this occasion?'

'Just put it on my account,' said Finch, trying to imitate Mr Pink's 'for customers' accent.

The manager hesitated for a moment before giving Finch a slight bow.

'See you on board then,' said Finch before picking up his brown paper bag and leaving the shop.

'Your bill comes to forty-one pounds, four shillings and six pence, Mr Mallory,' said Mr Pink.

George wrote out a cheque for the full amount.

'Thank you, sir. And may I say on behalf of all of us here at Ede and Ravenscroft that we hope *you* will be the first man to reach the summit of Everest, and not . . .'

Mr Pink did not finish the sentence. Both men looked out of the window and watched Finch as he strode off down the road.

BOOK FIVE

WALKING OFF
THE MAP

1922

36

George knew the moment he stepped on board the SS *Caledonia* at Tilbury that he was embarking on a journey for which he had been preparing all his life.

The climbing team spent the five-week sea voyage to Bombay getting better acquainted, improving their fitness and learning how to work together as a unit. Every morning for an hour before breakfast they would run circuits around the deck, with Finch always setting the pace. Occasionally George's ankle would play up a little, but he didn't admit it, even to himself. After breakfast he would lie out on the deck reading John Maynard Keynes's *The Economic Consequences of the Peace*, but not until he'd written his daily letter to Ruth.

Finch gave a couple of lectures on the use of oxygen at high altitudes. The team dutifully disassembled and reassembled the 32-pound oxygen sets, strapped them on each other's backs and adjusted the valves that regulated the amount of gas released. Few of them seemed enthusiastic. George watched intently. There wasn't any doubt that Finch knew what he was talking about, although most of the team disapproved of the idea of using oxygen on principle. Norton said that the sheer weight of the cylinders would surely nullify any advantage their contents might have to offer.

'What proof do you have, Finch, that we'll need these infernal contraptions to get to the summit?' he demanded.

'None,' admitted Finch. 'But should you find yourself at 27,000 feet and unable to progress any further, perhaps you'll end up being grateful for one of these infernal contraptions.'

'I'd rather turn back,' said Somervell.

'And fail to reach the summit?' queried Finch.

'If that's the price, so be it,' said Odell adamantly.

Although George was also against the idea of using oxygen, he didn't offer an opinion. After all, he wouldn't be expected to make a decision if Finch was proved wrong. His thoughts were interrupted by an unmistakable bark of, 'Time for PT, chaps.'

The team clambered to their feet and formed three orderly lines in front of General Bruce, who stood with his hands on his hips and his feet firmly on the ground, evidently having no intention of leading by example.

After an hour of furious exercise the General disappeared below deck for his morning snifter, leaving the rest of the team to their own devices. Norton and Somervell began a game of deck tennis, while Odell settled down to read EF Benson's latest novel. George and Guy sat cross-legged on the deck, chatting about the possibility of a Cambridge man winning the hundred metres dash at the Paris Olympics.

'I've seen Abrahams run at Fenners,' said George. 'He's good, damned good, but Somervell tells me there's a Scot called Liddell who's never lost a race in his life, so it will be interesting to see what happens when they come up against each other.'

'We'll be back well in time to find out which of them wins gold. In fact,' added Guy with a grin, 'it will be a good excuse to return to— oh my God.' Guy was looking over George's shoulder. 'What's he up to now?'

George swung round to see Finch standing with his arms folded, feet apart, staring up at the ship's funnels, which were belching out clouds of black smoke.

'Surely he can't be considering . . .'

'I wouldn't put it past him,' said George. 'He'd do anything to be one up on the rest of the team.'

'I don't think he gives a damn about the rest of the team,' said Guy. 'It's only you he wants to beat.'

'In which case,' replied George, 'I'd better have a word with the captain.'

◄◦►

George told Ruth in one of his daily letters that he and Finch were like two children, always striving to outdo each other to gain teacher's attention. In this case teacher was General Bruce, who, George confided: *may well be an old buffer, but he's no fool, and we've all happily accepted him as the expedition's leader.* He paused to look at Ruth's photograph, which he had remembered to bring with him this time, even though he'd forgotten his razor and left home with only one pair of socks. He continued to write:

> *I still spend so much of my time wondering if I made the right decision to come on this trip. When you've found Guinevere, why go in search of the Holy Grail? I've begun to realize that every day without you is a wasted day. God knows I hope I will exorcize this demon once and for all, so I can return to The Holt and spend the rest of my life with you and the children. I know how difficult you find it to put your true feelings into words, but please let me know how you really feel.*
>   *Your loving husband,*
>   *George*

Ruth read George's letter a second time. She still wondered if she had done the right thing in not letting him know before he left that she was pregnant again. She rose from her chair by the window, walked across to her little bureau and began to write, with every intention of answering his last question truthfully.

> *My darling,*
>   *I've never been able to properly express how I feel every time you leave home. This time it's no different from your*

trips to the Western Front or the Alps, when I spent every hour of the day wondering if you were safe, and if I would ever see you again. It's no different now. I sometimes envy other wives who were fortunate enough to see their husbands return in one piece from that misnamed Great War, and assumed that they would never have to face the same dread again in their lifetime.

Like you, I yearn for a successful outcome of this expedition, but only for the selfish reason that I have no desire to be put through such an ordeal again. You don't begin to understand how much I miss you, your company, your gentle humour, your kindness, your guidance in all things, but most of all your love and affection, especially when we are alone. I spend every waking hour wondering if you will return, if our children will have to grow up without a father from whom they would have learnt tolerance, compassion and wisdom, and if I will grow old having lost the only man I could ever love.

Your devoted wife,
Ruth

Ruth returned to her chair and read through the letter before placing it in an envelope. She looked out of the window at the open gate at the end of the drive, wondering, just as she had during the war, if she would ever see her husband come striding down that path again.

―◇―

Once the General had blown his whistle for the last time, most of the team remained flat on their backs as they tried to recover from the morning PT session. George sat up and glanced around the deck to be sure that none of his colleagues were showing any particular interest in him, then stood and sauntered off in the direction of his cabin.

He took the stairs down to the passenger deck, crossed the gangway and looked back for a moment before opening a door marked *Crew Only* and going down the crew's steps for another three levels, until he came to the engine room. He banged his fist on the heavy door, and a moment later the chief engineer stepped out to join him. The man nodded, but made no attempt to talk above the noise of the engines. He led George along a narrow corridor, stopping only when they came to a heavy steel door marked *Danger: No Entry*.

He removed a large key from a pocket in his boiler suit, unlocked the door and held it open.

'The captain gave me clear orders, Mr Mallory,' he shouted. 'You've got five minutes, and no longer.'

George nodded, and disappeared inside.

Guy Bullock started clapping the moment he saw George standing on top of the centre funnel. Norton and Somervell stopped playing deck tennis to see what the fuss was about. Odell looked up, closed his book, and joined in the applause. Only Finch, hands in pockets, feet apart, didn't respond.

'How did he manage that?' said Norton. 'You only have to brush up against one of those funnels and you'll get a blister the size of an apple.'

'And even if it weren't for the heat,' added Somervell, equally bemused, 'you'd need the suction of a limpet to climb that surface.'

Finch continued to stare up at Mallory. He noticed that for once there was no black smoke belching from the centre funnel, and glanced across at Bullock, who couldn't stop laughing. When Finch looked back up, Mallory had disappeared.

As George climbed back down the ladder on the inside of the funnel, he couldn't decide if he should tell Finch that every Thursday morning one of the funnels was taken briefly out of commission so that the ship's engineers could carry out a full inspection.

A few moments later, a plume of black smoke erupted from the centre funnel, and once again the rest of the team burst into spontaneous applause. 'I still can't work it out,' said Norton.

'The only explanation I can come up with,' said Odell, 'is that Mallory must have smuggled Mr Houdini on board.'

The rest of the team laughed, while Finch remained silent.

'What's more, he seems to have reached the top without the aid of oxygen,' Somervell added.

'I wonder how he managed that?' said Guy, a grin still fixed firmly on his face. 'No doubt our resident scientist will have a theory.'

'No, I don't have a theory,' said Finch. 'But I can tell you one thing. Mallory won't be able to climb up the inside of Everest.'

—◦—

Ruth sat by the window holding her letter, beginning to wonder if her forthright honesty might prove to be a distraction for George. After a few minutes of contemplation, she tore the letter into small pieces and dropped them into the crackling flames. She returned to her desk and began to write a second letter.

> *My darling George,*
>   *Spring is upon us at The Holt, and the daffodils are in full bloom. In fact, the garden has never looked more beautiful. Everything is just as you would wish it to be. The children are doing well, and Clare has written a poem for you, which I enclose . . .*

37

When the SS *Caledonia* docked in Bombay, the first person to disembark was General Bruce. He was dressed in the freshly ironed short-sleeve khaki shirt and neatly pressed khaki shorts that had become regulation kit for the British army serving in hot climates. He regularly reminded the team that it was Lord Baden-Powell who had followed his example when choosing the uniform of the Boy Scout movement, and not the other way round.

George followed closely in the General's wake. The first thing that struck him as he made his way down the wobbly gangplank was the smell – what Kipling had described as spicy, pungent, oriental, and like no other smell on earth. The second thing that hit him, almost literally, was the intense heat and humidity. To a pale-faced loon from Cheshire, it felt like Dante's fiery furnace. The third thing was the realization that the General had considerable clout in this far-off land.

Two groups of men were waiting at the foot of the gangplank to greet the expedition's leader, and not only did they stand far apart from each other, but they could not have been in greater contrast. The first group of three embodied 'the British abroad'. They made no attempt to blend in with the indigenous population, dressed as if they were attending a garden party in Tunbridge Wells and making no allowances for the inhospitable climate for fear it might suggest in some way that they and the natives were equals.

As the General stepped onto the dockside, he was greeted by

one of them, a tall young man wearing a dark blue suit and a white shirt with a stiff collar, and sporting an Old Harrovian tie.

'My name is Russell,' he announced as he took a step forward.

'Good morning, Russell,' said the General, and they shook hands as if they had known each other for years, whereas in reality their only bond was the old school tie.

'Welcome back to India, General Bruce,' said Russell. 'I'm the Governor-General's private secretary. This is Captain Berkeley, the Governor-General's ADC.' An even younger man in full dress uniform, who had been standing rigidly to attention since the General had stepped ashore, saluted. The General returned his salute. The third man, dressed in a chauffeur's uniform, stood by the side of a gleaming Rolls-Royce, and was not introduced. 'The Governor-General hopes,' continued Russell, 'that you and your party will join him for dinner this evening.'

'We shall be delighted to do so,' said Bruce. 'At what time would Sir Peter like us on parade?'

'He will be hosting a reception in the residence at seven o'clock,' said Russell, 'followed by dinner at eight.'

'And the dress code?' enquired the General.

'Formal, with medals, sir.'

Bruce nodded his approval.

'We have, as you requested,' continued Russell, 'secured fourteen rooms at the Palace Hotel, and I've also put a number of vehicles at your disposal while you and your men are in Bombay.'

'Most hospitable,' said the General. 'For the time being, perhaps you could arrange for my men to be transported to the hotel, billeted and fed.'

'Of course, General,' said Russell. 'And the Governor-General asked me to give you this.' He handed over a bulky brown envelope, which the General passed on to George as if he was his private secretary.

George smiled and tucked the envelope under his arm. He couldn't help noticing that the rest of the team, including Finch, were observing the exchange in awed silence.

'Mallory,' said the General, 'I want you to join me while the rest of the men are escorted to the hotel. Thank you, Russell,' he said to the Governor-General's private secretary. 'I look forward to seeing you at the reception this evening.'

Russell bowed and took a pace backwards, as if the General were minor royalty.

The General then turned his attention to the second group, also three in number, which was about the only thing they had in common.

The three locals, dressed in long, cool white gowns and white slippers, had waited patiently while Mr Russell carried out the formal welcome on behalf of the Governor-General. Now their leader stepped forward. 'Namaste, General Sahib,' he said, bowing low.

The General neither shook hands with the Sirdar nor saluted. Without preliminaries, he asked, 'Did you get my cable, Kumar?'

'Yes, General Sahib, and all your instructions have been carried out to the letter. I think I can say with some confidence that you will be well satisfied.'

'I'll be the judge of that, Kumar, and only after I've inspected the merchandise.'

'Of course, General,' said the Indian, once again bowing low. 'Perhaps you'd be kind enough to follow me.'

Kumar and his two compatriots led the General across a road teeming with people, rickshaws and hundreds of old Raleigh and Hercules bicycles, as well as the occasional contented-looking cow chewing its cud in the middle of the highway. The General marched through the bustling, noisy crowd, which parted as if he were Moses crossing the Red Sea. George pursued his leader, curious to discover what was next while at the same time trying to take in the unfamiliar sounds of the street traders plying their exotic wares: Heinz baked beans, Player's cigarettes, Swan Vesta matches, bottles of Tizer and Eveready batteries were continually thrust in front of his nose. He politely declined each new offer, while feeling overwhelmed by the energy and exuberance of the local people, but horrified by the poverty he saw all around him – the beggars far outnumbered the traders. He now understood why these people considered Gandhi to be a prophet, while the

British continued to treat the Mahatma as if he were a criminal. He would have so much to tell the lower fifth when he returned.

The General strode on, ignoring the dusty outstretched hands and the repeated cries of 'Pie, pie, pie.' The Sirdar led him into a square that was so packed it might have been a mass rally at Speaker's Corner, with the difference that everyone was talking, and no one was listening. The square was surrounded by unfinished concrete buildings. The curious and those with nothing better to do hung out of upper windows hoping to gain a bird's eye view of what was taking place below. Then George set eyes for the first time on what the General had described as 'the merchandise'.

On a dusty, sunburned patch of earth, one hundred mules awaited inspection. Behind them stood a large group of porters.

George stood to one side and watched as the General carried out his inspection, the crowd following his every move. He began by checking the mules' legs and teeth, and even sat astride several of the beasts to assess their strength. Two of them collapsed under his weight. It took him over an hour to select seventy of the animals that in his opinion passed muster.

Next, the General carried out exactly the same exercise with row upon row of the silent porters. First he inspected their legs, then their teeth, and in some cases, to George's astonishment, he even jumped on their backs. Once again, one or two of them collapsed under his weight. Despite this, before the second hour was up he had added sixty-two porters to the seventy mules he had already selected.

Although George had done little more than act as an observer, he was already sweating from head to toe, while the General seemed to take everything, including the heat, in his stride.

When the inspection had been completed, Kumar stepped forward and presented his demanding customer with two cooks and four dhobis. To George's relief, the General did not jump onto their backs. He did, however, check their teeth and legs.

Having completed his inspection, the General turned to Kumar and said, 'Be sure that every one of the coolies and mules are standing on the dockside at six o'clock tomorrow morning. If they are all on parade by that time you will be paid fifty rupees.' Kumar bowed and smiled. The General turned to George and put a hand out. George assumed he required the envelope. The General opened it, extracted a fifty-rupee note and handed it to the Sirdar to confirm that the deal had been struck. 'And instruct them, Kumar,' he added, pointing at the porters, 'that they will be paid ten rupees a week. Any of them who are still with us when we re-board the ship in three months' time will be given a bonus of twenty rupees.'

'Most generous, General Sahib, most generous,' Kumar replied, bowing even lower.

'Were you also able to comply with my other request?' demanded the General as he passed the envelope back to George.

'Yes, General Sahib,' said the Sirdar, with an even broader grin on his face.

One of the two men standing behind Kumar stepped forward, stood to attention in front of the General and then removed his slippers. George had given up trying to guess what would happen next. The General took a tape from a pocket in his shorts and proceeded to measure the young man, from the top of his head to the soles of his bare feet.

'I think you will find,' said Kumar with satisfaction, 'that the boy is exactly six feet.'

'Yes, but does he understand what is expected of him?'

'He does indeed, General Sahib. In fact he has been preparing for the past month.'

'I'm delighted to hear it,' said Bruce. 'If he turns out to be satisfactory, he will be paid twenty rupees a week, and on arrival at base camp will be given a bonus of fifty rupees.'

Once again the Sirdar bowed.

George was about to ask why the expedition required a youth who was exactly six feet tall, when the General pointed to the short, stocky man with Asiatic features who was standing at the back of the trio, and had not uttered a word. 'And who is that?'

The young man stepped forward before Kumar had a chance

to introduce him, and said, 'I am Sherpa Nyima, General. I am your personal translator, and will be the Sherpa leader when you reach the Himalaya.'

'Twenty rupees a week,' said the General, and marched out of the square without another word, his business completed.

It had always amused George that whenever generals marched off, they assumed that everyone else would follow. It was one of the reasons, he concluded, that the British had won more battles than they had lost. It took George several minutes to catch up with Bruce, because most of the crowd were still running after him, hoping to benefit from his largesse. When he finally managed to do so, Bruce simply said, 'Never become friendly with the natives. You'll regret it in the long run.' He didn't utter another word until they entered the driveway of the Palace Hotel twenty minutes later, leaving the pursuing horde behind them. As the General marched up the path through the manicured gardens, George spotted a third welcoming party standing on the top step of the hotel. He wondered how long they had been waiting.

The General came to a sudden halt in front of a beautiful young woman wearing a deep purple and gold sari. She was carrying a small bowl of sweet-smelling powdered herbs in her left hand and, after dipping the forefinger of her right hand into the powder, she gently pressed the tip of her finger to the General's forehead, leaving a distinctive red mark of respect. She took a pace back, and a second young woman, also in traditional dress, placed a garland of flowers over the General's head. He bowed and thanked them.

The ceremony over, a smartly dressed man wearing a black frock coat and pinstripe trousers stepped forward. 'Welcome back to the Palace Hotel, General Bruce,' he said. 'I have put your party in the south wing, overlooking the ocean, and your usual suite has been prepared.' He stood aside to allow his guest to enter the hotel.

'Thank you, Mr Khan,' said the General, walking straight past the check-in desk towards a lift that he assumed was being held open for him.

George followed him, and when they reached the top floor, the first thing he saw was Norton and Somervell standing at the far end of the corridor wearing their dressing gowns. He smiled and waved to let them know he would be joining them in a few minutes.

'I suppose, General,' said George, 'that this could be our last chance to have a bath for three months.'

'Speak for yourself, Mallory,' said Bruce, as Mr Khan held open the door of the Queen Victoria suite for him.

George was already discovering why the RGS had considered this short, plump, retired soldier to be head and shoulders above the rest.

38

'I'd like to post some letters, please,' said George.

'Of course, sir,' said the concierge. 'How many?'

'Seventeen,' said George. He had already posted eighteen letters when the ship had docked for a few hours at Durban to take on fuel and fresh food.

'All to the same country?' the concierge asked casually, as if this was an everyday occurrence.

'Yes, in fact all to the same address.' This time the concierge did raise an eyebrow. 'My wife,' explained George. 'I write to her every day, and I've only just disembarked, so . . .'

'Leave it to me,' said the concierge.

'Thank you,' said George.

'Are you coming to the Governor-General's shindig, George?' asked a voice behind him.

George turned to see Guy approaching. 'Yes,' he replied.

'Then let's share a taxi,' said Guy, as he headed towards the door.

'I intend to eat like a pig tonight,' said Guy as the rickshaw dodged obstacles in the crowded streets. 'I have a feeling this is likely to be the best spread we'll get before we return to England. Unless of course the Governor-General decides to invite us again on our way back.'

'That may depend on whether we return as conquering heroes or frostbitten failures,' said George.

'I'm not going to risk it either way,' said Guy. 'Especially as Bruce tells me that Sir Peter has the finest cellar in India.'

Two soldiers in full dress uniform snapped to attention and saluted as the rickshaw drove through the gates of the Governor-General's residence. Mallory and Bullock jumped out and walked beneath a high wooden arch into a long, ornate marble hall, where they took their place in the reception line. The General was standing by the Governor-General's side, introducing him to each member of the team.

'As you seem to be so well informed, Guy,' whispered George, 'who's the young lady standing by the Governor-General's side?'

'His second wife,' said Bullock. 'His first died a couple of years ago, and this one—'

'This is Guy Bullock, Sir Peter,' said the General. 'He's taken a sabbatical from the Foreign Office to join us.'

'Good evening, Mr Bullock.'

'And this is George Mallory, our climbing leader.'

'So this is the man who's going to be the first to stand on the summit of Everest,' said the Governor-General, shaking George warmly by the hand.

'He has a rival,' said Guy with a grin.

'Ah, yes,' said the Governor-General, 'Mr Finch, if I remember correctly. Can't wait to meet the fellow. And may I introduce my wife.'

After bowing to the young lady, George and Guy drifted into a packed room where the only Indians in sight were servants offering drinks. George selected a sherry wine and then headed for the one person he recognized.

'Good evening, Mr Mallory,' said Russell.

'Good evening, Mr Russell,' said George. 'Are you enjoying being posted out here?' He was never at ease when having to make small talk.

'Capital, enjoying every moment,' Russell replied. 'It's just a pity about the natives.'

'The natives?' repeated George, hoping Russell was joking.

'They don't like us,' whispered Russell. 'In fact, they loathe us. There's trouble brewing.'

'Trouble?' prompted Bullock, who had walked across to join them.

'Yes, ever since we put that fellow Gandhi in jail for creating unrest—' Suddenly, without warning, Russell stopped in mid-sentence and stared, his mouth hanging open. Mallory and Bullock turned to see what had caused him to be struck dumb.

'Is he one of yours?' asked Russell, barely able to hide his discomfort.

'I'm afraid so,' said George, stifling a grin as he turned to see Finch chatting to the Governor-General's wife. Finch was dressed in an open-necked khaki shirt, green corduroy trousers and brown suede shoes, with no socks.

'You should feel flattered,' chipped in Guy. 'He doesn't usually take that much trouble.'

The private secretary was clearly not amused. 'The man's a bounder,' he said as they watched Finch slip an arm around Lady Davidson's waist.

George didn't move as he spotted the General heading towards him, almost at a gallop.

'Mallory,' he said, his cheeks flushed, 'get that man out of here, and be quick about it.'

'I'll do my best,' said George, 'but I can't guarantee—'

'If you don't get him out, and now,' said the General, 'I will. And let me assure you it won't be a pretty sight.'

George handed his empty glass to a passing waiter before crossing the room to join Finch and the Governor-General's wife.

'Have you met Mallory, Sonia?' Finch asked. 'He's my only real rival.'

'Yes, we've been introduced,' replied the Governor-General's wife, pretending to be unaware of Finch's arm, draped around her waist.

'I'm sorry to interrupt you, Lady Davidson,' said George, 'but I need to have a private word with Mr Finch, as a small problem has arisen.'

Without another word he grabbed Finch firmly by the elbow and led him quickly out of the room. Guy slipped in next to Lady Davidson and started chatting to her about whether she intended to return to London for the season.

'So what's this small problem?' asked Finch once they were out in the hallway.

'You are,' replied George. 'At this moment I think you'll find the General is rounding up volunteers for a firing squad.' He guided Finch out of the door and onto the driveway.

'Where are we going?' asked Finch.

'Back to the hotel.'

'But I haven't had dinner yet.'

'I think that's the least of your problems.'

'You were ordered to get me out of there, weren't you?' said Finch as George shoved him into a rickshaw.

'Something like that,' admitted George. 'I have a feeling that will be the last time we're invited to one of the Governor-General's little soirées.'

'Speak for yourself, Mallory. If you and I get to stand on top of that mountain, you'll definitely be dining with the Governor-General again.'

'That doesn't mean you will be,' said George.

'No, I won't. I'll be upstairs in his lady's chamber.'

◄○►

George thought he heard a knock on the door, but then he could have been dreaming. It sounded a little louder the second time. 'Come in,' he said, still half asleep. George opened one eye to see the General staring down at him, still dressed in his uniform.

'Do you always sleep on the floor with the windows wide open, Mallory?' he asked.

George opened his other eye. 'It was either this or the veranda,' he said. 'And I can assure you, General,' he added, pushing himself up, 'this is luxury compared to what it's going to be like at 27,000 feet, stuck in a tiny tent with only Finch for company.'

'That's precisely what I wanted to speak to you about,' said the General. 'I felt you ought to be the first to know that I've decided to put Finch on the next boat back home.'

George put on his silk dressing gown and sat down on the

only comfortable chair in the room. He slowly filled his pipe with tobacco, and took his time lighting up.

'Finch's behaviour this evening was quite inexcusable,' the General continued. 'I now realize I should never have agreed to him being included in the team.'

George puffed away on his pipe for a few moments before he responded. 'General,' he said quietly, 'you don't have the authority to send any member of my team back to England without consulting me.'

'I am consulting you now, Mallory,' said the General, his voice rising with every word.

'No, you are not. You've barged into my room in the middle of the night to inform me that you've decided to send Finch back to England on the first available boat. That's not my idea of consultation.'

'Mallory,' interrupted the General, 'I don't have to remind you that I am in overall charge of this expedition. I will be the one who makes the final decision as to what happens to any member of my team.'

'Then you'll be making this one all on your own, General, because if you put Finch on that boat, then I and the rest of *my* team will be joining him. I'm sure the RGS will be fascinated to know why, unlike the Duke of York, you didn't even manage to take us to the top of the hill, let alone bring us down again.'

'But, but—' spluttered the General. 'Surely you agree that's not the way to treat a lady, Mallory, especially the Governor-General's wife.'

'No one knows better than I do,' said George, 'that Finch can be tiresome, and I'm sure he won't be teaching etiquette to any debs next season. But unless you're willing to take his place, General, I suggest you go to bed now, and just be grateful that Finch won't be attending any more cocktail parties for at least another three months. He's also unlikely to bump into any more ladies on his way to the Himalaya.'

'I'll have to think about it, Mallory,' said the General, turning to leave. 'I'll let you know my decision in the morning.'

'General, I'm not one of your coolies who's desperate for the

King's shilling, so please let me know now if I am to wake up my men and tell them they'll be returning to England on the first boat, or if I can allow them to rest before they set out on the most arduous journey of their lives.'

The General's face became redder. 'On your head be it, Mallory,' he said, before storming out of the room.

'Dear Lord,' said George as he took off his dressing gown and lay back down on the floor, 'please tell me, what did I do to deserve Finch?'

39

April 15th, 1922

My dearest Ruth,

We have begun the 1,000-mile trek to the Tibetan border. We boarded the train to Siliguri at the base of the Himalaya, which the timetable promised would be a 6-hour journey, but it took almost 16. I've often wondered what happens to old trains when they're pensioned off – well, now I know. They're sent to India, where they're reincarnated.

So, we all piled aboard an old Great Northern locomotive, Castle class, the Warwick Castle, to be precise. The seats in 1st class are now somewhat shoddy and worn, while third class still has wooden slats to sit on, and no loo, which meant we had to jump off when we stopped at a station and head for the bushes. The train also had cattle class, where Bruce put the mules and the porters. Both complained.

There is one big difference between travelling down from Birkenhead to London in comfort and going from Bombay to Siliguri: we used to keep the windows closed and turn the heating up on our way down from the north of England, but here, despite the fact that the rail company has dispensed with the glass windows, it feels as if you're travelling in an oven on wheels.

'Where's Daddy?' demanded Clare. 'Where is he now?'

Ruth put down the letter and joined her daughters on the floor so they could study the map her father had drawn for them, and follow his progress. She ran a finger across the ocean from Tilbury to Bombay, and then along a railway line, that finally came to a halt at Siliguri. She picked up the letter and continued to read it aloud to the children:

Imagine our surprise when we disembarked in Siliguri to be greeted by the sight of the Darjeeling Himalayan Railway Company's own miniature wonder of the world. Here the metre gauge ends, to be replaced by a unique two-foot gauge, which is why it is known affectionately by the locals as the toy train.

You step into a delightful little carriage which would be ideal for Beridge and Clare, but made me feel like Gulliver when he woke in the land of the Lilliputians. With a noise that is out of all proportion to its size, the little steam engine begins its upward journey from the foothills of Siliguri, at a mere 300 feet above sea level, to Darjeeling, 51 miles away, climbing to a height of 7,000 feet.

The children will be fascinated to learn that the gradient is so steep that a native has to sit on the front buffer of the engine so he can sprinkle sand on the tracks to make sure the wheels can grip as we climb higher and higher into the mountains.

I can't tell you how long the journey took, because every minute was such sheer delight that I didn't stop admiring the view even for a moment, for fear of missing some new wonder. In fact our intrepid cameraman, Captain Noel, became so infatuated by the whole experience that when we came to a halt at Tung to fill up with water – both the little engine and its passengers – he climbed up onto the roof of the carriage, from where he filmed the rest of the journey, while we mere mortals had to satisfy ourselves with looking out of the windows.

When we finally pulled into Darjeeling station after a 7-hour journey, I had only one thought: if only this little gem could transport us all the way to base camp, how much easier our lives would be. But no such luck, and within moments of our leaving the train, the familiar voice of General Bruce could be heard barking out orders as he lined up the mules and porters so we could begin the long journey into the jungle, and on to the plains of Tibet.

We have each been allocated our own pony to carry our personal possessions and equipment, and with the exception of the General we have to walk at least 20 miles a day. In the evening we try to set up camp near a river or lake if it's at all possible, which gives us the chance to swim, and for a few glorious moments rid ourselves of the flies, mosquitoes and leeches, which seem to prefer a diet of white men to natives.

The General has brought along his own bath, which is strapped to two mules, and every evening at around seven, half a dozen porters fill it with water that's been heated over a wood fire. I have a photograph of our leader sitting in his bath, a cigar in one hand and a glass of brandy in the other. He clearly sees no reason to change the habits of a lifetime simply because he's spending a few weeks in the Indian jungle.

We all dine together in the evening at a trestle table – the General sits at the top, perched on his shooting stick. Our menu rarely varies from stew and dumplings, but by the time we set up camp at the end of the day we're far too hungry to enquire which animal has been added to the pot.

The General has brought along a dozen cases of the finest Châteauneuf-du-Pape, as well as half a dozen cases of Pol Roger, which are carried by two of the sturdiest mules in the pack. The only complaint the General voices is that he can't keep the wine at room temperature. However, as the weather is becoming a little colder each day, it won't be too long before he'll be able to chill the champagne in a bath full of ice.

Everyone appears to be holding up well – a little fever and sickness are to be expected, although I seem to have escaped – so far – with just a few mosquito bites and a rather bad rash.

Three of the porters have already run away, and two of

*the mules have died of exhaustion – don't tell Clare.
Otherwise they all seem to be in pretty good shape. We've
already signed up our chief Sherpa. He's called Nyima, and
not only does he speak the King's English, but he is clearly a
serious climber – barefooted.*

*Somervell has been a real brick, as always. Not only is he
enduring the same hardships we all have to go through, but
he carries out his duties as our reserve quack without ever
grumbling about the extra workload. Odell is in his element,
discovering new types of rock by the day. No doubt once he
returns to Cambridge several volumes will be appearing on
the bookshelves, not to mention the dozens of well-attended
lectures he'll be delivering.*

*Norton, poor man, is six foot four inches tall, so he has to
have the largest mule, and still his feet touch the ground.
Finch always brings up the rear of the convoy – his choice as
well as ours – where he keeps a careful eye on his precious
oxygen cylinders, which he is still convinced will decide the
outcome of the expedition. I remain sceptical.*

*As we climb higher and higher, I'm monitoring how the
chaps handle the conditions, and I'm already beginning to
consider the composition of the individual climbing parties.
Finch assumes that he'll be the one who's selected for the
final assault on Everest, and frankly no one will be surprised
if he is. Hardly a civil word has passed between him and the
General since we left Bombay. However, as each day passes
the 'Sonia affair', as it's referred to by the lads, fades into
blessed memory.*

*One of our party has turned out to be an unexpected
revelation. I've always known that Noel was a first-class
alpinist, but I had no idea what an outstanding photographer
and film-maker he is. There can never have been an
expedition that's been better recorded, and as an added
bonus, Noel is one of the few members of the team who
speaks the local language.*

*One of the daily routines that Noel has been filming
wouldn't be believed unless he'd made a record of it.*

Morshead, who I don't believe you've met, is a cartographer who, as a member of the RGS team, is responsible for producing detailed maps of the area, and one of the things he's most assiduous about is recording distances accurately. To assist Morshead, the General has employed, at a cost of twenty rupees a day, a young Indian who is exactly six feet in height. Let me try to describe his responsibility, although you'll be able to see it on film for yourself once we return. He lies flat on the ground while another Sherpa makes a mark in the earth at the top of his head to record the distance. The six-foot man then stands up, placing his toes behind the mark (he's barefooted) while he repeats the entire exercise again and again, hour upon hour. That way, Morshead can measure the exact distance we cover each day – around 20 miles – which I've calculated means that the young man is standing up and lying down nearly 18,000 times a day. God knows he earns his twenty rupees.

My darling, it's time to stop writing and blow out my candle. I share my little tent with Guy. It's wonderful having an old friend on this trip, but it's not the same as being with you . . .

'Where's he reached?' demanded Clare, looking down at the map.

Ruth folded up the letter before joining Clare and Beridge on the floor again. She studied the map for a moment before pointing to a village called Chumbi. As George's letters took six or seven weeks to reach The Holt, she could never be quite sure where he actually was. She opened his latest letter.

Today we covered our usual 20 miles, and lost another mule, so we're now down to 61. I wonder what strategic decision the General would make if we were faced with a shortage of mules and he had to choose between ditching his wine or his bath.

He has the porters on parade, standing to attention for roll call, at six every morning. This morning we were down

to 37, *so another one has run away; the General describes*
them as deserters.

While we were on our march yesterday, we came across
a Buddhist monastery high in the hills. We stopped so that
Noel could film it, but the General advised us against
disturbing the monks at their worship. He's a strange
combination of wisdom and bombast.

Nyima tells me that once we've trudged up the Jelep La,
we should be setting up camp this evening at around 14,000
feet, under the peak of a mountain from which, if I were to
climb it, I would have a clear view of Everest. Tomorrow is
Sunday, which the General has designated as a day of rest,
to allow the porters and the mules a chance to recover their
strength, while some of us catch up with our reading or write
home to our loved ones. I'm currently enjoying TS Eliot's
The Waste Land, *though I confess I intend to climb that*
mountain tomorrow if there's the slightest chance of seeing
Everest for the first time. I shall have to rise early, as Nyima
estimates that the summit could be as high as 21,000 feet. I
didn't point out to the Sherpa leader that I've never climbed
to that height before.

'What happens if Daddy isn't allowed to cross the border?' asked
Clare, plonking a thumb on the thin red line that divided India
from Tibet.

'He'll just have to turn round and come back home,' said her
mother.

'Good,' said Clare.

40

George slipped out of camp just before sunrise, a knapsack on his back, a compass in one hand and an ice axe in the other. He felt like a schoolboy off to have a smoke behind the bicycle shed.

Through the early morning mist, he could just about make out the unnamed mountain rising high above him. He was estimating that it would take at least two hours before he could hope to reach its base when he heard an unfamiliar sound. He stopped and looked around, but couldn't see anything unusual.

By the time he reached the lower slopes of the mountain, he'd been able to consider several different routes to the summit. The first thrill for any mountaineer contemplating a climb is deciding which route to take. The wrong choice can result in disaster – or, at the least, in having to return another day. George didn't have another day.

He had just decided on what looked like the best route when he thought he heard the unfamiliar sound again. He looked back down the valley along which he had approached the mountain. Half of it was bathed in morning sunlight, while the shadow of the mountain made the rest of it appear as if it had not yet woken up, but he still didn't spot anything strange.

George double-checked his chosen route, then began to attack the stony, rough terrain at the foot of the mountain. For the next hour he made good progress, despite having to change direction several times whenever an obstacle blocked his way.

He could now see the peak ahead of him, and estimated that he would reach the top within the hour. That's when he made his first mistake. He had come up against a rock that not only blocked his path, but appeared to be insurmountable without a partner to assist him. George knew from bitter experience that much of mountaineering ends in frustration, and that he had no choice but to turn back and search for another route. He also knew that if he was to get back to camp before sunset, there would come a moment when he could no longer risk chasing the sun as it sank beneath the unfamiliar horizon.

And then he heard the sound again, closer this time. He swung round, and saw Nyima approaching. George smiled, flattered that the Sherpa leader had followed him.

'We'll have to turn back,' George said, 'and try to find another route.'

'That won't be necessary,' said Nyima, who simply jumped up onto the rock and began to scale it effortlessly, his arms and legs working as one unit as he moved across the uneven surface. George watched as the Sherpa followed a route he'd so clearly taken before, and George wondered if he'd seen Everest before. Moments later, Nyima had reached the top of the obstacle, and all George could see was a hand beckoning him to follow.

George tracked the route the Sherpa had taken, and grabbed a ledge he had not noticed before, but that opened up a direct path all the way to the summit. This simple manoeuvre had saved him an hour, perhaps two, while at the same time Nyima had become George's climbing leader. It was not long before he had joined the Sherpa, and as they made their way up the mountain it was clear to George that Nyima was familiar with the terrain, as he set a pace George could only just keep up with.

When they reached the summit, they sat down and looked towards the north, but everything was enveloped in a bank of thick cloud. George reluctantly accepted that he would not be introduced to Chomolungma today. He opened his knapsack, took out a bar of Kendal Mint Cake, broke it in half and handed a piece to Nyima. The head Sherpa did not take a bite until he had seen George chewing away for some time.

As they sat staring at the unmoving clouds, George concluded that Sherpa Nyima was the ideal climbing partner – experienced, resourceful, brave and silent. He checked his watch, and realized they would have to leave soon if they were to be back in camp before sunset. He rose, tapped his watch and pointed down the mountain.

Nyima shook his head. 'Just a few more minutes, Mr Mallory.'

As the Sherpa had proved right about which route they should take, George decided to sit back down and wait for a few more minutes. However, there comes a moment when every climber has to decide if the reward is worth the risk. In George's opinion, that moment had passed.

George rose and, without waiting for Nyima to join him, began to descend the mountain. He must have covered about 150 feet when he felt the breeze picking up. He turned round to see the clouds drifting slowly away. He quickly retraced his steps and rejoined the silent Sherpa at the summit, when he found that, like Salome, Chomolungma had already stripped away four of her seven veils.

As the breeze grew stronger, Chomolungma removed yet another veil, revealing a small range of mountains in the foreground that reminded George of the French Alps, and then another. He didn't believe that such beauty could possibly be surpassed, but then a gust of wind removed the final veil, proving him wrong.

George was lost for words. He stared up at the highest mountain in the world. Everest's radiant summit dominated the skyline, making the other peaks of the mighty Himalaya look like a kindergarten playground.

For the first time, George was able to study his nemesis more closely. Below her furrowed brow projected a sharp Tibetan nose made up of uneven ridges and unapproachable precipices below which wide nostrils belched out a wind so fierce that even on level ground you would have been prevented from advancing a single stride. But worse, far worse, this goddess was two-faced.

On her west face, the cheekbone was made up of a pinnacle of rock that stretched high into the heavens, far higher than George's imagination had ever dared to soar, while the east face displayed a mile-long sheet of ice that never thawed, even on the longest day of the year. Her noble head rested on a slim neck, nestling in shoulders of granite. From her massive torso hung two long supple arms, attached to large flat hands that offered a slight hope until you saw her ten thin, icy fingers, one of the nails of which was where they hoped to set up base camp.

George turned to see Nyima gazing at Chomolungma with the same fear, respect and admiration that he himself felt. George doubted if, alone, either of them would be capable of climbing onto even the shoulders of this giant, let alone scaling her granite ice face – but perhaps together . . .

41

After their midnight dispute in Bombay, George was relieved that the General invited him to be a member of the diplomatic mission that would present their credentials at the border post.

Thirteen members of the expedition team, thirty-five porters and forty-eight mules had bedded down for the night on a flat piece of land by a fast-flowing river on the India–Tibet border. George and the rest of the party spent a convivial evening enjoying the General's excellent wine and cigars over dinner.

At 5.45 the following morning, the General was standing outside George's tent in full dress uniform, carrying a black leather attaché case. Sherpa Nyima stood a pace behind him, wearing his traditional woollen *bakhu* and carrying a large black box with the words *LOCK'S of London* printed on the lid. George crawled out of his tent a few moments later, dressed in the suit he'd worn for the Governor-General's reception and his old school tie. He accompanied Bruce out of the camp towards the border post.

'Now, I am not expecting any problems, Mallory,' said the General, 'but should any misunderstanding arise, leave everything to me. I've dealt with these natives in the past, and have the measure of them.'

George accepted that the General had many great strengths, but feared he was about to witness one of his weaknesses.

When they reached the border post, George was taken by surprise. The little bamboo hut was well camouflaged by the dense undergrowth, and certainly didn't look as if it welcomed strangers. A few paces later, George spotted a soldier, and then another, ancient rifles pointing in their direction. This show of hostility didn't cause the General to slacken his pace – if anything, he speeded up. On balance, George felt he would have preferred to die on the top of a mountain rather than at the bottom. A few paces further on, George could see exactly where the Tibetan border lay. At the only break in the bamboo barrier that stretched across the narrow path, two more soldiers sat in a dug-out fortified by sandbags, their rifles also aimed directly at the advancing British army. Still undaunted, the General marched straight up the wooden steps of the hut and through the open door, as if the border post was under his command. George followed cautiously in his wake, Nyima a pace behind.

Inside the hut, the General came to a halt in front of a wooden counter. A young corporal seated behind the desk stared at the three strangers in disbelief and, although he opened his mouth, he didn't speak.

'I wish to speak to your commanding officer,' barked the General. Sherpa Nyima translated in a soft voice.

The corporal quickly disappeared into a little room behind him and closed the door. It was some time before the door opened again, and a short, thin man with sunken cheeks and a battle-hardened face stepped out and glared at the General as if his private territory had been invaded. The General smiled when he noticed that the post commander only held the rank of captain. He saluted, but the Tibetan did not return the compliment. Instead, he looked directly at Sherpa Nyima and, pointing at the General, said in his native tongue, 'I am the Dzongpen of the district of Phari. Who is this?'

Once Sherpa Nyima had translated his words, only adding the final word 'gentleman', the General replied, 'I am General Bruce,' then opened his attaché case and removed some papers, which he placed firmly on the desk. 'These are the official permits that authorize my party to enter the district of Phari Dzong.' After Nyima had translated the General's words, the Dzongpen gave the documents a cursory glance, then shrugged his shoulders. 'As you can see,' said the General, 'they have been signed by Lord Curzon, the British Foreign Secretary.' The General waited for Sherpa Nyima to complete his translation before the Dzongpen came back with a question.

'The Dzongpen wishes to know if you are Lord Curzon.'

'Of course I'm not,' said the General. 'Tell this fool that if he doesn't allow us to cross the border immediately, I will have no choice but to . . .'

It was clear that the Tibetan commander didn't need the General's words translated, as his hand moved swiftly to the gun in his holster.

'The Dzongpen says that he will allow Lord Curzon to cross the border, but no one else,' translated Nyima.

Bruce banged a fist on the desk, and shouted, 'Doesn't the stupid man realize who I am?'

George bowed his head and began to think about the long journey home as he waited for the Dzongpen's response. He could only hope that the General's words would be lost in translation, but the Dzongpen had removed his pistol from its holster and was pointing the barrel at the General's forehead before Sherpa Nyima had completed his translation.

'Tell the General he can go home,' said the commander quietly. 'I will give my men orders to shoot on sight if he comes anywhere near this border post again. Do I make myself clear?'

The General didn't flinch, even after Nyima had translated the border commander's words. Although George had given up any chance of being allowed to cross the border, he still rather hoped they might get out alive.

'May I speak, General?' he whispered.

'Yes, of course, Mallory,' replied the General.

George wondered if he should have held his tongue, because the commander's gun was now pointing at his forehead. He looked the Dzongpen straight in the eye. 'I bring gifts of friendship from my country to yours.'

Sherpa Nyima translated, and the Dzongpen slowly lowered his gun and put it back in its holster, before placing his hands on his hips. 'I will see these gifts.'

George removed the lid of the Lock's box and took out a

black Homburg hat which he handed across to the Dzongpen. The commander placed it on his head, looked at himself in a mirror on the wall and smiled for the first time. 'Please tell the Dzongpen that Lord Curzon wears a Homburg to work every morning,' said George, 'as do all gentlemen in England.' When the commander heard these words he leant over the desk and peered into the box. General Bruce bent down, took out another Homburg and passed it to the commander, who in turn placed it on the head of the young corporal standing by his side. This time the Dzongpen burst out laughing, then grabbed the box, left the hut and began to distribute the remaining ten Homburgs among his guards.

When the commander returned to the hut, he began to study the General's documents more carefully. He was about to rubber stamp the last page when he looked up, smiled at the General and pointed to his half-hunter gold watch. The General wanted to explain that he had inherited the watch from his father, Lord Aberdare, but he thought better of it, and without a word handed it over. George was relieved that in his haste that morning he had forgotten to put on the watch Ruth had given him for his birthday.

The Dzongpen was now eyeing General Bruce's thick leather belt – then his brown leather shoes – and finally his knee-length woollen socks. Having stripped the General, he turned his attention to George, and appropriated his shoes, socks and tie. George could only wonder when and where the Dzongpen would wear an Old Wykehamist tie.

At last the Dzongpen smiled, stamped the last page of the entry permits and handed them back to the General. Bruce was just about to place the documents in his attaché case when the Dzongpen shook his head. The General left the case on the desk, and stuffed the documents into the pockets of his trousers.

The barefooted Bruce held up his trousers with one hand and saluted with the other. This time the Dzongpen returned the compliment. Sherpa Nyima was the only person who left the hut fully dressed.

An hour later the expedition party, led by General Bruce,

advanced towards the border, and the barrier was raised to allow them to enter the district of Phari Dzong.

After checking the time on his half-hunter gold watch, the Dzongpen smiled at the General, raised his Homburg and said, 'Welcome to Tibet, Lord Curzon.'

Nyima didn't translate his words.

42

May 4th, 1922

My dearest Ruth,

Having crossed the border into Tibet, we are now approaching the Himalaya – a range of a thousand mountains that surround and protect their mistress like armed guards, do not accept the authority of the local Dzongpen and have never heard of Lord Curzon. Despite their frosty welcome and cold demeanour, we battle on.

When we arrived and set up base camp, some 17,000 feet above sea level, we saw the General at his best. Within hours the porters – down to 32 – had erected the team tent, about the size of our drawing room, which made it possible for us to sit down for dinner. By the time coffee and brandy had been served, 15 other tents were in place, which meant we could all bed down for the night. When I say 'all', I should point out that the porters, including Nyima, are still sleeping outside in the open air. They curl up on the rough ground with only stones for their pillows. I sometimes wonder whether, if I'm to have any chance of conquering this infernal mountain, I ought to join them.

Sherpa Nyima is proving invaluable when it comes to organizing the natives, and the General has agreed to raise his pay to thirty rupees a week (about sixpence). Once we reach the slopes of Everest, it's going to be fascinating to find out just how good a climber he really is. Finch is convinced that he'll be the equal of any one of us. I'll let you know.

This evening the General will officially hand over command to me until the moment we begin to retrace our steps back to England . . .

'His Majesty the King,' said the General, raising his glass.

'The King,' responded the rest of the team.

'Gentlemen, you may smoke,' said the General, sitting back down and clipping off the end of his cigar.

George remained standing, as did the rest of the team. He raised his glass a second time. 'Gentlemen,' he said. 'Chomolungma, Goddess Mother of the Earth.'

The General was quickly back on his feet, and joined his colleagues as they raised their glasses, while the Sherpas fell flat on the ground and lay facing the mountain.

A moment later, George tapped his glass and called for order. Command had changed hands.

'I should like to begin, gentlemen,' he said, 'by thanking General Bruce for ensuring that we all arrived in one piece. And, to quote you, sir,' he added, turning to the General, 'burly and fit.'

'Hear, hear,' chorused the rest of the team, a sentiment with which even Finch felt able to join in.

George unfurled a parchment map, cleared a space in front of him and placed it on the table. 'Gentlemen,' he began, 'we are currently here.' He pointed the handle of his coffee spoon at 17,500 feet. 'Our immediate aim is to progress to here,' he added, moving the spoon up the mountain and coming to a halt at 21,000 feet, 'where I hope to set up Camp III. If we are to succeed in conquering Chomolungma, we must establish three more camps at altitude. Camp IV should be on the North Col around 23,000 feet while Camp V will be at 25,000 feet, and Camp VI at 27,000 feet, just 2,000 feet from the summit. It is imperative to discover a route along the crest or skirting the North-East Ridge, that could lead us to the summit.

'But for now,' he continued, 'we must remember that we have no idea what lies ahead of us. There are no reference books to consult, no maps to pore over, no old fogies sitting at the bar of the Alpine Club who can regale us with anecdotes of their past triumphs, real or imagined.' Several members of the team smiled and nodded. We must therefore chart a course that will allow *us* to one day be the old fogies who pass on *our* knowledge to the next generation of climbers.' He looked up at his team. 'Any questions?'

'Yes,' said Somervell. 'How long do you think it will take to establish Camp III? And by that I mean fully stocked and occupied.'

'Ever the practical one,' said George with a smile. 'In truth, I can't be sure. I'd like to cover two thousand feet a day, so by tomorrow evening I hope to have set up Camp II at 19,000 feet and be back here at base camp before sunset. The following day we push for 21,000 feet, where we set up Camp III before returning to Camp II for the night. It will take at least a couple of weeks to become acclimatized to altitudes none of us has ever experienced before. Never forget: climb high, sleep low.'

'Will you be dividing us up into teams before we set out?' asked Odell.

'No, not yet,' said George. 'We'll remain as one unit until I know which of you acclimatize best to the conditions. However, I suspect that in the end it won't be me who decides on the final composition of the teams, but the mountain itself.'

'Couldn't agree more,' said Finch. 'But have you given any further thought to the use of oxygen above 25,000 feet?'

'Again, I expect the mountain will dictate that decision, and not me.' George waited for a moment before he asked, 'Any more questions?'

'Yes, skipper,' said Norton. 'What time do you want us on parade tomorrow morning?'

'Six o'clock,' replied George. 'And that means all kitted up and ready to move. Remember, tomorrow, we must have the courage to think like Columbus and be prepared to walk off the map.'

‑◇‑

George couldn't make up his mind if it was the responsibility of leadership, or the sheer thrill of knowing that from this moment on, every pace he took would be the highest he'd ever climbed, that meant he emerged from his tent the next morning some time before the rest of the team.

A few minutes before six o'clock, on a clear morning with little wind and the sun inching its own path above the highest peak, George was delighted to find that all eight of his climbers were waiting patiently outside their tents. They were dressed in a variety of garments: woollen waistcoats, probably knitted by their wives or girlfriends, Jaeger trousers, windproofs, silk shirts, cotton smocks, climbing boots, Burberry scarves and Canadian moccasins, making one or two of them look as if they were about to embark on a skiing holiday in Davos.

Standing behind the climbers were the local Sherpas Nyima had recruited. They each carried as much as 80 pounds of equipment strapped to their backs: tents, blankets, spades, pots and pans, Primus stoves and food, as well as a dozen oxygen cylinders.

At six o'clock precisely, George pointed upwards, and his men set off on the first stage of a journey of which none of them could predict the outcome. He looked back at his team and smiled at the thought of the General sitting in his warm bath at base camp having to read through endless telegrams from Hinks demanding to know how much progress had been made, and whether Finch was behaving himself.

George set a steady pace for the first hour, tramping over the barren, stony ground that stretched along the side of the valley above base camp, regularly passing the sacred blue sheep of the Rongbuk valley, which, however hungry the local tribesmen became, could not be slaughtered. He was well aware that the real challenges wouldn't arise until they'd skirted the North Ridge, at around 23,000 feet, where not only would the air be thinner and the temperature fall to levels few of them had ever experienced, but far worse, they would have no way of knowing which route they should take if they hoped to progress.

As they tramped on, George became awestruck by colours he had never seen before – a faint blue light that changed to a rich yellow and seemed bent on parching their pale English skins. In the distance he could see the Kangshung face, its vast icy fangs pitted with crevasses and dark, unfathomable ridges perpetually threatening them with an unwelcome avalanche.

Once they'd established Camps II and III, George could only wonder just how many days they would have to spend searching for a safe route on the North Col, only to find that at the end of every illusory path there would be signposts announcing, *No Entry, Dead End*. George was beginning to wonder if it would even prove possible for a human to reach the summit. Those members of the RGS who had predicted that Chomolungma would be just like Mont Blanc, but a little higher, were already looking foolish.

At the end of the second hour, George called the caravan to a halt so that everyone could enjoy a well-earned rest. As he walked among the team he noticed that Morshead and Hingston were breathing heavily. Nyima had to report that three of the Sherpas had dumped their loads in the snow and headed back down the mountain to return to their villages. George wondered how many Sherpas would be standing on the dockside in Bombay waiting to claim their twenty-rupee bonus from General Bruce. 'You'll be able to count them on one hand,' Bruce had warned him, though even the General couldn't have predicted that one of his colleagues wouldn't even be able to do that.

Thirty minutes later the group continued on their way, and didn't stop to rest again until the sun had reached its zenith. During the lunch break they chewed on mint cake, ginger biscuits and dried apricots, and drank reconstituted powdered milk before setting off once again.

After another hour's climbing they had to cross a stream surrounded by tufts of green grass. On its bank stood a willow tree teeming with giant butterflies that rose into the air as they approached; an oasis, the memory of which soon became a mirage as they climbed higher and higher.

The time had come for George to look for a suitable place to pitch Camp II. He finally chose a piece of flat, stony ground in the middle of the East Rongbuk Glacier, among the giant pinnacles of ice that had the advantage of being sheltered from the wind. He checked his altimeter – just above 19,000 feet. Under Nyima's watchful eye the Sherpas deposited their loads in the snow, and levelled off the rocky debris before they could set about erecting the first tent. After unloading equipment and boxes of provisions destined for Camp III and meant to last them at least a month, they finally raised the team tent.

George told his men over dinner back at base camp – goat stew and dumplings once again, no need for a menu, because water biscuits and cheese were certain to follow – that he thought the first day could not have gone much better. However, he still had no idea how long it would take to identify a route beyond the Rongbuk Glacier, and they must be prepared to expect a number of false dawns.

Before George blew out his candle that night, he read a few pages of *The Iliad*, having just finished another long letter to Ruth. She would read it two months later, some time after the tragedy had taken place.

—◇—

George's letters often turned up at The Holt several weeks after the news they carried had been reported in *The Times*. Ruth knew she would eventually receive a letter that would give George's side of the story of what had taken place on that fateful June morning, but until then she could only follow the drama in instalments, like reading a Dickens novel.

May 8th, 1922

My dearest Ruth,

I'm sitting in my little tent, writing to you by candlelight. The first day's climb went well, and we found an ideal site on which to set up a temporary home. However, it's so cold that when I go to bed I have to wear those mittens you knitted for me last Christmas, as well as a pair of your father's woollen long johns.

The mountain has already left me in no doubt that we were not properly prepared for such a demanding venture. Frankly, many of the team are too old, and only a few are fit enough to continue. Like me, they must wish they'd been given the chance to attempt this in 1915, when we were all so much younger. Damn the Germans.

My darling, I miss you so much that . . .

Ruth stopped reading, and knelt down beside Clare and Beridge to study the map that had taken up permanent residence on the drawing-room floor. When she drew the figure of a man in goggles leaning on an ice axe at 19,400 feet, Clare started clapping.

43

June 16th, 1922

My dearest Ruth,

We have now spent just over a month searching for a route which will take us beyond the East Rongbuk Glacier and I was beginning to become downcast, after Sherpa Nyima reminded me that the monsoon season will soon be upon us, and we'll then have no choice but to return to base camp and begin the long journey back to England.

However, the breakthrough came today, when Morshead located a route beyond the Rongbuk Glacier that curves around Changtse and onto the other side of the North Col. So tomorrow Norton, Somervell and Morshead will return, and if they can find a large enough platform, and assuming the wind – gale force up there, Morshead warns me – allows them, they'll try to pitch a tent and discover if it's possible to spend a night under canvas on top of the North Col, some 6,000 feet below the summit.

If it is, Norton and Somervell will make the first attempt on the summit the following day. I know 6,000 feet doesn't sound much – indeed, I can hear Hinks telling the committee that it's not much higher than Ben Nevis. But Ben Nevis doesn't consist of pinnacles of insurmountable black ice, or temperatures that fall to minus 40 degrees, and a wind that insists that for every four strides you take, you will only advance a single step. On top of that, we are only breathing one-third of the oxygen you are enjoying in Surrey. And, as

*coming back down will undoubtedly be even more hazardous,
we can't take unnecessary risks just so Hinks can inform his
committee that one of us has climbed heights no man has
ever reached before.*

*Several of the team are suffering from altitude sickness,
snow blindness and, worst of all, frostbite. Morshead has lost
two fingers and a toe. It would be worth two fingers and a
toe if he'd reached the summit, but for the North Col? If
Norton and Somervell fail to reach the summit the day after
tomorrow, Finch, Odell and I will try the following day. If
they do succeed, then we'll be on our way home long before
you open this letter. In fact I might even arrive ahead of it –
let's hope so.*

*I have a feeling that it may be Finch and I who end up
sleeping in that tiny tent some 27,000 feet above sea level,
although there's one other member of the team who has
matched us stride for stride.*

*My darling, I write this letter with your photograph by
my side, and . . .*

Once again, Ruth joined her daughters on the drawing-room
carpet, only to find that Clare already had her thumb firmly
planted on the North Col.

◄○►

'They should have been back over an hour ago.'

Odell didn't comment, although he knew George was right.
They stood outside the team tent and stared up at the mountain,
willing Norton, Somervell and Morshead to appear.

If Norton and Somervell had reached the summit, George's
only regret – although he would never have admitted it to anyone other than Ruth – would be not putting himself in the first
team.

George checked his watch again, and calculated that they
could wait no longer. He turned to the rest of his team, all of
whom were peering anxiously up the mountain. 'Right, it's time
to put together a search party. Who wants to join me?'

Several hands shot up.

A few minutes later, George, Finch, Odell and Sherpa Nyima were fully kitted out and ready to go. George set off up the mountain without another word. A biting cold wind was whistling down the pass and tore into their skin, covering them in a thin wafer of snow that immediately froze onto their parched cheeks.

George had never faced a more determined or bitter enemy, and he knew that no one could hope to survive a night in these conditions. They must find them.

'Madness, this is nothing but madness!' he shouted into the howling gale, but Boreas didn't heed him and kept on blowing.

After more than two hours of the worst conditions George had ever experienced, he could hardly place one foot in front of the other. He was about to give the order to return to the camp when he heard Finch cry out, 'I can see three little lambs who've lost their way, baa, baa, baa.'

Ahead of them, almost invisible against the rocky background, George could just make out three lost climbers shuffling slowly down the mountain. The rescue party moved as quickly as they could towards them. Desperate as they all were to find out if Norton and Somervell had reached the summit, they looked so exhausted that no one attempted to ask them. Norton was holding a hand over his right ear, and George took the poor fellow by the elbow and guided him slowly back down the mountain. He glanced over his shoulder to see Somervell a few feet behind. His face gave no clue as to the success or failure of their mission. He finally looked at Morshead, whose face remained expressionless as he staggered on.

It was another hour before the camp came into sight. In the murky twilight, George guided the three climbers into the team tent, where mugs of lukewarm tea awaited them. The moment Norton stepped into the tent he collapsed on his knees. Guy Bullock rushed to his side and began to examine his frostbitten ear, which was black and blistered.

While Morshead and Somervell knelt over the flame of the Primus stove trying to thaw out, the rest of the team stood around in silence, waiting for one of them to break the news. It was Somervell who spoke first, but not until he'd drunk several gulps of tea laced with brandy.

'We couldn't have made a better start this morning, having put up the tent at Camp V,' he began, 'but after about a thousand feet, we walked straight into a snow storm,' he added between breaths. 'My throat became so bunged up I could hardly breathe.' He paused again. 'Norton thumped me on the back until I was violently sick, which temporarily solved the problem, but by then I didn't have the strength to take another step. Norton waited for me to recover before we struck out across the North Face.'

Norton picked up the story while Somervell took another gulp of tea. 'It was hopeless. We made a little more progress, but the snow storm didn't ease up, so we had no choice but to turn back.'

'What height did you reach?' asked George.

Norton passed the altimeter to his climbing leader. 'Twenty-six thousand, eight hundred and fifty feet,' gasped George. 'That's the highest any man has ever climbed.'

The rest of the team burst into spontaneous applause.

'If only you'd taken oxygen,' said Finch, 'you might have reached the summit.'

No one else offered an opinion.

'This is going to hurt, I'm afraid, old fellow,' said Bullock, picking up a pair of scissors and warming them over the Primus. He bent down and carefully began trimming off parts of Norton's right ear.

—◦—

The following morning, George rose at 6.00am. He stuck his head out of his tent to see a clear sky, without the slightest suggestion of wind. Finch and Odell were sitting cross-legged on the ground, devouring a hearty breakfast.

'Good morning, gentlemen,' said George. He was so keen to be on the move that he ate breakfast standing up, and was ready to set off ten minutes later. Bullock, Morshead and Somervell crawled out of their tents to wish them Godspeed. Norton remained flat on his back.

George took Norton's advice on which route they should take and led Finch and Odell slowly towards the North Ridge. Despite the clear, windless conditions, every pace seemed more demanding than the last because they had to take three breaths for each stride they advanced. Finch had insisted on strapping two cylinders of oxygen to his back. Would he prove to be right, and end up the only one who could keep going?

Hour after hour, they trudged on up the mountain in silence. It was not until the late afternoon that they felt the first breath of icy wind, that met them like an unwelcome guest. Within minutes the gentle breeze had turned into a gale. If George's altimeter hadn't confirmed that they were only a hundred yards from Camp V, at 25,000 feet, he would have turned back.

One hundred yards became an hour as the wind and snow lashed relentlessly at their bodies, tearing into their garments as if searching mercilessly for any exposed skin, while trying to blow them back down the mountain whence they'd come. When they finally reached the tent, George could only pray that the bad weather would have cleared by the morning, otherwise they would have to return, as they couldn't hope to survive such conditions for two nights in a row; in fact, George feared that if they fell asleep, all three of them might freeze to death.

The three men attempted to settle down for the night. George noticed that their condensed breath froze and turned into icicles that hung from the roof of the tent like chandeliers in a ballroom. Finch spent every moment checking and re-checking the dials on his precious oxygen cylinders, while George attempted to write to Ruth.

June 19th, 1922

My dearest Ruth,
Yesterday three brave men set out to try to reach the summit of Everest, and one of them, Norton, climbed to a

height of 26,850 ft before sheer exhaustion got the better of
them. They finally had to turn back, and Norton lost parts of
his right ear to frostbite. He sleeps tonight in the knowledge
that he has climbed higher than any man on earth.

Tomorrow three more of us will attempt to follow in their
footsteps, and perhaps one of us might even . . .

'After what we've been through today, Mallory, surely you'll
reconsider using oxygen tomorrow?'

'No, I won't,' replied George, putting his pen down. 'I'm
determined to give it a go without any artificial aids.'

'But your handmade boots are an artificial aid,' said Finch.
'The mittens your wife knitted for you are an aid. Even the sugar
in your tea is an aid. In fact, the only thing that isn't an aid is our
partner,' said Finch, glaring at the sleeping Odell.

'And who would you have chosen in his place? Norton or
Somervell?'

'Neither,' replied Finch, 'although they're both damned good
climbers. But you made it clear right from the start that the final
push should only be attempted by someone best acclimatized to
the conditions, and we both know who that is.'

'Nyima,' said George quietly.

'There's another reason why you should have invited Nyima
to join us, and I would certainly have done so if I'd been climbing
leader.'

'And what might that be?'

'The pleasure of seeing Hinks's face when he had to report
to the Everest Committee that the first two men to place a foot
on the summit of Everest were an Australian and a Sherpa.'

'That was never going to happen,' said George.

'Why not?' demanded Finch.

'Because Hinks will be reporting to the committee that an
Englishman was the first to reach the summit.' George gave
Finch a brief smile. 'But I can't see any reason why an Australian
and a Sherpa shouldn't manage it at some time in the future.' He
picked up his pen. 'Now go back to sleep, Finch. I've got a letter

to finish.' Once again George began to move the nib across the paper, but no words appeared; the ink had frozen.

◄◦►

At five o'clock the following morning the three men clambered out of their sleeping bags. George was the first to emerge from the tent, to be greeted by a cloudless blue sky, the colour of which JMW Turner would have marvelled at, although the great artist would have had to climb to 25,000 feet before he could hope to paint the scene. There was only the slightest suggestion of a breeze, and George filled his lungs with the cold morning air as he looked up at the peak, a mere 4,000 feet above him.

'So near . . .' he said as Finch crawled out of the tent with 32 pounds of oxygen cylinders strapped to his back. He also looked up at the summit, and then beat his chest.

'Shh,' said George. 'We don't want to wake her. Let her slumber, and then we can take her by surprise.'

'That's hardly the way to treat a lady,' replied Finch with a grin.

George began pacing up and down on the spot, unable to hide his frustration at having to wait for Odell to appear.

'Sorry to keep you waiting, chaps,' Odell said sheepishly when he eventually crawled out of the tent. 'I couldn't find my other glove.' Neither of his companions showed any sympathy.

They roped up, George taking the lead, with Finch behind him and Odell bringing up the rear. 'Good luck, gentlemen,' said George. 'The time has come for us to court a lady.'

'Let's hope she doesn't drop her handkerchief right on top of us,' said Finch, turning the valve of one of his oxygen cylinders and adjusting his mouthpiece.

George had taken only a few steps before he knew that this was going to be like no other climb he'd ever experienced. Whenever he'd approached the summit of a mountain in the past, there were always places where it was possible to stop and rest. But here there was no chance of respite. The slightest movement was as exhausting as if he was trying to run a 100-yard dash, although he progressed at a tortoise's pace.

He tried not to think about Finch, only a few strides behind, contentedly taking in his oxygen. Would he prove them all wrong? George battled on but with each step his breathing became more and more laboured. He had practised a special deep-breathing technique every day for the past seven months – four seconds in through the nose, fill up your chest, followed by four seconds out through the mouth, but this was the first opportunity he'd had to try the technique out above 25,000 feet. He glanced back to see that Finch, despite carrying an extra 32 pounds on his back, still appeared relaxed. But if they both reached the top, there would be no doubt which one of them would be considered the victor.

George struggled on inch by inch, foot by foot, and didn't stop until he came across Norton's Burberry scarf, which had been left as a marker to proclaim the new – now old – world record altitude for any climber. He looked back to see Finch still climbing strongly, but Odell was clearly struggling and had already fallen several yards behind. Would Finch prove to be right? Should George have chosen the best climber available to accompany them?

George checked his watch: 10.12. Although their progress had been slower than he had anticipated, he still believed that if they could reach the summit by midday, they would have enough time to return to the North Col before sunset. He counted slowly to sixty – something he'd done on every climb since he was a schoolboy – before checking the altimeter to see how far they'd progressed. He didn't need an altimeter to know the distance was becoming less and less by the minute, but he still remained confident that they could make it to the top when they reached 27,550 feet at 10.51. That was when he heard a cry that sounded like a wounded animal. He knew it wasn't Finch.

George looked back to see Odell was on his knees, his body racked with coughs, his ice axe buried beside him in the snow. He clearly wasn't going to advance another inch. Reluctantly,

George slithered back down to join him, losing twenty hard-earned feet in the process.

'I'm so sorry, Mallory,' gasped Odell. 'I can't go any further. I should have let you and Finch set off without me.'

'Don't give it a second thought, old chum,' George said between breaths. He placed an arm around Odell's shoulders. 'I can always have another crack at it tomorrow. You couldn't have done more.'

Finch didn't waste any time with words of sympathy. He removed his mouthpiece and said, 'If you're going to stick around looking after Odell, can I at least carry on?'

George wanted to say no, but knew he couldn't. He checked his watch – 10.53 – and nodded. 'Good luck,' he said, 'but you must turn back by midday at the latest.'

'That should be quite long enough,' said Finch, before replacing his mouthpiece and releasing himself from the team's rope. As he eased his way past Mallory and Odell, neither could see the grin on his face. George could only watch as his rival progressed slowly on up the mountain, inching his way towards the summit.

However, long before the hour was up, Finch could no longer place one foot in front of the other. He stopped to release the valve on the second gas cylinder, but he could still only manage a few more feet. He cursed as he thought how close he was to immortality. He checked his altimeter: 27,850 feet, a mere 1,152 feet from shaking hands with God.

Finch stared up at the glistening peak, took out his mouthpiece and shouted, 'It was Mallory you were expecting, wasn't it? But it will be me who comes back tomorrow!'

44

June 28th, 1922

My dearest Ruth,

We so nearly reached the summit, but within hours of returning to the North Col the foul weather set in again with a vengeance. I can't make up my mind if the Gods are angry because we failed to reach the top, or that we came too close so they decided to slam the door in our face.

The following day the conditions were so dreadful that we only just got back to Camp II, and we've had to sit around for the past week waiting for a break in the weather. I'm still determined to have one final crack at the summit.

Norton has had to return to base camp, and I suspect the General may decide to send him back to England. God knows he's played his part.

Finch has been struck down with dysentery and also returned to base camp but is still well enough to remind anyone who cares to listen that he is the man who climbed higher than anyone else on earth (27,850 feet) – myself included. Morshead has had to join him as his frostbite has become unbearable. Odell has fully recovered from our first attempt on the summit, when he suffered badly, and tells me that he wants to be given another chance, but if we do make another attempt I'm not going to risk climbing with him again. So with Finch, Norton and Morshead no longer available to join me for the final climb, only Somervell among the recognized climbers is still on his feet, and he has every right to be given a second chance.

If the weather breaks, even for a couple of days, I'm determined to give it one more go, before the monsoon season is upon us. I don't care for the idea of returning to Britain in second place, not while I'm convinced that if Odell hadn't held me up, I could have gone far higher than 27,550, especially with Finch snapping at my heels – possibly even to the top. Now that he's laid low, I may even experiment with his foul oxygen cylinders, but I won't tell him until I've returned triumphant.

However, the real reason I'm so determined to put an end to this life-long obsession is that I have no interest in coming back to this desolate place, and every interest in spending the rest of my life with you and the girls – I even miss the lower fifth.

I hope that long before you open this letter, you will have read in The Times *that your husband has stood on top of the earth and is on his way back home.*

I can't wait to hold you in my arms.

Your loving husband,

George

George was sealing the envelope when Nyima appeared by his side with two mugs of Bovril.

'You will be pleased to learn, Mr Mallory,' he said, 'that we are about to have three clear days in a row, but no more. So this will be your last chance, because the monsoon season will follow close behind.'

'How can you be so sure?' asked George, warming his fingers on the mug before taking a sip.

'I'm like a cow in your country,' Nyima replied, 'that knows when to shelter under a tree because it's about to rain.'

George laughed. 'You have a considerable knowledge of my country.'

'More books have been written about England than any country on earth.' Nyima hesitated for a moment before saying, 'Perhaps if I had been born an Englishman, Mr Mallory, you might have considered including me in your climbing party.'

'Please wake me at six,' said George, folding his letter. 'If you're right about tomorrow's weather, I'd like to try to reach the North Col Camp by sunset, so we can have one final crack at the summit the following day.'

'Would you like me to take your letter down to base camp, so it can be posted immediately?'

'No, thank you,' said George. 'Someone else can do that. I have a more important role than postman in mind for you.'

—◦—

When Nyima woke him the following morning, George's spirits were high. Ascension Day. A day for making history. He ate a hearty breakfast, aware that he would only be able to nibble Kendal Mint Cake for the next couple of days.

When he stepped out of his tent he was delighted to see Somervell and Odell already waiting for him, along with nine Sherpas, including Nyima, who all looked equally determined to be on their way.

'Good morning, gentlemen,' said George. 'I think the time has come to leave our calling card on top of the earth.' Without another word he set off up the mountain.

The weather was perfect for climbing: a bright, clear day, not a breath of wind, just a carpet of overnight snow that reminded him of the Swiss Alps. If Nyima's prediction turned out to be correct, George's only problem would be selecting who to team up with for the final assault. But he'd already made up his mind to follow Finch's advice and invite the most competent climber to join him tomorrow.

—◦—

George made better progress in the first hour than he had thought possible, and when he turned to see how his team was faring, he was delighted to find that no one was lagging behind. He decided not to stop while they were progressing so well; a decision that was to save his life.

No one flagged during the second hour, at the end of which George called for a break. He was pleased to see that even the

Sherpas, despite each having 80 pounds of supplies on their backs, were still smiling.

When they set off again, their pace dropped a little as the slope steepened. The snow was deep, often above his knees, but George's spirits remained high. He was pleased that Somervell and Odell were keeping up with the pace, no doubt both assuming that they would be joining him tomorrow for the final climb. He'd already decided that, this time, only one of them would. A little further down the mountain, the Sherpas were managing a slow shuffle up the slope, with Nyima bringing up the rear. A contented smile remained on George's face, as he now believed he could defeat both Finch and Hinks.

They were within 600 feet of the North Col when George heard what sounded like a car backfiring somewhere above him. He instantly recalled when he'd last heard that unmistakable, unforgiving sound.

'Please God, not again,' he shouted as a wave of rocks, snow and rubble came crashing down from a cliff-face some 200 feet above him. Within seconds he, Somervell and Odell were completely buried. George frantically fought his way to the surface in time to see the avalanche continuing its ruthless course down the mountain, gathering momentum as it engulfed everything in its path. He could only watch helplessly, still buried up to his shoulders in snow, as first his colleagues, and then the Sherpas, disappeared below the surface, one by one. The last to be buried was Nyima, an image that would remain with George for the rest of his life.

An eerie silence fell, before George cried out. He prayed that he wasn't the only member of the party still alive. Odell answered his call, and moments later Somervell surfaced. The three of them dug themselves out of the snow and hurried down the mountain, hoping against hope that they could save the Sherpas who had served them so faithfully.

George spotted a glove on the surface and tried to run towards it, but with each step he sank deeper into the thick snow. When he finally reached the glove, he began frantically shovelling at the snow around it with his bare hands. He was beginning to despair when a blue gloveless hand appeared, followed by an arm, a neck, and finally a head, gasping for breath. Behind him he heard a cry of relief as Odell rescued another Sherpa who had not expected to see the light of day again. George waded on down the mountain through the thick powdery snow searching for a rucksack, a boot, an ice axe, anything that might lead him to Nyima. For what seemed like hours he dug desperately at even the slightest hint of life. He found nothing. At last he collapsed, exhausted, forced to accept that he could do no more.

When the sun set an hour later, only two of the nine Sherpas had been rescued. The other seven, including Nyima, remained buried in undug graves. George knelt in the snow and wept. Chomolungma had laughed at the impertinence of these mortals.

◄○►

It would be days before the loss of those seven Sherpas was not constantly on George's mind, even when he slept. No matter how hard his colleagues tried to console him, they were unable to convince George that his ambition had not been the cause of the Sherpas' deaths. General Bruce had ordered that a memorial cairn be erected on a moraine close to a Tibetan monastery. As the team stood around it, heads bowed, Somervell said quietly, 'It would have been better if one of us were buried alongside them.'

Bruce led a broken band of men back to Bombay. They had been on board the ship sailing for England for several days before anyone smiled, and weeks passed before anyone laughed. George could only wonder what lay ahead of them when they docked at Liverpool.

Every member of the team had vowed that he would not return to Everest for, to quote their climbing leader, all the gold in Arabia.

BOOK SIX

BACK TO EARTH

45

Monday, September 4th, 1922

George leant over the railing of the SS *Caledonia* and, along with the rest of the team, stared down at the dockside in disbelief. None of them could believe what they were witnessing. As far as the eye could see, the dockside was crowded with people clapping, cheering and waving Union Jacks.

'Who are they cheering for?' asked George, wondering if perhaps some American film star was on board.

'I think you'll find, George, that they're welcoming you home,' said Somervell. 'They must be suffering from the delusion that you reached the summit.'

George continued to stare down at the clamouring crowd, but there was only one person he was looking for. It wasn't until they had tied up to the dock that he finally caught a fleeting glimpse of her: a lone figure who kept appearing and disappearing among the vast mêlée of raised hats, waving hands and Union Jacks.

George would have been the first down the gangplank if Finch hadn't beaten him to it. The moment he placed a foot on the dockside he was engulfed by a mass of out-thrust arms which brought back vivid memories of Bombay – except that this time they were trying to slap him on the back rather than begging or proffering second-hand goods.

'Do you still hope to be the first man to conquer Everest, Mr

Mallory?' shouted a journalist with his notepad open, his pencil poised.

George made no attempt to reply, but fought his way through the crowd towards the spot where he'd last seen her.

'*I'll* certainly be going back,' shouted Finch, as the press surrounded him. 'After all, I only have just over a thousand feet left to climb.' The man with the poised pencil wrote down his every word.

'Do you think *you'll* make it to the top next time, Mr Mallory?' a pursuing journalist persisted.

'There isn't going to be a next time,' mumbled George under his breath. And then he saw her, just a few yards in front of him.

'Ruth! Ruth!' he called, but she clearly couldn't hear him above the clamour of the crowd. At last their eyes met, and he saw that smile she reserved only for those she truly cared for. He stretched out a hand, and several strangers tried to shake it. He finally lunged forward and took her in his arms.

'How are we ever going to escape from this lot?' he shouted in her ear.

'The car's just over there,' she said, clinging on to his hand and pulling him away from the crowd, but his new-found friends were unwilling to let him escape quite that easily.

'Have you accepted the position as climbing leader for next year's trip?' shouted another journalist.

'Next year's trip?' asked George, taken by surprise. But by then Ruth had reached the car, opened the door and pushed him into the passenger seat. George couldn't hide his astonishment when she climbed behind the wheel.

'When?' he asked.

'A girl has to find something to occupy her time when her husband is off visiting another woman,' Ruth said with a smile.

He took her in his arms again, and kissed her gently on the lips.

'I've spoken to you before about kissing strange women in public, George,' she said, not letting go of him.

'I remember,' George replied, kissing her again.

'Let's get moving,' said Ruth reluctantly, 'before this becomes the closing scene of a Lillian Gish picture.'

She switched on the ignition and cranked the gear lever into first, then tried to inch her way through the crowd, but it was another twenty minutes before she was able to change into second gear and leave the baying pack behind her, and even then one last admirer banged the bonnet with his hand and shouted, 'Well done, sir!'

'What was all that about?' asked George, looking out of the rear window as some of the mob continued to pursue them.

'You had no way of knowing, but the press has been covering your progress since the day you left, and over the past six months they've turned you into something of a national figure.'

'But I failed,' said George. 'Didn't anyone take that into account?'

'They don't seem to care. The fact that you remained behind with Odell after he'd collapsed, and let Finch go on, is what caught the public's imagination.'

'But it's Finch whose name's in the record books – he climbed at least three hundred feet higher than I managed.'

'But only with the aid of oxygen,' said Ruth. 'In any case, the press thinks you would have climbed far higher than Finch if you'd had the opportunity – possibly even made it to the top.'

'No, I wouldn't have been able to climb much further than Finch that day,' said George, shaking his head. 'And it was because I wanted to prove that I was better than him that seven good men lost their lives. One of them just might have stood by my side on the summit.'

'But surely all the climbing team survived?' said Ruth.

'He wasn't part of the official party,' said George. 'But I'd already decided that he and Somervell would accompany me on the final assault.'

'A Sherpa?' said Ruth, unable to mask her surprise.

'Yes. Sherpa Nyima. I never did find out his family name.' George remained silent for some time before he added, 'But I know that I was responsible for his death.'

'No one blames you for what happened,' said Ruth, taking his hand. 'You obviously wouldn't have set out that morning if you had thought even for a moment there was the slightest chance of an avalanche.'

'But that's the point,' said George. 'I didn't think. I allowed my personal ambition to cloud my judgement.'

'Your latest letter only turned up this morning,' said Ruth, wanting to change the subject.

'And where was I?' George asked.

'In a small tent 25,000 feet above sea level, explaining to Finch why you wouldn't consider using oxygen.'

'If I'd taken his advice,' said George, 'I might have reached the top.'

'There's nothing to stop you trying again,' said Ruth.

'Never.'

'Well, I know someone who'll be delighted to hear that,' she said, trying not to reveal her own feelings.

'You, my darling?'

'No, Mr Fletcher. He called this morning and asked if you could drop in and have a word with him at ten o'clock tomorrow.'

'Yes, of course I will,' said George. 'I can't wait to get back to work. I know you won't believe it, but I even missed the lower fifth and, more important, I need to start earning a salary again. Heaven knows we can't go on living off your father's largesse for ever.'

'I've never heard him complain,' said Ruth. 'In fact, he's very proud of what you've achieved. He never stops telling all his friends at the golf club that you're his son-in-law.'

'That's not the point, my darling. I must get back behind my desk in time for the first day of term.'

'No chance of that,' said Ruth.

'But why not?'

'Because the first day of term was last Monday,' replied Ruth, smiling. 'Which is no doubt why the headmaster's so keen to see you.'

'Now tell me about our son,' said George.

—◇—

When they finally drove through the gates of The Holt some six hours later, George said, 'Slow down, my darling. I've been thinking about this moment for the past two months.'

They were halfway down the drive when George saw his daughters waving from the steps. He couldn't believe how much they'd grown. Clare was cradling a small bundle in her arms.

'Is that who I think it is?' said George, turning to smile at Ruth.

'Yes. At last you're going to meet your son and heir, Master John Mallory.'

'Only a complete fool would ever leave you for a day, let alone six months,' said George as the car came to a halt in front of the house.

'Which reminds me,' said Ruth, 'someone else phoned and asked you to call him urgently.'

'Who?' asked George.

'Mr Hinks.'

46

Ruth helped George on with his gown before handing him his mortar board and umbrella. It was as if he'd never been away.

After he'd kissed her and said goodbye to the children, he marched out of the front door and began to stride down the path towards the main road. Beridge asked, 'Is Daddy going away again?'

George checked his watch, interested to see how long it would now take him to reach the school gate. Ruth had made certain that he left well in time for his appointment with the headmaster.

The Times had been particularly generous that morning, giving extensive coverage to the *triumphant homecoming* of the Everest team. It didn't seem to concern their correspondent that no one had reached the summit, although he reported Finch as saying that he had every intention of going back next year to do just that. Towards the end of the article there was a guarded quote from Mr Hinks, hinting that George would be the Everest Committee's first choice as climbing leader for the second expedition, which was no doubt what Hinks wanted to speak to him about so urgently. But George intended to tell Hinks exactly what he would be telling the headmaster in a few minutes' time: his climbing days were over. He was looking forward to a life of domesticity, while at the same time continuing to teach the lower fifth about the exploits of Elizabeth, Raleigh, Essex and . . .

A smile crossed George's face when he thought about the

dilemma Hinks would face when it came to selecting who would take his place as climbing leader. The obvious choice was Finch – he was unquestionably the most skilled and experienced climber, and was the man who had reached the highest point on the last expedition. But George was in no doubt that Hinks would come up with some utterly compelling reason to resist any such suggestion, and that the committee would end up by appointing either Norton or Somervell as climbing leader. Even Hinks, however, wouldn't be able to stop Finch reaching the summit well ahead of both of them, particularly if he was assisted by his faithful oxygen cylinders.

When the school chapel came into view, George checked his watch again. He might be thirty-six years old, but he'd lost none of his speed. As he marched through the school gates, he might not have set a new record, but he was damned close.

George strolled across the main quad in the direction of the headmaster's study, smiling at a couple of boys he didn't recognize. It was clear from their response that they had no idea who he was, which brought back memories of his first days at Charterhouse, and of how nervous he had felt whenever he came face to face with a pupil, let alone the headmaster.

Mr Fletcher was a stickler for punctuality, and would no doubt be pleased, and possibly even surprised, that George was five minutes early. George straightened his gown and took off his mortar board before knocking on the door of the outer office.

'Come in,' said a voice. George entered the room to find Fletcher's secretary, Miss Sharpe, seated at her desk. Nothing changes, he thought. 'Welcome back, Mr Mallory,' she said. 'May I say,' she added, 'how much we've all been looking forward to seeing you again following your triumph on Everest.' On Everest, thought George, but not on top of it. 'I'll let the headmaster know you're here.'

'Thank you, Miss Sharpe,' said George as she went into the adjoining room. A moment later the door opened. 'The headmaster will see you now,' she said.

'Thank you,' George repeated, and marched into Mr Fletcher's study. Miss Sharpe closed the door behind him.

'Good morning, Mallory,' said the headmaster as he rose from behind his desk. 'Good of you to be so punctual.'

'Not at all, headmaster,' said George. 'Can I say how nice it is to be back,' he added as he sat down.

'Allow me to begin,' said the headmaster, 'by congratulating you on your achievements during the past six months. Even allowing for the press's tendency to exaggerate, we all feel that given a little more luck, you would undoubtedly have made it to the top.'

'Thank you, headmaster.'

'And I'm sure I speak for everyone at the school when I say that I'm in no doubt that you'll fulfil your ambition next time.'

'There won't be a next time,' George replied. 'I can assure you that my climbing days are over.'

'However, as I'm sure you'll appreciate, Mallory,' continued the headmaster as if he hadn't heard him, 'running a school like Charterhouse necessitates being able to rely on all members of staff at all times.'

'Yes, of course, headmaster, but—'

'Your decision to join the armed forces despite the fact that you were exempt, although commendable in itself, severely disrupted the school timetable, as I made clear at the time.'

'You did indeed, headmaster, but—'

'And then your decision, rightly taken in my view, to accept the invitation from the Everest Committee caused even more disruption to the running of the school, especially as you had recently been appointed senior history master.'

'I do apologize, headmaster, but—'

'As you know, I had to appoint Mr Atkins to take over from you in your absence, and I'm bound to say that he has carried out his duties with commendable diligence and authority, and has shown unswerving commitment to the school.'

'I'm glad to hear that, headmaster. However—'

'I'm also bound to say, Mallory, that when you failed to report for the first day of term, no doubt through no fault of your own, I was left with little choice but to offer Atkins a permanent appointment as a full member of staff, which ipso facto means, regrettably, that there is no position for you at Charterhouse at the present time.'

'But—' spluttered George, trying not to sound desperate.

'I have no doubt that many of our leading schools will jump at the opportunity of adding Mallory of Everest to their numbers. Indeed, were I to lose a member of the history staff, you would be among the first candidates I would consider interviewing.'

George no longer bothered to interrupt. He felt as if Everest's relentless east wind was hitting him in the face again.

'Do let me assure you, Mallory, that you leave Charterhouse with the respect and affection of both the staff and the pupils. It goes without saying that I will be delighted to supply you with a reference confirming that you were a valued member of staff.'

George remained silent.

'I'm sorry it had to end this way, Mallory, but allow me to add on behalf of myself, the governing body and all of us at Charterhouse, that we wish you good fortune in whatever it is you decide to do in the future. Should that turn out to be one more stab at Everest, our thoughts and prayers will be with you.'

Mr Fletcher rose from behind his desk. George stood up, dutifully shook hands, doffed his mortar board and left the study without another word.

◄o►

Ruth was reading about her husband in *The Times* when the phone rang. Only her father ever called at that time of the day.

'Hello,' she said cheerfully as she picked up the phone. 'Is that you, Daddy?'

'No, it isn't, Mrs Mallory. It's Hinks of the RGS.'

'Good morning, Mr Hinks,' she said, her tone of voice immediately changing. 'I'm afraid my husband isn't here at the moment, and I'm not expecting him back until this evening.'

'I'm pleased to hear that, Mrs Mallory, because I was hoping to have a private word with you.'

Ruth listened carefully to what Mr Hinks had to say, and assured him that she would think it over and let him know her decision. She had just returned to reading the paper when she heard the front door open. She feigned surprise when George marched into the drawing room and slumped down on the sofa opposite her.

'That bad?' she ventured.

'It couldn't have been much worse,' he said. 'The damned man sacked me. It seems I'm so unreliable that he's offered my job to Atkins, who he assured me is diligent, conscientious and, more important, reliable. Can you believe it?'

'Yes, I can,' said Ruth. 'In fact, I can't pretend that it comes as a great surprise,' she added, folding the paper and placing it on a side table.

'What makes you say that, my darling?' asked George, looking at her more closely.

'It worried me that the headmaster asked to see you at ten o'clock.'

'Why was that important?'

'Because that man's whole life is dominated by a timetable. If all had been well, my darling, he would have invited both of us for a drink at six in the evening. Or he would have arranged your morning meeting for eight o'clock, so that you could accompany him in triumph when he presided over assembly.'

'So why did he ask to see me at ten?'

'Because at that time all the boys and staff would be safely in their classrooms, and he'd be able to get you on and off the premises without anyone having the chance to speak to you. He must have planned the whole exercise down to the minute.'

'Brilliant,' said George. 'You'd have made a first-class detective. Do you have any clues about what's going to happen to me next?'

'No,' admitted Ruth. 'But while you were out, I had a call from Mr Hinks.'

'I hope you made it clear to him that I'm not available to play any part in next year's expedition.'

'That wasn't why he called,' said Ruth. 'It seems that the American Geographical Society wants you to do a lecture tour of the East Coast – Washington, New York, Boston . . .'

'Not a hope,' said George. 'I've only just got home. Why would I want to troop off again?'

'Possibly because they're willing to pay you a thousand pounds for half a dozen lectures on your experiences of climbing Everest.'

'A thousand pounds?' said George. 'But that's more than I'd earn at Charterhouse in three years.'

'Well, to be accurate,' said Ruth, 'the AGS think the lectures could bring in as much as two thousand pounds, and the RGS is willing to split the profits with you fifty-fifty.'

'That's unusually generous of Hinks,' said George.

'I think I can also explain that,' said Ruth. 'It seems that if you turn down the offer, there's only one other person the Americans would consider inviting in your place.'

'And Hinks would never agree to that,' said George. 'So what did you tell him?'

'I said I'd discuss the idea with you, and then let him know your decision.'

'But why did he call *you* in the first place? Why didn't he want to speak to me?'

'He wondered if I might like to join you on the trip.'

'The cunning old devil,' said George. 'He knows that's the one thing that might clinch the deal for me.'

'But not for me,' said Ruth.

'But why not, my darling? You've always wanted to visit the States, and we could turn this into a second honeymoon.'

'I knew you'd come up with some reason why I should agree to the idea, and so, obviously, did Mr Hinks. But you seem to forget that we have three children.'

'Can't nanny take care of them while we're away?'

'George, the girls haven't seen you for six months, and John didn't even know who you were. Now, no sooner has his father returned than he disappears off to America with their mother for another six weeks. No, George, that's no way to bring up children.'

'Then you can tell Hinks that I'm not interested.'

'Good,' said Ruth, 'because heaven knows I don't want you to leave again when you've only just come home.' She hesitated before saying, 'In any case, we can always go to America another time.'

George looked directly at her. 'There's something you haven't told me.'

Ruth hesitated. 'It's just that Hinks did say that before you turn down such a lucrative offer, you mustn't forget that, to quote the Americans, you're hot property at the moment and they're evidently a nation whose enthusiasms cool fairly quickly. And frankly, I doubt if you'll find an easier way to earn a thousand pounds.'

'And if I don't go,' said George quietly, 'I may well have to make another appointment to see your father, and end up being even more indebted to him.'

Ruth said nothing.

'I'll agree to do it, on one condition,' said George.

'And what might that be?' asked Ruth suspiciously.

'That you'll let me take you to Venice for a few days. And this time,' he added, 'just the two of us.'

1923

47

George had been on deck for over an hour by the time the SS *Olympic* steamed into New York harbour. During the five days of the Atlantic crossing, Ruth had been constantly in his thoughts.

She had driven him down to Southampton, and once he had reluctantly left her to board the ship, she'd remained on the dockside until it had sailed out of the harbour and become a small speck on the horizon.

Mr and Mrs Mallory had spent their promised break in Venice, which turned out to be something of a contrast from the last visit George had made to that city, because on this occasion he booked a suite at the Cipriani Hotel.

'Can we afford it?' Ruth had asked as she looked out of the window of the lagoon-side suite her father usually occupied.

'Probably not,' George replied. 'But I've decided to spend a hundred of the thousand pounds I'm going to earn in America on what I intend to be an unforgettable holiday.'

'The last time you went to Venice, George, it *was* unforgettable,' Ruth reminded him.

The newlyweds, as most of the other guests assumed they were, because they came down so late for breakfast, were always holding hands and never stopped looking in each other's eyes, did everything except climb St Mark's Tower – inside or out. After such a long time apart, the few days really did feel like a honeymoon, as they got to know each other again. By the time the Orient Express pulled into Victoria Station a week later, the last thing George wanted to do was leave Ruth again and sail away to the States.

If his bank statement hadn't been among the unopened post on their arrival back at The Holt, he might even have considered cancelling the lecture tour and staying at home.

There was one other letter George hadn't anticipated, and he wondered if he ought to accept the flattering invitation, given the circumstances. He'd see how the tour went before he made that decision.

◄◦►

George's overwhelming first impression of New York, as the ship came into the harbour, was the sheer size of its buildings. He'd read about skyscrapers, even seen photographs of them in the new glossy magazines, but to see them standing cheek by jowl was beyond his imagination. The tallest building in London would have appeared as a pygmy among this tribe of giants.

George leant over the ship's railing and looked down at the dock, where a boisterous crowd were smiling and waving as they waited for their loved ones and friends to disembark. He would have searched among the throng for a new friend, had he had the slightest idea what Lee Keedick looked like. Then he spotted a tall, elegant man in a long black coat holding up a placard that read *Mallory*.

Once George had stepped off the ship, a suitcase in each hand, he made his way towards the tall impressive figure. When he was a stride away, he pointed to the board and said, 'That's me.'

That's when George saw him for the first time. A short, plump man who would never have made it to base camp stepped forward to greet him. Mr Keedick was wearing a beige suit and an open-necked yellow shirt with a silver cross dangling from a chain around his neck. It was the first time George had ever seen a man wearing jewellery. Keedick must have stood a shade over five feet, but only because his crocodile-skin shoes had higher heels than those Ruth usually wore.

'I'm Lee Keedick,' he announced, after removing the stub of an unlit cigar from his mouth. 'You must be George. Is it OK to call you George?'

'I think you just did,' said George, giving him a warm smile.

'This is Harry,' said Keedick, pointing to the tall man. 'He'll be your chauffeur while you're in the States.' Harry touched the rim of his hat with the forefinger of his right hand, then opened the back door of what George had thought was a small omnibus.

'Somethin' wrong?' asked Keedick, as George remained on the sidewalk.

'No,' said George as he stepped inside. 'It's just that this is the biggest car I've ever seen.'

'It's the latest Caddie,' Lee told him.

George thought a caddie was someone who carried a golfer's clubs, but then recalled George Bernard Shaw once telling him, 'England and America are two nations divided by a common language.'

'It's the finest darn car in America,' added Keedick, as Harry pulled away from the kerb to join the morning traffic.

'Are we picking up anyone else on the way?' asked George.

'I just love your English sense of humour,' said Keedick. 'Nope, this is all yours. You gotta understand, George, it's important for people to think you're a big shot. You gotta keep up appearances, or you'll never get anywhere in this town.'

'Does that mean the bookings for my lectures are going well?' asked George nervously.

'They're just swell for the opening at the Broadhurst Theater tomorrow night.' Keedick paused to light his cigar. 'And if you get a good write-up in the *New York Times*, we'll do just fine for the rest of the tour. If it's a rave, we'll sell out every night.'

George wanted to ask him what 'rave' meant, but satisfied himself with looking up at the skyscrapers as the car inched its way through the traffic.

'That's the Woolworth Building,' said Keedick, winding down the window. 'It's seven hundred and ninety-two feet tall. The tallest building in the world. But they're planning one that will be over a thousand feet.'

'That's just about how much I missed it by,' said George as the limousine came to a halt outside the Waldorf Hotel.

A bellboy rushed forward to open the car door, with the manager following close behind. He smiled the moment he saw Keedick step out onto the sidewalk.

'Hi, Bill,' said Keedick. 'This is George Mallory, the guy who conquered Everest.'

'Well, not quite,' said George. 'In fact—'

'Don't bother with the facts, George,' said Keedick. 'No one else in New York does.'

'Congratulations, sir,' said the manager, thrusting out his hand. George had never shaken hands with a hotel manager before. 'In your honour,' he continued, 'we've put you in the Presidential Suite, on the seventeenth floor. Please follow me,' he added as they walked across the foyer.

'May I ask where the fire escape is?' asked George, before they'd reached the elevator.

'Over there, sir,' said the manager, pointing to the other side of the lobby, a puzzled look appearing on his face.

'The seventeenth floor, you say?'

'Yes,' confirmed the manager, looking even more puzzled.

'I'll see you up there,' said George.

'Don't they have elevators in English hotels?' the manager asked Keedick as George strode across the lobby and through a door marked *Fire Escape*. 'Or is he mad?'

'No,' replied Keedick. 'He's English.'

The elevator whisked both men up to the seventeenth floor. The manager was even more surprised when George appeared in the corridor only a few minutes later, and didn't seem to be out of breath.

The manager unlocked the door to the Presidential Suite, and stood aside to allow his guest to enter the room. George's immediate reaction was that there must have been some mistake. The suite was larger than the tennis court at The Holt.

'Did you think I was bringing my wife and children with me?' he asked.

'No,' said Keedick, laughing, 'it's all yours. Don't forget, the press may want to interview you, and it's important that they think this is how they treat you back in England.'

'But can we afford it?'

'Don't even think about it,' said Keedick. 'It all comes out of expenses.'

◄◦►

'How nice to hear from you, Geoffrey,' said Ruth when she recognized the familiar voice on the other end of the line. 'It's been far too long.'

'And I'm the one to blame,' said Geoffrey Young. 'It's just that since I took up my new post at Imperial College, I don't get out of town much during term-time.'

'Well, I'm afraid George isn't at home at the moment. He's in America on a lecture tour.'

'Yes, I know,' said Young. 'He dropped me a line last week to say he was looking for a job, and that if anything came up I should let him know. Well, a position has arisen in Cambridge that just might be ideal for him, but I thought I'd run it past you first.'

'That's very thoughtful of you, Geoffrey. Shall we try and meet up when I'm next in London?'

'No, no,' said Young, 'I can always pop down to Godalming.'

'When did you have in mind?'

'Would next Thursday suit you?'

'Of course. Will you be able to stay for the night?'

'Thank you, I'd like that, if it's not inconvenient.'

'If you were able to stay for a month, Geoffrey, it wouldn't be inconvenient.'

◄◦►

George couldn't sleep on his first night in New York, and the time difference wasn't to blame, because the five-day Atlantic crossing had taken care of that. It was just that he'd never spent a night in a city before where the traffic never came to a halt and police and ambulance sirens screamed incessantly. It reminded him of being back on the Western Front.

He finally gave up, climbed out of bed and sat at a large desk by the window overlooking Central Park. He went over his lecture once again, then checked all the large glass slides. He was delighted to find that none of them had been broken during the voyage from England.

George was becoming more and more apprehensive about what Keedick kept referring to as 'opening night'. He tried not to think of the consequences of it being a flop, another of Keedick's words, even though the agent kept assuring him that there were only a few seats left unsold, and all that mattered now was what the *New York Times* thought of the lecture. On balance, George decided he preferred mountains. They didn't give a damn what the *New York Times* thought of them.

He crept back into bed a couple of hours later, and eventually fell asleep at around four o'clock.

◄○►

Ruth sat in her chair by the window enjoying George's first letter from America. She laughed when she read about the Caddie and the Presidential Suite with its central heating, aware that George would have been quite content to pitch a tent on the roof, but she doubted if that was an option at the Waldorf. When she turned the page, she frowned for the first time. It worried her that George felt that so much rested on the opening night. He ended his letter by promising to write and let her know how the lecture had been received just as soon as he returned to the hotel later that evening. How Ruth wished she could have read the review in the *New York Times* before George saw it.

◄○►

There was a knock on the door, and George answered it to find a smiling Lee Keedick standing in the corridor. He was dressed in his usual open-necked shirt, but this time it was green, while his suit was a shade of light blue that would have been more appropriate if worn by a blade in Cambridge. The chain around his neck had turned from silver to gold, and the shoes from crocodile to white patent leather. George smiled. Lee Keedick would have made George Finch look elegant.

'How are you feelin', old buddy?' asked Keedick as he stepped into the room.

'Apprehensive,' admitted George.

'No need to,' said Lee. 'They're gonna love you.'

An interesting observation, George thought, considering Keedick had only known him for a few hours and had never heard him speak in public. But then he was beginning to realize that Lee Keedick had a set of stock phrases whoever his client was.

Outside the hotel, Harry was standing by the car. He opened the back door, and George jumped in, feeling far more nervous than he ever did before a demanding climb. He didn't speak on the journey to the theatre, and was grateful that Keedick remained silent, even if he did fill the car with cigar smoke.

As they drew up outside the Broadhurst Theater, George saw the poster advertising his lecture. He burst out laughing.

Book Now!

GEORGE MALLORY

*The man who conquered Everest
single-handed*

Next week: Jack Benny

He smiled at the photograph of a young man playing a violin, pleased that he would be followed by a musician.

George stepped out onto the sidewalk, his legs trembling and his heart beating as if he was a few feet from the summit. Keedick led his client down a side alley to the stage door, where a waiting assistant accompanied them up a stone staircase to a door with a silver star on it. Keedick told George before he left that he'd see him before he went on stage. George sat alone in the cold, slightly musty dressing room lit by several naked light bulbs surrounding a large mirror. He went over his speech one last time. For the first time in his life, he wanted to turn back before he'd reached the top.

There was a tap on the door. 'Fifteen minutes, Mr Mallory,' said a voice.

George took a deep breath, and a few moments later Keedick walked in. 'Let's get this show on the road, pal,' he said. He led George back down the stone steps, along a brick corridor and into the wings at the side of the stage, leaving him with the words, 'Good luck, buddy. I'll be front of house, cheering you on.'

George paced up and down, becoming more nervous by the minute. Although he could hear loud chattering coming from the other side of the curtain, he had no idea how many people were in the audience. Had Keedick exaggerated when he said there were only a few unsold tickets?

At five minutes to eight, a man dressed in a white tuxedo appeared at George's side and said, 'Hi, I'm Vince, the compère. I'll be introducing you. Is there some special way of pronouncing Mallory?'

This was a question George had never been asked before. 'No,' he replied.

George looked around for someone, anyone, to talk to while he waited nervously for the curtain to rise. He would even have been happy to see Keedick. He realized for the first time how Raleigh must have felt just before he had his head chopped off. And then suddenly, without any warning, the curtain rose and the compère marched out onto the stage, tapped the microphone and announced, 'Ladies and gentlemen, it's my pleasure to present to you for your entertainment this evening, George Mallory, the man who conquered Everest.'

At least he didn't add 'single-handed', thought George as he walked onto the stage feeling desperately in need of oxygen. But he quickly recovered when he was greeted by warm applause.

George began his lecture hesitantly, partly because he couldn't see the audience, who must have been out there somewhere, but while several spotlights were trained on him it was impossible to see beyond the front row. However, it took only a few minutes for him to become accustomed to the strange experience of being treated like an actor rather than a lecturer. He was encouraged by intermittent bursts of applause, and even the occasional roar of laughter. After a bumpy start, he battled on for nearly an hour. It wasn't until he called for questions, and the lights went up, that he saw just how many people he had been addressing.

The stalls were almost full, even if the dress circle remained in darkness. George was relieved by how many people seemed keen to ask questions, and it quickly became clear that there were some seasoned alpinists and genuine enthusiasts among the audience, who offered observations that were both thoughtful and relevant. However, George was nearly stumped – not that the questioner would have known the derivation of the word – when a slim blonde seated in the third row asked, 'Mr Mallory, could you tell us how much it costs to mount such an expedition?'

It was some time before George replied, and not just because he didn't know the answer. 'I've no idea, madam,' he finally managed. 'The financial details are always handled by the RGS. However, I do know that the Society will be launching an appeal in the near future to raise funds for a second expedition that will set out for the Himalaya early next year with the sole purpose of putting an—' he stopped himself just in time from saying 'an Englishman' – 'a member of that team on the summit.'

'Can those of us who might consider donating to that fund,' the young lady enquired, 'assume that you will be a member of the team, in fact its climbing leader?'

George didn't hesitate. 'No, madam. I have already assured my wife that the Society will have to look for someone else to lead the team next time.' He was surprised when several groans of disappointment emanated from the audience, even one or two muffled cries of 'Shame!'

After a couple more questions, George recovered, and was

even a little disappointed when Lee stage-whispered from the wings, 'Time to wrap it up, George.'

George immediately bowed and quickly left the stage. The audience began to applaud.

'Not so fast,' said Keedick, pushing him back onto the stage to laughter and even louder applause. In fact, he had to send him back three times before the curtain finally came down.

'That was great,' said Lee as they climbed into the back of the limousine. 'You were fantastic.'

'Did you really think so?' asked George.

'Couldn't have gone better,' said Lee. 'Now all we have to pray for is that the critics love you as much as the public do. By the way, have you ever come across Estelle Harrington before?'

'Estelle Harrington?' repeated George.

'The dame who asked if you were going to lead the next expedition.'

'No, I've never seen her before in my life,' said George. 'Why do you ask?'

'She's known as the cardboard-box widow,' said Lee. 'Her late husband, Jake Harrington, the inventor of the cardboard box, left her so much money she can't even count it.' Lee inhaled deeply and puffed out a plume of smoke. 'I've read a ton of stuff about her in the gossip columns over the years, but I never knew she took any interest in climbing. If she was willing to sponsor the tour, we wouldn't have to worry about the *New York Times*.'

'Is it that important?' asked George.

'More important than all the other papers put together.'

'So when will it deliver its verdict?'

'In a few hours' time,' replied Lee, blowing out another cloud of smoke.

48

'The Workers' Educational Association,' said Geoffrey Young as they strolled around the garden.

'I've never heard of them,' said Ruth.

'It was founded in the early days of the Labour movement, and its aim is to assist people who weren't given the chance of a decent education in their youth, but would benefit from it in later life.'

'That sounds very much in line with George's Fabian principles.'

'In my opinion,' said Geoffrey, 'the job was made for him. It would allow George to combine his teaching experience with his views on politics and education.'

'But would it also mean us having to move to Cambridge?'

'Yes, I'm afraid so. But I can think of worse places to live,' responded Geoffrey. 'And don't forget that George still has a lot of old friends there.'

'I think I should warn you, Geoffrey, that George is becoming quite anxious about what he describes as his financial predicament. In his latest letter he hinted that the tour wasn't going quite as well as he'd hoped.'

'I'm sorry to hear that,' said Young. 'However, I do know that the basic salary for the job is three hundred and fifty pounds a year, with the opportunity to earn a further hundred and fifty through extra tuition fees, which would make it up to around five hundred pounds.'

'In that case,' said Ruth, 'I think George will jump at the opportunity. When would they want him to start?' she asked.

'Not until next September,' said Young. 'Which would mean, dare I mention it, that George could even reconsider—'

'Not now, Geoffrey,' Ruth said, as they walked back towards the house. 'Let's discuss that particular matter over dinner. For now, why don't you go and unpack, and then join me in the drawing room around seven.'

'We don't have to talk about it, Ruth.'

'Oh yes we do,' she replied as they strolled back into the house.

—◇—

'Taxi!' shouted Keedick, and when it screeched to a halt he opened the back door to allow his client to climb in. Harry and his Caddie were nowhere to be seen.

'So, how bad is it?' asked George as he slumped down in the back seat.

'Not good,' admitted Lee. 'Even though the *New York Times* gave you a favourable review, the out-of-town bookings have still been –' he looked out of the window – 'let's say, disappointing, although you seem to have attracted at least one huge fan.'

'What are you talking about?'

'Come on, George, you must have noticed that Estelle Harrington's turned up to every one of your lectures. I'd be willing to bet good money she'll be there again tonight.'

'Well, at least tonight's lecture is sold out,' said George, not wanting to dwell on the ever-present Mrs Harrington.

'"Sold" would be the wrong word,' said Lee. 'They refused to sign the contract unless we agreed to let students in gratis – not a word I'm comfortable with.'

'What about Baltimore and Philadelphia?' asked George, as the taxi swung off the main road and drove onto a campus George had always wanted to visit, but had never imagined he would be invited to lecture at.

'Sorry, old buddy,' said Lee between puffs, 'but I had to cancel both, otherwise we might have lost what little dough we've made so far.'

'That bad?' said George.

'Worse. I'm afraid we're gonna have to cut the tour short. In fact I've booked you onto the *Saxonia*, which sails outta New York on Monday.'

'But that means—'

'This'll be your last lecture, George, so be sure to make it a good one.'

'So how much profit have we made?' asked George quietly.

'I can't give you an exact figure at the moment,' said Lee as the taxi drew up outside the private residence of the President of Harvard. 'There are one or two out-of-pocket expenses I still have to calculate.'

George thought about the letter that had arrived at The Holt the day before he sailed. Once Hinks learnt that the tour had failed to make the anticipated profit, would George's invitation to deliver the Society's annual memorial lecture be withdrawn? Perhaps the best solution would be for George to decline the invitation, and save the Society unnecessary embarrassment.

—◄○►—

'You've been avoiding the subject all evening,' said Ruth as she led Young through to the drawing room.

'But it was such a magnificent meal,' said Geoffrey, sitting down on the sofa. 'And you're such a wonderful hostess.'

'And you're such an old flatterer, Geoffrey,' said Ruth as she passed him a cup of coffee. She sat down in the chair opposite him. 'So, were you hoping to try to persuade me that George should reconsider leading the next expedition to the Himalaya? Because I'm not altogether convinced that's what he really wants.'

'Are we telling each other the truth?' asked Geoffrey.

'Yes, of course,' said Ruth, looking a little surprised.

'When George wrote to me just before he sailed, he made it clear that, to quote him, he still wanted one more crack at his wildest dream.'

'But—' began Ruth.

'He also said that he wouldn't consider leaving you again unless he had your complete support.'

'But he's already told me that he wouldn't go back again under any circumstances.'

'He also begged me not to let you know how he really felt. By telling you, I've betrayed his confidence.'

'Did he give you one good reason why he would want to put himself through all that again?' asked Ruth.

'Apart from the obvious one? If he were to succeed, just think about the extra income that would generate.'

'You know as well as I do, Geoffrey, that he didn't do it for money.'

'It was you who reminded me that he's anxious about his current financial predicament.'

Ruth didn't speak for some time. 'If I were to agree to lie to George about how I really feel,' she eventually said, ' – and it would be a lie, Geoffrey – you must promise me that this will be the last time.'

'It would have to be,' said Geoffrey. 'If George were to take the job as director of the WEA, the board won't want him to be disappearing for six months at a time. And frankly, my dear, he'll be too old by the time the RGS considers mounting another expedition.'

'I just wish there was someone I could turn to for advice.'

'Why don't you seek a second opinion from the one person who will understand exactly what you're going through?'

'Who do you have in mind?' asked Ruth.

When Young told her, Ruth simply said, 'Do you think she'd agree to see me?'

'Oh yes. She'll see the wife of Mallory of Everest.'

—◦—

George immediately recognized the attractive woman who was chatting to Keedick on the far side of the room. She was not someone he was likely to forget.

'Congratulations, Mr Mallory, most stimulating,' said the president of Harvard. 'Most stimulating. May I also say that I hope you pull it off next time?'

'That's kind of you, Mr Lowell,' said George, not bothering to repeat once again that he wouldn't be going on the next expedition. 'And allow me to thank you for organizing this reception.'

'My pleasure,' said the president. 'I'm only sorry that Prohibition prevents me from offering you anything other than orange juice or a Coca-Cola.'

'An orange juice will be just fine, thank you.'

'I know that many of the students are keen to ask you questions, Mr Mallory,' said the president, 'so I won't monopolize you.' He walked off to join the woman speaking to Keedick.

Within moments, George was surrounded by eager young faces that brought back memories of his days at Cambridge.

'Have you still got all your toes, sir?' asked a young man who was peering down at George's feet.

'They were all there when I checked in the bath this morning,' said George, laughing. 'But my friend Morshead lost two fingers and a toe, and poor Captain Norton had half his right ear trimmed off after he'd set a new altitude record.'

A voice from behind him asked, 'Are there any mountains in America, sir, that you might consider a worthy challenge?'

'Most certainly,' said George. 'I can assure you that Mount McKinley presents as great a challenge as any to be found in the Himalaya, and there are several peaks in the Yosemite Valley that would test the skills of the most experienced climber. If it's rock climbing that interests you, you need look no further than Utah or Colorado, if you hope to prove your worth.'

'Something has always puzzled me, Mr Mallory,' said an intense-looking young man. 'Why do you bother?'

The president, who had just returned to George's side, coughed and tried to hide his embarrassment.

'There's a simple answer to that,' said George. 'Because it's there.'

'But—'

'I apologize for interrupting you, Mallory,' said Mr Lowell, 'but I know that Mrs Harrington is keen to meet you. Her late husband was an alumnus of this university, and indeed a generous benefactor.'

George smiled as he shook hands with the young woman who

had asked him about the expedition's finances in New York and had since attended every one of his lectures. She didn't look much older than some of the undergraduates, and George assumed that she must have been at least the third Mrs Harrington, unless the cardboard king, as Keedick kept describing him, married very late in life.

'I confess, Estelle,' said the President, 'I had no idea you were interested in mountaineering.'

'Who could fail to be entranced by Mr Mallory's charisma?' – a word George had never heard used in that way before, and would have to look up in his dictionary to find out if in fact it had a second meaning. 'And of course, we all hope,' she gushed, 'that he will be the first person to stand on top of his mountain, and then he can come back and tell us all about it.'

George smiled and gave her a slight bow. 'As I explained in New York, Mrs Harrington, I shall not—'

'Is it true,' continued Mrs Harrington, who clearly wasn't in the habit of being interrupted, 'that this evening's lecture was your last before your return to England?'

'I'm afraid so,' replied George. 'I take the train back to New York tomorrow afternoon, and then sail for Southampton the following morning.'

'Well, if you're going to be in New York, Mr Mallory, perhaps you might care to join me for a drink tomorrow evening.'

'That's extremely kind of you, Mrs Harrington, but sadly—'

'You see, my late husband was a very generous benefactor, and I feel sure he would have wanted me to make a substantial donation to your cause.'

'Substantial?' repeated George.

'I was thinking about –' she paused – 'ten thousand dollars.'

It was some time before George said, 'But I won't get back to New York until around seven tomorrow evening, Mrs Harrington.'

'Then I'll send a car to pick you up from your hotel at eight. And, George, do call me Estelle.'

◄◊►

After breakfast had been cleared and nanny had taken the children off for their morning walk, Ruth went through to the drawing room. She sat down in her favourite chair by the window and opened George's latest letter.

March 22nd, 1923

My dearest Ruth,

I'm sitting on a train travelling between Boston and New York. Some good news for a change. Harvard was everything I could have hoped for. Not only was the Taft Hall packed – hanging from the rafters is how Keedick described the audience – but the undergraduates and the dons couldn't have made me feel more welcome.

I came away from the president's reception in high spirits, despite not being allowed to drink more than an orange juice because of Prohibition. But when I woke this morning, reality set in once again. My tour has been cut short, and I'll be returning to England far earlier than expected. It's a pity I didn't talk you into coming with me, since the whole trip has turned out to be less than a month. Mind you, our short holiday in Venice was unforgettable, despite not climbing St Mark's. This is to warn you that I'll be back some time next week. I'll cable you from the ship with details of when we dock at Southampton.

The second piece of good news is that I'm to be given one last chance to top up the Society's funds in New York this evening.

The only good thing about the trip being cut short is that I'll be able to see you and the children earlier than expected. But back to reality. The first thing I'll have to do when I return is to start looking for a job.

See you soon, my darling.

Your loving husband,
    George

Ruth smiled as she put the letter back in the envelope and placed it in the top drawer of her desk, along with all the letters George had written to her over the years. She glanced at the clock on the mantelpiece. Her train to London wasn't due to leave Godalming for another hour, but Ruth felt she ought to set out for the station fairly soon, as this was an appointment for which she mustn't be late.

49

George knocked on the front door of a brownstone on West 64th Street a few minutes before nine o'clock. A butler dressed in a long black tailcoat and white tie answered the door.

'Good evening, sir. Mrs Harrington is expecting you.'

George was shown into the drawing room, where he found Mrs Harrington standing by the mantelpiece below a Bonnard oil of a nude woman stepping out of a bath. His hostess was wearing a bright red silk dress that didn't quite cover her knees. There was no sign of an engagement or wedding ring, although she was wearing a necklace of diamonds with a matching bracelet.

'Thank you, Dawkins,' said Mrs Harrington, 'that will be all.' Before the butler had reached the door she added, 'And I won't be requiring you again this evening.'

'As you wish, madam,' said the butler, bowing before closing the door behind him. George could have sworn he heard a key turning in the lock.

'Do have a seat, George,' said Mrs Harrington, gesturing him towards the sofa. 'And let me fix you a drink. What would you like?'

'I suppose I'll have to settle for orange juice,' said George.

'Certainly not,' said Mrs Harrington. She walked across to the other side of the room, touched a leather-bound volume of *Hard Times* and the bookcase immediately swivelled round to become a drinks cabinet. 'Scotch and soda?' she suggested.

'Is there anything you don't know about me?' asked George with a smile.

'One or two things,' said Mrs Harrington as she took a seat next to him on the sofa, her dress rising several inches above the knee. 'But given a little time, I should be able to remedy that.' George nervously touched his tie. 'Now, do tell me, George, how my little donation might help your next expedition?'

'The truth is, Mrs Harrington,' said George, taking a sip of his Scotch – it was even his favourite blend – 'we need every penny we can lay our hands on. One of the things we learnt from the last trip was that we just weren't well enough prepared. It was the same problem Captain Scott faced on his journey to the South Pole, and it resulted in him losing his life along with the rest of his polar party. I'm not willing to take that risk with my men.'

'You're so very serious, George,' said Mrs Harrington, leaning over and patting him on the thigh.

'It's a serious business, Mrs Harrington.'

'Do call me Estelle,' she said, as she crossed her legs to reveal the top of her black stockings. 'Do you think you'll reach the top this time?'

'Possibly, but you always need a bit of luck,' said George, 'not least with the weather. If you can get three, or perhaps even two, clear days in a row with no wind, you're in with a chance. Just when I thought I had my chance, sadly a disaster befell me.'

'I do hope that if I get my chance,' said Mrs Harrington, 'a disaster won't befall me.' Her hand was now resting on George's thigh. George turned the colour of Mrs Harrington's dress, and decided the time had come to look for an escape route. 'There's no reason to be nervous, George. This is one little adventure that no one need find out about, and it certainly doesn't have to end in disaster.'

George was just about to get up and leave when she added, 'And when you do stand on top of your mountain, George – and I'm sure you will – do spare a thought for me.'

She reached into her sleeve and drew out a slip of paper, which she unfolded and placed on the table in front of her. George looked down at a cheque which read *Pay: The Royal*

Geographical Society $10,000. He thought about Mr Hinks, and remained seated.

'Now, you just think about that for a moment, George, while I slip into something a little less formal. Do help yourself to another drink while I'm away. Mine's a gin and tonic,' she added before leaving the room.

George picked up the cheque, and was about to place it in his wallet when he saw the edge of a small photograph sticking out between two dollar bills. He pulled out the picture of Ruth he had taken during their honeymoon, and which he always carried with him on his travels. He smiled, put the photograph back in his wallet and tore the cheque in half. He walked across to the door and slowly turned the handle, only to discover that it was locked. What a pity the RGS hadn't selected Finch for the American tour, he thought, because then the Society's coffers would undoubtedly have been swelled by $10,000, and he felt confident Mrs Harrington would have considered it a good investment.

George walked across to the other side of the room, slipped the latch on the sill and quietly slid open the window. He stuck his head out, and considered the best possible route. He was pleased to see that the façade of the building was made up of large rough stone slabs, evenly placed. He stepped out onto the ledge and began to make his way slowly down the building, and when he was five feet from the ground, he jumped down on to the sidewalk. George walked quickly across the street. He knew that a climber should never look back, but he couldn't resist it, and was suitably rewarded. There, standing by an open upper-storey window, was a beautiful woman wearing only a sheer negligee that left little to the imagination.

'Damn,' said George when he remembered he hadn't bought a present for Ruth.

◄○►

Ruth knocked gently on the front door of No.37 Tite Street; a moment later it was opened by a maid, who curtsied and said, 'Good morning, Mrs Mallory. Would you be kind enough to follow me?'

When Ruth entered the drawing room, she found her hostess standing by the fireplace beneath an oil painting of her late husband approaching the South Pole. She was wearing a simple long black dress, no make-up, and no jewellery other than an engagement and wedding ring.

'What a pleasure to meet you, Mrs Mallory,' said Kathleen Scott as they shook hands. 'Please come and join me by the fire,' she added, ushering her to a comfortable chair opposite her.

'It's extremely kind of you to agree to see me,' said Ruth. As she sat down the maid reappeared, carrying a silver tray laden with tea and biscuits, which she placed on a table by her mistress's side.

'You can leave us, Millie,' said Captain Scott's widow. 'And I don't wish to be disturbed.'

'Yes, of course, my lady,' said the maid, leaving the room and closing the door quietly behind her.

'Indian or China, Mrs Mallory?'

'Indian, please.'

'Milk and sugar?'

'Just milk, thank you,' said Ruth.

Mrs Scott completed the little ceremony and passed Ruth a cup of tea. 'I was intrigued by your letter,' she said. 'You indicated there was a personal matter that you wished to discuss with me.'

'Yes,' replied Ruth tentatively. 'I need your advice.'

Ruth's hostess nodded before giving her a warm smile.

'My husband,' began Ruth, 'is currently on a lecture tour in the United States, and I'm expecting him back any day now. Although he's told me several times that he doesn't wish to lead the next RGS expedition to Everest, I have no doubt that that is exactly what he does want.'

'And how do you feel about him returning to the Himalaya?'

'After his long absence during the war, followed by the expedition to Everest and now his trip to America, I really don't want him to be away for another six months.'

'I can appreciate that, my dear. Con was exactly the same – just like a child, never able to settle in the same place for more than a few months at a time.'

'Did he ever ask how you felt about that?'

'Constantly, but I knew he only wanted reassurance, so I told him what he wished to hear, that I believed he was doing the right thing.'

'And did you?'

'Not always,' the older woman admitted with a sigh. 'But however much I yearned for him to stay at home and lead a normal life, that was never going to be a possibility, because just like your husband, Mrs Mallory, Con wasn't a normal man.'

'Surely you must now regret not telling him how you really felt?'

'No, Mrs Mallory, I do not. I would rather have spent two years with one of the most exciting men on earth, than forty with someone who thought I had prevented him from fulfilling his dream.'

Ruth tried to compose herself. 'I can bear the thought of being apart from George for another six months.' She paused. 'But not for the rest of my life.'

'No one understands that better than I do. But your husband is no ordinary man, and I'm sure you knew about his overriding ambition long before you agreed to be his wife.'

'Yes, I did, but—'

'Then you cannot, indeed must not, stand in the way of his destiny. If he were to see some lesser mortal achieve his dream, it could be you who spends the rest of your life regretting it.'

'But does it have to be *my* destiny to spend the rest of my life without him?' asked Ruth. 'If he only knew how much I adore him . . .'

'I can assure you he does know, Mrs Mallory, otherwise you would not have asked to see me. And because he knows, you will have to convince him that you believe it is nothing less than his duty to lead the next expedition. And then, my dear, all you can do is pray for his safe return.'

Ruth raised her head, tears streaming down her face. 'But your husband didn't return.'

'If I could turn the clock back,' came the quiet reply, 'and Con were to ask me, "Do you mind me going off again, old gal?"

I would still reply as I did thirteen years, one month and six days ago. "No, my darling, of course I don't mind. But do remember to take your thick woollen socks with you this time."'

—◇—

George was up, packed and ready to leave by six the following morning. When he checked out of the hotel, he wasn't altogether surprised to find that Keedick hadn't settled the bill. He was only relieved that his final night was spent in a single room in a guest house on the Lower East Side, and not the Presidential Suite at the Waldorf.

When George stepped out onto the sidewalk, he didn't hail a cab, for more than one reason. He strode off on the 43-block route march, a suitcase in each hand, dodging the natives as he crossed the sweating, teeming jungle of Manhattan.

When he reached the dockside just over an hour later he saw Keedick standing by the ship's gangway, cigar in mouth, smile etched on his face and the appropriate line ready. 'When you make it to the top of your mountain, George, gimme a call, 'cause that could be the clincher.'

'Thank you, Lee,' said George, and after hesitating for a moment he added, 'for an unforgettable experience.'

'My pleasure,' said Keedick, thrusting out his hand. 'Delighted to have been of assistance.' George shook hands, and was stepping onto the gangway when Keedick called out after him, 'Hey, don't go without this.' He was holding out an envelope.

George turned and walked back down, not something he enjoyed doing.

'It's your share of the profits, old boy,' he said, trying to imitate George's English accent. 'Fifty per cent, as agreed.'

'Thank you,' said George, placing the envelope in an inside pocket. He had no intention of opening it in front of Keedick.

When George went in search of his berth, he wasn't surprised to discover that he'd been downgraded to steerage, four levels below the main deck, and that he and three others were sharing a cabin which wasn't much larger than his tent on the North Col. He stopped unpacking when he heard the first blast of the foghorn announcing their departure, and made his way quickly up on deck so he could follow the ship's slow progress out of the harbour.

Once again he leant over the railing and looked down on the dockside; friends and families were now waving goodbye. He didn't bother to look for Lee Keedick, whom he knew would have long gone. George watched as the giant skyscrapers became smaller and smaller, and when the Statue of Liberty was finally out of sight, he decided the time had come to face reality.

He took the envelope out of his pocket, tore it open and extracted a cheque. *Pay: The Royal Geographical Society $48.* He smiled, and thought about Estelle for a moment, but only for a moment.

BOOK SEVEN

A WOMAN'S PRIVILEGE

50

They strolled down King's Parade together hand in hand, looking like a couple of undergraduates.

'Don't keep me in suspense any longer,' said Ruth. 'How did the interview go?'

'I don't think it could have gone much better,' said George. 'They seemed to agree with all my views on higher education, and didn't baulk when I suggested the time has come to award degrees to women who are taking the same courses as men.'

'About time too,' said Ruth. 'Even Oxford has managed to come to terms with that.'

'It may take another world war before Cambridge budges,' said George as a couple of crusty old dons strolled past.

'So do you think there's a chance they'll offer you the job? Or are there still other candidates to interview?'

'I don't think so,' said George. 'In fact, Young led me to believe that I was on a shortlist of one, and the chairman of the interviewing board rather gave the game away when he asked if I'd be able to start work next September.'

'That's wonderful,' said Ruth. 'Congratulations, my darling.'

'But won't you find it a terrible bore having to up roots and move to Cambridge?'

'Good heavens, no,' said Ruth. 'I can't think of a better place to bring up the children, and you still have so many friends here. Let's be grateful they don't need you until next September, which will give me more than enough time to look for a new house and plan the move while you're away.'

'While I'm away?' said George, looking puzzled.

'Yes, because if the job doesn't start until next year, I can't see any reason why you shouldn't go off and climb your mountain.'

George stared at her as if he couldn't believe what he was hearing. 'Are you telling me, my darling,' he eventually managed, 'that you wouldn't object if I were to sign up for the return expedition?'

'On the contrary, I'd welcome it,' said Ruth. 'The idea of you hanging around the house for months like a bear with a sore head isn't worth thinking about, and I certainly wouldn't want to be around if Finch ends up standing on top of your mountain and all you can do about it is send him a telegram of congratulations. Of course,' she continued, 'it's possible that they may not be willing to offer you a place on the climbing team.'

'And why not?' demanded George.

'Well, you may still look like an undergraduate, my darling, and at times even behave like one, but if they were to check your curriculum vitae more carefully, they'd soon see that you're no spring chicken. So you'd better let them know you're available pretty quickly, because this will undoubtedly be your last chance.'

'You cheeky little minx,' said George. 'I don't know whether to kiss you or spank you. I think I'll settle for a kiss.'

When he finally released her, all Ruth had to say was, 'I've had to speak to you before, Mr Mallory, about kissing me in public.' She couldn't remember when she'd last seen him looking so exhilarated.

'Thank you, my darling,' he said. 'It's such a relief to know how you really feel about me having one last crack at Everest.'

Ruth was glad that George took her back in his arms, for fear he would look into her eyes and discover what she really felt.

◄○►

No one was surprised that George was late for his brother's birthday party, but his sister Mary did tick him off when she discovered that he'd left Trafford's present back at The Holt.

'What did you get him?' asked Mary. 'Or can't you remember that either?'

'A watch,' said George. 'I picked it up when I was last in Switzerland.'

'That's a surprising choice, considering it's an instrument you've shown scant interest in for the past thirty-seven years,' she said as Trafford came across to join them.

'I can always pick it up at Christmas,' said Trafford. 'Just as I did last year,' he added with a smile. 'But more important, I need to settle an argument between Cottie and Mother about the highest point George reached on Everest.'

George looked across the room to see Cottie chatting to a man he didn't recognize. He hadn't seen her since they had visited the Monet exhibition at the Royal Academy a year or two ago. She gave him that familiar smile he remembered from their climbing days, and he felt even more guilty that he hadn't been in touch since her father had gone bankrupt. Not that he could have offered any financial help, but . . .

'Twenty-seven thousand, five hundred and fifty feet,' said Mary, 'as every schoolboy knows.'

'Then it's higher than any pilot has ever managed,' said Trafford, 'otherwise I'd try and land on top of the damn mountain.'

'That would save us all a lot of trouble,' said George, turning back. 'Until then, someone will still have to go up the hard way.' Trafford laughed. 'How's Cottie?' George asked. 'Is she still having to work for a living?'

'Yes,' replied Mary. 'But thankfully she's no longer serving behind the counter at Woolworth's.'

'Why?' asked Trafford. 'Have they made her the manager?'

'No,' said Mary, laughing. 'She's just had her first book published, and the reviews have been most favourable.'

George felt even more guilty. 'I'll have to take a copy with me on my next trip,' he said without thinking.

'Your next trip?' said Trafford. 'I thought you'd decided not to be part of the next Everest expedition.'

'Can Cottie make a living from writing?' asked George, not

wanting to respond to his brother's question. 'I only earned a miserable £32 in royalties from my book on Boswell.'

'Cottie's written a romantic novel, not a stuffy biography,' said Mary. 'What's more, the publishers have offered her a three-book contract, so someone must believe in her.'

'More than one person, it would seem,' said Trafford, looking more closely at the man Cottie was talking to.

'What do you mean?' asked George.

'Cottie's just got married,' said Mary. 'A diplomat from the Foreign Office. Didn't you know?'

'No, I didn't,' admitted George. 'I wasn't invited to the wedding.'

'Hardly surprising,' said Mary. 'If you read *Peking Picnic*, you might understand why.'

'What are you getting at?'

'The hero of the novel is a young schoolmaster who was educated at Cambridge and climbs mountains in his spare time.'

Trafford laughed. 'What? No mention of his dashing younger brother, the fearless flying ace who, after beating off the Germans, returns to his homeland to become the youngest flight commander in the RAF?'

'Only one paragraph,' said Mary. 'But she does suggest that, like his more handsome older brother, he's destined for higher things.'

'That might depend on which one of us is the first to reach 29,000 feet,' suggested Trafford.

'Twenty-nine thousand and *two* feet,' said George.

1924

51

The rest of the committee were studying the RGS's latest map of the Himalaya when General Bruce began his report.

'Most of the back-up party should have reached 17,000 feet by now,' said the General, tapping the map with his monocle to indicate the position. 'Their job will be to make sure that everything is ready for Mallory and his team of climbers by the time they turn up at base camp in twelve weeks' time.'

'Good,' said George. 'And as I've already identified the route I intend to take, that will give us more than a month to get bedded in and have a crack at the summit before the monsoon season sets in.'

'Can we assume, Mallory,' said Sir Francis, 'that we've dealt with most of the anxieties you raised following the previous expedition?'

'You certainly can, Mr Chairman,' George replied. 'But after my desultory efforts in the United States, I'm bound to ask where the money has come from to make all this possible.'

'We had an unexpected windfall,' explained Hinks. 'Although all may not have gone to plan for you in America, Mallory, Noel's film, *The Epic of Everest*, was a huge success here. So much so that he's offered the Society eight thousand pounds for the exclusive, I think the expression is "cinematography rights", for the next expedition, with only one proviso.'

'And what might that be?' asked Raeburn.

'That Mallory be appointed as climbing leader,' said Hinks.

'And as I've already agreed to that,' said Mallory, 'all that's left for me to do is settle the composition of the rest of my climbing party.'

'Which quite frankly, Mr Chairman,' interjected Geoffrey Young, 'selects itself.'

George nodded, and took a piece of paper from his jacket pocket. 'May I present the list of names for the committee's approval, Mr Chairman?'

'Yes, of course, old boy,' said Sir Francis. 'Damn it all, it's your team.'

George read out the names that he and Young had agreed on at the previous meeting of the Alpine Club. 'Norton, Somervell, Morshead, Odell, Finch, Bullock, Hingston, Noel and myself.' He looked up, expecting to receive the committee's unanimous approval.

There was a long silence before the chairman responded. 'I'm sorry to have to tell you, Mallory, that I received a letter only this morning from Mr Finch saying that he felt that, given the circumstances, he would have to withdraw his name for consideration as a member of the 1924 expedition.'

'Given the circumstances?' repeated George. 'What circumstances?'

Sir Francis nodded in Hinks's direction. Hinks opened one of the files in front of him, extracted a letter and passed it to George.

George read it twice before he said, 'But he gives no specific reason for having to withdraw.' He passed the letter to Geoffrey Young, then asked, 'Is he ill, by any chance?'

'Not that we are aware of,' said Sir Francis guardedly.

'And it can't be a financial problem,' said Young, passing the letter back to Hinks, 'because thanks to Noel, we have more than enough money to cover any expenses Finch might require for his passage and equipment.'

'I'm afraid, Mallory, the truth is that the situation is a little more delicate than that,' said Hinks, as he closed the minute book and screwed the top back onto his fountain pen.

'Surely it can't be anything to do with that business with the Governor-General's wife?' said George.

'No, I fear it's far worse than that unsavoury incident,' said

Hinks, taking off his half-moon spectacles and placing them on the table. George waited impatiently for Hinks to continue. 'Without informing the RGS,' Hinks eventually said, 'Finch accepted several speaking engagements up and down the country. These resulted in him making a considerable sum of money, of which the Society has not received one penny.'

'Was the Society entitled to one penny?' asked Young.

'It most certainly was,' said Hinks, 'as Finch had signed a contract, just as you did, Mallory, to pass over fifty per cent of any earnings he received as a consequence of the Everest expedition.'

'How much money is involved?' asked Young.

'We have no idea,' admitted Hinks, 'as Finch refuses to submit any accounts, despite several requests for him to do so. In the end, the Society had no choice but to issue a writ demanding what is rightfully ours.'

'I always said he was a cad from the start,' interjected Ashcroft. 'This latest incident only proves that I was right.'

'Do you think the matter will come to court?' asked Young.

'I would hope not,' said Hinks. 'But were it to do so, the case would probably be heard when the expedition is already in Tibet.'

'I'm sure the Sherpas will get very worked up about that,' said George.

'This is no laughing matter,' said Sir Francis gravely.

'Is there anyone around this table who believes this latest misdemeanour will in any way affect Finch's climbing ability?' asked Young.

'That's not the point, Young,' said Hinks, 'and you know it.'

'It will be the point,' said George, 'when I'm standing at 27,000 feet and have to decide who to select to partner me for the final climb.'

'You'll still have Norton and Somervell to choose between,' Hinks reminded him.

'And they would be the first to admit they aren't in Finch's class.'

'Surely, Mallory, you must accept that the RGS has been left with no choice following this latest incident.'

'It is not the RGS's God-given right to make the decision as to who should and should not be in the climbing party,' said Mallory. 'Just in case you've forgotten, Mr Hinks, this is the Everest Committee.'

'I say, Mallory,' interjected Ashcroft, 'I think that was a bit ripe.'

'Then let me ask you, Commander,' George spat out, 'with all your vast experience of being above sea-level, who do you consider would be the obvious choice to take Finch's place?'

'I'm glad you raised that question, Mallory,' interjected Hinks, 'because I believe we have come up with a suitable replacement.'

'And who might that be?' asked Mallory.

'A young man called Sandy Irvine. He's an Oxford rowing blue, and has agreed to stand in despite the short notice.'

'As it's not my intention to row up Everest, Mr Hinks, perhaps you could let us know what climbing experience Mr Irvine has, because I've never heard of him.'

Hinks smiled for the first time. 'It seems that your friend Odell was very impressed with the lad when they climbed together inside the Arctic Circle last year, and Irvine was the first to reach the summit of the highest peak on Spitsbergen.' Hinks looked rather pleased with himself.

'Spitsbergen,' interjected Young, 'is for promising novices, and in case you didn't know, Mr Hinks, its highest peak is about 5,600 feet.'

'So when I'm next looking for someone to keep me company for the first 5,600 feet,' said George, 'let me assure you, Mr Hinks, that Irvine's will be the first name that springs to mind.'

'I should also point out, Mallory,' said Hinks, 'that Irvine is reading chemistry at Oxford, and is well-acquainted with the oxygen apparatus Finch experimented with on the last trip. In fact, I'm reliably informed that he's in regular touch with the manufacturers about possible improvements to the system.'

'Finch is also a dab hand when it comes to the use of oxygen, and he's got a first-class honours degree to prove it,' George reminded him. 'And just in case the committee has forgotten, he's already experimented with oxygen above 27,000 feet, which you were extremely critical of at the time, Mr Hinks. Perhaps even more relevant is that Finch is the current holder of the world altitude record at 27,850 feet, as I know to my cost.'

'Gentlemen, gentlemen,' said Sir Francis, 'we must try to resolve our differences with some degree of decorum.'

'What do you have in mind, Mr Chairman?' asked George. 'As clearly Mr Hinks and I are never going to agree on this particular subject.'

'That we should allow the majority to prevail, as has always been our custom at the RGS.' Before George could interrupt, Sir Francis added, 'As I'm sure is also the case at the Alpine Club.'

Young kept his counsel, and as no one else ventured an opinion Sir Francis continued, 'May I therefore suggest, somewhat reluctantly, that the time has come for us to take another vote on this matter?' He waited for any objections to be voiced, but the rest of the committee remained silent. 'Will you please officiate, Mr Secretary?'

'Certainly, Mr Chairman,' said Hinks. 'Those in favour of Mr Finch being reinstated as a member of the climbing party, please raise your hand.'

Mallory, Young and, to everyone's surprise, General Bruce, raised their hands. Before Hinks registered the General's vote in the minute book he stared across at him and said, 'But I thought you detested the man?'

'Yes, I do, old boy,' said Bruce. 'But the highest point I managed on the last trip was 17,400 feet, and I can assure you, Hinks, that I have no intention of putting my name forward to join Mallory when he reaches 27,000 feet and has to decide who will join him for the final climb.'

Hinks reluctantly registered the General's vote. 'Those against?' Raeburn and Ashcroft joined the secretary when he raised his hand. 'I fear that it's three all, Mr Chairman, so once again you have the casting vote.'

'On this occasion,' said Sir Francis without hesitation, 'I vote against Finch being reinstated.'

Hinks immediately entered the result in the minute book and, before the ink was dry, announced, 'The Everest Committee has decided, by four votes to three, that George Finch should not be reinstated as a member of the climbing party.' He closed the minute book.

'May I ask what caused you to change your mind on this occasion, Mr Chairman?' asked George calmly.

'Not keeping to his agreement with the RGS was the final straw for me,' said Sir Francis, glancing at the portrait of the Society's president. 'However, I also suspect that His Majesty would not be pleased to be told that a divorced man was the first person to stand on top of the world.'

'What a pity Henry the Eighth wasn't your president when the first attempt on Everest was considered,' said George quietly. He slowly gathered up his papers and rose from his place. 'I must apologize, Mr Chairman, but you have left me with no choice but to resign as a member of this committee, and to withdraw my name as climbing leader. Naturally I wish my successor every good fortune. Good day, gentlemen.'

'Mr Mallory,' said Hinks, before George had reached the door. 'I hope your decision will not prevent you from delivering the memorial lecture to the RGS this evening. The event has been sold out for weeks, and indeed the—'

'I shall of course honour my agreement,' said Mallory. 'But should anyone ask me why I have resigned from this committee and will not be leading the forthcoming expedition to Everest, I shall not hesitate to tell them that I was overruled when it came to the selection of the climbing party.'

'So be it,' said Hinks. Mallory left the room and closed the door quietly behind him.

'Bang goes Noel's eight thousand pounds,' said Raeburn as he stubbed out his cigar. 'Which leaves us with little choice but to cancel the whole damn shindig.'

'Not necessarily,' said Hinks quietly. 'You will have noticed, gentlemen, that I did not record Mallory's resignation in the minute book. I still have a couple of cards up my sleeve, which I intend to play before the evening is out.'

—◦—

George quickly made his way out of the hall and across the corridor to the speaker's room. He didn't stop to chat to anyone on the way, for fear they might ask him a question that he didn't want to answer until after he'd given his lecture. He also needed to use the forty minutes to compose his thoughts, as he knew he was about to deliver the most important speech of his life.

When he walked into the speaker's room he was surprised to find Ruth waiting for him.

'What happened?' she asked when she saw the expression of anger on his face.

George paced up and down the room while he gave Ruth a blow-by-blow account of what had taken place at the committee meeting. He finally came to a halt in front of her. 'I did do the right thing, didn't I, darling?'

Ruth had anticipated the question, and knew that all she had to say was, Yes, of course you were right to resign, my darling. Hinks behaved disgracefully, and unless Finch is reinstated, you'll be taking far too great a risk. And don't let's forget it's your life, not his, that will be at risk.

George stood there, waiting for her reply.

'Let's hope that you won't live to regret your decision,' was all she said. She jumped up from her chair before George could press her further. 'I'll leave you now, my darling. I only popped by to wish you luck. I realize you'll need these last few minutes to prepare yourself for such an important occasion.' She gave him a gentle kiss on the cheek, and left without another word.

George sat at the little desk and tried to go over his notes, but his thoughts kept returning to the committee meeting, and Ruth's ambiguous response to his question.

There was a gentle tap on the door. George wondered who it could possibly be. It was one of the Society's golden rules that a speaker must not be interrupted during his final moments of preparation. When he saw Hinks come marching through the door, he could have happily punched the damn man on the nose, until he noticed who was following close behind him. George leapt to his feet and bowed.

'Your Royal Highness,' said Hinks, 'may I have the honour of presenting Mr George Mallory, who, as you know, sir, will be delivering tonight's lecture.'

'Yes, indeed,' said the Prince of Wales. 'I apologize for barging in on you like this, Mallory, but I have a message from His Majesty the King that I've been entrusted to deliver to you in person.'

'It's extremely kind of you to take the trouble, sir.'

'Not at all, old fellow. His Majesty wanted you to know how delighted he is that you have agreed to lead the next expedition to Everest, and he looks forward to meeting you on your return.' Hinks gave a thin smile. 'And may I say, Mallory, that those are also my sentiments, and add how much I am looking forward to your lecture.'

'Thank you, sir,' said George.

'Now I'd better leave you in peace,' the Prince said, 'otherwise this show may never get off the ground.'

George bowed again as the Prince of Wales and Hinks left the room.

'You bastard, Hinks' he muttered as the door closed behind them. 'But don't imagine even for one moment that your little subterfuge will change my mind.'

52

'Your Royal Highness, my lords, ladies and gentlemen, it is my privilege as chairman of the Royal Geographical Society and the Everest Committee to introduce tonight's guest speaker, Mr George Mallory,' announced Sir Francis Younghusband. 'Mr Mallory was the climbing leader on the last expedition, when he reached a height of 27,550 feet – a mere 1,452 feet from the summit. Tonight, Mr Mallory will be telling us about his experiences on that historic adventure in a lecture entitled "Walking Off the Map". Ladies and gentlemen, Mr George Mallory.'

George was unable to speak for several minutes because the audience rose to their feet as one and applauded until he finally had to wave them down. He looked down at the front row and smiled at the man who should have been giving the memorial lecture that evening, had it not been for the injury he sustained in the war. Young returned his smile, clearly proud that his pupil was representing him. Norton, Somervell and Odell sat beside him.

George waited for the audience to settle before he delivered his first line. 'When I was recently in New York,' he began, 'I was introduced as the man who had conquered Everest single-handed.' He waited for the laughter to die down before he went on, 'Wrong on both counts. Although one man may end up standing alone on top of that great mountain, he could not hope to achieve such a feat without the backing of a first-class team. And by that I mean, you'd better have everything from seventy Indian mules to a General Bruce if you hope even to reach base camp.' This was the cue for the lights to go down and the first slide to appear on the screen behind him.

Forty minutes later, George was back at base camp and once again receiving rapturous applause. He felt that the lecture had gone well, but he still needed to answer questions, and feared that the wrong response could well put *him* back at base camp.

When he called for questions he was surprised that Hinks didn't rise from his place, as tradition allows the secretary of the RGS to ask the first question. Instead, he remained resolutely in his place in the front row, arms folded. George selected an elderly gentleman in the second row.

'When you were stranded at 27,550 feet, sir, and saw Finch moving away from you, did you not wish at the time that you had taken a couple of oxygen cylinders along with you?'

'Not when we first set out I didn't,' replied Mallory. 'But later, when I couldn't progress more than a few feet without having to stop for a rest, I came to the conclusion that it would be nigh on impossible to reach the summit under one's own steam.'

He pointed to another hand.

'But wouldn't you consider the use of oxygen to be cheating, sir?'

'I used to be of that opinion,' said George. 'But that was before a colleague who shared a tent with me at 27,000 feet pointed out that you might argue that it was cheating to wear leather climbing boots or woollen mittens, or even to put a lump of sugar in your lukewarm tea, all of which undoubtedly give you a better chance of success. And let's be honest, why travel five thousand miles if you have no hope of covering the last thousand feet.'

He selected another raised hand.

'If you hadn't stopped to assist Mr Odell, do you think you might have reached the top?'

'I could certainly see the top,' George replied, 'because Mr Finch was 300 feet ahead of me.' This was greeted with warm laughter. 'I confess that the summit seemed to be tantalizingly close at the time, but even that can be deceptive. Never forget that on a mountain, 500 feet is not a couple of hundred yards. Far from it — it's more likely to be over a mile. However, that experience convinced me that given enough time and the right conditions, it is possible to reach the summit.'

George answered several more questions during the next twenty minutes, without giving any hint that he had just resigned as climbing leader.

'Last question,' he said finally, with a relieved smile. He pointed to a young man near the middle of the hall, who was standing up and waving a hand, hoping to be noticed. In a voice that had not yet broken, the boy asked, 'When you have conquered Everest, sir, what will be left for the likes of me?'

The whole audience burst out laughing, and Mallory recalled how nervous he had been when he had asked Captain Scott almost the same question. He looked up at the gallery, delighted to see Scott's widow in her usual place in the front row. Thank God his decision earlier that evening meant that Ruth would no longer have to worry about suffering the same fate. Mallory looked back down at the young man and smiled. 'You should read HG Wells, my boy. He believes that, in time, mankind will be able, like Puck, to put a circle round the earth in forty minutes, that someone will one day break the sound barrier, with consequences we have yet to comprehend, and that in your lifetime, though perhaps not in mine, a man will walk on the moon.' George smiled at the young man. 'Perhaps you'll be the first Englishman to be launched into space.'

The audience roared with laughter, and applauded again as George took his final bow. He felt confident that he'd escaped without anyone suspecting what had taken place at the committee meeting earlier that evening. He smiled down at Ruth, who was sitting in the front row, his sisters Avie and Mary on either side of her; another small triumph.

When George raised his head, he saw his oldest friend standing and applauding wildly. Within moments the rest of the audience had joined Guy Bullock and seemed quite unwilling to resume their seats, however much he gestured that they should do so.

He was about to leave the stage, but when he turned, he saw Hinks climbing the steps towards him, carrying a file. He gave Mallory a warm smile as he approached the microphone, lowered it by several inches, and waited for the applause to die down and for everyone to resume their seats before he spoke.

'Your Royal Highness, my lords, ladies and gentlemen. Those of you who are familiar with the traditions of this historic Society will be aware that it is the secretary's privilege on these occasions to ask the lecturer the first question. I did not do so this evening, thus breaking with tradition; but only because my chairman, Sir Francis Younghusband, rewarded me with an even greater prize, that of giving the vote of thanks to our guest speaker and my dear friend, George Mallory.'

George had never heard Hinks call him by his Christian name before.

'But first, allow me to tell you about a resolution that we passed at the Everest Committee this evening in Mr Mallory's absence, and which we feel is something we should share with every member of this society.' Hinks opened the file, extracted a piece of paper, adjusted his spectacles and began to read. 'It was unanimously agreed that we should invite Mr George Leigh Mallory to be climbing leader for the 1924 expedition of Everest.' The audience burst into loud applause, but Hinks raised a hand to silence them, as he clearly had more to say.

George stood a pace behind him, seething.

'However, the committee is only too aware that there might be reasons why Mr Mallory would feel unable to take on this onerous task a second time.'

Cries of 'No!' came from the audience, causing Hinks to raise a hand once again. 'Reasons you may not be aware of, but when I tell you what they are, you will appreciate his dilemma. Mr Mallory has a wife and three young children whom he may not wish to abandon for another six months. Not only that, but I learnt today that he is about to be appointed to a most important position at the Workers' Educational Association that will allow him to put into practice the beliefs he has held passionately for many years.

'If that were not enough,' continued Hinks, 'there is a third reason. I must be very careful how I word this, as I am only too aware that several gentlemen of the press are among us tonight. Your society learnt today that Mr Finch, Mr Mallory's colleague on the last Everest expedition, has had to withdraw his name from the climbing team for personal reasons, which I fear the newspapers will be reporting in greater detail tomorrow.' The room was now silent. 'With this in mind, your committee has decided that if Mr Mallory felt, quite understandably, unable to take his place as leader of the 1924 expedition, we would be left with no choice but to postpone – not abandon, but postpone – that expedition until such time as a suitable replacement as climbing leader could be found.'

George suddenly realized that the King and the Prince of Wales were only a side show. Hinks was about to deliver the knock-out punch.

'Let me end by saying,' Hinks said, turning to face George, 'that whatever decision you come to, sir, this society will be eternally grateful for your unswerving commitment to its cause, and, more important, your service to this country. We naturally hope that you will accept our offer of the position of climbing leader, and that this time you will lead your team to even greater glory. Ladies and gentlemen, I ask you all to join me in thanking our guest speaker this evening, Mallory of Everest.'

The audience rose as one. Men who would normally offer courteous and respectful applause to the guest speaker leapt from their seats, some cheering, some pleading, all hoping that Mallory would accept the challenge. George looked down at Ruth, who was also on her feet, joining in the applause. When Hinks took a pace back to join him, George said for the second time that evening, 'You bastard.'

'Quite possibly,' Hinks replied. 'However, when I bring the minute book up-to-date later this evening, I presume I'll be able to record your acceptance of the position of climbing leader.'

'Mallory of Everest! Mallory of Everest!' the audience chanted in unison.

'You bastard,' George repeated.

53

George leant over the railing of the SS *California*, searching for his wife. He smiled when he spotted her among the cheering crowd. The moment she realized he had found her, she began to wave. She was only glad that he could not see the tears streaming down her face.

By the time the crew had raised the gangway, the ropes had been untied and the ship had begun to ease away from the dockside, he was already missing her. Why did he always have to go away to realize how much he loved her? For the next six months all he would have to remind him of her beauty was a frayed sepia photograph taken during the first week of their honeymoon. If she had not been adamant that he should go, he would have stayed at home, content to follow the progress of the expedition in *The Times*. He knew that Hinks had no intention of postponing the expedition, but as every word of his speech had been reported in the 'Thunderer' the following morning, he also realized that his bluff had been called. Hinks had proved to be a far better poker player.

So now he was on his way back to India without Finch to challenge his every move. And Sherpa Nyima would not be standing on the dockside waiting to greet him when he stepped off the ship on the far side of the world.

And then George saw him standing at the back of the crowd, slightly to one side, as befits a loner. He didn't recognize him to begin with, until the man raised his hat to reveal that thick, wavy fair hair that so many women had swooned over. George returned the compliment, only surprised that Finch hadn't smuggled himself on board. But Hinks had made certain that he couldn't show his face in public until the scandal had died down, let alone make a solo appearance on the highest stage on earth.

George searched for Ruth once again and, having found her, he never let her out of his sight until she could no longer be seen among the vast crowd of well-wishers waving from the dockside.

◄o►

When finally a column of black, belching smoke was all that could be seen on the horizon, Ruth reluctantly walked slowly to her car. She drove out of the dock and began the long journey back to The Holt. This time there were no adoring crowds to prevent her from escaping.

Ruth had never craved adoring crowds. She simply wanted her husband to return alive. But she had played the game so well that everyone was convinced she wanted George to be given one last chance to fulfil his dream. In truth, she didn't care if he succeeded or failed, as long as they could grow old together, and today would become nothing more than a fading memory.

◄o►

When George could no longer see his homeland, he retired to his little cabin. He sat at the desk below the porthole and began to write a letter to the only woman he had ever loved.

My dearest Ruth . . .

BOOK EIGHT

ASCENSION DAY

54

March 12th, 1924

My dearest Ruth,

The long sea voyage has only served to remind me what a fine bunch of chaps I have the privilege of leading. I think too often of the sacrifices I have made, and not enough about these fine men who have been willing to join me in this capricious adventure, and what tribulations they must also have been through with their families and friends during the past two years.

Despite my initial misgivings, Sandy Irvine turns out to be a very singular fellow. Although he's only 22, he has a shrewd northern head screwed firmly onto his broad shoulders, and the coincidence of us both hailing from Birkenhead would not be acceptable on the pages of a novel.

Of course, I'm still anxious about the fact that he's never climbed much above 5,500 feet, but I have to admit that he is far fitter than any of us, as passengers have been able to witness at our morning PT sessions conducted by the redoubtable General Bruce. Bruce is happy enough to remain our conductor, while still having no desire to be part of the orchestra.

I must also confess that Hinks did not exaggerate Irvine's chemistry skills. He's quite the equal of Finch in that department, even though Norton and Odell still refuse to countenance the idea of using oxygen, let alone agreeing to strap those bulky cylinders onto their backs. Will they

347

in the end accept that we cannot hope to reach the summit without the aid of this infernal heresy, or will they remain, in Finch's words, blessed amateurs who must therefore fail? Only time will tell.

*

Our ship docked at Bombay on March 20th, and we immediately boarded the train for Darjeeling, where we selected our ponies and porters. Once again General Bruce performed miracles, and the following morning we set off on the long trek for Tibet, along with 60 ponies and more than a hundred porters. Before leaving Darjeeling on the Toy Train, we dined with Lord Lytton, the new Governor-General, and his wife, but as Finch wasn't present there is nothing of interest to report, other than the fact that young Irvine took more than a passing interest in the Governor-General's daughter, Lynda. Lady Lytton seemed happy to encourage him.

There was a letter awaiting me at the embassy from my sister Mary. Bit of luck her husband being posted to Ceylon, because she'll be able to warn us in advance when the monsoon season will be upon us, as it travels across that island about ten days before it's due to reach us.

The following morning we set off on the 80-mile journey to the border, which passed without incident. Sadly, General Bruce caught malaria and had to return to Darjeeling. I fear we won't see him again. He took with him his bath, a dozen boxes of cigars and half his cases of wine and champagne – but he kindly left us with the other half, not to mention all the gifts he had so carefully selected for the Dzongpen, when we present our credentials at the border.

The General's deputy, Lt Col Norton, has taken over his responsibilities. You may recall Norton as the man who held the world altitude record for 24 hours before Finch so rudely snatched it away from him. Although he never mentions the subject, I know Norton is keen to put the record straight, and I must admit that if only he would agree to using oxygen once we have reached 27,000 feet, he would be the obvious choice *to accompany me to the summit. However, Somervell is wavering when it comes to oxygen, so he may well turn out to be the alternative, as I wouldn't consider attempting the last 2,000 feet with Odell again.*

We sailed across the border on this occasion, even if we were all wearing our oldest boots and watches picked up cheaply in Bombay. However, we were still able to shower the Dzongpen with gifts from Harrods, Fortnum's, Davidoff and Lock's, including a black opera cane mounted with a silver head of the King, which I assured him was a personal gift from His Majesty.

We were all taken by surprise when the Dzongpen told us how disappointed he was to learn that General Bruce had been taken ill, as he had been looking forward to seeing his old friend again. I couldn't help noticing that he was wearing the General's half-hunter and chain, even if there was no sign of my Old Wykehamist tie.

＊

This morning as we passed over Pang La, the clouds suddenly lifted and we saw the commanding heights of Chomolungma dominating the skyline ahead of us. Once again, her sheer beauty took my breath away. A wise man would surely resist her alluring charms and immediately turn back, but like Euripides' sirens, she draws one towards her rocky and treacherous terrain.

As we climbed higher and higher, I kept a watchful eye on Irvine, who appears to have acclimatized to the conditions as well as any of us. But then, I sometimes forget that he's 16 years younger than I am.

＊

This morning, with Everest in the background, we held a service in memory of Nyima and the other six Sherpas who lost their lives on the last expedition. We must reach the summit this time, if for no other reason than to honour their memory.

I only wish Nyima was standing by my side now, because I

would not hesitate to invite him to join me on the final climb, as it must surely be right that a Sherpa is the first person to stand on top of his own mountain. Not to mention that it would be the sweetest revenge on Hinks after his Machiavellian behaviour on the night of the memorial lecture. But sadly a Sherpa will not reach the top on this occasion, as I have searched among his countrymen and have not found Nyima's equal.

We finally arrived at base camp on April 29th, and to be fair to Hinks – something I've never found easy – everything I requested has been put in place. This time we will not be wasting precious days erecting and dismantling camps and continually moving equipment up and down the mountain. I've been assured by Mr Hazard (an unfortunate name for someone with the responsibility of organizing our daily lives) that Camp III has already been established at 21,000 feet, with eleven of the finest Sherpas awaiting our arrival under the command of Guy Bullock.

One must never forget that it's Noel's £8,000 that has made all this possible, and he's filming anything and everything that moves. The final documentary of this expedition will surely rival Birth of a Nation.

✲

I am writing this letter in my little tent at base camp. In a few minutes' time I will be joining my colleagues for dinner, and Norton will hand over the responsibility of command to me. I will then brief the team on my plans for the ascent of Everest. And so, my dearest, the great adventure begins once again. I am much more confident about our chances this time. But as soon as I conquer my magnificent obsession, I shall press a button, and moments later I will be standing by your side. From this you will gather that I am currently re-reading HG Wells's The Time Machine. Even if I can't press his mythical button, I will nevertheless return as quickly as humanly possible, as I have no desire to be away from you a moment longer than necessary. As I promised, I still intend to leave your photograph on the summit . . .

55

Thursday, May 1st, 1924

And then there were eight. 'Gentlemen, His Majesty the King,' said Lieutenant Colonel Norton as he rose from his place at the head of the table and raised his tin mug.

The rest of the team immediately stood up and, as one, said, 'The King.'

'Please remain standing,' said George. 'Gentlemen, Chomolungma, Goddess Mother of the Earth.' The team raised their mugs a second time. Outside the tent, the Sherpas fell flat on the ground, facing the mountain.

'Gentlemen,' said George, 'you may smoke.'

The team resumed their places and began to light cigars and pass the port decanter around the table. A few minutes later George stood up again and tapped his glass with a spoon.

'Allow me to begin, gentlemen, by saying how sorry we all are that General Bruce is unable to be with us on this occasion.'

'Hear, hear. Hear, hear.'

'And how grateful we are to him for the fine wine he has bequeathed to us, which we have enjoyed this evening. Let us hope that in time, God willing, we will have good reason to uncork his champagne.'

'Hear, hear. Hear, hear.'

'Thanks to General Bruce's foresight and diligence, we have been left with only one task, that of finally taming this monster so that we can all return home and begin leading normal lives. Let me make it absolutely clear from the outset that I haven't yet decided the composition of the two teams that will join me for the final ascent.

'One aspect that will not differ from the previous expedition is that I will be keeping a close eye on each one of you, until I decide who has best acclimatized to the conditions. With that in mind, I expect all of you to be up and ready to leave by six o'clock tomorrow morning, in order that we can reach 19,000 feet by midday, and still return to base camp by sunset.'

'Why come back down,' asked Irvine, 'when we're trying to get to the top as quickly as possible?'

'Not as quickly as possible,' said George, smiling when he realized just how inexperienced young Sandy Irvine was. 'Even you will take a little time to become acclimatized to new heights. The golden rule,' he added, 'is climb high, sleep low. When we've become fully acclimatized,' he continued, 'it's my intention to move on to 23,000 feet, and set up Camp IV on the North Col. Once we've bedded in, we will move on and establish Camp V at 25,000 feet, and Camp VI around 27,000 feet, from where the final assault will be launched.' George paused for some time before he delivered his next sentence. 'I want all of you to know that whoever I invite to join me will be part of the team making the *second* attempt on the summit, as I intend to allow two of my colleagues the first opportunity to make history. Should the first team fail, my partner and I will make our attempt the following day. I feel sure that every one of us has the same desire, to be the first to place his foot on the brow of Chomolungma. However, it's only fair to let you know, gentlemen, that it's going to be me.'

This was greeted by the whole team with laughter and banging of mugs on the table. When the noise had died down, George invited questions.

'Is it your intention to use oxygen for the second attempt on the summit?' asked Norton.

'Yes it is,' replied George. 'I've reluctantly come to the

conclusion that Finch was right, and that we cannot hope to scale the last 2,000 feet without the aid of oxygen.'

'Then I'll have to make sure I'm in the first party,' said Norton, 'and prove you wrong. It's a shame, really, Mallory, because that means I'll be the first man to stand on top of Everest.'

This was greeted with even louder cheers, and more banging of mugs on the table.

'If you manage that, Norton,' retorted George, 'I'll abandon the use of oxygen the following day, and climb to the top in my bare feet.'

'That will be of little significance,' said Norton, raising his mug to George, 'because no one will remember the name of the second man to climb Everest.'

—◇—

'Howzat!'

'Not out.'

Mallory wasn't sure if he was dreaming, or if he really had just heard the sound of leather on willow. He stuck his head out of the tent to see that a square of snow in the Himalaya had been transformed into an English village cricket pitch.

Two ice axes had been planted in the snow 22 yards apart, serving as stumps. Odell, ball in hand, was bowling to Irvine. Mallory only needed to watch a few deliveries to realize that bat was on top of ball. It amused him to see the Sherpas standing around in little huddles, chatting among themselves, clearly puzzled by the English at play, while Noel filmed the event as if it were a Test Match.

Mallory crawled out of his tent and strolled across to join Norton behind the stumps, taking up his place at first slip.

'Irvine's not at all bad,' said Norton. 'The lad's only a few runs off his half century.'

'How long has he been at the crease?' asked Mallory.

'Best part of thirty minutes.'

'And he's still able to run between the wickets?'

'Doesn't seem to be a problem. He must have lungs like

bellows. But then, you have to remember, Mallory, he does have at least fifteen years on the rest of us.'

'Wake up, skipper,' shouted Odell as the ball shot past Mallory's right hand.

'Sorry, Odell, my mistake,' said Mallory. 'I wasn't concentrating.'

Irvine hit the next ball for four, bringing up his fifty, which was greeted with warm applause.

'I've seen enough of this bloody Oxford man,' said Guy Bullock as he took over the bowling from Odell.

Guy's first effort was a little short, and Irvine dispatched it to the boundary for another four runs. But his second sizzled off an icy patch, caught the edge of Irvine's bat and George, falling to his right, took the ball one-handed.

'Well caught, skipper,' said Guy. 'Pity you didn't turn up a little earlier.'

'All right, chaps, let's get moving,' said Mallory. 'I want to be out of here in half an hour.'

Suddenly the pitch was deserted, as the village cricketers reverted to seasoned mountaineers.

Thirty minutes later nine climbers and twenty-three Sherpas were all ready to move. Mallory waved his right arm like a traffic policeman, and set off at a pace that would soon sort out those who would be unlikely to survive at greater heights.

One or two Sherpas fell by the wayside, dropping their loads in the snow and retreating down the mountain. However, none of the climbing party seemed to be in trouble, with Irvine continually dogging his leader's footsteps despite having two large oxygen cylinders strapped to his back.

Mallory was puzzled because he didn't seem to have a mouthpiece attached. He beckoned the young man to join him. 'You won't be needing oxygen, Irvine,' he said, 'until we reach at least 25,000 feet.'

Irvine nodded. 'I was hoping not to use one precious ounce of the stuff until at least 27,000 feet, but if I'm lucky enough to be selected to join you for the final climb, I want to become accustomed to the extra weight. You see, I'm planning to be sitting on top,' he said, pointing to the peak, 'waiting for you to join me. After all,' he added, 'it's nothing more than the duty of an Oxford man to hammer a tab whenever possible.'

George gave a slight bow. 'Fix me up with two of your cylinders tomorrow,' he said. 'It's not just getting used to the extra weight that's important, but once we have to tackle sheer rock faces and sheets of ice, even the slightest shift of balance could prove fatal.'

After a couple of hours, George allowed the team a short break to enjoy a digestive biscuit and a mug of tea before setting off again. The weather couldn't have been more conducive to climbing, apart from a brief shower of snow that wouldn't have distracted a child building a snowman, and they maintained a steady pace. George wondered just how long the weather would remain so docile.

He prayed. His prayers were not answered.

56

May 17th, 1924

My dearest Ruth,

   *Disaster. Nothing has gone right for the past two weeks.
The weather has been so foul that there have been days when
the relentless heavy snow has made it impossible to see more
than a few feet in front of your nose.*

   *Norton, always as brave as a lion, somehow managed to
reach 23,400 feet, where he and Somervell set up Camp IV
and spent the night. However, the following day the two of
them only just made it back to Camp III before nightfall.
It took them over eight hours of downhill trekking into the
driving snow to cover 2,400 ft. Think about it – that's an
average speed of 100 yards an hour, a distance Harold
Abrahams covered in 9.6 seconds.*

   *The following day Odell, Bullock and I reached 25,300 ft
and somehow managed to pitch Camp V on an icy ledge.
But after spending the night there, the weather gave us no
choice but to return here, to Camp III. When we arrived,
Dr Hingston greeted me with the news that one of the
Sherpas had broken his leg, while another had suspected
pneumonia. I didn't bother to tell him that my ankle's been
playing up again. Guy and Odell kindly volunteered to
accompany the walking wounded down to base camp, from
where they were escorted back to their villages.*

   *When Guy returned the following day, he reported that
our cobbler had died of frostbite, a Gurkha NCO had*

developed a blood clot on the brain and 12 more Sherpas
had run away; on the equivalent of less than a shilling a
week, who could blame them? Apparently morale at base
camp is pretty low. What do they imagine it's like up here?

*

Norton and Somervell finally reached the North Col after
three more attempts, and even managed to set up camp
despite the temperature being minus 24 degrees. But when
they were on their way back down, four of the Sherpas lost
their nerve and, fearing an avalanche, returned to spend a
second night on the North Col.

The following morning, Norton, Somervell and I mounted
a rescue party, and somehow managed to reach the Sherpas
and bring them back to the relative safety of Camp III. My
bet is that we've seen the last of them.

If that wasn't enough, our meteorologist informed me
over breakfast this morning that, in his opinion, the monsoon
will soon be upon us. However, he did remind me that, last
time, the monsoon was preceded by three days of clear skies.
It's hardly a pattern one can rely on, but it didn't stop me
from offering up a prayer to whichever god is in charge of
the weather.

◄o►

George should have seen it coming, but he had been so preoccupied with the desire to be given one more chance that he had
failed to notice what was taking place around him. That was until
Norton called a council of war.

'I think it would be wise, given the circumstances, gentlemen,' said Norton, 'for us to cut our losses and turn back now,
before we lose anyone else.'

'I don't agree,' said George immediately. 'If we were to do
that, we would have sacrificed six months of our lives, with
nothing to show for it.'

'At least we would live to fight another day,' said Somervell.

'None of us is going to be given the opportunity to fight

another day,' said George tersely. 'This is our last chance, Somervell, and you know it.'

Somervell was momentarily stunned by the vehemence of Mallory's words, and it was some time before he responded. 'But at least we'd be alive,' he managed.

'That's not my idea of living,' responded George. Before anyone had a chance to offer an opinion, he turned to his oldest friend and asked, 'How would you feel about turning back, Guy?'

Bullock didn't respond immediately, though the rest of the team waited for his reply.

'I'm still willing to back your judgement, George,' he finally said, 'and to hang about for a few more days to see if the weather breaks.'

'Me too,' said Irvine. 'But then, I have no qualms about turning back either. After all, I'm the only one here young enough to fight another day.'

The rest of the team burst out laughing, which helped to ease the tension.

'Why don't we give it another week before we decide to shut up shop?' suggested Odell. 'If the weather hasn't improved by then, perhaps we should admit defeat and return home.'

George looked around the group to find his colleagues nodding. He recalled AC Benson's sage advice: *when you know you're beaten, give in gracefully.*

'So be it,' said George. 'We'll stick it out for another seven days, and if the weather doesn't improve, Norton will resume command and we'll return to England.'

George felt he had won the day – or to be more accurate, seven days. But would that be enough?

—◇—

May 29th, 1924

So, unless the weather turns on its head in the next few days, you can expect me back in England towards the end of August, or the beginning of September at the latest.

Please thank Clare for her wonderful poem – Rupert

Brooke would have been proud of her – and Beridge for her drawing of a cat, or was it a dog? – not to mention John's good wishes, short but appreciated.

I'm glad that you've found time to visit Cambridge and start looking for a home, and thanks for the warning that it gets very cold in the Fens at this time of the year.

My dearest, I'm looking forward to starting the new job, and to sleeping in a bed with a woman I want to hold, and not a man I have to cling on to just to stay alive. When I return home this time, there will be no crowds at the dockside to welcome Mallory of Everest, just a young lady waiting for a middle-aged man who is looking forward to spending the rest of his life with the woman he loves.

Your loving husband,
George

57

Monday, June 2nd, 1924

And then there were five. George was having breakfast on a clear, windless morning, when a Sherpa arrived from base camp and handed him the cable. He tore it open, read its contents slowly, and smiled as he considered its implications. He glanced at Norton, who was sitting cross-legged on the ground beside him.

'Could we have a word, old chap?'

'Yes, of course,' said Norton, putting aside his sliced ham and tongue.

'I'm going to ask you one last time,' said George. 'If I were to offer you the chance to partner me on the final climb, would you be willing to consider the use of oxygen?'

'No, I would not,' said Norton firmly.

'So be it,' said George quietly, accepting that no amount of further discussion on the subject was going to persuade Norton to change his mind. 'In that case, you will lead the first assault, without oxygen. If you succeed . . .'

◄○►

'Gentlemen,' George said, after calling the team together, 'I'm sorry to interrupt your breakfast, but I've just received a message from my sister in Colombo.' He looked down at Mary's cable. '*One week, possibly ten days of good weather before monsoon season upon you. Good luck.*' Mallory looked up. 'We don't have a moment to waste. I've had a good deal of time to consider my options, and I will now share my thoughts with you. I've selected two teams for the attempts on the summit. The first will be Norton and Somervell. They will set out in an hour's time, and attempt to reach Camp V, at 25,300 feet, by nightfall. Tomorrow they will have to rise early if they hope to skirt the North-East Ridge, establish Camp VI at around 27,000 feet, and be bedded down before the sun sets. They will have to grab as many hours of sleep as possible, because on the following morning they will have to make the first attempt on the summit. Any questions, gentlemen?'

Both Norton and Somervell shook their heads. They had spent the past month endlessly discussing every possible scenario. Now all they wanted to do was get on with it.

'Meanwhile, the rest of the team,' Mallory said, 'will just have to sit around twiddling their thumbs while we wait for the return of the conquering heroes.'

'And if they fail?' asked Irvine with a grin.

'Then you and I, Sandy, will make the second attempt using oxygen.'

'And if we succeed?' asked Norton.

Mallory gave the old soldier a wry smile. 'In that case, Odell and I will make the second ascent without the aid of oxygen.'

'In your bare feet, remember,' added Somervell.

While the rest of the team laughed, Mallory gave his two colleagues a slight bow. He waited for a moment before he spoke again.

'Gentlemen,' he said, 'this is not the occasion on which to make a speech about what being the first man to stand on the top of this mountain would mean to our fellow countrymen throughout the Empire, or to dwell on the possible garlands that would be placed on our heads. There will be time enough to sit at the bar of the Alpine Club and bore young climbers with tales of our past glories, but for now, if we are to succeed, we cannot afford to waste a precious moment. So good luck, gentlemen, and Godspeed.'

Thirty minutes later, Norton and Somervell were fully

equipped and ready. Mallory, Odell, Irvine, Bullock, Morshead and Hingston were standing in line to see them off, while Noel went on filming them until they were out of sight. He didn't see Mallory look up to the heavens and say, 'Just give me one more week, and I'll never ask you for anything else again.'

—◦—

George matched Norton and Somervell stride for stride as he sat alone in his tent. He regularly checked his watch, trying to imagine what height his two colleagues would have reached.

After a prolonged lunch of macaroni and prunes with the rest of the team, George returned to his tent. He wrote his daily letter to Ruth, and another to Trafford – Wing Commander Mallory: another man interested in reaching great heights. He then translated a few lines of *The Iliad*, and later managed a round of bridge against Odell and Irvine, with Guy as his partner. After the last rubber was decided, Odell dug out a tin of bully beef from rations and, once it had thawed over a candle, divided the contents into four portions. Later, all the remaining members of the climbing party sat and watched the moon replace the sun, which had flickered across the snow on what had turned out to be a perfect day for climbing. They all had only one thought on their minds, but no one spoke of it – where were they?

George climbed – the only climbing he managed that day – back into his sleeping bag just before eleven o'clock, exhausted by hour upon hour of doing nothing. He fell into a deep sleep, wondering if he would live to regret allowing Norton and Somervell the first crack at the summit. Would he be returning to England in a week's time having captained the winning team, only to be forever reminded of Norton's words, *No one will remember the name of the second man to climb Everest*?

—◦—

Irvine was the first to rise the following morning, and immediately set about preparing breakfast for his colleagues. George vowed that when he returned home, he would never eat another sardine in his life.

Once breakfast had been cleared away, Irvine lined up the nine oxygen cylinders and, like his leader, selected the best pair for the final climb. George watched as he went about the slow, methodical business of tapping cylinders and adjusting knobs, and wondered if they would ever be used, or simply discarded here on the North Col along with their owner. Odell went off in search of rare rocks and fossils, happy to escape into a world of his own.

In the afternoon the three of them came together to pore over Noel's photographs of the upper reaches, searching for any piece of new information that might assist their attempt to reach the summit. They earnestly discussed whether they should follow the ridgeline and tackle the Second Step head-on, or simply strike out onto the North Face across the limestone slabs of the Yellow Band, and skirt around the Second Step. In truth, all three of them knew that the final decision couldn't be made until Somervell and Norton had returned, and were able to pass on the first-hand knowledge that would allow them to fill in so many empty spaces on the map, and so many gaps in their knowledge.

After supper, George returned to his tent, a drink made from powdered milk in one hand, *Ulysses* in the other. He fell asleep at page 172, determined to finish Joyce's masterpiece on the sea voyage back to England.

◄○►

The next morning Odell rose early, and to his colleagues' surprise pulled on his rucksack, gloves and goggles.

'Just off to Camp V to make sure the tent's still in place,' he explained as George crawled out of his sleeping bag. 'And I may as well leave them some provisions, as they're sure to be famished.'

George would have laughed at such a casual remark delivered at 25,000 feet, but it was typical of Odell to consider the plight of others, and not the dangers he might be facing. He watched as Odell, accompanied by two Sherpas, headed up the mountain as if he was on an afternoon stroll in the Cotswolds. George was beginning to wonder if Odell wouldn't be the best choice to accompany him on the final climb, as he seemed to have acclimatized to the conditions far better than any of them had this time, himself included.

Odell was back in time for a lunch of two sardines on a wholemeal biscuit – wholemeal meant whole meal – and he didn't appear to be even out of breath.

'Any sign of them?' George asked before he had pulled off his rucksack.

'No, skipper,' Odell replied. 'But then, if they reached the summit by midday and returned to spend the night at Camp VI, I wouldn't expect them to be back at Camp V much before two, in which case they should be with us some time around four this afternoon.'

'Just in time for tea,' George said.

After a six-minute lunch, George returned to *Ulysses*, but spent most of his time staring up the mountain waiting for two specks to appear from the wasteland of the North Face, rather than turning the pages of the novel. He checked his watch: just after two. If they turned up now, they could not have reached the summit; if they arrived around four, the prize must surely be theirs. If they had not returned by six . . . he tried not to think about it.

Three o'clock passed, to become four, followed by five, by which time small talk had been replaced by more serious discussion. No one mentioned supper. By six, the moon had replaced the sun, and they were all becoming apprehensive. By eight, they were beginning to fear the worst.

'I think I'll just head back up the North Ridge,' said Odell casually, 'and see if they've decided to bed down for the night.'

'I'll join you,' said George, leaping up. 'I could do with the exercise.' He tried to sound as if there was nothing to be worried about, but in truth they all knew he was leading a search party.

'Me too,' said Irvine, dumping his oxygen cylinders in the snow.

George was grateful for a full moon, and a still night with no wind or snow. Twenty minutes later, Odell and Irvine were fully equipped and ready to accompany him as he set out in search of their colleagues.

Up, up, up they went. George was becoming more despondent with each step he took. But he didn't consider turning back, even for a moment, because they might just be a few feet away from . . .

It was Irvine who spotted them first, but then, he had the youngest eyes. 'There they are!' he shouted, pointing up the mountain.

George's heart leapt when he saw them, even if they did resemble two old soldiers limping off a battlefield. Norton, the taller of the two, had one arm draped around Somervell's shoulder, the other covering his eyes.

George moved as quickly as he could up the slope to join them, with Irvine only a pace behind. They each threw an arm under Somervell's shoulders, and almost carried him back across the finishing line. Norton transferred an arm to Odell's shoulder, the other still covering his eyes.

Mallory and Irvine guided Somervell into the team tent before lowering him gently to the ground and covering him with a blanket. Norton followed a moment later, and immediately fell to his knees. Bullock had already prepared two mugs of lukewarm Bovril. He passed one to Somervell as Norton eased himself onto a mattress and lay flat on his back. No one spoke as they waited for the two men to recover.

George undid Somervell's laces and gently pulled off his boots, then began to rub his feet to get some circulation back. Bullock held one of the mugs of Bovril to Norton's lips, but he was unable to take even a sip. Although George had never believed patience was a virtue, he somehow managed to remain silent, despite being desperate to know if either of them had reached the summit.

To everyone's surprise, it was Somervell who spoke first. 'Long before we reached the Second Step,' he began, 'we decided not to climb it, but to skirt round the Yellow Band. A longer route, but safer,' he added between breaths. 'We traversed across it until we came to a massive couloir. I thought that if we were able to cross it, we could progress all the way to the final pyramid, where the gradient would be less demanding. Our progress was slow, but I still believed we had enough time to make it to the top.'

But did you? George wanted to ask, as Somervell sat up and took another sip of now cold Bovril.

'That was until we reached 27,400 feet, when my throat started to play up again. I began coughing up phlegm, and when Norton slapped me on the back with all the force he could muster, I brought up nearly half my larynx. I tried to struggle on, but by the time we reached 28,000 feet I couldn't put one foot in front of the other. I had to stop and rest, but I could see the peak ahead of me, so I insisted that Norton carried on. I sat there watching him climb towards the summit, until he was out of sight.'

George turned to Norton and quietly asked, 'Did you make it?'

'No, I didn't,' said Norton. 'Because when I stopped to rest, I made the classic mistake.'

'Don't tell me you took your goggles off?' said George in disbelief.

'How many times have you warned us never to do that, in any circumstances?' said Norton as he removed the arm that was covering his eyes. 'By the time I replaced them, my eyelids had almost frozen together and I couldn't see a pace in front of me. I called out to alert Somervell, he yodelled to let me know where he was, and I slowly made my way back down to join him.'

'Some glee club,' said Somervell, attempting a smile. 'With the aid of my torch we were able to make our way back down, if somewhat slowly.'

'Thank God for Somervell,' said Norton as Odell placed a handkerchief that he'd soaked in warm water over his eyes.

It was some time before either man spoke again. Norton drew a deep breath. 'I don't believe that there's ever been a better example of the blind leading the blind.'

This time George did laugh. 'So what height did you reach?'

'I've no idea, old man,' Norton said, and passed his altimeter to Mallory.

George studied the altimeter for a moment before he

announced, 'Twenty-eight thousand, one hundred and twenty-five feet. Many congratulations, old chap.'

'For failing to climb the final 877 feet?' said Norton, sounding desperately disappointed.

'No. For making history,' said George, 'because you've regained the altitude record. I can't wait to see Finch's face when I tell him.'

'It's kind of you to say so,' said Norton, 'but Finch would be the first to remind me that I should have listened to him and agreed to use oxygen.' He paused before adding, 'If this weather holds, I expect to be nothing more than a footnote in history, because, if you'll forgive the cliché, old fellow, you should walk it.'

George smiled, but made no comment.

Somervell added, 'I agree with Norton. Frankly, the best thing you, Odell and Irvine can do is make sure you get a good night's sleep.'

George nodded, and although they had all been together for over three months, he shook hands with both his colleagues before returning to his own tent to try to capture that good night's sleep.

He might even have succeeded if one of Norton's remarks hadn't remained constantly on his mind: *If this weather holds . . .*

58

Friday, June 6th, 1924

And then there were three.

George rose long before dawn to witness a full moon glistening on the snow, making it look like a lawn of finely cut diamonds. Despite the temperature being minus thirty degrees, he felt a warm glow, and a confidence that they would succeed, even if he hadn't made up his mind who *they* would be.

Did he really need to bother with oxygen after Norton and Somervell had come so close? And hadn't Odell proved to be better acclimatized than either of them? Or would Odell once again fall by the wayside just when the prize was within his grasp? Would Irvine's inexperience become a liability when they stepped into uncharted territory? Or perhaps his enthusiasm, supported by those blessed oxygen cylinders, would be the only thing that would guarantee success?

'Good morning, sir,' said a voice behind him.

George swung round, to be greeted by Irvine's infectious grin. 'Good morning, Sandy,' he replied. 'Shall we go and have some breakfast?'

'But it's only five o'clock,' said Irvine, checking his watch. 'In any case, Odell is still asleep.'

'Then wake him up,' said George. 'We must be on our way by six.'

'Six?' said Irvine. 'But at your final briefing yesterday evening you told us to be up in time for breakfast at eight, ready to move off at nine, because you didn't want to spend any longer than necessary perched on a ledge at 27,000 feet.'

'Six thirty, then,' conceded George. 'If Odell isn't up by then, we'll leave without him. And while you're at it, young man, why don't you do something useful for a change?'

'Like what, sir?'

'Go and make my breakfast.'

The infectious grin returned. 'I can offer you sardines on biscuit, lightly grilled, sardines off the bone with raisins, or the speciality of our tent, sardines—'

'Just get on with it,' said George.

◄○►

Mallory, Odell and Irvine, accompanied by five Sherpas carrying tents, equipment and provisions, left the North Col just after 7.30 on the morning of June 6th. Odell had missed breakfast, but he didn't complain. Guy Bullock was the last to shake hands with George before he left. 'See you in a couple of days, old friend,' he said.

'Yes. Keep the kettle boiling.'

As George's old housemaster Mr Irving – George wondered if he was still alive – used to say, you can never start too early, only too late. George set off like a man possessed, at a pace Odell and Irvine found difficult to match.

He kept peering suspiciously up at the clear blue sky, trying to detect the slightest suggestion of wind, the appearance of a single wisp of cloud or the first flake of snow that might alter all his best laid plans, but the sky remained resolutely calm and undisturbed. However, he knew from bitter experience that this particular lady could change her mind in the blink of an eye. He also kept a close watch on his two companions to see if either of them appeared to be in any trouble, almost hoping that one of them would fall behind, and take the final decision out of his hands. But as hour succeeded hour, he reluctantly concluded that there was nothing to choose between them.

The party reached Camp V a few minutes after three that

afternoon, well ahead of schedule. George checked his watch and tried to make a calculation. When Hannibal crossed the Alps, he had always allowed the sun to make such decisions for him. Should he press on to Camp VI, and try to save a day? Or would that result in them being so exhausted that they wouldn't be able to take on the more important challenge ahead? He chose caution, and decided on an early night so they could set out for Camp VI first thing in the morning. But who would he set out with? Which one of them would accompany him to the summit, and which would be accompanying the Sherpas back to the North Col?

Turning in early didn't guarantee a night's sleep for George. Every hour or so he would wake, poke his head out of the tent and check if he could still see stars few others had witnessed with such clarity. He could. Irvine slept like a child, and Odell even had the nerve to snore. George looked across at them while he continued to wrestle with the problem as to who should join him for the final climb. Should it be Odell, who after years of dedication had surely earned his chance – probably his last chance? Or should it be Irvine? After all, it would only be human for the young man to be dreaming of his place in the sun, but if he were not selected, he would still have many years ahead of him in which to try again.

George was certain of only one thing. This was his last chance.

—◇—

Just after four o'clock the following morning, with the moon still shining peacefully down on them, the three men set off again. Their pace slowed with each hour that passed, until it was no more than a shuffle. If either Odell or Irvine was suffering from the experience, neither gave the slightest hint of it as they continued doggedly in their leader's footsteps.

The sun was beginning to set by the time the North-East Shoulder came into sight. George checked his altimeter: 27,100 feet. Half an hour and 230 feet later, the three of them collapsed exhausted, and mightily relieved to find Norton and Somervell's small tent still in place. George could no longer put off making his final decision, because three men weren't going to be able to sleep in that small space, and there certainly wasn't enough room on the ridge to pitch a second tent.

George sat on the ground and scribbled a note to Norton to inform him of their progress, and that they would attempt the final ascent in the morning. He stood up, and looked at both silent men before handing the note to Odell. 'Would you please take this back down to the North Col, old fellow, and see that Norton gets it?'

Odell betrayed no sign of emotion. He simply bowed.

'I'm sorry, old chap,' added George. He was about to explain his reasons when Odell said, 'You've made the right decision, skipper.' He shook hands with George, and then with the young man he had recommended to the RGS should replace Finch as a member of the climbing team. 'Good luck,' he said, before turning his back on them to begin the lonely journey down to Camp V to spend the night, before returning to the North Col the following morning.

And then there were two.

59

June 7th, 1924

My darling,

 I'm sitting in a tiny tent some 27,300 feet above sea level, and almost 5,000 miles from my homeland, seeking the paths of glory . . .

'Don't you ever sleep?' asked Irvine as he sat up and rubbed his eyes.

'Only on the way down,' said George. 'So by this time tomorrow I'll be sound asleep.'

'By this time tomorrow they'll be hailing you as the new St George after you've finally slain your personal dragon,' said Irvine, adjusting an indicator on one of the oxygen cylinders.

'I don't recall St George having to rely on oxygen when he slew the dragon.'

'If Hinks had been in charge at the time,' said Irvine, 'St George wouldn't even have been allowed the use of a sword. "Against the spirit of the amateur code, don't you know, old chap,"' added Irvine as he touched an imaginary moustache. 'You must strangle the wretched beast with your bare hands.'

George laughed at Irvine's plausible imitation of the RGS secretary. 'Well, if I'm going to break with the amateur spirit,' he said, 'I'll need to know if your blessed oxygen cylinders will be up and running by four o'clock tomorrow morning. Otherwise I'll be sending you back to the North Col to ask Odell to take your place.'

'Not a chance,' said Irvine. 'All four of them are in perfect working order, which should give us more than enough oxygen, assuming you don't plan to take longer than eight hours to cover a mere 2,000 feet and back.'

'You'll find out what a *mere* 2,000 feet feels like only too soon, young man. And I'd have a darn sight better chance of achieving it if you were to go back to sleep so I can finish this letter to my wife.'

'You write to Mrs Mallory every day, don't you?'

'Yes,' replied George. 'And if you're lucky enough to find someone half as remarkable, you'll end up feeling exactly the same way.'

'I think I already have,' said Irvine, lying back down. 'It's just that I forgot to tell her before I left, so I'm not absolutely sure if she knows how I feel.'

'She'll know,' said George, 'believe me. But if you're in doubt, you could always drop her a line – that's assuming writing is still a form of communication they're using at Oxford.'

George waited for a barbed riposte, but none followed, as the lad had already fallen back into a deep slumber. He smiled and continued his letter to Ruth.

After he'd shakily scribbled *your loving husband, George*, and sealed the envelope, he read Gray's *Elegy Written in a Country Churchyard*, before finally blowing out the candle and falling asleep.

Sunday, June 8th, 1924

'Would you like me to remove the scarf, old chum?' asked Odell.

'Yes, please do,' said Norton.

Odell lifted the silk scarf gently off Norton's face.

'Oh Christ, I still can't see a thing,' said Norton.

'Don't panic,' said Somervell. 'It's not unusual for it to take two or three days for your sight to begin to recover following a bout of snow blindness. In any case, we're not going anywhere until Mallory comes back down.'

'It's not down I'm worried about,' snapped Norton. 'It's up. Odell, I want you to return to Camp VI, and take a jar of Bovril and a supply of Kendal Mint Cake with you, because you can be sure that Mallory's forgotten to pack something.'

'I'm on my way,' said Odell. He peered out of the tent. 'I've never known better conditions for climbing.'

◄○►

George woke a few minutes after four to find Irvine preparing breakfast.

'What's on the menu for Ascension Day?' he asked as he poked his head out of the tent to check on the weather. Despite being hit by a blast of cold air that made his ears tingle, what he saw brought a smile to his face.

'Macaroni and sardines,' replied Irvine.

'An interesting combination,' said George. 'But I have a feeling it won't make the next edition of Mrs Beeton's cookbook.'

'I might have been able to offer you a little more choice,' said Irvine with a grin, 'if you'd remembered to pack your rations.'

'I do apologize, old chap,' said George. 'Mea culpa.'

'No skin off my nose,' said Irvine, 'because frankly I'm far too nervous to even think about eating.' He pulled on an old flying jacket, not unlike the one George's brother Trafford had been wearing when he'd last visited The Holt on leave. George wondered how Irvine had acquired it, because he was far too young to have served in the war.

'My housemaster's,' explained Irvine as he did up the buttons, answering George's unasked question.

'Stop trying to make me feel so old,' said George.

Irvine laughed. 'I'll fix up your oxygen cylinders while you're having breakfast.'

'A couple of sardines and a short note to Odell, and I'll be with you.'

Outside the tent, the morning sun almost blinded Irvine as it shone down from a clear blue sky.

Once George had eaten what was left of the sardines, having ignored the macaroni, he scribbled a quick note to Odell and left it on his sleeping bag. He'd have put money on Odell returning to Camp VI that day.

George had slept in four layers of clothes, and he now added a thick woollen vest and a woven silk shirt, followed by a flannel shirt and another silk shirt. He then put on a cotton Burberry jacket known as a Shackleton smock, before pulling on a pair of baggy gaberdine trousers. He strapped a pair of cashmere puttees around his ankles, pulled on his boots and slipped on a pair of woollen mittens that had been knitted by Ruth. He finally put on his brother's leather flying cap before grabbing the latest pair of goggles, donated by Finch. He was glad there wasn't a mirror available, although Chomolungma would have agreed that he was correctly dressed for an audience with Her Majesty.

George crawled out of the tent to join Irvine, who helped him on with a set of oxygen cylinders. Once they were strapped to his back, George wondered if the extra weight would prove more of a disadvantage than not being able to breathe regularly. But he'd made that decision when he sent Odell back. The last ritual the two men carried out was to smear zinc oxide all over the exposed parts of each other's faces. Before setting off up the mountain they squinted at the summit, which looked so close.

'Be warned,' said George, 'she's a Jezebel. She grows even more alluring the closer you come to her, and this morning she's even tempting us with a spell of perfect weather. But like any woman, it's her privilege to change her mind.' He checked his watch: 5.07. He would have liked to start a little earlier. 'Come on, young man,' he said. 'In the words of my beloved father, it's time to put our best foot forward.' He adjusted his mouthpiece and turned on the oxygen supply.

◄○►

If only Hinks could see me now, thought Odell as he climbed the last few feet to Camp VI. When he reached the tent he fell on his knees and pulled back the flap, to encounter the sort of mess one might expect after having left two children to spend the night in a treehouse: a plate of unfinished macaroni, an empty sardine tin and a compass that George must have left behind. Odell chuckled as he crawled in and set about tidying up. It wouldn't have been Mallory's tent if he hadn't left something behind.

Odell was placing the Bovril and a couple of bars of Kendal Mint Cake on George's sleeping bag when he spotted the two envelopes – one addressed to 'Mrs George Mallory, The Holt, Godalming, Surrey, England', which he put in an inside pocket, and one with his own name scrawled across it. He tore the envelope open.

> *Dear Odell,*
>   *Awfully sorry to have left things in such a mess. Perfect weather for the job. Start looking for us either crossing the rock band or going up the skyline.*
>   *See you tomorrow.*
>   *Yours ever,*
>   *George*

Odell smiled, and once he'd double-checked that everything was in place for the returning heroes, he crawled out of the tent backwards, then stood and stretched his arms above his head as he looked up at the highest peak in the world. The weather was so perfect that for a moment he was even tempted to follow them, as he couldn't help feeling a little envious of his two colleagues who must by now be approaching the summit.

And then suddenly he spotted two figures silhouetted against the skyline. As he watched, the taller of the two walked across to join the other. He could see that they were standing on the Second Step, about 600 feet from the summit. He checked his watch: 12.50. They still had more than enough time to reach the top and be back in their little tent before the last rays of sunlight disappeared.

He couldn't stop himself from leaping up and down with joy as he watched them stride into a cloud of mist, and disappear from sight.

◄○►

Once Irvine had reached the top of the Second Step, he clambered over a jagged piece of rock and joined George.

'We've got about another six hundred feet to go,' said George, checking his altimeter. 'But remember, that's equivalent to at least a mile, and without oxygen Norton could only manage about 125 feet an hour. So it could take us another three hours,' he added between breaths, 'which means we can't afford to waste any time, because when we start back down that rock face later this afternoon,' he said, pointing upwards, 'I want to be sure I can still see several feet in front of me.'

As George replaced his mouthpiece, Irvine gave him the thumbs-up sign. Then they began the slow trek along a ridgeline no man had ever trodden before.

60

When George looked up again, it appeared as if the peak was within touching distance, despite the altimeter warning him that they still had over 300 feet to climb. So breathtakingly close, even if it had taken far longer than he had bargained for.

Once they had conquered the Second Step, the two of them chipped, pushed and pulled their way slowly up the narrow north-east ridgeline, aware that the snow on either side of them was like the eaves of a roof, with nothing below but air. They would only have to stray a few feet either way, and . . .

The inviting-looking fresh, untrodden snow had turned out to be two feet deep, making it almost impossible to take a step forward, and when they did, their feet only advanced a few inches before sinking once again into the snow.

Two hundred and eleven steps later – George counted every one of them – and they were finally released from the snowdrift, only to be confronted by a sheer rock face that would have been a challenge for him on a warm summer's morning at 3,000 feet, let alone when his body was soaked with sweat, his limbs almost frozen and he was so exhausted that all he wanted to do was lie down and sleep, even though he knew that at minus forty degrees, if he was to stay still for more than a few moments, he would freeze to death.

George even considered turning back while there was still a

good chance that they would be safely under canvas before sunset. But then he would have had to spend the rest of his life explaining why he'd let the prize slip from his grasp at the last moment and, worse, when he fell asleep, each night he would dream of climbing those last 300 feet, only to wake from the nightmare in a cold sweat.

He turned round to see an exhausted Irvine pulling his foot out of the snow, only to stare in disbelief at the rock face that stood in front of them. For a moment George hesitated. Did he have the right to risk Irvine's life as well as his own? Should he, even now, suggest that the young man turn back while he went on alone, or rest and wait for him to return? He banished the thought from his mind. After all, Irvine had surely earned the right to share the spoils of triumph with him. George removed his mouthpiece and said, 'We're nearly there, old chap. This rock will be the last obstacle before we reach the top.' Irvine gave him a thin smile.

George turned round to face a vertical rock, covered with ice that never melted from one year to the next. He searched for somewhere he could gain a toehold. Normally, he would place his first step at about eighteen inches, perhaps even two feet, but not today, when a few inches would prove a mountain in itself. With a trembling hand he grasped a ledge inches above his head and pulled himself slowly up. He lifted a boot and searched for a foothold so he could raise his other arm and progress a few more inches on the vertical journey to the top of the rock. He tried not to think what it was going to be like on the way down. His brain screamed *turn back*, but his heart whispered *carry on*.

Forty minutes later he heaved himself up onto the top of the rock and pulled the rope taut to make his colleague's task a little easier. Once Irvine had clambered up to join him, George checked the altimeter: 112 feet left to climb. He looked up, this time to be faced with a sheet of ice that had built up over the years into a cornice overhanging the East Face, which would have prevented even a four-legged animal with spiked hooves from progressing any further.

George was trying to secure a foothold when a flash of

lightning struck the mountain below him, followed moments later by a clap of thunder. He assumed they were about to be engulfed by a storm, but as he looked down, he realized that they were far above the tempest, which must have been venting its fury on his colleagues some 2,000 feet below them. It was the first time George had viewed a storm from above, and he could only hope that by the time they descended it would have moved on, leaving in its wake the still, clear air that so often follows such anger.

Once again, George lifted his boot and tried to gain some purchase on the ice. The surface immediately cracked, and his heel skidded back down the slope. He almost laughed. Could things get any worse? He thrust his axe into the ice in front of him. This time it didn't crack quite so easily, but when it did, he placed a foot in the hole. It still slithered back a few inches. He didn't laugh when he recalled the saying, two paces forward, one pace back. He was now having to satisfy himself with one foot forward, six inches back. After a dozen such steps, the narrow ridge became even thinner until he had to fall on all fours and begin crawling. He didn't look to his left or right, because he knew that on both sides of him was a sheer drop of several hundred feet. Look up, ignore everything around you and battle on. Another yard forward, another half yard back. Just how much could the body endure? Then, suddenly, he felt solid rock below him, and was able to climb out of the bed of ice and stand on rough, stony ground only fifty, perhaps sixty feet from the summit. He turned round to see an exhausted Irvine still on his hands and knees.

'Only fifty feet to go,' he shouted, as he untied the rope so that both men could continue at their own pace.

It was another twenty minutes before George Leigh Mallory placed a hand, his right hand, on the summit of Everest. He pulled himself slowly up onto the top and lay flat on his stomach. 'Hardly a moment of triumph,' was his first thought. He pushed himself up onto his knees, and then, with a supreme effort, he somehow managed to stand up. The first man to stand on top of the earth.

He looked across the Himalaya, admiring a view no man had

ever seen before. He wanted to leap up and down with joy and shout triumphantly at the top of his voice, but he had neither the energy nor the breath to do so. Instead he turned a slow circle; the biting wind which seemed to come at him from every direction did not allow him to move any faster. A myriad of unconquered mountains stood proudly around him, heads bowed in the presence of their monarch.

A strange thought crossed his mind. He must remember to tell Clare that the top of Everest was about the same size as their dining-room table.

George checked his watch: 3.36pm. He tried to convince himself that they had more than enough time to return to the safety of their little tent at Camp VI, especially if it turned out to be a clear night with no wind.

He looked back down to see Irvine moving ever closer, even if it was at a snail's pace. Would he falter at the last step? Then, like a child who couldn't yet walk, Irvine crawled up onto the summit.

Once George had helped him to his feet, he fumbled around in the pocket of his Shackleton smock, only hoping that he hadn't forgotten what he was looking for. His fingers were so numb with cold that he nearly dropped his Vest Pocket camera over the side. Once he'd steadied himself, he took a photograph of Irvine, arms held high above his head as if he'd just won the boat race. He passed the Kodak to his companion, who took a photo of him trying to look as if he'd been for a bracing walk in the Welsh hills.

George checked his watch again, and frowned. He pointed firmly down the mountain. Irvine placed the camera in a trouser pocket and buttoned up the proof of what they had achieved.

George was about to take the first step back down, when he recalled his promise to Ruth. With heavy, ice-covered fingers, he clumsily pulled out his wallet and extracted the sepia photograph that he always took with him on every trip. He gave his wife one last look and smiled, before placing her image on the highest point on earth. He put his hand back in his pocket and began rummaging around.

'The King of England sends his compliments, ma'am,' he said, giving a bow, 'and hopes that you will grant his humble subjects safe passage back to their homeland.'

George smiled. George cursed.

He'd forgotten to bring Geoffrey Young's sovereign.

61

5.49pm, Sunday, June 8th, 1924

When Odell arrived back at Camp IV, he was unable to conceal his excitement. He crawled into Norton's tent and told him what he'd seen.

'About six hundred feet from the summit, you say?' said Norton, still lying flat on his back.

'Yes,' said Odell, 'I'm certain of it. They were standing on the Second Step when I saw one of them walk towards the other before going strong for the top.'

'Then nothing should stop them now,' said Bullock as he placed a fresh warm cloth over Norton's eyes.

'Let's hope you're right,' said Somervell. 'But I still think it would be wise for Odell to write down the details of everything he saw while they're fresh in his mind. It might turn out to be significant when the history of the expedition is written.'

Odell crawled across to his rucksack and took out his diary. He sat in a corner of the tent and for the next twenty minutes wrote down everything he had witnessed that morning. Exactly where he'd seen the two figures, the time at which they continued up the mountain, and the fact that they appeared to be in no difficulty as they disappeared into the mist. When he'd finished, he checked his watch: 6.58pm. Were Mallory and Irvine safely back in their tent at Camp VI, having stood on top of the earth?

◄○►

Once they'd roped up, George's first thought as he stepped off the summit of Everest was to wonder how long his oxygen would last. Irvine had joked about them not taking more than eight hours, but they must surely be approaching that deadline. His second thought was to wonder how many hours were left in the sun's rays, because that was something you couldn't alter with the twiddling of a valve. Finally, he hoped it would be a clear night, which would allow the moon to accompany them on the last steps of their journey home.

He was surprised to find that once they had attained the prize, the rush of adrenaline had deserted him, and all he had left was the will to survive.

After covering a mere fifty feet, George wanted to sit down and rest, but with his body so fatigued and racked with pain, he knew that if he closed his eyes even for a moment, he might never open them again.

He jabbed his ice axe into the cracked surface, took a step backwards and immediately felt the rope tighten. Irvine must be finding the journey down even more difficult than he was, if that was possible. George tentatively placed his left foot back onto the icy slope that was now even more treacherous than before. He tried to take advantage of the finger and toeholds he'd left behind on the way up, but they were already icing over. Despite losing his balance and falling on his backside several times, he managed to keep moving until he had safely reached the patch of stony ground, only to find himself once again standing above a sheer icy rock face, this time looking down. George knew that this would be the most dangerous part of the climb, and he had to assume that Irvine was in an even worse state than he was. If either of them made the slightest error, they would both tumble to their deaths. He turned to his companion and smiled. For the first time, Irvine did not return his smile.

George gripped the top of the rock with both hands and slowly lowered himself a few inches, searching for the slightest indentation that might secure a toehold. Once his toe had found a step, he lowered his other leg. Suddenly he felt the rope go slack. He looked up to see that Irvine had lost his grip on an icy ledge, and was falling backwards. His body passed George a moment later.

George knew that he couldn't hope to cling onto an icy, vertical rock face while the six-foot-two-inch, sixteen-stone man to whom he was roped was falling through the air. An instant later he was pulled off the rock. He didn't even have a chance to think about death as he followed Irvine down, down, down . . .

A second later, they both landed in the two feet of thick snow that had so bedevilled them on the way up, and which now acted as a cushion to save their lives. After a brief, stunned silence, they both began laughing, like two naughty schoolboys who'd fallen out of a tree and were buried in Christmas snow.

George rose slowly and checked his limbs. He stood unsteadily, pleased to see Irvine already on his feet. The two men collapsed into each other's arms, and George began slapping his young colleague on the back. He finally released him and gave Irvine the thumbs-up before once again setting off down the mountain.

George knew nothing was going to stop him now.

62

When Odell rose at five the following morning, the first thing he saw was Noel setting up his tripod on a small, flat ridge. The massive lens of his camera was pointing in the direction of Camp VI, ready to roll at the slightest sign of life. A moment later, Norton crawled out to join them.

'Good morning, Odell,' he said cheerfully. 'I confess that for the moment you're no more than a blur, but at least I can tell the difference between you and Noel – just.'

'That's good news,' said Noel, 'because I hope it won't be too long before we see George and Sandy coming over the skyline.'

'Don't count on it,' said Norton. 'Mallory's never been an early riser, and I expect young Irvine will still be fast asleep.'

'I can't hang around waiting for them any longer,' said Odell. 'I'm going up to cook them some breakfast, and then I'll escort them back down in triumph.'

'Before you leave, old man,' said Noel, 'once you get up there would you do something for me?' Odell turned to face him. 'Could you drag their sleeping bags out of the tent and lay them side by side in the snow, and then we'll know they reached the summit?'

'And if they didn't?' He paused. 'Or worse?'

'Place the bags in the sign of a cross,' said Noel quietly.

Odell nodded, pulled on his rucksack and began the climb

back to Camp VI for the second time in three days. But this time the weather was becoming worse by the minute. Within moments he was battling against a savage wind that was whipping down the valley, a clear warning that within hours the monsoon would be upon them. He kept looking up anxiously, hoping to see his two triumphant colleagues on their way down.

As he came closer and closer to Camp VI, he tried to dismiss from his mind the thought that they might have come to any harm. But when he finally spotted the small tent, it was covered in a layer of fresh snow, with no telltale footprints in sight, and its green canvas flapping in the wind.

Odell attempted to quicken his pace, but it was pointless, because his heavy boots just sank deeper and deeper into the fresh snow until it felt as if he was treading water. He finally gave up, fell on his knees and began to crawl the last few feet towards the tent. He poked his head inside and took off his goggles, hoping to see an untidy mess left by two exhausted men who were fast asleep. But in truth, he already knew that was wishful thinking. He stared in disbelief. Odell would tell his friends for many years to come that it was like looking at a still-life painting. The sleeping bags had not been slept in, the jar of Bovril was unopened and the bars of Kendal Mint Cake had not been unwrapped, while beside them stood a candle that had not been relit.

Odell put on his goggles and backed out of the tent. He pushed himself up off his knees and looked up towards the mountain peak, but could no longer see more than a few feet in front of him. He screamed, 'George! Sandy!' at the top of his voice, but the lashing wind and drifting snow beat his words back. He kept on shouting until his voice was just a whimper and he could barely hear himself above the noise of the gale. He finally gave up, but not until he accepted that his own life was in danger. He crawled back towards the tent, and reluctantly pulled out one sleeping bag and placed it on the side of the mountain.

◄◦►

'Someone's dragging out one of the sleeping bags,' announced Noel.

'What's the message?' cried Norton.

'Not sure yet. Ah, he's dragging the other one out now.'

Noel focused on the moving figure.

'Is it George?' shouted Norton, looking hopefully up the mountain, a hand shielding his eyes from the driving snow. Noel didn't reply. He just bowed his head.

Somervell shuffled across the ridge as quickly as he could, and took Noel's place behind the camera. He peered through the viewfinder.

The whole lens was filled with the sign of a cross.

EPILOGUE

He who would valiant be 'gainst all disaster

If George Leigh Mallory had been surprised by the reception he received on returning to England following the 1922 expedition, what would he have made of the memorial service that was held in St Paul's Cathedral in his honour? No body, no casket, no grave, yet thousands of ordinary citizens had travelled the length and breadth of the land to line the streets and pay homage.

Let him in constancy follow the master

His Majesty the King, the Prince of Wales, the Duke of Connaught and Prince Arthur were all represented, with the Prime Minister, Ramsay MacDonald, the former Foreign Secretary Lord Curzon, the Lord Mayor of London and the Mayor of Birkenhead in attendance.

There's no discouragement shall make him once relent

General Bruce stood at the east end of the cathedral and lined up Lieutenant Colonel Norton, Dr Somervell, Professor Odell, Major Bullock, Major Morshead, Captain Noel and Geoffrey Young to form the guard of honour. They carried silver ice axes under their right arms as they followed the Dean of St Paul's down the nave past the crowded pews, and took their places in the front row next to Sir Francis Younghusband, Mr Hinks, Mr Raeburn and Commander Ashcroft, who were there to represent the Royal Geographical Society.

His first avowed intent to be a pilgrim

When the Bishop of Chester mounted the pulpit steps to address the packed congregation, he opened his eulogy by trying to articulate the people's feelings of affection and admiration for the two lads from Birkenhead, who, on Ascension Day, had captured the imagination of the world.

'We will never know,' he went on to say, 'if together they reached the summit of that great mountain. But who among us can doubt that if the prize was within his grasp, George Mallory would have battled on whatever the odds, and that young Sandy Irvine would have followed him to the ends of the earth?'

Ruth Mallory, who was seated in the front row on the other side of the aisle, was in no doubt that her husband wouldn't have turned back if there was even the slightest possibility of achieving his wildest dream. Nor did the Reverend Herbert Leigh Mallory, who sat beside his daughter-in-law. Hugh Thackeray Turner, seated on the other side of his daughter, would go to his grave without offering an opinion.

Who so beset him round with dismal stories

After the Dean of St Paul's had given the blessing, and the captains and the kings had departed, Ruth stood alone by the north door, shaking hands with friends and well-wishers, many of whom told her how their lives had been enriched by this gallant and courageous gentleman.

She smiled when she saw George Finch, waiting in line to speak to her. He was dressed in a dark grey suit, white shirt and black tie that looked as if they were being worn for the first time. He bowed as he shook her hand. Ruth leant forward and whispered in his ear, 'If it had been you who was climbing with George, he might still be alive today.'

Finch didn't voice his long-held opinion that had he been invited to join the expedition, he and Mallory would surely have reached the summit together and, more importantly, returned home safely. Although Finch accepted that if they had been in any trouble, Mallory might have ignored his advice and carried on, leaving him to return alone.

Do but themselves confound, his strength the more is

At last Ruth's father felt the time had come to take his daughter home, despite the fact that so many mourners still wished to pay their respects.

On the drive back to Godalming, hardly a word passed between them. But then, Ruth had lost the only man she had ever loved, and old gentlemen do not expect to attend the funerals of their sons-in-law. As they passed through the gates of The Holt, Ruth thanked her father for his kindness and understanding, but asked if she could be left alone to grieve. He reluctantly departed, and returned to Westbrook.

No foes shall stay his might, though he with giants fight

When Ruth opened the front door, the first thing she saw lying on the mat was an envelope, addressed to her in George's unmistakable hand. She picked it up, painfully aware that it must be his last letter. She walked through to the drawing room and poured herself what George would have called 'a stiff whisky' before taking her seat in the winged chair by the window. She looked up at the driveway, somehow still expecting George to come striding through the gates and take her in his arms.

He will make good his right to be a pilgrim

Ruth tore open the envelope, took out the letter and began to read her husband's last words.

June 7th, 1924

My darling,

I'm sitting in a tiny tent some 27,300 feet above sea level, and almost 5,000 miles from my homeland, seeking the paths of glory. Even if I were to find them, it would be as nothing, if I am unable to share the moment with you.

I should not have needed to travel halfway round the world to discover that without you I am nothing, as many less fortunate men with envy in their eyes have oft reminded me, and they do not know the half. Ask any one of them what he would sacrifice for that first moment of passion to last a lifetime, and he would tell you half his days, because no such woman exists. They are wrong. I have found that woman, and nothing will ever take her place, certainly not this ice-cold maiden that slumbers above me.

Some men boast of their conquests. The truth is, I've had but one, as I loved you from the moment I first saw you. You are my waking morning, you are my setting sun.

And if that were not enough, I still marvel at my good fortune, for I have been thrice blessed.

The first blessing came on the day you became my wife and agreed to share the rest of your life with me. That night you became my lover, and since have become my closest friend.

The second blessing came when you unselfishly encouraged me to fulfil my wildest dream, always allowing my head to remain in the clouds while you, somehow, managed with wisdom and common sense, to keep your feet firmly on the ground.

And thrice you have blessed me with a wonderful family, who continue to bring unending joy to my life, although there are never enough minutes in each day to share their laughter and brush away their tears. I often regret depriving myself of so much of their brief years of childhood.

Clare will follow me to Cambridge, where she will not only outwit untested men, but when put to the test herself will surely succeed where I failed. Beridge has been gifted with your grace and charm, growing daily in your image so that when she blossoms into a woman, many men will bend low to seek her hand, but for me, none will be worthy. And as for little John, I cannot wait to read his first school report, watch his first football match, and be by his side when he has to face up to what he imagines to be his first disaster.

My darling, there is so much more that I want to say, but my hand grows shaky, and the flickering candle reminds me *that I still have some purpose on the morrow, when I intend to place your photograph on the highest point on earth so that I might exorcize this demon for ever, and finally return to the only woman I have ever loved.*

I can see you at The Holt, sitting in your winged chair by the window, reading this letter and smiling as you turn each page. Look up, my darling, for at any moment you will see me march through those gates and come striding down the path towards you. Will you leap up and rush to greet me, so that I can take you in my arms and never leave your side again?

Forgive me for having taken so long to realize that you are more important to me than life itself.

Your loving husband,
   George

At the same time every day for the rest of her life, Ruth Mallory would sit in the winged chair by the window and reread her husband's letter.

On her deathbed, she told her children that not a day had passed when she hadn't seen George march through those gates and come striding down the path towards her.

POST 1924

George Leigh Mallory

George's body was discovered on May 1st, 1999 at 26,760 feet. The photo of his wife Ruth was not in his wallet and there was no sign of a camera. To this day, the climbing fraternity are divided as to whether he was the first person to conquer Everest. Few doubt that he was capable of doing so.

Sandy Irvine

When Irvine's death was announced in *The Times*, three women came forward claiming to be engaged to him.

Despite several expeditions in search of his body, it has not been found. However, in 1975 a Chinese mountaineer, Xu Jing, told a colleague that he'd come across a body, which he described as *the English dead*, frozen in a narrow gully at 27,230 feet. A few days later, before he could be questioned more closely, Xu Jing was killed by an avalanche.

Ruth Mallory

After George's death, Ruth and the children remained in Surrey, where Ruth spent the rest of her life. She died of breast cancer in 1942, aged fifty.

Air Chief Marshal Sir Trafford Leigh Mallory KCB

Mallory's brother Trafford died when his plane crashed in the Alps in November 1944, while he was on his way to take command of Allied Air Operations in the Pacific. It was thought he might have been piloting the aircraft at the time.

Trafford died at the age of fifty-two.

Arthur C Benson

Mallory's tutor became Master of Magdalene College, Cambridge in 1915, and remained in that position until 1925. He wrote a moving tribute for Mallory's memorial service at Cambridge, but was too ill to deliver it. He is best remembered for having written the words of 'Land of Hope and Glory'.

Benson died in 1925, aged sixty-three.

THE CLIMBERS

Brigadier General CG Bruce CB MVO

Although severely wounded at Gallipoli, Bruce commanded his regiment on the North West Frontier until 1920.

He was President of the Alpine Club from 1923 to 1925, and appointed Hon. Colonel of the 5th Gurkha Rifles in 1931.

Bruce died in 1939, aged seventy-three.

Geoffrey Young D.Litt FRSL

Appointed as a consultant to the Rockefeller Foundation in 1925. Reader in Education at London University in 1932. President of the Alpine Club from 1940 to 1943. Young climbed the Matterhorn (14,692 feet) in 1928 aged fifty-two, and Zinal Rothorn (11,204 feet) in 1935 aged fifty-nine, despite being burdened with an artificial leg.

Young died in 1958, aged eighty-two.

George Finch FRS MBE

Appointed a Fellow of the Royal Society in 1938. President of the Alpine Club from 1959 to 1961. In 1931 three of Finch's friends fell to their deaths in the Alps, and he never climbed again.

Finch died in 1970, aged eighty-two.

His son, Peter Finch, became an actor. Peter died before he found out that he'd won the 1976 Academy Award for Best Actor in the film *Network*.

Lt General Sir Edward Norton KBE DSO MC
Continued his career as a professional soldier, and after being ADC to King George VI was appointed Military Governor of Hong Kong. In 1926, awarded the Founder's Medal of the Royal Geographical Society.

Held the world altitude record, 28,125 feet, until 1953, when Sir Edmund Hillary and Sherpa Tensing conquered Everest.

Norton died in 1954, aged seventy.

T Howard Somervell OBE MA MB B.Ch FRCS
Spent the rest of his professional life as a surgeon in a mission hospital in Travancore, southern India, where he became one of the world's leading authorities on duodenal ulcers. In 1956 he retired and returned to England. President of the Alpine Club from 1962 to 1965.

Somervell died in 1975, after a bracing walk in the Lake District, aged eighty-five.

Professor Noel Odell
The Everest Committee turned down Odell's request to be a member of the 1936 expedition to Everest on account of his age, fifty-one. That same year, he scaled Nanda Devi at 25,645 feet, the highest mountain to have been climbed at that time. No member of the 1936 Everest expedition managed to reach 24,000 feet.

Odell spent the rest of his professional life as a geologist, holding professorships at Harvard and McGill. He retired to Cambridge where he was made an Honorary Fellow of Clare College.

Odell died in 1981, aged ninety-six.

Lt Colonel Henry Morshead DSO
The tops of three fingers of Morshead's right hand were amputated after returning from the Everest expedition of 1924. He returned

to India in 1926 as a surveyor. He was shot dead while out riding one evening in 1931, in Burma, by his sister's lover.

Morshead was forty-nine when he was murdered.

Captain John Noel

Continued his career as a professional photographer and film-maker. His film *The Epic of Everest* was seen by over a million people in Britain and America. His life's work is preserved in the National Film Archive.

Noel died in 1987, aged ninety-nine.

THE ROYAL GEOGRAPHICAL SOCIETY

Sir Francis Younghusband KCSI KCIE

Continued to serve on the Everest Committee as its chairman until 1934. In 1925 he wrote a bestselling book entitled *The Epic of Mount Everest*. All the proceeds were donated to the RGS. In 1936 he founded the World Congress of Faiths.

Younghusband died in 1942, aged seventy-nine.

Arthur Hinks FRS CBE

In 1912 Hinks was awarded the Gold Medal of the Royal Astronomical Society. In 1913, he was elected a Fellow of the Royal Society. In 1920, he was awarded the CBE for services to mountaineering. In 1938, he was awarded the Victoria Medal of the Royal Geographical Society, and remained Secretary to the Everest Committee until 1939.

Hinks died in 1945, aged seventy-two.

MALLORY'S FRIENDS

Guy Bullock

In 1938 Bullock was appointed Britain's resident minister in Ecuador. In 1944 he was appointed as Consul General to Brazzaville.

Bullock died in 1956, aged sixty-nine.

Mary Ann 'Cottie' Sanders

After her father was declared bankrupt, Cottie worked as a shop assistant in Woolworth's. She later became a bestselling novelist, writing under the pseudonym Ann Bridge. Several of her fictional heroes were thinly disguised versions of George Mallory. She married a diplomat, Sir Owen O'Malley, and remained a close friend of the Mallory family.

Cottie died in 1974, aged eighty-six.

THE REST OF THE MALLORY FAMILY

The Reverend Herbert Leigh Mallory MA

In 1931 George's father became a canon of Chester Cathedral. He died in 1943, aged eighty-seven.

Mrs Annie Mallory

Annie outlived her husband, both her sons and both of her daughters-in-law. She died in 1946, aged eighty-three.

Mallory's sisters

Mary, Mrs Ralph Brook, died in 1983, aged ninety-eight.

Avie, Mrs Harry Longridge, died in 1989, aged one hundred and two.

Mallory's children

Clare gained a first-class honours degree at Cambridge University. She married an American scientist, Glenn Millikan. They lived in California and had three sons. Clare's husband died in a climbing accident in Tennessee in 1947 and, like her mother, she was left to bring up three children.

Clare died in 2001, aged eighty-five.

Beridge became a doctor, and married David Robertson, a professor of English at Columbia University and the author of

George Mallory. They had two daughters and a son. Berry, like her mother, contracted breast cancer.

Beridge died in 1953, aged thirty-six.

John emigrated to South Africa, where he worked as a water engineer. He is married, and has five children. One of those children is George Leigh Mallory II.

George Leigh Mallory II
Mallory's grandson is a senior water engineer working on water supply projects in Victoria, Australia.

At 5.30am on May 14th, 1995, George Leigh Mallory II placed a laminated photograph of his grandparents, George and Ruth, on the summit of Everest. In his own words, he was *completing a little outstanding family business.*

THE END

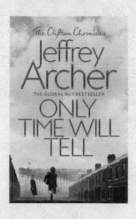

MAISIE CLIFTON

1919

PRELUDE

THIS STORY WOULD never have been written if I hadn't become pregnant. Mind you, I had always planned to lose my virginity on the works outing to Weston-super-Mare, just not to that particular man.

Arthur Clifton was born in Still House Lane, just like me; even went to the same school, Merrywood Elementary, but as I was two years younger than him he didn't know I existed. All the girls in my class had a crush on him, and not just because he captained the school football team.

Although Arthur had never shown any interest in me while I was at school, that changed soon after he'd returned from the Western Front. I'm not even sure he realized who I was when he asked me for a dance that Saturday night at the Palais but, to be fair, I had to look twice before I recognized him because he'd grown a pencil moustache and had his hair slicked back like Ronald Colman. He didn't look at another girl that night, and after we'd danced the last waltz I knew it would only be a matter of time before he asked me to marry him.

Arthur held my hand as we walked back home, and when we reached my front door he tried to kiss me. I turned away. After all, the Reverend Watts had told me often enough that I had to stay pure until the day I was married, and Miss Monday, our choir mistress, warned me that men only wanted one thing, and once they'd got it, they quickly lost interest. I often wondered if Miss Monday spoke from experience.

The following Saturday, Arthur invited me to the flicks to

see Lillian Gish in *Broken Blossoms*, and although I allowed him to put an arm around my shoulder, I still didn't let him kiss me. He didn't make a fuss. Truth is, Arthur was rather shy.

The next Saturday I did allow him to kiss me, but when he tried to put a hand inside my blouse, I pushed him away. In fact I didn't let him do that until he'd proposed, bought a ring and the Reverend Watts had read the banns a second time.

My brother Stan told me that I was the last known virgin on our side of the River Avon, though I suspect most of his conquests were in his mind. Still, I decided the time had come, and when better than the works outing to Weston-super-Mare with the man I was going to marry in a few weeks' time?

However, as soon as Arthur and Stan got off the charabanc, they headed straight for the nearest pub. But I'd spent the past month planning for this moment, so when I got off the coach, like a good girl guide, I was prepared.

I was walking towards the pier feeling pretty fed up when I became aware someone was following me. I looked around and was surprised when I saw who it was. He caught up with me and asked if I was on my own.

'Yes,' I said, aware that by now Arthur would be on his third pint.

When he put a hand on my bum, I should have slapped his face, but for several reasons I didn't. To start with, I thought about the advantages of having sex with someone I wasn't likely to come across again. And I have to admit I was flattered by his advances.

By the time Arthur and Stan would have been downing their eighth pints, he'd booked us into a guest house just off the seafront. They seemed to have a special rate for visitors who had no plans to spend the night. He started kissing me even before we'd reached the first landing, and once the bedroom door was closed he quickly undid the buttons of my blouse. It obviously wasn't his first time. In fact, I'm pretty sure I wasn't the first girl he'd had on a works outing. Otherwise, how did he know about the special rates?

I must confess I hadn't expected it to be all over quite so

quickly. Once he'd climbed off me, I disappeared into the bathroom, while he sat on the end of the bed and lit up a fag. Perhaps it would be better the second time, I thought. But when I came back out, he was nowhere to be seen. I have to admit I was disappointed.

I might have felt more guilty about being unfaithful to Arthur if he hadn't been sick all over me on the journey back to Bristol.

The next day I told my mum what had happened, without letting on who the bloke was. After all, she hadn't met him, and was never likely to. Mum told me to keep my mouth shut as she didn't want to have to cancel the wedding, and even if I did turn out to be pregnant, no one would be any the wiser, as Arthur and I would be married by the time anyone noticed.

HARRY CLIFTON

1920–1933

1

I WAS TOLD my father was killed in the war.

Whenever I questioned my mother about his death, she didn't say any more than that he'd served with the Royal Gloucestershire Regiment and had been killed fighting on the Western Front only days before the Armistice was signed. Grandma said my dad had been a brave man, and once when we were alone in the house she showed me his medals. My grandpa rarely offered an opinion on anything, but then he was deaf as a post so he might not have heard the question in the first place.

The only other man I can remember was my uncle Stan, who used to sit at the top of the table at breakfast time. When he left of a morning I would often follow him to the city docks, where he worked. Every day I spent at the dockyard was an adventure. Cargo ships coming from distant lands and unloading their wares: rice, sugar, bananas, jute and many other things I'd never heard of. Once the holds had been emptied, the dockers would load them with salt, apples, tin, even coal (my least favourite, because it was an obvious clue to what I'd been doing all day and annoyed my mother), before they set off again to I knew not where. I always wanted to help my uncle Stan unload whatever ship had docked that morning, but he just laughed, saying, 'All in good time, my lad.' It couldn't be soon enough for me, but, without any warning, school got in the way.

I was sent to Merrywood Elementary when I was six and I thought it was a complete waste of time. What was the point of school when I could learn all I needed to at the docks? I wouldn't have bothered to go back the following day if my mother hadn't dragged me to the front gates, deposited me and returned at four o'clock that afternoon to take me home.

I didn't realize Mum had other plans for my future, which didn't include joining Uncle Stan in the shipyard.

Once Mum had dropped me off each morning, I would hang around in the yard until she was out of sight, then slope off to the docks. I made sure I was always back at the school gates when she returned to pick me up in the afternoon. On the way home, I would tell her everything I'd done at school that day. I was good at making up stories, but it wasn't long before she discovered that was all they were: stories.

One or two other boys from my school also used to hang around the docks, but I kept my distance from them. They were older and bigger, and used to thump me if I got in their way. I also had to keep an eye out for Mr Haskins, the chief ganger, because if he ever found me loitering, to use his favourite word, he would send me off with a kick up the backside and the threat: 'If I see you loiterin' round here again, my lad, I'll report you to the headmaster.'

Occasionally Haskins decided he'd seen me once too often and I'd be reported to the headmaster, who would leather me before sending me back to my classroom. My form master, Mr Holcombe, never let on if I didn't show up for his class, but then he was a bit soft. Whenever my mum found out I'd been playing truant, she couldn't hide her anger and would stop my halfpenny-a-week pocket money. But despite the occasional punch from an older boy, regular leatherings from the headmaster and the loss of my pocket money, I still couldn't resist the draw of the docks.

I made only one real friend while I 'loitered' around the dockyard. His name was Old Jack Tar. Mr Tar lived in an abandoned railway carriage at the end of the sheds. Uncle Stan told me to keep away from Old Jack because he was a stupid, dirty old tramp. He didn't look that dirty to me, certainly not as dirty as Stan, and it wasn't long before I discovered he wasn't stupid either.

After lunch with my uncle Stan, one bite of his Marmite

sandwich, his discarded apple core and a swig of beer, I would be back at school in time for a game of football; the only activity I considered it worth turning up for. After all, when I left school I was going to captain Bristol City, or build a ship that would sail around the world. If Mr Holcombe kept his mouth shut and the ganger didn't report me to the headmaster, I could go for days without being found out, and as long as I avoided the coal barges and was standing by the school gate at four o'clock every afternoon, my mother would never be any the wiser.

◄◘►

Every other Saturday, Uncle Stan would take me to watch Bristol City at Ashton Gate. On Sunday mornings, Mum used to cart me off to Holy Nativity Church, something I couldn't find a way of getting out of. Once the Reverend Watts had given the final blessing, I would run all the way to the recreation ground and join my mates for a game of football before returning home in time for dinner.

By the time I was seven it was clear to anyone who knew anything about the game of football that I was never going to get into the school team, let alone captain Bristol City. But that was when I discovered that God had given me one small gift, and it wasn't in my feet.

To begin with, I didn't notice that anyone who sat near me in church on a Sunday morning stopped singing whenever I opened my mouth. I wouldn't have given it a second thought if Mum hadn't suggested I join the choir. I laughed scornfully; after all, everyone knew the choir was only for girls and cissies. I would have dismissed the idea out of hand if the Reverend Watts hadn't told me that choirboys were paid a penny for funerals and tuppence for weddings; my first experience of bribery. But even after I'd reluctantly agreed to take a vocal test, the devil decided to place an obstacle in my path, in the form of Miss Eleanor E. Monday.

I would never have come across Miss Monday if she hadn't been the choir mistress at Holy Nativity. Although she was only five feet three, and looked as though a gust of wind might blow her away, no one tried to take the mickey. I have a feeling that even the devil would have been frightened of Miss Monday, because the Reverend Watts certainly was.

I agreed to take a vocal test, but not before my mum had handed over a month's pocket money in advance. The following Sunday I stood in line with a group of other lads and waited to be called.

'You will always be on time for choir practice,' Miss Monday announced, fixing a gimlet eye on me. I stared back defiantly. 'You will never speak, unless spoken to.' I somehow managed to remain silent. 'And during the service, you will concentrate at all times.' I reluctantly nodded. And then, God bless her, she gave me a way out. 'But most importantly,' she declared, placing her hands on her hips, 'within twelve weeks, you will be expected to pass a reading and writing test, so that I can be sure you are able to tackle a new anthem or an unfamiliar psalm.'

I was pleased to have fallen at the first hurdle. But as I was to discover, Miss Eleanor E. Monday didn't give up easily.

THE
CLIFTON CHRONICLES

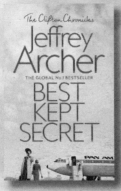

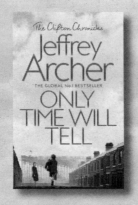

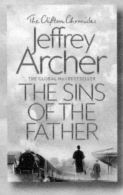

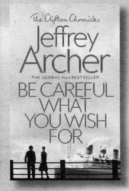

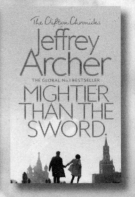

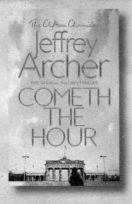

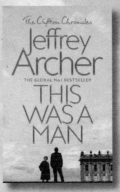